Operation Snowflake

Book #6 Max & Olivia Series

The final Story in the Max & Olivia Series

Books In This Series

Operation Underpants (2016)

Claudia (2017)

Operation OBE - Over Bloody Eighty (2018)

St. Mary's Dating Agency (2020)

Operation Origami - The Ire of Claudia (2021)

Operation Snowflake (2021)

Other books by Mark A. Biggs

Above and Beyond: 2nd edition (2014)

Love Letters From Dresden: Book #1 Artōrius Series (2019)

Silent Trail: Book #2 Artōrius Series (2024) (Set on the famous Camino de Santiago).

Operation Snowflake

Copyright

A CIP catalogue record for this book is available from the National Library of Australia.

First published in Australia 2021.

mbkbooks

62 Sunnybrook Ave

Warragul Victoria 3818

Australia

www.markabiggs.com

Dedication

Lacy and Craig, who shared the Max and Olivia journey with me.

Max and Olivia Story

The Max and Olivia story is a six-part series. While the first two books lay the foundation for their journey, the subsequent instalments can be enjoyed as stand-alone tales. However, readers will find a greater depth in the characters and themes through the overarching narrative that connects them all.

The Max and Olivia story is a tribute to the vibrant lives of older adults. As Abraham Lincoln wisely observed, "In the end, it's not the years in your life that count. It's the life in your years." Max and Olivia personify this sentiment, embodying the joy, wisdom, and vitality that come with experience. Their journey serves as a testament to the richness of life at any age.

Although the author recounts the early days of Max and Olivia, their wartime service, and then as cold war spies, the narrative is set in the here and now. With a backdrop of current geopolitical happenings, in their eighties, Max and Olivia return to the world of espionage.

Each book in the series is a little different. Most use a measured dose of humour to broach topical subjects, or to lighten what otherwise would be dark scenes. The result is a rewarding read.

The age of the main characters lends the books to an older audience. However, Max and Olivia are ably assisted by Claudia and a host of other people who give the stories a much broader appeal.

In a world where much of what we read is 'same, same but different', the Max and Olivia series is refreshingly unique, and just a little quirky.

CHAPTER 1
London

'Welcome home Claudia,' James said, as she entered the outer office. 'Stephen and Inspector Axel are expecting you.'

'Thank you, James.'

'Tea? English Breakfast?'

'That would be most kind of you, James.'

As was her way, Claudia knocked on the door before opening it. Inside, Stephen and Inspector Axel were seated. They smiled warmly as they rose to their fee. To Claudia, the greeting appeared genuine. Stephen gestured towards a vacant chair while saying, 'It's good to have you back, Claudia.'

'Thank you. It's good to be home.'

As they settled into their seats, Claudia chose the vacant one beside them. Inspector Axel turned to her and asked, 'How are Max and Olivia?'

'They were in good spirits, but Max had a niggling cough and a temperature. I was surprised when Stephen suggested they remain in Spain. When I left, there were unthinkable numbers of people, the elderly in particular, dying of COVID-19 every day. Yesterday the fatality rate exceeded one thousand again. Surely Britain, with its National Health Service, would be a safer place for them to see out the pandemic?'

There was a knock on the door which paused the conversation. James entered saying, 'Excuse me, Sir. I have a cup of tea for Claudia. Would anyone else like a refill while I am here?'

When Stephen and the Inspector declined, James left.

Stephen looked at Claudia. 'The pandemic is one item that Inspector Axel and I were discussing before you arrived, though perhaps lamenting would be a better description.' Stephen hesitated, considering his words. 'I seem to recall having this discussion with you over the phone before you left for Spain. Unfortunately, our R-value remains too high. Pandora's box is well and truly open and Britain is in for a difficult time. Max and Olivia are safest in Spain; besides travel is too dangerous.'

Claudia nodded.

'I'm afraid, Claudia,' Stephen said. 'We will all be affected by this virus in one way or another. We'll bring Max and Olivia home once Spain relaxes its lockdown rules and before it faces the inevitable second wave. By then, I hope Britain will be better prepared.'

Claudia nodded.

Inspector Axel sighed. 'In a genuine disaster, fault is rarely simple. The contagious nature of the virus makes containment difficult for even the most proactive of countries.'

There was a pause in the conversation before Stephen asked, 'How was the handover with Chen Li?'

Claudia stared at Stephen, then raised her hands in exasperation. 'You might have told me that Britain had back-flipped over allowing Huawei into its 5G network and that you're drawing up plans to strip out existing Huawei gear by the end of the year. Chen Li stopped short of calling it an act of war, but his language was provocative. He was blunt, telling me that there would be consequences. Stephen, you know it was Davros and H1 Technologies and not the Chinese who were behind the recent tensions. The outcome is what Davros wanted. We've played into his hands.'

Stephen considered his answer for a moment before saying, 'As you know, GCHQ has, for some time, advised the Government against even limited use of Huawei equipment but they approved its use in January. They did not want a dispute with China at the same time as the Brexit negotiations were happening in Europe. That broader geopolitical game has changed, with China imposing national security laws on Hong Kong and enforcing sterilisation on Uighurs and other minorities to curb the Muslim population. This has altered our government's perspective. What China sees as its internal affairs, we perceive as gross and egregious human rights abuse and yet another example of its aggression and wish to dominate world affairs.'

'So, what of Davros?'

'The Government's priority, post-Brexit and responding to an increasingly assertive China, is to strengthen its military and economic ties with India. We have satellite imagery in the remote reaches of the Himalayas, on the disputed border between China and India. China is doing what it did in the South China sea, incrementally extending its footprint. China's behaviour is serving to strengthen the developing Indo-British alliance, which means the Government is reluctant to take action against Davros or H1 Technologies at this point in time for fear of impeding its relations with India.'

'Even if that means signing contracts with H1 Technologies?'

'Yes,' Stephen raised an eyebrow and tilted his head to one side as he said, 'Although I needn't remind you, Claudia, government priorities can change.'

'And what about Adele?' Claudia asked. 'She tried to kill Inspector Axel?'

'The Inspector and I both agree that what occurred is an occupational hazard. Now, if I may ask you another question, Claudia. The Crane. Why the help in Montserrat and the warning in Pi-Ski?'

Claudia shrugged her shoulders. 'I can only guess it was because of Linda Orr; the Crane, not appreciating an impersonator.'

'I see.' Stephen let the silence hang in the air before saying. 'Which means the Crane is one member of the St Mary's Parish Council?'

Claudia considered her reply. *What do I say?* 'That would seem a logical conclusion, Stephen, but which one, I couldn't say.'

Stephen pursed his lips. 'Couldn't or wouldn't?'

Claudia looked at Inspector Axel. 'Perhaps the Inspector's insights are wiser than mine.'

Inspector Axel finished the remains of his coffee and, placing his cup down on the table, said, 'Sorry, Stephen, the Crane could be any of them.'

Annoyance present in his voice, Stephen asked, 'Any, Inspector?'

'Well, yes. The legacy of the Crane could pass from mother to daughter, so it could even be the Vicar.'

Claudia bit her lip, trying to stop herself from smiling.

Stephen shook his head. 'Why do I feel you are both being deliberately misleading? For the time being, at least, I will accept that you have your reasons.' After a moment's silence, Stephen continued, 'Okay, let's move on. How are the Liew's after their ordeal?'

Claudia smiled as she remembered what Olivia had told her and said, 'They're an effective team.'

Stephen and Inspector Axel glanced at each other, the subtlety of the message flying over their heads.

Claudia felt a sense of satisfaction watching her colleagues' puzzlement. Suppressing a grin, she asked, 'How is Daniel Tinkov? Did he make it safely to the UK?'

Stephen nodded. 'Yes, thanks to you. He's still with us for the time being and, when he's moved, even I won't know of his new identity. What we learned from Daniel Tinkov and the information you gathered from Linda Orr has awakened the security service to the threat posed by The Firm and The Seven. We are slowly unravelling the identities of the seven. Hopefully, this will lead us to the Principal, the head of this new organisation. We know Sergey Rutskoy is Jasper, and that Azim Singh is Davros. There is also an avatar called Cosy Bear; who the actual individual is, we don't yet know. However, we assume that he, or she, has links to the Russian Intelligence Services hacking group, Cozy Bear.' Stephen paused. He gave Claudia an inquisitorial look before asking. 'Your ex-boyfriend, the Russian Mafia Boss, Monya; is he the avatar Cosy Bear, perhaps?'

Claudia chuckled. 'Were the hackers successful in securing the information about Britain's ongoing COVID-19 vaccine research?'

The question caught Stephen by surprise, which showed in the tone of his voice as he said, 'No.'

'Well, that's your answer.'

Stephen shifted uncomfortably in his seat before saying, 'Identifying the person calling themselves The Principal and the remaining members of The Firm is a priority. Taking down Jasper will be a victory, but there's more to be done.'

Claudia, thinking of Davros, muttered, 'When it suits you!'

'Indeed Claudia,' Stephen replied, a smile creeping across his face. 'I recall you like ancient proverbs. What is it they say? *The enemy of my enemy is my friend.*'

'Indeed, Stephen. Did you find Charles Scott from Barra Island, Inspector?'

Inspector Axel shook his head. 'No, and we can only assume that he's dead. Perhaps you could ask Linda Orr when you see her this evening?'

Oh, they know I'm seeing Linda. Now, that's interesting.

'Yes, I can do that for you, Inspector. When I was at Montserrat, Linda promised me a drink, and she's paying.'

'Did she indeed?' Stephen said. 'At The Windsor Castle I understand. I take it you won't be lending her your phone again!'

Claudia raised her hands, a sign of defeat, as she chuckled and said, 'What can I say, Stephen, other than sorry?'

Stephen nodded. 'Under the circumstances, Claudia, considering the murder of John Moss, your apology is accepted.' Stephen breathed out slowly, 'I must ask Claudia, what are your intentions for Linda?'

Claudia thought for a moment before answering.

Two octogenarians, Saint Vladimir, seven-year-old Molly, Snowflake the cat, and a man named John Moss have all left their mark on my life in ways that will forever change it. I will not seek retribution.

'To savour a glass of Rose Gold Methuselah–anything else is a decision for MI6.'

'Indeed, it is Claudia. Indeed, it is.'

CHAPTER 2
Rose Gold Methuselah

Linda Orr placed a bottle of chilled Dom Perignon and two champagne flutes on the table in front of her. Seated, she pondered how her once best friend and ex-Mafia colleague would react after her betrayal. Linda had, posing as the Chinese State Security Service, murdered John Moss, Claudia's lover, then framed Claudia for retaliatory killings which sparked an international incident. Her ruthless deception was performed while pretending to be Claudia's trusted friend. Waiting at the Windsor Castle pub for Claudia to arrive, Linda sighed, recalling the flippant promise she'd made to Claudia as she abandoned her friend to certain death in the prison cell hidden deep below Montserrat Abbey in Spain.

Claudia had called out after her, 'I'll see you at the Castle Hotel, seven o'clock Saturday night for dinner, and you're paying.'

Linda turned and grinned, not expecting Claudia to survive, saying, 'That's the spirit, Claudia. I'll be there with a bottle of your favourite, 1996 Dom Perignon.'

Waving a finger towards Linda, Claudia had replied, 'Don't over chill it.'

'I'll keep that in mind.' Linda remembered saying. She'd made the promise, never expecting to honour it. Yet here she was, Max and Olivia had seen to that.

Those interfering, meddling old people have been the bane of my existence.

The pub door opened and Linda glanced up. Claudia entered and Linda smiled and waved at her. Claudia reciprocated, but her welcoming smile drifted from her face as she approached the table, becoming a frown. The rapid change in demeanour took Linda by surprise. Claudia peered at the bottle of Dom Perignon resting in the chiller bucket and shook her head as she said, 'What did I say, Linda?'

Linda raised an eyebrow. 'Claudia, you will find the bottle is a perfect nine degrees Celsius.'

Claudia's demeanour softened as she said, her tone lighter than Linda had expected, 'Leaving me for dead, killing my friends and murdering my lover, I can forgive. Over-chilling a bottle of Dom Perignon would be inexcusable. Any cooler than nine degrees numbs the taste buds, which would be such a waste.'

Continuing the banter, once a hallmark of their friendship, Linda replied. 'I was going to cool it to absolute zero but, on reflection, thought better of it. Given recent events, I feared that your sense of humour and tolerance for my mischief may not be as it once was.'

Claudia took the seat opposite Linda and made herself comfortable. 'I would call that wise and a fair observation.' Claudia hesitated, pursing her lips, contemplating her next move. 'I wondered if you would be here. You made the promise expecting me not to live, plus, given how events turned out, I assume that every man and his dog are after you. Here is not the safest of place for you.'

Exaggerating her facial expressions to feign surprise, Linda said, 'Au contraire, Claudia. I had every faith in your abilities, rightly so because, look - here you are! Your observation about being the centre of unwanted attention is regrettably true, although not from my employer. After tonight, it's goodbye to Britain, for a while at least.' Linda tilted her head to one side. 'Unless you have plans for me?'

'Tempting. If I were a bitter woman, Linda, I might have come here tonight seeking retribution for John's murder.'

'Are you?'

'A bitter woman, or seeking retribution?'

'Either.'

'Um. Maybe.'

Linda Orr laughed. 'I will take that as a no, not tonight anyway.'

Claudia smiled. Linda was right, not tonight. She let a moment's silence linger between them before saying, 'If you leave that bottle of champagne any longer, it will be too cold and that just won't do.'

Linda nodded. 'Let me do the honours.' She took the bottle from the ice bucket and, examining it in her hand said, 'You are right Claudia. A bottle of champagne must not be over chilled but it also needs to be cold enough, otherwise the pressure inside the bottle will release the cork too quickly, sending a geyser of the precious golden liquid spraying into the air. That is barely acceptable on a podium when sporting champions spray each other with cheap plonk. It would certainly not do here.' Linda picked up a wine key from the table. 'It annoys me when people use their fingers like barbarians to rip the foil away from the bottle, leaving an ugly mess.' Using the key, Linda cut an even clean line around the bottle before removing the foil to reveal the cork and cage. Placing the wine key back on the table, holding the bottle at precisely forty-five-degrees, she untwisted the cage all the way around the bottle, while keeping pressure on the cork. 'We don't want the cork to pop prematurely Claudia, the sound is something to savour.' Twisting the bottle and not the stopper, Linda Orr pulled the cork away from the bottle, accompanied by a satisfying POP!

She filled their champagne flutes, passing one to Claudia, before putting the opened bottle back into the chiller. Lifting her glass, Linda said, 'To what shall we toast?'

Claudia thought for a moment. 'How about to old friends?'

Linda grinned, recognising the double meaning within the words. 'Yes, that's quite clever. To "old" friends.' They clinked glasses and sipped their golden contents.

Claudia dropped her head to one side in silent contemplation as she savoured the taste, thinking something was not quite as it should be. 'That's not a 1996 vintage!'

Linda chucked, 'No, I thought a six-litre bottle was, even for you and me, a little much.'

Claudia grinned. 'Yes, that was for our younger days. Nevertheless, the bottle you have chosen is superb, an exceptional vintage. Well done, Linda.'

Linda nodded. 'I had an excellent teacher.' She took another sip from her glass. 'Undeniably, an excellent teacher.'

'Why thank you,' Claudia said, before hesitating as if searching for the right words. 'After your... debacles in A Coruña and then Montserrat, I imagine it's not only our side hunting you. The Principal would undoubtedly want your head on a plate.'

Repeating her earlier words, Linda said, 'Au contraire Claudia, not from my employer. It's the outcome that matters and that is that the British and others have dumped Huawei. Governments are preventing their telecom companies from buying Huawei equipment and legislating that existing Huawei products are to be stripped from existing infrastructure. H1 Technologies are poised to fill the void and will assist Western Governments in the roll-out of 5G across their networks. My dear Claudia, that was the goal all along. Between you and me, we reached that conclusion via a spurious route; in the end, that doesn't matter as the Firm's strategy is to exploit the complexities of tensions between the world's largest economic and military powers for its own advantage. This venture was successful. For the time being, it's only MI6 that I need to watch.'

Claudia took another sip of champagne and glanced up. 'Linda, I think The Firm is over estimating its influence. China is kicking own goals without your help. Its diplomatic blunders are strengthening international alliances. For example, the Chinese embassy in Australia publicly sharing a detailed list of fourteen grievances that Beijing has against the country. The fabricated image it tweeted that purported to show an Australian special forces soldier slitting the throat of a small Afghan child wrapped in an Australian flag, caused international outrage. Then there is Beijing's wrath against Norway, Canada, Britain, Japan, U.S., the list goes on.'

'Claudia, Claudia, Claudia. Where do you think wolf warrior diplomacy came from? Surely not the Chinese? The Firm seeks to ensure there is no unity of purpose, so taking advantage of Sino-Western mistrust and tension is one of its endeavours. Speaking of endeavours, how long do I have?'

'What do you mean?'

Linda laughed, 'Claudia, you said it yourself. Every man and his dog are after me. The British authorities will not have turned a blind eye to my antics, particularly what happened on the Isle of Barra. It's reasonable to assume that MI6 knows we are catching up.'

'Maybe.'

'I will take that as a yes!'

Claudia shrugged her shoulders. 'We all have choices, Linda. If you were to share your knowledge of the Firm and The Principal, MI6 may call off its dogs of war.'

'Ha! If I were to do that Claudia, then I would truly have no friends left.'

'I thought you were freelancing, Linda?'

'I was, but there comes a time when you have to choose sides. What is it you just told me? We all have choices. Why don't you come and join me?'

Claudia released a gasp of incredulity. 'Is that a threat?'

Linda shook her head and her tone became serious. 'No, a warning. The authorities have no idea what's coming. The Principal is an adversary, the likes of which the world has never faced before. Using your metaphor, when the dogs of war are unleashed, you want to be on the winning side. Join us!'

'Interesting proposition. Have you met the Principal?'

Linda shook her head. 'No, not yet, but soon. Claudia, there's a place for someone like you in The Firm.' Linda pursed her lips. 'I repeat: the world has no idea what's coming. Using modern jargon, The Firm is a disruptor.'

Claudia sighed. 'Linda, you know what they say... if you lay with dogs, you'll get fleas.'

Linda chuckled. 'You're really into the animal references tonight. Do you know who the disruptor is that I fear tonight, Claudia? Your MI6. They might bother us before we enjoy our meal together and finish the champagne, and that would be a shame.'

Claudia shrugged shoulders. 'Who knows? Maybe they will.'

Linda rubbed her chin. 'Um. I don't think you know what's going to happen. Your precious MI6 is keeping you in the dark. The job offer, it stands.'

'As does mine, Linda.' Claudia took a sip from her champagne flute. 'If MI6, the police, or someone else is coming for you Linda, then your observation is correct. I am not part of the plan and do not wish to spoil our meal, but given what you did, I do hope they arrive.'

'Your candour is appreciated.'

Claudia glanced around the pub, counting its patrons. 'It's busy in here tonight. I can't imagine any action while you're inside the pub.' Motioning with her head, Claudia nodded towards a man and woman seated on the opposite side of the room. 'I recognise two of your associates, Linda. If the authorities are worth a pinch of salt, they would know that you wouldn't come alone and attempting to arrest you inside would invoke a bloodbath. They are bound to wait until you leave.' Claudia paused before shaking her head from side to side. 'Sorry Linda, you're not getting out of it that easily.'

Linda shot Claudia an inquisitive look. 'What do you mean?'

'Paying ... there's plenty of time for us to eat.'

Linda smiled. 'I wondered where you were going with all that risk assessment rubbish. Do you know, I have missed our banter. We were a good team and could be again. Paying, that sounds fair.'

Claudia and Linda queued, placing their order before returning to the table. Claudia, taking a sip of her fizz, said, 'Linda, you told me you can't remain in the UK. Where will you go?'

Linda chuckled. 'Now, now, Claudia, would you be fishing?'

Lifting both of her arms in unison, displaying the palms of her hands, a sign of someone being open and truthful, Claudia said, her tone contradicting her body language. 'Who me? Of course, I'm fishing, it is my job sweetie.'

Linda opened her mouth ready to reply, when her phone beeped, alerting her to a text message. Lifting one finger, she said, 'Uno momento por favor, I need to check this.' The message was from Cindy, one of her two associates, telling Linda to check the outside camera feed. In readiness for the meeting with Claudia, Linda and Cindy had placed Wi-Fi cameras to monitor the street. Linda opened the app to study the live feeds. She held the image up for Claudia to see. Police were evacuating nearby houses and cordoning off the surrounding streets.

Linda said, 'This is most annoying, Claudia. I thought you told me we would have time to enjoy our dinner.'

'We may have to eat quickly or, at least, you will!'

'I love your sense of humour. Did you see the personnel in black? They looked like SAS, the Special Air Service.'

Claudia nodded. 'It seems, my old friend, someone is taking your capture seriously. The British SAS are reputed to be among the best in the world and they will not underestimate you, as you did with Max and Olivia.'

'I will take MI6 committing the SAS as a compliment and it's not true. I did not underestimate your geriatric friends. And I use the phrase geriatric as a term of endearment and not insult.' Linda removed the champagne bottle from the chiller. 'A top up?'

'Please.'

Linda refilled their glasses. 'Ah, to think I once drank alco-pops. Makes me shiver to think of it. Where was I? Oh, yes. The

Firm did not underestimate Max and Olivia at all. The Principal understood the risk they posed to the plan, which is why a team was sent to neutralise them.' Linda placed her champagne glass on the table, lifting both hands in a gesture of frustration. 'The mercenaries, on the other hand,' Linda shook her head. 'Despite being warned to the contrary, they allowed themselves to be deceived by Max and Olivia's doddering personas. They let their eyes and egos bamboozle them, and they paid the ultimate price, their lives.'

It had been Claudia who introduced Max and Olivia into the conversation but, when Linda recalled trying to eliminating them, Claudia was irritated. The previously suppressed anger grew. Claudia thought to calm herself:

Don't become annoyed, girly. Rage is never helpful.

Regaining her calm demeanour, Claudia pushed the tide of fury down deep inside. Linda, having known Claudia for a long time, spotted the glint of ire in her eyes and was not deceived by her act of composure. 'I will make you this promise, Claudia. If I'm engaged again to target your friends, Max and Olivia, I will tell you.' Linda paused and smiled. 'I've become fond of those oldies myself. A fondness borne out of respect.'

Claudia tightened her lips and then repeated Linda's words. 'I will make you this promise, Linda. If you do anything to harm Max and Olivia, I will come for you, sanctioned or not.'

Lifting her champagne flute and holding it in front of her, Linda said, 'That's fair. Let's drink to Max and Olivia.'

'To Max and Olivia,' Claudia said as she moved the glass towards her lips, closing her eyes as she put her nose into the flute to savour its aroma. Taking a sip, Claudia said, 'I find excellent wine irresistible, champagne in particular, like good friends.'

Linda looked at Claudia, her expression becoming serious. 'It's not only I who would like you to join The Firm. The invitation is from the Principal.'

'Really? In that case, if you have an address, I'll make a house call and discuss the offer in person.'

Linda laughed. 'I love your flippancy, Claudia. It is something that I have missed. The Principal has asked Tomoe to make the arrangements.'

Claudia huffed. 'You don't accept no, do you? I'm not sure that attending such a job interview would bear well with my current employers. Tomoe, is she nice? A good sense of humour, I mean.'

'She? What makes you think Tomoe is a woman?'

'Simple. Tomoe is the name of an ancient female warrior. It makes sense that Tomoe is female so, is she nice?'

Linda smiled. 'Ah, you clever woman. Nice-ish, but I wouldn't say that we are pals. Which, my old friend, is why I give you a word of warning.'

Old friend, Claudia thought, *I no longer believe you are my friend.*

Linda continued, 'Tomoe is a dangerous woman and you can't trust her. As the old saying goes, be prepared to duck and watch out for the curve ball.'

'You've met her, I take it?'

'Yes, recently, after our adventure in Spain.'

'After the debacle.'

Linda shook her head. 'I've told you, there was no debacle and besides, debacle is such a loaded term. Regardless, my warning stands.'

Claudia gave Linda a sideways glance. 'Tomoe is one of the Seven, so I take it you want her job, and for me to kill her for you?'

Linda raised an eyebrow. 'Opportunities multiply as they are seized. Besides Claudia, killing is something you are good at.' Linda took a sip of champagne. 'I've always been an ambitious woman and can see when an opportunity presents itself. I know Tomoe's type. She will want to test you, prove her superiority, but I have faith in your abilities.'

Claudia gave Linda a confused look. 'You told me that the Principal wants me to join The Firm so I fail to see a conflict with Tomoe, except in your imagination.'

Linda laughed. 'To be accepted into The Firm, you need to prove yourself. Too gladiatorial for my liking.'

Claudia sensed Linda was lying. 'Why would I fight Tomoe?'

Linda grinned. 'That's easy because, when the invitation comes, you won't be able to resist.'

'Ha! You want Tomoe's job, but don't want to be bloodied in the arena.'

Linda shrugged her shoulders and smiled. 'Let's say I'm open to all possibilities. If I were one of the Seven, Claudia, and we were to work together, imagine the possibilities.'

Claudia shook her head. 'As Bast and Athena, we could rule the world. Although I doubt you are a virgin, Linda.'

'Sometimes your humour is lost on me, Claudia, but seriously, we should work together.'

'These are courageous words from you Linda, particularly when the trust between us is so low.'

Linda shrugged her shoulders and lifted her champagne flute. 'We live in a complex world but, if we were on the same side ... all I ask is that you consider it. Cheers.'

'Cheers.' In the silence, as the champagne trickled across her taste buds, Claudia wondered if Tomoe would contact her and when. She could ask Linda, but thought better of it, knowing that Linda was playing with her. Linda was being contrary and contriving, to rile and then smooth her; a strategy of control, as old as time itself. Anger surfaced again and Claudia suppressed it, trying to avoid Linda's trap. 'I wonder how our meals are coming along, Linda?'

'That's a good question, but the one that's burning in my mind is how are preparations going for my capture?'

'Or execution,' Claudia added with a wry grin.

'This is Britain, Claudia. Not even the SAS do executions here. That's left for people like you and me, sanctioned psychopaths. And we are both here.'

Claudia raised an eyebrow at Linda's comments, a sign she did not agree.

'Ha, Claudia, that's right. You've lost the blood lust. And here I was, thinking that you would eliminate Tomoe for me. Compassion is a weakness that your enemies will exploit. Get in their way and they will threaten the people you care about and, I hear, that your list keeps getting larger.' Linda put her champagne flute on the table and lifted her right hand, making it into a fist. As she started speaking, she raised a finger at each name she uttered. 'Max... Olivia... Penny....' Linda tilted her head in contemplation. After a moment, she said, 'I watched you spy on Molly, Richard

Liew's daughter. You were, um, how can I describe it? Smitten. After the time you spent with her at Montserrat, I knew we must add her to the list.' Linda lifted her little finger, saying, 'Molly. That makes four.'

Claudia took a sip of her bubbly. 'Are you trying to antagonise me?'

'Not at all, Claudia. I'm reminding you why, for people like us, blood lust is a good thing. It keeps our friends safe.'

'If that's the case, then you've forgotten someone.'

'Really. Who?'

'That's my secret.'

'Best keep it that way, Claudia. As I told you, your enemies will exploit your weakness.'

Claudia shrugged. 'They wouldn't want to poke the bear.'

Linda resisted the urge to point out the reality that she had killed John Moss, the man Claudia had fallen in love with, yet was still alive to tell the tale. Smiling, knowing that she was manipulating Claudia skilfully, Linda bit her tongue.

Don't poke the bear. Not yet, anyway. Now is the time to be conciliatory, by proffering something of value. Information that Claudia would want.

'I have a confession to make.'

Claudia raised an eyebrow, uncertain what to expect.

'I was rather taken by Molly and even Snowflake, the cat, myself. So, as a friend, I think you will want to know this. Richard Liew is being recalled to China, and his family is to accompany him. I think you understand what this will mean... for Molly.'

Claudia stroked her chin. 'How do you know this?'

'The Firm has sources.'

'When?'

'Sorry, I don't have an exact date, but I'm told it's soon.'

Claudia breathed out heavily, not knowing what to believe. 'Why are you telling me this?'

'As I mentioned, I was taken by Molly. After all, she is just a child.'

Claudia sensed Linda was being truthful for a change about Richard Liew's return to China, at any rate. Her motivation was another matter entirely. 'Be careful Linda, people will start talking. They'll say you're going soft.' As Claudia uttered the words, her thoughts turned to protecting Molly, knowing that the Chinese State Security Service will be watching the family.

Linda laughed, 'Ha, ha, it's not me, but that is what some say about you, except the Principal who thinks otherwise.' The beeping of the phone interrupted Linda, who checked its screen and then held it for Claudia to see. 'It seems our time together is ending, as your friends are moving quicker than I expected. I assumed they would allow sufficient time for you to interrogate me and you are yet to begin.'

Claudia lifted her champagne flute and let the light filter through its golden liquid. 'Or time for dinner. Tut, tut, what is MI6 becoming?'

'Yes. What is MI6 coming to? You don't belong here, Claudia... You don't belong anywhere, least of all here. Think about the offer.'

'A moment ago, you were telling me I'd gone soft.'

'No Claudia, you misunderstand. The Principal is offering you a way out.'

Ignoring Linda, Claudia glanced at the live feed on Linda's phone and started a running commentary. 'Um, they've already cordoned off the streets... Tick Tock. You'd better shake a leg.'

'You always were the joker. I will give the British one thing. If there's a job to be done, they get in there and do it.' Turning the phone to herself, away from Claudia, Linda, with a flurry of thumbs and fingers, switched between the numerous camera feeds. 'Good Claudia, there's nothing too surprising, but where is the incident centre?'

'You'd better watch out, Linda. Who knows what goodies they've installed for you?'

Linda grinned and gave Claudia a sly look. 'What you meant to say is, what surprises do I have in store for them? Oh, my goodness, Claudia, I see armed officers, cars and an armoured personnel carrier. Talk about a welcoming committee. This is some operation. I am flattered, humbled, even.'

Claudia rolled her eyes. 'Spare me.'

'Where are those Special Air Service soldiers?' Linda scrolled through the pictures while muttering to herself. 'Come to mama. Got you! It seems the SAS is about to storm the pub. I call that a ballsy move, not cricket. So unlike the British.'

Claudia laughed. 'Clearly they have the Windsor Castle public house confused with the Iranian Embassy.'

'Your wicked sense of humour again Claudia, but I know that one, even though the 1980 embassy siege in London was before my time. For once, I appreciate your wit. On that occasion, the SAS were victorious, but not so today, they will be humiliated.'

Claudia shrugged her shoulders. 'Or you will.'

Ignoring Claudia's comment, Linda returned her focus to the screen. A moment later, she burst out laughing as she turned the phone towards Claudia. 'Look at this. We can see them, watching us, watching them.' Linda waved at the fibre optic camera hidden directly above their table, stood and disconnected it.

'I'm surprised, Linda.'

'At what?'

'At you. For not checking earlier.'

Feigning annoyance, Linda said, 'It was your fault.'

'How so?'

'For guessing I would choose our favourite table. I take it the camera is your doing. Is there no one I can trust these days?'

Claudia smiled and held up her hand with her fingers splayed. 'I would make you number five, but as you said, that would only put you in greater danger. By the way, you still owe me dinner.'

Linda picked up her champagne glass and drained its contents. 'Yes, I do still owe you dinner. Before I leave, a serious question. In my escape, do I need to worry about you?'

'Not tonight, Linda. I'm a spectator.'

Linda nodded. 'I'll take you on your word.'

'It's called trust, Linda, something we once shared.'

'Join me and we will again.' Linda took in a deep breath. 'Time to exit, stage right, as they say in the movies. Oh Claudia, you will want to stay and watch as I've prepared quite a reception that will gain your approval. The master's apprentice at work.'

'I'm not going anywhere. I wouldn't miss this for the world.'

Linda switched on her concealed lapel microphone and inserted an ear piece she plucked from under her jacket.

'We have company,' Linda said.

Cindy, the associate seated across the room, replied, 'Yes, we've been watching.'

Claudia picked up the remnants of the bottle of champagne. 'If you will excuse me Linda, I will find a seat out of harm's way.' She scanned the room. 'Over there, I think, a nice table away from the front and windows. I will finish this lovely bubbly and enjoy the show, but I'll be close enough to that solid oak bar in case things become too lively. If you don't mind, I won't wish you good luck.'

'Not a surprise but, for what it's worth, I am sorry I crossed you.' Linda paused and lowered her voice as she added. 'And for John.'

Without acknowledging Linda's apology, Claudia moved away, while Linda began whispering into her lapel microphone. Reaching her new seat, Claudia placed the champagne bottle on the table.

No, Claudia that won't do!

She moved the bottle to the floor. Satisfied, she turned her attention to Linda in time to see her signal her accomplices.

Here we go.

BANG!... The buzz of chatter, which had hitherto bathed the room in a warm hum, was silenced by a piercing noise coming from the kitchen. The explosion was followed by a flash of brilliant yellow light, accompanied by a wave of hot air rushing through the bar and lounge. Claudia's trained ear recognised the fraud; a simulation, like those used in stage productions, an electronically detonated pyrotechnic device, giving the pretence of a blast. Linda's two accomplices sprung to their feet and called out in a commanding yet reassuring tone.

'Do not panic, there is no need to panic. We have a fire in the kitchen. Please evacuate in an orderly fashion.' Moving from their table, they shepherded the puzzled, agitated patrons towards the front door. Amidst the confusion, Claudia watched Linda trigger a smoke bomb, reinforcing the illusion of a fire.

'Keep moving. Do not run!' Linda's colleagues called.

Claudia scratched her head in thought.

This is very interesting. I didn't expect Linda to attempt an escape through the front door by blending in with the crowd. I wouldn't rate her chances highly, unless... unless there are more surprises outside. Yes, that must be it.

Claudia shrugged her shoulders at her own musings and stood.

I'd better join the queue and wait for the next instalment. If I know Linda, it will be impressive.

Claudia looked at the half empty bottle of expensive champagne on the floor.

Oh, why not?

She picked up her champagne flute and then the bottle, but changed her mind, returning them both to the table.

Hang on girly, don't be silly. Keep your hands free, in case this turns ugly.

Claudia strolled towards the front door. Linda was still near the table they had shared, so Claudia paused and said, 'It's a pleasant light and sound show, although I doubt the authorities are deceived.' As Claudia spoke, there was another loud BANG from the kitchen.

'Quick, keep moving,' Claudia heard Linda's colleagues calling out.

Linda smiled. 'The theatricals are not for the authorities. They are for these lemmings. Look at them.' Linda waved her arm towards the crowd, rushing and pushing against each other as they tried to escape through the door. 'You will enjoy what I have in store for them once they are outside.'

'I'm sure I will.' Amid the excitement, the animosity Claudia felt towards Linda faded, replaced by anticipation. 'Linda, I will look forward to it, but I wasn't expecting you to "exit stage right" through the main entrance. If you were a bloke, I'd call it a ballsy move.'

Linda scoffed. 'I may be gutsy, but I'm not stupid.' Pointing her finger towards the ceiling, Linda said, 'It's upstairs and then onto the roof for me.' Before Claudia could respond, Linda added. 'Yes, yes, I'm aware they'll be watching for that as well. I hope they are, because that's also part of my plan. Now, if you'll excuse me, Claudia, it's time to shake a leg. Until we meet again.'

Claudia gave a slight bow of her head. 'Indeed, until we meet again.'

Oh, dear, I've started using Stephen's expressions. What is the world coming to? Maybe the Principle is right, I need a way out.

Outside the hotel, the commotion had caught the police off-guard, and they were busy trying to herd the fleeing people, trying to avoid Linda melting into the crowd before she vanished. Intending to be the last to leave, Claudia stood back, waiting before she moved towards the open door. When she was a couple of feet away, the sounds of cascading explosions erupted outside, accompanied by a fog of smoke. Claudia recognised the voices of Linda's associates, bellowing, 'RUN FOR YOUR LIVES!'

The patrons that the police had corralled, along with those still to be gathered, were spooked and ran in all directions. Claudia moved into the doorway for a better view and watched as the law enforcers worked furiously in a futile attempt to control, then contain, the crowd.

Nice one, Linda. The police seem to have the roads blocked. Eventually, they'll gather the patrons together, but it's an excellent distraction. I wonder if they had planned for this?

Claudia watched the police officer approaching but pretended not to notice. The officer put her hand on Claudia's shoulder while pulling her to one side as he said, 'Madam, Madam, you must move.' Claudia allowed herself to be guided as heavily armed SAS personnel rushed past and inside the pub. A moment later, Claudia heard a soldier shout out, 'CLEAR!' She knew they would now begin searching upstairs.

It's round one to you, Linda, although I am wondering what the next part of your scheme entails.

Before going onto the roof, Linda waited for the telltale sound of SAS soldiers searching and securing the floor below. She wanted her opponents in the building and off the street as she made her escape from the roof. She knew there would be others stationed outside, watching and waiting, but it was a numbers game. Her strategy aimed to reduce the number of people who could immediately pursue her.

A tall tree with a full canopy of foliage overshadowed the outdoor area at the back of the pub and its mass of leaves hid Linda from the SAS snipers positioned on buildings in Peel Street and Campden Hill Road, overlooking the Castle as she climbed onto the roof. Linda hummed as she climbed onto a branch which overhung the roof, shuffled across it to the trunk of the tree. Earlier that day, Linda and Cindy had made a flying-fox zip line using invisible aerial cable, the type magicians use when performing levitation illusions. One end was secured to the tree and the other to another tree two hundred feet away. Linda planned to descend the incline using a pulley system. She calculated that her destination—the rear of a residential dwelling—would be on the far side of the police roadblocks. Once she began her descent, she knew she would be visible to her pursuers; however, she hoped the speed of her plunge would carry her away faster than they could react. At the other end of the line awaited a 750W, 48V off-road, non-speed-restricted e-bicycle with a thumb throttle—the perfect getaway vehicle. A wolf in sheep's clothing, it could exceed thirty-five miles per hour, yet equally comfortable meandering along paths at six miles per hour.

The flying-fox and bicycle were only part of Linda's escape plan. Immediately following the phoney pub explosion, text messages had been sent to three associates who were driving in rental cars. At Linda's signal, they would each proceed to a designated central London intersection and abandoned their vehicles. Their role was to create traffic mayhem to impede the authority's pursuit of her.

The day prior to Linda's dinner with Claudia, MI6 surveillance teams had spotted Linda Orr scouting an escape route from The Windsor Castle pub. The analysts believed she was planning to avoid capture by riding a bike through the green spaces of central London: Hyde Park, Green Park, Buckingham Palace Garden, and St James's Park, an area of four-square miles, leaving a short dash through a busy part of London to reach the Thames. Here, they suspected a speedboat would whisk her away.

Kensington Gardens, the western extent of the neighbouring Hyde Park, was a half a mile from The Windsor Castle, Linda's entry point to the network of green spaces, or so the analysts concluded.

Linda familiarised herself with the route, including the key landmarks that would guide her when the chase began, by cycling the entire route, occasionally using electric pedal assist on the e-bike. She had broken the journey into five zones: Kensington Gardens/Hyde Park, Hyde Park Corner, Green and St James Park, Parliament Square, and The River Thames. Each zone had a defined boundary, with way-points that had to be reached within a given time. She had also scanned the adjoining areas, in case, on the day, her movement along the path was disrupted, and she needed to adjust the plan.

Unseen by MI6, Linda started her journey where the flying-fox finished. She rode east along the residential street of Campden, before crossing Kensington Church Street, a busy arterial road, mounted the footpath on the other side and turned right. Thirty meters later, she took a left onto Berkeley Gardens before a right onto Brunswick Gardens, following it to Vicarage Gate.

I do so love the names of these streets and roads. The British are such funny people.

Vicarage Gate took Linda to the entrance of Saint Mary Abbots, a church built in 1872 to the design of Sir George Gilbert Scott. From inside the grounds of the church Linda rode cross country for a hundred meters before linking up with Kensington Palace Gardens, a private roadway within Kensington Gardens which, if she turned left, would take her to the Embassy of the Russian Federation. Linda stopped and checked the physical map of the gardens she had printed. A paper map let Linda view the gardens in their entirety, something her smart phone wouldn't to the same level of detail. Having gained her bearings, satisfied that she'd been stationary long enough to be seen, Linda folded the map and put it away. She turned right onto Kensington Palace Gardens and peddled to Palace Avenue, where she took a left and then, rather than following it to join Studio Walk, rode diagonally on the lawns, crossing Dial Walk and Broad Walk, before coming to a stop on the Flower Walk, where she checked the map again.

Perfect. I hope you're watching because I'm giving you plenty of opportunities. Mustn't linger too long or I'll give the game away.

From Flower Walk, Linda rode past The Albert Memorial, an ornate pavilion fifty-four metres tall in the style of a Gothic ciborium over the high altar of a church sheltering a statue of the Prince facing south towards Serpentine Lake, a forty-acre recreation lake in Hyde Park created in 1730 at the behest of Queen Caroline. The spire of the Albert Memorial was an important navigational beacon for Linda. If for any reason she couldn't follow the intended route, she would aim for the spire and then ride past the Memorial and onto Kensington Road, disappearing into the city. Staying on Flower Walk, Linda peddled past Kensington Gardens Mount Gate toilets, before crossing West Carriage Drive, a street in Hyde Park.

'There you are,' Linda said, seeing Serpentine Lake. 'Now, according to the map, if I follow its southern bank to the eastern end, I will ride past the next way-point, the Serpentine Waterfall, Hyde Park Holocaust Memorial, and the Huntress Fountain, which I must keep on my left.'

Peddling slowly, Linda rode past the markers one after another, making her way to the next landmark, an architectural structure, the Screen at Hyde Park Corner Entrance, a Colonnade of Greek Ionic pillars pierced by three entrances and flanked by iron railings with stone piers. Approaching the structure, Linda slowed, coming to a standstill under the central archway. The large green wrought-iron gate on the arch was open, but a security fence blocked her path.

I wasn't expecting that, which Linda, is why we do reconnaissance.

Back-peddling, Linda checked the entrances under the other arches. The one to her right was also open but without a security fence to impede her progress.

When the time comes, stay right.

Leaving Hyde Park, Linda paused on the footpath, lingering longer than she really needed in order to check her directions.

'Ah. That's a pretty sight,' Linda said, while resisting the urge to point, an exaggerated gesture that would have let the cat out of the bag. From where she stood, Linda had a clear view of the next way-point, Wellington Arch, originally built as the entrance to Buckingham Palace, later becoming Victory Arch, proclaiming Wellington's defeat of Napoleon. It is the centrepiece of Hyde Park Corner, standing on a large traffic island between the corners of Hyde Park and Green Park, with crossings for pedestrians. Six streets converge at the road junction: Park Lane from the north, Piccadilly, the northeast, Constitutional Hill, the southeast, Grosvenor Place, the south, Grosvenor Crescent, southwest and Knightsbridge to the west. The entrance to Hyde Park Corner underground railway station is also located near the junction. Linda wheeled her bike from the park, across the pedestrian crossing and onto the large traffic island. Mounting again, she rode past Victory Arch before dismounting as she reached Duke of Wellington Place pedestrian crossing that led to the next destination, Constitutional Hill, a long straight road connecting the western end of The Mall, in front of Buckingham Palace, with Hyde Park Corner and bordering Buckingham Palace Gardens to the south, and Green Park Gardens to the north.

As she waited for the pedestrian lights to turn green, Linda grinned.

I could be delayed trying to cross these roads, which is an obvious weakness in my plan. Sometimes Linda, you're too clever by half.

The lights changed colour and Linda crossed the road before mounting the e-bike to cycle along the footpath which ran parallel to Constitutional Hill. She rode passed Canada Gate, an entrance to Green Park near Buckingham Palace, before crossing The Mall, briefly entering St James Park, before exiting on to Birdcage Walk which she followed east-west to reach the café at Storey's Gate, and Horse Guard Road, the boundary of the central London green spaces. Linda dismounted in preparation to cross the road and sighed, looking about her.

I'm going to miss you, old London town, for your rich history, stunning architecture, and vibrant culture on every corner—but most of all, for your beloved pubs.

Okay Linda, all that remains is the dash to the River Thames, the most dangerous part of the plan so far, somewhere that MI6 will believe they can capture you.

The next part of the journey took Linda along Great George Street, through Parliament Square and past Big Ben, collectively one of the most heavily policed areas in Great Britain. Having crossed Horse Guard Road, Linda rode along the footpath. Pedestrians made progress at any speed difficult.

What were you expecting, Linda? This is central London, after all.

When she reached Westminster bridge, Linda bumped her bike down the first of three sets of steps near the statue of Boadicea and Her Daughters, Queen of the Celtic Iceni tribe, who led an uprising in Roman Britain, leading to Westminster Millennium Pier. She stopped on the steps, breathing out.

I've made it, but I'm not as fit as I thought. It's a damn good job that this bike has batteries.

She peered out over the river.

Hopefully, my MI6 lovelies. You will see a speedboat as it approaches the pier. It will pull in close, and I leap from the steps, over the wall and into the waiting boat, driven by Miss Adele.

Linda took a firm hold of the flying-fox pulley, ready for the descent on a line that would deposit her on the other side of the Campden Street police road closure. As she launched herself from the trees and raced down the cable at breakneck speed, the wind running through her hair, Linda said, 'This is perfect, just perfect. Let the fun begin.'

'There,' Stephen Walls said, pointing to one of the large monitors hanging on the wall in the incident room at MI6 headquarters. It displayed a live satellite feed over the Windsor Castle pub.

'A flying-fox, that's ingenious.' Inspector Axel said. 'I wondered how she would try to escape our ring of steel.' He relayed what they were seeing to the Operational Commander at the Windsor Castle.

Having dropped safely from the zip line, Linda secured a helmet, donned her yellow jacket, and calmly pushed the e-bike out onto the street. She glanced at the roadblock, laughing at the authority's incompetence when the police paid her no attention. She mounted the bike and cycled towards Kensington Gardens.

Stephen Walls said, 'Is that an electric bicycle she's taken?'

'Can you zoom in?' Inspector Axel asked.

Melissa, who was controlling the satellite surveillance, nodded. 'We can do that.'

'Stop there.' Inspector Axel said as he hesitated, waiting for Linda to reappear from the tree cover. 'It's as we hoped Stephen, the same bike that we tracked her using yesterday, and yes, it's electric.'

Stephen nodded. 'A wise choice for central London, better than a motorbike, where you may get snarled up in the traffic.'

Melissa raised her hand to attract the attention of Stephen and Inspector Axel. They both glanced at her. 'We have reports coming in of vehicles being abandoned in the middle of three of London's busiest intersections. Traffic chaos is cascading out quickly.'

'Indeed,' Stephen said. 'Is this another element in Linda's escape plan?'

'I imagine so,' Inspector Axel said, his tone brisk. A traffic jam hadn't been part of their planning, so he was annoyed. Yesterday, they could have arrested Linda Orr at Westminster Millennium Pier, but Stephen, on the phone from Brussels, had rejected the idea. Stephen wanted intelligence from Linda on The Firm and he expected Claudia to deliver it. Inspector Axel was irritated because Stephen Walls had shut down the Windsor Castle meeting early, and now they risked losing Linda Orr for little or no gain.

Ignoring the Inspector's abruptness, Stephen Walls said, 'You believe Linda Orr is making for Hyde Park on her way to Westminster Millennium Pier?'

Inspector Axel, annoyed at himself for showing his vexation, said politely, 'Yes, Sir. The surveillance teams tracked her from Kensington Gardens to Westminster Millennium Pier, but we don't know her route from the pub to the gardens.'

After a pause, Stephen Walls continued. 'Inspector, I assume that you've considered whether the route of yesterday may have been a ploy, a ruse to lead you away from her intended escape route.'

Inspector Axel smiled and maintained his professional tone. 'That's a possibility Stephen and, if indeed that is the case... well, we will respond to the situations as they arise.'

Which is why I wanted to apprehend Linda when we had the opportunity, Stephen. Enough Axel, it's time to put your frustration to bed and focus on capturing Linda Orr.

Inspector Axel pointed towards another TV monitor. 'We are tracking a speedboat piloted by Miss Adele, currently heading towards Westminster Pier and so we have confidence that this is Linda Orr's destination.'

'Where is the intercept to take place, Inspector?'

'Victory Arch Stephen, on Hyde Park Corner, the traffic island, as she crosses from Hyde Park to Saint James Park.'

'An interesting choice.'

Inspector Axel nodded. 'Perhaps ordinarily Sir. We've installed technology from the Netherlands, which can automatically reduce or cut off an electric bicycle's power. Once on the traffic island, we can use this technology to pen Linda in.'

'You can do that, Inspector?'

'Yes, Stephen.'

'Theoretically Inspector, you could do the same with an electric car?'

Inspector Axel thought for a moment. 'That's an interesting observation. I imagine in time, that electric cars will be automatically speed limited when they enter a city or town's limits.'

'Excuse me gentlemen,' Melissa said.

Inspector Axel and Stephen Walls looked up in anticipation, but did not speak.

'The three abandoned cars are creating significant traffic difficulties.'

'Will this pose a problem, Inspector?'

With the dumped cars no longer a surprise, Inspector Axel remained calm. 'It may work to our advantage by limiting Linda's options.'

Let's hope so,' Stephen said as they turned their attention to the live satellite feed. When Linda Orr reached Kensington Palace Gardens, Inspector Axel instructed the Ground Commander to send in the Mounted Branch.

'Horses, Inspector?'

Inspector Axel nodded. 'We want to keep Linda moving towards Hyde Park Corner; horses give the impression we've been surprised.'

For Linda Orr, the trip from The Windsor Castle pub drop point into the Kensington Gardens went as planned. The pedal assist on her e-bike had been set to maximum, in readiness for any eventuality. Cycling down Studio Drive, as she approached Broad Walk ready to cut across the lawn and towards The Albert Memorial, Linda spotted two mounted police offices galloping towards her.

'Horses,' Linda said and laughed out loud, fighting the urge to look skyward towards the satellites watching her, saying, 'I didn't see that one coming.'

With a touch of the thumb throttle, not bothering to peddle, Linda used the power of the bike to speed away. The next part of the journey went without incident and as she neared the Screen at Hyde Park Corner entrance, she slowed.

'Where has she gone?' Inspector Axel said.

'We've lost her under the trees,' Melissa replied. Five seconds later she added, 'Look, she's leaving the gardens.'

'I can't see her.'

Melissa pointed at the screen. 'She's stopped at Knightsbridge and it looks like she's checking to see if the coast is clear before crossing the road and onto the traffic island.'

'Yep, I've got her.' Inspector Axel relayed Linda's position to the ground commander, adding, 'We don't want the target to suspect a trap. Wait for my command before cutting the electric motor.'

'Yes Sir,' the radio crackled.

'Commander, she's crossing Knightsbridge.'

'We have her in sight, Sir.'

'Good. Wait for my order.'

Those in the MI6 incident room watched in silence as Linda crossed the road, mounted her bike and cycled towards the Arch. Inspector Axel waited until she was twenty feet from Wellington Arch before instructing the commander, 'Do it now, cut the motor.'

Linda felt the full effort of peddling the bicycle when the electric assist failed and said, irritated, 'What's happening?' She glanced down at the electric motor, wondering why it had ceased working.

'Go, go, go,' Inspector Axel barked into the radio.

Linda heard the wailing of police sirens and tried the thumb throttle, but nothing happened.

They've disabled the electric motor. I wasn't expecting that!

In the sky above, the whooshing noise of a helicopter was accompanied by the appearance of heavily armed officers blocking her path to Constitutional Hill. Realising that MI6 wanted her trapped on the traffic island, Linda gritted her teeth, and said, 'Okay, if you want to play games, bring it on'.

With all the strength she could muster, Linda swung the bike to her right, away from the officers, and cycled furiously across the grass towards the Australian War Memorial in the southernmost corner, a curved wall that formed an amphitheatre, a memorial dedicated to the 102,000 Australians who died in the First and Second World Wars. From there, Linda could cross Duke of Wellington Place, a busy multi-lane road between Grosvenor Place and Constitutional Hill, and into Green Park. Nearing the Australian War Memorial, two armed officers appeared, one at each end, to block her path. Swinging right and leaning the bike hard over, the front wheel on the cycle slipped, almost unseating Linda as she struggled to regain control. Straightening the bike, Linda rode toward the only remaining escape option. She changed up gears, increasing speed.

As Linda approached the perimeter of the traffic island, she noticed her path was obstructed by a five-foot-high steel security fence. Ordinarily, Linda would jump her bike over the fence, a skill most mountain bikers had. Her approach would have been to ride towards the obstacle in a high-ready position, stop pedalling, relax, and raise up a little. Next, she would transition down into her ready position, with her elbows out and knees bent, she would compress the bike with a short powerful compression resulting in an equal and opposite explosion as she reached the takeoff point, thrusting the bike into the air, then throwing her weight forward as she sailed over the obstacle. Because the bike carried the added weight of a battery and electric motor, she knew that, from a flat start, it would be impossible to clear the fence. Slamming on the brakes, the bike skidded to the side and Linda leaned the bike over and let go of the handlebars, sending it crashing into the fence with a thud. She slid to a stop on the grass.

Inspector Axel and Stephen Walls heard over the radio, 'We have her.'

Heavily armed officers surrounded Linda, yelling, 'Armed police, stay on the ground!'

Two officers ran towards the prostrate Linda and secured her hands behind her back.

While Stephen and Inspector Axel watched the events unfold, the radio in the incident room crackled. 'She's secure.'

Inspector Axel felt uneasy; something wasn't right. Melissa, can we switch the view to the officers' body cameras, please? He studied the screen, then scrunched up his face.

'What's wrong Inspector?'

'Take the bike helmet off,' Inspector Axel said into the radio as he and Stephen watched the screen.

Inspector Axel sighed in frustration and then shook his head. 'It looks like her, but it's not Linda Orr. Check and see if she's wearing a wig Commander.'

They watched as a blond wig was removed to reveal a woman with jet black hair.

'Damn it Inspector,' Stephen Walls said, 'where did Linda make the swap?'

It wasn't Inspector Axel's intention to ignore Stephen, but his eyes were drawn to the satellite tracking live feed of a speedboat on the River Thames, piloted by Miss Adele. As the wig had been removed, the speedboat, heading towards Westminster Millennium Pier, slowed, turned around. The SAS helicopter tracking the boat radioed the MI6 incident room, providing intel that Inspector Axel had already seen, asking, 'Shall we intercept her?'

Inspector Axel thought for a moment before replying in the negative. 'We have no lawful reason to detain Miss Adele, not today anyway.' He looked at Stephen, who nodded in agreement, saying,

'Unfortunately, Inspector, we can't prove that it was Miss Adele who tried to kill you in Oxford, though we know without question that it was.'

Inspector Axel raised an eyebrow and, tilting his head slightly to one side, said, 'Miss Adele will make a mistake. Criminals always do and, when she does, I'll be there waiting for her.'

'Indeed, Inspector. Now, where did Linda Orr make the swap?'

Inspector Axel breathed out heavily, a sign of his frustration at losing his target. 'It's only a guess Sir. My money is on the Screen at the Hyde Park Corner entrance. If you recall, we lost sight of her under the trees. Linda Orr knew we were watching.'

***

The double, a bicycle helmet secured to her head and holding a light green jacket was waiting for Linda Orr at Hyde Park Corner. She was already wearing a matching yellow top, and the changeover was smooth and efficient, taking less than five seconds. As Linda watched her electric bike disappear across the road, she removed her helmet, placed it on the ground donned a green jacket. From the pocket she took a face mask, a common site on public transport since the pandemic, and a pair of elegant tortoiseshell rimmed spectacles. With her facial features now hidden, Linda walked casually towards the Hyde Park Corner tube station, yards away from where the switch had taken place. Humming, Linda passed through the subway turnstile, boarded a train, travelled two stations and alighted at South Kensington.

She glanced at her watch.

Perfect timing.

She was out of the underground system before the decoy could be apprehended. With the mask and glasses in place, Linda strode away from the station, confident that she had outwitted MI6. Wanting to avoid the traffic chaos, Linda walked two blocks before hailing a cab. Safely inside the taxi, feeling smug at her success, Linda peered out of the side window and said, 'You haven't seen the last of me!'

Believing his passenger was speaking to him, the taxi driver said, 'Sorry, Madam? I didn't quite get that.'

'It's a song by Cher,' she said and started singing. When she reached the title of the song, Linda raised her voice and shouted out, 'You haven't seen the last of me.'

You haven't seen the last of me, Stephen Walls and MI6.

The taxi driver, in his late sixties and a Sikh in a turban, stole a glance at Linda in the rear vision mirror. 'I'm afraid I don't know that one, Madam.'

'Really. It was nominated for a Grammy. For best song ever.'

'Sorry, it eludes me. Where to, Madam?'

'Second star to the right and straight on till morning.'

The taxi driver smiled. 'Ha, I know that one, Madam. When they were young, I would read that story to my children.'

Linda grinned. 'It's a classic and something an old friend of mine would always say.' She paused, before adding, 'To the Royal Observatory, please, driver.'

'Greenwich, Madam?'

'Yes, Greenwich.'

As the taxi pulled away from the curb, Linda broke into song, giving another rendition of, "You haven't seen the last of me".

***

'Yes, Inspector,' Stephen Walls said, 'the trees. They are near the subway station entrance, so I assume that Linda Orr donned a disguise and caught a train.'

'I would say so, Stephen.'

There were other people in the incident room, so Stephen chose his words and tone of delivery carefully. 'Inspector, had we considered that possibility?'

'Yes, Sir. We had people in place at the station. There were no reported sightings.'

'Umm.'

'Linda is gone Sir.' Inspector Axel said.

'Yes, Inspector.' Stephen paused before adding, 'Stand everybody down.'

'We haven't seen the last of her, Stephen.'

Stephen pursed his lips before nodding in agreement, his face sombre.

Claudia, I hope you've learned something that makes this worthwhile. It was my decision not to arrest Linda when Inspector Axel had the chance, and I hope I won't come to regret that choice.

Speaking into the radio, Inspector Axel said, 'All units, stand down.'

Stephen straightened his tie. 'Inspector. I want a full briefing in the morning, nine-thirty, my office, and Claudia will join us.'

'Yes, Sir.'

Leave me this mess to clean up.

Stephen started to leave, but after taking three steps toward the door, he paused, turning to face Inspector Axel.

'In hindsight, Inspector, it might have been wiser to follow your recommendation.'

Without waiting for a reply, Stephen swivelled on his heals and departed.

CHAPTER 3
Oh John

Claudia slipped past the Windsor Castle Road blocks set up to capture Linda and headed towards her new home, a flat she'd purchased in Chelsea, an exclusive and desirable area of London, located to the west of the city, bound by the River Thames, Knightsbridge to the north, Fulham to the northwest and Battersea to the south. Claudia had bought the top-floor apartment for its uninterrupted view overlooking the Thames and the city. Her days of staying at the St Ermin's Hotel when visiting London were over.

For Britain, it was an unusually balmy evening so, after leaving The Windsor Castle, Claudia decided she would walk the three and a half miles to her apartment, besides a taxi in London traffic, made worse by Linda's escape plan, would have been a nightmare. Strolling, enjoying the evening air which Claudia sucked deep into her lungs, she mused. Linda would avoid capture, she was sure of that, and imagined the authorities participation in the wild goose chase her old partner had created before slipping away, leaving MI6 with egg on its face. The thought of a flustered Stephen Walls made Claudia smile but, having been betrayed by Linda, she wanted her captured. Claudia pondered terminating Linda Orr herself after she'd tracked her relentlessly, a thought that brought a grin to her face. Forty minutes later, she punched the security code into the keypad that secured the front door and entered her four-bedroom flat. The wealth needed to purchase an apartment that most would describe as an architectural masterpiece was a consequence of Claudia's income from the time she worked for the Russian Mafia, certainly not from the miserly MI6 salary.

The front door opened into an entry gallery which led to a breath-taking open plan dining room and kitchen with floor to ceiling windows soaring over four metres. There were two terraces with unobstructed panoramic views over the river and of the London skyline. The kitchen boasted a granite island bench, a double refrigerator, a Miele double oven, six burner cook top with a vented hood and a pair of dishwashers. Oak and satin-etched glass cabinets provided abundant storage space. Off the kitchen was a five-hundred-and-fifty bottle wine closet and a marble bar, both hidden behind oak doors. On the second story was a library with windows framing the River Thames and finally the master bedroom. This featured a fireplace, a sitting room, a terrace, an enormous walk-in closet and a limestone bathroom with a heated floor, double sink, shower, and deep soaking tub. The four bedrooms all had en-suite bathrooms. Before moving in, Claudia had the latest in high-tech AV and security systems installed. If Linda hadn't murdered John Moss, she would have married him and lived a more austere existence, perhaps in the country. This purchase was a statement, like her decision to adopt again her old Mafia name of Claudia.

Closing the door behind her, she took a deep breath, leaving the events of the day outside. She kicked off her shoes, took out her smart phone and switched off the security system before the alarm was activated by her presence. A last task remained before she could relax, an IT scan, to ensure the security measures hadn't been compromised by hackers, and that there had been no unwanted visitors during her absence. Because she was using advanced technology, both scenarios were unlikely. Nevertheless, the ritual born out of habit was difficult to break. Everything was as it should have been, so Claudia put on slippers from next to the front door and entered the kitchen, releasing an audible sigh of relief, 'Ahhhh.'

Opening the oak doors, she plucked a wineglass from the bar before selecting from the wine closet a vintage Sauvignon Blanc. Studying the label, she replaced it, taking instead an aged Riesling.

'That's a better choice for tonight.'

Claudia poured the mellow yellow contents into the glass, holding it up to let the light filter through. Placing the glass on the bar, she screwed the top back onto the bottle and, as she was about to put it to sleep in the wine closet, changed her mind, removed the top and added more of the nectar to her glass. Examining the new level, Claudia smiled in satisfaction. Taking her companion upstairs, Claudia settled into a comfortable chair in the sitting room where she could take in the view and enjoy the taste and fragrance of her drink. After a couple of sips, she placed the glass on a side table, stretched her legs and relaxed, vibrant dreams filling her mind as she fell asleep. In one, a conversation earlier that night with Linda replayed itself. Linda said,

'I was rather taken by Molly and even Snowflake the cat myself. So, as a friend, I think you will want to know this. Richard Liew is being recalled to China, and his family is to accompany him. I think you understand what this will mean... for Molly.'

When? Claudia heard herself ask.

'Sorry, I don't have an exact date, but I'm told it's soon. Very soon.'

Claudia awoke with a jerk and glanced at her watch. She'd been asleep only ten minutes, but felt revived. With the dream fresh in her mind, Claudia took a further sip of wine.

'How do I protect you, my young Molly, if I don't know when I'm needed?'

Claudia recalled a conversation with Olivia. Samantha, Molly's mother, had told Olivia that she was going to demand Richard resign from the Chinese State Security Service. Olivia had counselled against it, telling her that the family must be an effective team, particularly to the spying eyes of the Chinese. Claudia feared the prediction Olivia had made, that returning to China would be dangerous for Samantha and Molly, something to be avoided. She examined the wine in her glass, still one-third full. Claudia tilted the glass so that the wine rolled towards its edge, letting the light of the room exposed the Riesling's complete colour range. She gave the wine a swirl and, as it moved around the edge of the glass, she considered the conundrum. Claudia gave the wine a further swirl and, without burying her nostrils inside, her nose hovered like a hummingbird surveying the nectar in a beautiful flower. She took some quick sniffs, then pulled away, letting her brain ponder. The ritual worked and ideas started to form.

Operation Snowflake. That's how I will protect you, Molly.

Claudia took another sip of wine and closed her eyes.

Would Samantha believe me if I said that she and Molly were in imminent danger and should leave Richard? No, because she blames me. Can I trust what Linda Orr told me? Did she tell the truth?

Claudia opened her eyes and said aloud, 'You have to believe Linda is telling the truth, but you can't tell Samantha, because she loathes you.' Claudia closed her eyes again.

Okay, but what happens when you're overseas on a mission and Molly needs you? How can you protect her? Max and Olivia. I will ask Max and Olivia to be her guardian angels when I'm away. They're the only people I really trust.

Opening her eyes, Claudia swirled her glass again before finishing the last of its contents, satisfied that she had the bones of a plan.

After a shower to wash away the grime of the day, Claudia retired to her bedroom for the night. As was her way in the warmer months when the days were longer, she left the curtains open so that the dawn light filtered in and woke her in time for a six-kilometre run before breakfast, after which she had a nine-thirty meeting with Stephen Walls at MI6 headquarters. In the en suite, Claudia changed into a silky translucent white nightdress with red sexy underwear beneath, worn the night she first slept with John Moss. Pulling back the silk duvet and the one-thousand thread count Egyptian cotton bed sheets on her king size bed, Claudia paused. Thinking of John, she ran her hands slowly over her body, tracing the shape of her breasts before letting her fingers linger on her leg. Lifting her hand slowly, the nightdress lifted, leaving her fingers to rest on the outside of her red panties. Squeezing her hand to feel her curve, her fingers penetrated between her legs, causing her to gasp.

'Oh, John.'

She lingered for a moment, savouring the sensation before releasing her grip. Claudia straightened her nightgown before climbing into bed. She let the sensation of the bed sheets resting on her exposed arms and legs blanket her. Closing her eyes, Claudia sought a companion and searched her memory for John, but it was Daniel Tinkov, Saint Vladimir, that she pictured. Claudia smiled. Since the passing of John Moss, she'd been intimate with no one. However, while guarding Daniel Tinkov on the Canary Islands, she felt a rekindling of desire. Before she'd met John Moss, her sexual appetite was purely physical, devoid of attachment. During her time with Daniel Tinkov, Claudia had relaxed, smiled again and felt a tenderness she'd known only with John. It was Saint Vladimir who became her imaginary companion, as Claudia drifted into a restful sleep.

The hairs on the back of Claudia's neck bristled, sending adrenaline pumping through her veins and in an instant, she underwent a transformation, from deep sleep to hyper-alert. Controlling the urge to jump from her bed, ready to fight, Claudia maintained the rhythmic breathing of a person in slumber while probing the room, scanning through half-opened eyes, listening for signs of danger.

Moving her hand slowly, Claudia felt for the pistol she kept under the pillow.

Where are you? There you are, my trusty friend.

Nothing stirred in the room, everything sounded as it should, never-the-less, Claudia knew something wasn't right!

Moving stealthily like a cat stalking its prey, Claudia gripped the butt of her gun, her finger poised on the trigger. With the speed of a rattlesnake, she retrieved the weapon, sat up in bed, and, with the city lights filtering through the window to dimly to illuminate her surroundings, she swept the barrel left and right as she scanned the room.

She saw nothing.

With the agility of a leopard, Claudia slipped from beneath the sheets, her feet touching the floor in silence. With knees slightly bent, ready to respond, and with only the light from the windows to guide her, she drifted through the apartment, checking each room in turn. Thirty minutes later, at three-fifty in the morning, Claudia was satisfied that she was alone. Next, she ran a scan of her security system. There was no sign of an intruder or any compromise by a hacker. Claudia shook her head. She trusted her instincts and regardless of what the IT system told her; she was certain that someone had been in the apartment.

Go back to bed, girly. Whoever was here has gone and there's nothing you can do now.

At the foot of Claudia's bed, an envelope was lying on the duvet.

Was that there before?

Claudia raised her pistol, its barrel sweeping across the bedroom in a steady arc.

She was alone; she was sure.

Claudia checked the lock on the sliding window leading to the upstairs terrace. It was locked from the inside.

Shaking her head in frustration, she said, 'How did you buggers get in?'

Returning to the foot of the bed, Claudia picked up a premium quality invitation envelope and turned it over in her hand. The front and back were blank, but there was something inside. Opening it, Claudia removed a white card on which was printed a silhouette of a female Samurai warrior, accompanied by two words.

Altindere Vadisi

'Well, I suppose this at the least proves you don't want me dead, not yet anyhow.'

She read the words again: Altindere Vadisi.

'Um. I don't recognise you. The name of a person? An address? More likely a location.'

Claudia picked up her phone, ready to enter Altindere Vadisi into an internet search engine, however changed her mind. 'I'll look you up in the morning.' Claudia raised her voice as if calling out to someone hiding in the apartment. 'Tomoe, I will work out how you achieved this feat of magic. Somehow, you managed to enter and leave without me knowing, which is a worthy achievement.'

After a last glance about the bedroom, Claudia placed the pistol back under the pillow and climbed into bed, falling into a fitful sleep, one eye open alert for danger. The fantasy of Daniel

Tinkov was forgotten, replaced by the truth of the life she lived, one on the edge.

61

CHAPTER 4
The Great Game

MI6 Headquarters

'Good morning Claudia,' James said as she entered the outer office, 'Stephen and Inspector Axel are expecting you.'

'Thank you, James.'

'Tea? English Breakfast?'

Claudia smiled, wondering if she should stick to their well-rehearsed script, or change it by saying something like, 'Earl Grey, please.' She followed their routine.

'That would be most kind of you, James.'

It was James's turn to smile.

Claudia knocked on Stephen's door and, as she was expected, opened it before he answered.

'Ah, Claudia,' Stephen said. He and Inspector Axel rose from their chairs. 'Please, join us' Stephen pointed to a vacant chair next to where Inspector Axel was seated, both positioned in front of Stephen's desk.

Inspector Axel bowed his head in greeting. 'Good morning, Claudia.'

'Inspector.'

Both men waited for Claudia to be seated before resuming their positions. 'I take it that James has offered you a beverage?'

'Yes, he has Stephen. Thank you.'

'How was,' Stephen paused, searching for the right words. 'Your dinner with Linda?'

Grinning, her voice light, Claudia said, 'Unfortunately, the authorities were overly enthusiastic so Linda fled before we could eat.' Her voice became more serious. 'Linda eluded the net, am I correct?'

'She did.' Stephen waited a moment. 'Did you learn anything illuminating?'

'Nothing you didn't hear, Stephen.'

Stephen nodded. 'Indeed. As you know, Claudia, context is everything. Your perspective on what Linda told you is of much interest.' Stephen handed Claudia a transcript of their conversation. 'The Inspector and I have some questions. If I may start with...' There was a knock at the door.

'Come,' Stephen called.

James entered, carrying a cup and saucer. 'Your tea, Claudia. I'll put it on the table.'

'Ah. Thank you, James.'

Claudia placed her copy of the transcript on Stephen's desk and sipped her tea.

They waited for James to leave and when the door was closed before Stephen said, 'Where was I? Yes, if I could start with two related items, the offer for you to join The Firm, and Tomoe. I found that part of the transcript confusing.'

Claudia nodded. 'Me too. On reflection, I believe the Firm is sowing seeds of doubt within MI6 over my loyalties, perhaps to encourage me to join them. Tomoe may want to entice me into a trap, but I have my reservations. Then there's Linda's suggestion that I kill Tomoe. In the underworld Stephen, rivalries play out differently than that of the public service. I took her inference at face value. Linda is, after all, an ambitious woman and probably wishes to trigger a power struggle, then fill the vacuum.'

Inspector Axel tilted his head to one side, picking up on an inflection in Claudia's voice. 'You mentioned that you have reservations. Could you explain?'

Claudia smiled. 'Inspector, you are a perceptive man. Last night I had an intruder in my apartment who I believe was Tomoe. If she'd wanted me dead, I would not be here talking to you now.'

Inspector Axel scratched his head. 'Are you certain, Tomoe?'

Claudia handed Inspector Axel the white card she'd left, with its silhouette of a female samurai warrior.

'Have you considered that your friend Linda Orr is leading you to Tomoe for her own purposes? It is her modus operandi, after all.'

'In the world of espionage, Inspector, nothing is as it seems.'

Inspector Axel nodded, then read the words on the card and passed it to Stephen Walls, 'Altindere Vadisi.'

'What or where is Altindere Vadisi?' Stephen Walls asked.

Claudia shrugged her shoulders. 'I assume Tomoe wants me to go there, Stephen.'

'Does it mean anything to you, Claudia?'

'I hadn't heard of the place until last night.'

As Stephen and Claudia talked, Inspector Axel entered *Altindere Vadisi* into a search engine on his smart phone. 'Have you looked it up, Claudia?'

'Yes. It's a national park in Turkey.'

Stephen Walls rubbed his chin. 'A national park! There must be more to this, surely. Inspector, read out what you've found.'

'The Altindere National Park is the best-known park in the Black Sea region and lies to the west of Trabzon in Turkey. The Sumela Monastery is one of the major sites of the Altindere National Park. Also known as Meryemana, because it was dedicated to the Virgin Mary and was the centre of Christianity in the region. The Sumela Monastery is a Greek Orthodox monastery and is also a significant place in history and art. It was thought the monastery was constructed in the 4th century, although Alexios III, (1349-1390) can be named as the real founder. It was extended in the 19th century, when it enjoyed its most popular period. The national park can be reached via the 48 km road connecting Trabzon to Macka.'

Stephen scrunched up his face. 'You have a thing for monasteries, Claudia.'

'Ha, they have a thing for me.'

'A major tourist attraction is an unlikely lair for Tomoe, don't you think?'

Inspector Axel raised his eyebrows.

'Something on your mind, Inspector?'

While I don't recall Altindere National Park, Sumela Monastery is a different story. While researching Melk Abbey for our operation there, I sifted through the MI6 files on abbeys and monasteries—believe it or not; we have them. The Sumela Monastery is situated on Melá Mountain, built into a steep cliff at an altitude of about 3,900 feet. In 2015, because of increasing rock falls, it was closed to the public for a year, which was later extended to three years. It finally reopened in 2019. There were reports of extensive earthworks that went beyond what was necessary for stabilization, leading to speculation that a secret complex lies hidden within the monastery, an important historical and tourist site in Trabzon. Why such a complex would be there remains unanswered, but as I said, it was only speculation.

Claudia looked at Stephen. 'Do you want me to go?'

He shook his head. 'Not for the time being. I have another pressing operation to discuss with you, but tell me, how did the intruder gain access to your home?'

Claudia shrugged her shoulders. 'It's equipped with our latest security systems.'

Inspector Axel gave Claudia a sideways glance and Claudia returned the gesture, a non-verbal expression that questioned the Inspector's knowledge,

'Is the security managed through your smart phone?'

Claudia nodded.

'The one you lent to Linda.' A statement, not a question.

'No, Inspector.'

'Sorry, Claudia, I thought...'

Claudia interrupted. 'It's possible, I suppose, that when Linda Orr cloned my phone, The Firm set up a backdoor that gives them access to my data when I do an upload.'

Stephen Walls shook his head and breathed out heavily in frustration. 'Can we be sure that your night time visitor wasn't Linda Orr?'

Claudia shrugged her shoulders. 'With no CCTV footage, anything is possible.'

Inspector Axel nodded before repeating Claudia's last words. 'Anything is possible, but the *who* gives insight into the *why* - the motive, and the *how*, the method. The identity of the intruder is something we shouldn't dismiss too lightly.'

'Inspector, your policing perspective is understood. Yes, identifying the intruder is important to understand the motive, but we have debated this enough. We'll take things on face value until time reveals otherwise. In the interim Claudia, have James organise our boffins to check your phone for malware and, for heaven's sake, use one of our secure terminals to change your passwords and not the phone. What we don't need is an MI6 agent accused of funding an insurrection in some failed state, with a money trail leading back to your accounts.'

Claudia bit her lip. With the Chinese State Security Service having hacked into the MI6 systems, she resisted the urge to say, *Are our computers safe?*

You've been sloppy, Claudia, sloppy. Pick up your game girly and don't let this happen again.

Claudia nodded her agreement to Stephen.

'Good,' Stephen said. 'Now, to discuss a pressing matter that requires your unique skills.'

Flattery from Stephen. This must be serious.

Stephen rubbed his chin. 'The conjecture about your phone being hacked is a good segue into what I want to discuss. A major cyber-attack has penetrated the U.S. federal government, leading to a series of data breaches. The U.S. Office of the Director of National Intelligence has warned of a grave threat to critical infrastructure. The department has also discovered long-undetected intrusions into government and private computer systems. The Department of Energy, Treasury and Commerce and Microsoft, to name a few, have been infiltrated. The attack was so serious that it led to a National Security Council meeting at the White House. While the Government's Cybersecurity and Infrastructure Security Agency (CISA) is working with the FBI to investigate, it is suspected that Russian hackers are behind the attack. It was originally thought they used network management software from Texas-based SolarWinds to infiltrate computer networks but now believe they used other methods too.'

'Reassuringly, our U.S. colleagues assure us that their national security operations have not been compromised, including the agency that manages the nation's nuclear weapons stockpile.'

'As we know from the UK experience, these sophisticated cyber-attacks are not limited to the United States. While this latest incident appears to be part of an ongoing espionage and information gathering campaign against the Five Eye partners, it is suspected that the same operatives have also targeted public and private computer systems around the world with ransomware. In the continuing analysis of the SolarWinds attack, the FBI has found elements of the attack share some features with Kazuar, a .NET backdoor linked to a Russian hacking group, Cozy Bear. I am told they include the victim UID generation algorithm, the sleeping algorithm and the extensive usage of the FNV-1a hash.'

'As part of their ongoing investigation into Cozy Bear, the CIA has intercepted what they have classified as a real and present threat of a cyber breach in the world's financial systems. If that was to occur, it could create an economic downturn as disastrous as the global financial crisis and the coronavirus recession combined. If I can quote the U.S. President, "There is a lot we don't yet know, but what we know is a matter of great concern"'.

'I have informed our U.S. counterparts that the Russian Intelligence Services hacking group, Cozy Bear, may have a rogue operative in its midst. A person or persons working for The Firm under the avatar of Cosy Bear. The similarity between the two names, spelt differently but pronounced the same, is undoubtedly deliberate. Part of the subterfuge.'

Stephen paused and looked at Inspector Axel. 'You're smiling, Inspector. Care to share your thoughts?'

Inspector Axel rubbed his chin. 'Attributing a cyber-attack, Sir, is a complex technical challenge, rarely straightforward.'

'Indeed, Inspector, which is why we need to keep an open mind. It is likely Cozy Bear works on different projects with disparate user groups, which makes attribution more difficult. For the time being, we will proceed with what we know, or if you prefer, Inspector, what we believe we know.'

Inspector Axel nodded his agreement.

Stephen Walls continued, 'Today, coming hot on the heels of the U.S. Federal Government data breaches, an unknown actor seized control of the computers of a water treatment plant in Tampa Bay City, Oldsmar, Florida. They tried to poison the water supply by cranking up the sodium hydroxide from about 100 parts per million to more than 11,100 parts per million. Fortunately, a plant operator monitoring the facility noticed the breach and returned the settings to normal.'

'You suspect Cozy Bear?' Claudia asked.

'It's too early to tell. This has all the hallmarks of a ransomware attack without a ransom demand, which is unusual. It could be a demonstration of ability aimed at other utility providers. The UK and U.S. anticipate a string of extortion demands to follow. It is the view of the CIA that, by spreading its activities beyond espionage and into the criminal world of ransomware attacks, Cozy Bear has made a strategic error.'

Claudia scratched the back of her neck before saying, 'If this is a Russian extortion attempt, it's more likely to be coming from The Firm's Cosy Bear than from the Kremlin.'

Stephen Walls nodded in agreement. 'For the time being, Claudia, we are not separating the two and hope the confusion will work to our advantage. By targeting The Firm's Cosy Bear, we also hit the Kremlin's Cozy Bear ... Which is why Claudia, the CIA, has sought our assistance, and this is where you come in.'

Cocking her head slightly to one side, Claudia glanced at Stephen.

'Bronwyn, my counterpart in the CIA, would like you to talk to your former employer, Russian Mafia boss Monya Mogilevick and enlist his help to bring down Cozy Bear.'

Claudia raised an eyebrow.

'Stephen, the cyber-attack may well have originated from the North Korea Military Intelligence Agency for all we know. They regularly initiate hacks at the behest of the government to use stolen funds to benefit their regime. I recall MI6 previously accusing the Russians, only later discovering that it was North Korea who had carried out the attack.' Claudia shook her head. 'Even if this is the work of the Russians, why would Monya assist the Western Intelligence Services?'

Stephen Walls hesitated and considered his response. 'I asked Bronwyn the same question, and she had a powerful argument, to which I concur. By branching out into ransomware, Cozy Bear has become Monya's competitor. Helping us would be a simple business decision.'

Claudia pulled on her hair as she weighed Stephen's remarks. 'We support this approach, do we?'

'The British Government wants MI6, the SAS, and other Special Forces Groups to play a more active role in disrupting Russian meddling around the world. We've been tasked with directly tackling "hostile state actors". The Firm's meddling in Cozy Bear may be to our advantage.'

'Only if I persuade Monya to help.'

'Yes.'

'He's in league with the Russian security services Stephen... He won't compromise that relationship, even if it costs him money.'

Stephen raised his head. 'I trust in your powers of persuasion.'

'Stephen, Monya has no sympathy for the aims of MI6 or the CIA. If I were to persuade him, he would bite off your left hand, while taking from the right. An alliance, if it were to happen, will create a greater threat another day.'

Stephen picked a pen up from his desk and twirled it in his fingers. 'Perhaps, Claudia. Regardless, the CIA knows what they are asking and is aware of the consequences.'

Claudia knew this was a poor decision and felt her anger rising.

Settle girly.

She shifted uncomfortably in her chair. 'With due respect, Stephen, I can think of many cases where the CIA has underestimated the consequences, as you put it. Operation Cyclone, the CIA program in Afghanistan to arm and finance the Mujahideen against the Soviets.' Claudia paused, testing if Stephen was going to close off the discussion. When he remained silent, she continued. 'If my memory serves me correctly, the Mujahideen were also supported by MI6.'

Stephen's facial features hardened, a sign he was displeased with Claudia. 'The United Kingdom has a long history in Central Asia. It dates back hundreds of years to Victorian Britain.'

'Yes, the great game played out between Russia and Britain and not much has changed. The Taliban was formed in the early 1990s by the Afghan Mujahideen. The rest, as they say, is history.'

Stephen curled his lips and nodded, an acknowledgement of sorts. 'Claudia, it's important to understand the context of the decision at the time. In the West, the Soviet invasion of Afghanistan was considered a threat to global security and oil supplies from the Persian Gulf.'

'An intelligence failure.'

Stephen replied in a matter-of-fact tone, 'The failure was not anticipating the Soviet invasion of Afghanistan in the first place.'

'I understand that, Stephen, but the intelligence community, MI6 included, by overestimating the threat to global security and oil supplies, made decisions that turned out to be to our detriment.'

Stephen folded his arms. 'The threat was real at the time.'

Claudia scoffed, a noise escaping from her nose as Stephen fixed her with a cautionary glare, a warning to remain respectful.

Claudia softened her tone. 'I'm not suggesting that the British and U.S. support of the Mujahideen against the Soviets gave rise to the Taliban. Yet, out of fear of another 9/11 attack, and the Taliban giving sanctuary to al-Qaeda, the British, U.S., Dutch, Canadian, Australian, and other NATO forces were next to follow Russia into Afghanistan. The U.S. is still bogged down years later and when they leave, Kabul will fall to the Taliban. Stephen, what I'm suggesting is that intelligence failures...' Claudia cut herself off in mid-sentence. 'With respect, Sir, let me highlight a couple of our other security failures that will help make my point.'

Stephen's patience was waning.

I wish you wouldn't, Claudia.

Ordinarily, he would not tolerate such insubordination, but two points were encouraging his forbearance. First, Claudia had defected from the Russian Mafia to MI6, so sending her back was dangerous, but, as Monya Mogilevick's ex-lover, she was best placed to persuade him. Second, he had news to share with Claudia that would be difficult for her to handle; he would cut her some slack.

'Our pre-war judgments of Iraq's alleged weapons of mass destruction and, more recently, the CIA wanting Max to assassinate Monya to stave off World War Three. It's ironic. Now Bronwyn wants Monya's help.'

Stephen nodded. 'Intelligence analysis is not an exact science. Claudia, you know this, so we make the best judgements on the information available at the time.'

Claudia smiled. 'Yes. Hindsight is a wonderful thing.'

Stephen shifted in his chair. 'So, it would seem... The truth, Claudia, is different individuals and groups will make different assessments and arrive at different decisions, and often there will be no objectively right answer, either before or after the event. You see, things may have turned out worse had we not acted as we did. Then again, they may have turned out better had we not been involved.' Stephen took a deep breath, searching for the right words.

'Espionage, the Great Game, a turn of phrase made famous by novelist Rudyard Kipling in his novel Kim, is surrounded by uncertainty, the consequence, a proactive-reactive balancing act.'

Claudia crossed her legs, then uncrossed them again, as she reflected on Stephen's words. 'You are right, Stephen. It's not possible to know the future. I remind you what the President of the United States said about the recent cyber-attacks and the threat to the world's financial systems. "There is a lot we don't yet know". I fear that, by rushing into an alliance with Monya, we risk repeating previous mistakes. It's a hasty decision that we may later regret.'

'Perhaps.'

Claudia looked at Inspector Axel, her mien saying silently, 'What do you think?'

Inspector Axel glanced at Stephen Walls, seeking his permission to speak. Stephen nodded.

'You are the student of history, Claudia. I remind you of the ancient proverb. "The enemy of my enemy is my friend". Ask yourself, when has this not been so?'

Claudia sighed. 'True, Inspector.'

Inspector Axel sat forward in his chair. 'In keeping with your historical imperatives, the Allies' alliance with the Soviet Union during the Second World War, without which the outcome of the war would have been quite different. Both sides distrusted each other, and the tension was rife. Despite their differences, they recognised a need to work together to meet a common threat. Logic dictated that the West and the Soviets would *never* remain allies once the foe was neutralised, and they have not. Despite the separation of Europe and the lowering of the iron curtain after World War Two, few would argue that the alliance wasn't necessary. You know Monya better than anyone and you are right to caution MI6 and the United States. If an alliance can be formed, it will be fraught, but current events dictate it may be necessary.'

Claudia nodded her agreement.

Stephen Walls said, 'Claudia, your advice is noted. In directing you to meet with Monya in Russia, are we sending you into harm's way?'

'It's difficult to be certain, Stephen. I don't think so, but there is no guarantee that Monya will meet with me.'

'Understood, Claudia. Regardless, I'd like you to leave soon.' Stephen noticed a look of hesitation wash across Claudia's face. Hoping it wasn't a rerun of previous objections, he asked. 'Is there something on your mind?'

'Yes, Molly. The daughter of Richard and Samantha Liew.'

Stephen tapped his hand on his desk three times before saying, 'You are referring to Linda's warning that Richard Liew and his family are to be recalled to China. In the transcript Linda said, "I think you understand what this will mean".'

Claudia picked up her cup and took a sip of tea, scrunching up her face because it was now cold. 'Yes, I believe that's what she said. The Chinese State Security will want Samantha and Molly to go with Richard to ensure their silence.' She put the cup back on its saucer. 'If the way China has controlled the information surrounding COVID-19 is anything to go by, I fear for their safety.'

Stephen cocked his head to one side. 'I'm not sure I follow your analogy.'

'China detained health professionals, citizens and journalist who sounded the alarm about the virus in its early days and those who exposed the Government's attempts to cover it up, or criticised its early response to control it.'

'Go on, Claudia.'

'Beijing is paranoid, fearing that Samantha, Molly even, may speak out against Richard and the Communist Party's espionage activities in Britain. They will want to ensure their silence. Once Molly and Samantha are in China, they will vanish and our attempts to investigate will be thwarted.'

'Does Samantha have information that may be of benefit to the British Government?'

'I don't know. If she did, Stephen, Samantha wouldn't speak out for fear of the consequences. Allowing them to be taken to China is an unnecessary risk.'

'Are you advocating the British Government put the family into protection?'

'No, not the entire family, Stephen, only Samantha and Molly.'

'I'm yet to be convinced that this is necessary.'

'It was because of me they came to be in harm's way. It's not their fault, Stephen, and they are British citizens.'

Stephen tapped his fingers in contemplation.

Filling the silence, Claudia said, 'Molly is a child.'

'Okay, but I can't make any promises, Claudia. I will raise the matter with the Foreign Secretary but she may not share your concern. Samantha and Molly hardly pose a threat to China, do they? The Secretary may think your concern...'

Claudia interjected, saying. '... is exaggerated?'

Stephen shook his head. 'No, not at all. Perhaps overstated is a better word. The Secretary is keen to reduce tensions with China. I will ensure your concerns are aired.'

Claudia gave Stephen Walls a respectful smile.

Stephen, that will not do, not at all. I'll have to make my own plans.

Giving a wry smile, Claudia said, 'Thank you, Stephen. I can ask for no more. If I may return to the matter at hand, my visit to Monya. It would be unwise to make an unannounced visit. He may not even be there.'

'Tell me what's on your mind, Claudia.'

'Monya formed a special relationship with Max and Olivia, so it would be prudent to ask them to broker the meeting.'

Stephen's eyes betrayed him, and Claudia knew that something was amiss.

CHAPTER 5
Good Night Sweet Man

Stephen looked at Inspector Axel. 'Would you mind excusing us, Inspector?'

'Yes, certainly.' Inspector Axel turned to Claudia. 'I'll wait for you outside.' As he stood, Claudia noticed a hollow expression written on his face and felt her heart miss a beat. Inspector Axel knew what Stephen was going to tell her, and it wasn't good.

Stephen Walls waited for Inspector Axel to leave before he said, 'I have some tough news to share with you.'

Claudia was a trained assassin; little could touch her emotionally. Stephen understood this; for him to say the news was difficult to share could mean only one or two things.

'Is it Max and Olivia?'.

'Yes.'

Claudia bit her lip discretely. The next obvious question to ask was whether they were dead. Instead, Claudia remained silent, waiting for Stephen to continue. The pause hung heavily in the air.

'Olivia is okay.' He clasped his hands together. 'Unfortunately, Claudia, the niggling cough and a temperature you reported Max as having was COVID-19. He experienced breathing difficulties and was admitted to a Barcelona hospital, then transferred to the Intensive Care Unit and placed on a ventilator. Despite the best efforts of the hospital staff, he deteriorated and passed away in the early hours of this morning.'

Please, no! This can't be happening, it's a ploy. People like Max don't die, not of an illness anyway. Max is adopting a new identity for another mission. That is what he's up to. He can't be dead, not like this!

In her mind, Claudia saw the anonymous images from the nightly news; men and women dying alone in hospital, mass graves in Brazil, funeral pyres in India, hundreds of bodies stored in freezer trucks at a disaster morgue in New York City, body bags laid out in preparation, distressed relatives unable to grieve properly.

Claudia studied Stephen's face. He was telling the truth. Her voice low and fearing the answer, Claudia asked. 'Was Olivia with him?'

Stephen shook his head. 'No, COVID restrictions prevented it. Olivia wanted to be there, despite knowing that, at her age, catching the disease was certain death. The authorities wouldn't permit it, for anyone.'

Claudia nodded. 'Was anyone with him, someone who held his hand? I've heard it's an unpleasant end.'

Stephen swallowed, trying to hide his sorrow. His voice, normally coldly professional, wavered. 'I'm sorry Claudia. Like many others during this awful pandemic, strict infection control meant that he died without Olivia, family, or a friend to comfort him or say goodbye. These are distressing times.'

Despite hearing Stephen, Claudia couldn't stop herself from asking again, though she knew the answer would be the same. 'Was nobody present at all, not even a nurse or hospital Chaplain?'

Stephen knew Max had died alone, accompanied only by those on breathing machines. The early gains that Spain had made in containing the spread of COVID-19 had faded and hospitals were overwhelmed, the ICUs at capacity overloaded with severely sick patients. He desperately wanted to say Max shared his death in the presence and love of another to help ease the pain of his isolation, but he could not. Max's end was a tragedy, to be faced night after night by many families in the coming months.

'No. I'm truly sorry.'

Why she wanted details, Claudia, did not know; there was no reason. She rocked herself gently back and forth in the chair before mumbling a question. 'Was he conscious during the last hours?' Grief welled up from depths within her and she fought back her tears. For the briefest of moments, a flicker of the pain she felt showed in her eyes until she regained control. Stoic with an emotionless face.

Stephen pretended not to hear and remained silent, not wanting to add to Claudia's pain.

Claudia asked again, her voice cold. 'Was he conscious?'

Stephen shook his head. 'No. Max was placed in an induced coma when connected to the ventilator.'

A tube going in through his mouth and down his windpipe.

Claudia's character demanded, as with John Moss, that sorrow was private. However, the news of Max's passing caught her by surprise. For a moment, her true feelings were on display. A solitary teardrop escaped from her eye and trickled down her face. Grief, sadness, mourning. They were signs of weakness, to be hidden until she was alone.

Claudia whispered to herself as she wiped the tear away,

My precious man, I'm not a woman of faith, but please hear my prayer.

There will be no sorrow, no weeping or pain
but fullness of peace and joy.
Through the mercy of God,
rest in peace.

Amen.

'Thank you, Stephen. I appreciate your candour.' Claudia moved uncomfortably in her chair. 'Do we understand why the elderly are most at risk of dying from COVID-19?'

Stephen rested his cheek on his closed hand, a sign that he was evaluating the best way to respond. He understood Claudia's question was a diversion, an opportunity to gather herself. She was intellectualising, avoiding uncomfortable emotions by focusing on facts and logic.

Each of us deals with the inner turbulence in our own way, and this is Claudia's method.

He was aware Max was the second loved one that Claudia had lost in a short time and, despite her annoying tendencies, like questioning his decisions, a habit he put down to cultural differences, he was fond of her, something he couldn't always say about his other agents. She had a way of sliding under one's skin; nobody can afford to have too many like Claudia on their team, but one is a bonus. He sighed; he'd once had three: Claudia, Max, and Olivia, and now there were only two. All too soon, there would be one. Olivia's time was also nearing its end.

'A good question, Claudia. It's partly explained because the elderly are most likely to have underlying health conditions like cardiovascular disease and diabetes, which makes it more difficult to fight off the COVID-19 infection. A challenge governments have faced around the world is encouraging young people to comply with their health warnings and directives. In part, that's because for every 1,000 people infected under the age of 50, almost none die. For people in their fifties and early sixties, it's about four, impacting men more than women, it turns out. The risk climbs steeply as the years accrue and men face twice the risk than women.' At the mention of women, Stephen spotted the opportunity to move the conversation to Olivia. He hoped Claudia was ready.

'We believe Olivia will be okay.'

How can you say that, Stephen?

Claudia checked herself. 'That sounds like good news, Stephen. May I ask, what gives you this confidence?'

'The infection pathway, the spread of the virus, is driven by only a small percentage of those who become infected, super spreaders. Young people and children, especially in households, are efficient transmitters, although there are a lot of variables. Olivia's close contact with Max doesn't necessarily place her at any greater risk. You will have undoubtedly read about the race to produce a COVID vaccine. The United States, with their Pfizer-BioNTech and Britain's Oxford-AstraZeneca, have entered stage three trials. The results for both are promising, with the U.S. Food and Drug Administration set to approve the Pfizer-BioNTech vaccine for public use in the coming weeks. Approval has been given for Olivia to participate in the Oxford-AstraZeneca trial and she won't receive a placebo dose.'

Claudia gave Stephen a worried look. 'Apart from being a guinea pig, doesn't that undermine the integrity of the scientific trial?'

'I've chosen my words poorly. Olivia is not part of the scientific trial–the vaccine is to be administered as an emergency measure–outside of the trial. Olivia has already agreed.'

'When?'

Unlike the Pfizer-BioNTech vaccine, which uses strands of genetic material known as mRNA and must be stored at minus 70° Celsius or 94° Fahrenheit, the Oxford-AstraZeneca is an adenovirus-vectored vaccine. It can be kept in a fridge, between 2° and 8° Celsius for up to six months. It's already on a plane and on its way to Barcelona. Olivia will have the first of her two jabs this afternoon.'

Claudia crossed her legs, making herself more comfortable, and, with a voice overflowing with conviction, asked, 'Is it safe?'

'Safe, yes. The vaccine is in stage three trials. That doesn't mean administering the vaccine to frail older adults like Olivia is without risk because many older people are already seriously ill. For her age, Olivia is still in good health and, even in this trial phase, COVID-19 is far more dangerous than the vaccine.'

Claudia gave a slight nod of her head in acknowledgement. She thought for a moment before saying, 'I suppose it's too early yet, but do you know what the funeral arrangements are likely to be?'

Stephen dropped his head slightly to one side and sighed.

Understanding his body language, Claudia nodded. 'COVID?'

'Yes. The restrictions in place to prevent the spread of the virus means only three people can attend.'

Claudia shook her head in disappointed acceptance.

This great man should be honoured.

Stephen read her mind. 'There will be a memorial service here in the UK when this wretched pandemic is over. That's a promise Claudia, and fear not, time won't diminish our memories of him.'

'No. Time won't diminish our memories.' Claudia hesitated for a moment before saying, 'We don't appreciate the heartbreak of families all over the world who could not say goodbye meaningfully, not until you are touched yourself.'

Stephen nodded. 'Losing someone you love changes your perspective. Even when we think we understood their pain, the reality is always different.'

'Does the family know? Penny, the children?'

Stephen raised his hands, palms out, while giving a slight shrug of his shoulders, gesturing to Claudia, that he didn't know.

Claudia nodded again. 'You'll bringing Olivia home, to the UK, I mean.'

'I know Claudia, that's what you wanted from the start, for them both to be brought back to the UK. However, despite what's occurred, I believe it's still in Olivia's best interest to remain where she is.'

Claudia resisted the urge to glare at Stephen, instead giving him an inquisitive look while remaining silent, afraid her words would betray her anger.

Aware of Claudia's unease, Stephen considered his response. He shifted uncomfortably in his seat. 'There's been a new discovery, reported to the World Health Organisation (WHO), yet to be made public. Scientist have detected a mutated strain, a SARS-CoV-2 variant in Britain named VUI. It's also known as B.1.1.7. Early indications are that it's between 50 to 70 percent more transmissible. Those currently infected are over sixty–the most vulnerable. The new variant was picked up as part of an epidemiological and virological investigation following an unexpected rise in COVID-19 cases in South East England. These are early days, but emerging evidence suggests it could be 30 percent more deadly. We may be among the first countries to identify a variant, but we won't be the last. There are rumours circulating of a South African and Indian delta mutant.' Stephen picked up a piece of paper from in front of him and read from it. 'N501Y.V2 and B.1.617.J. Virus mutation is a natural and expected process, caused by random changes, errors made to genetic code as the virus copies itself, more common in RNA viruses like SARS-CoV-2. It's unclear yet how effective antibodies from the AstraZeneca vaccine will be at neutralising the British and other variants.' Stephen looked at Claudia, and when she remained quiet, he continued.

'The scientists are also concerned about another emerging variant from Brazil, P.1. These are evolving to be fitter and more transmissible, better able to avoid immunity. As I have said, we knew the virus would change, however, the more virus there is, the faster this is occurring. The concern, Claudia, is the degree and speed of change. The South African variant is believed to have nine changes to its spike protein alone.'

Stephen's explanation settled on Claudia. 'Are these new strains of the virus?'

'No. My understanding is a strain is a whole new virus type, whereas a variant, like B.1.1.7, is a virus with a collection of mutations, a mutation being a random change in the organism's genetic code. I'm told variants are common, part of the virus's widening family tree. However, B.1.1.7 has a worrisome mutation called E484K. The mutation alters the structure of the virus spike protein, the target for vaccines and many naturally produced antibodies. The mutation may help the virus elude detection, both from the human immune system and vaccines. This is going to be a challenging year, Claudia. The COVID-19 pandemic will continue to cast a long shadow over Britain, the economy, businesses, and individuals.' Stephen shook his head and sighed. 'Sadly, some countries will seize upon these dark times to accelerate their ideological and political agenda. It is also my fear that one of these COVID variants will be vaccine resistant. Claudia, it's no exaggeration to say that I am gravely concerned. We face the prospect of huge infections rates and being overwhelmed by the disease. Despite having been vaccinated, it is best for Olivia to remain in Spain.'

Claudia stroked her chin and weighed up Stephen's words. 'I understand the good intention, to leave Olivia where she is, never-the-less, when I talk with her today. If she requests or insists on coming back to the UK, you will facilitate it, yes?'

Stephen thought for a moment. 'If that is her wish, then of course.' He looked directly into Claudia's eyes and said with conviction. 'Yes, I will.'

'Thank you.'

Stephen picked up a pen from his desk and twirled it twice between his fingers before placing it back on his desk. 'With the news of Max, will you still ask Olivia to facilitate your meeting with Monya?'

Claudia's response was unequivocal. 'Yes. With the death of Max, it's more important than ever that she feels useful. Which is why Stephen, she needs to be here.'

Despite having already promised to bring Olivia to the UK, Stephen held the palms of his hands towards Claudia, a sign of surrender. 'Yes, yes, I agree.'

Claudia gave a slight nod of her head. 'Do you know when Britain will start its national vaccination program?'

Stephen pondered the question for a moment. 'Not exactly, although planning is well underway. We expect the Pfizer vaccine to be approved first. The program will start then and be ramped up once the Oxford-AstraZeneca vaccine becomes available. The Health Secretary has told me that the UK will be the world's biggest supporter of the global programme to ensure equitable access to COVID-19 vaccines. We here at MI6 fear that Russia and China will seek to gain an economic and diplomatic advantage by rolling out their vaccines, Sputnik and Sinovac, to strategic partners like Indonesia, Morocco, Brazil, Turkey and those they wish to influence: India and Arab countries for example. For China, we see the foreign distribution of Sinovac as an extension of its Belt and Road policy—a jab with strings attached. China's foreign policy direction will give attention to those countries neglected by Western powers in the multilateral arena. It is in Britain's and the West's interest to ensure that there's not a catastrophic moral failure because of unequal Covid-19 vaccine distribution. China will exploit our failure.'

'Are Sputnik and Sinovac effective?'

'Both Russia and China skipped final state clinical trials, but unlike Sinovac, there are some peer-reviewed articles for Sputnik, so we believe it is. China's data has been less robust. Thirty-four countries are using Sinovac, which makes up a decent chunk of the vaccination race and if it fails, it could leave parts of the world exposed. Gauging Sinovac's impact would be pure speculation, but let's hope so. We are all still in the trial stages.'

Remembering that he had another meeting, Stephen glanced at the clock on his table. 'I'll expect a call from you this afternoon, after you've spoken to Olivia. Please pass on my condolences.'

'Yes, Sir.'

'Before you leave, Claudia, when you meet Monya, you are at liberty to negotiate terms, but they will be subject to the Home Secretaries approval.'

'Monya will extract a high price.'

'As always, Claudia, we have every faith in you.'

Ha! When has that ever been the case?

'Thank you, Sir. I appreciate your confidence.'

Glancing at his clock again, Stephen said, 'That is all, Claudia. Will you send James in, please?'

Claudia stood and began moving towards the office door. Stephen called out after her.

'Yes, Sir.'

'I am truly sorry. Max was a man of dignity, tradition, and informality. We will not see the likes of him again. The world is a lesser place for his passing.'

Claudia acknowledged Stephen's condolences with a bow of her head and, thinking of Max, whispered to herself, '*Good night, my sweet, sweet man.*'

***

Inspector Axel was waiting, chatting with James in the outer office, when Claudia came out. 'Are you alright?' he asked.

'Of course,' she answered stoically, adding while looking to James, 'Stephen requests your company.'

'Thank you, Claudia,' James replied. When he'd left, Claudia said, 'Inspector, I need to talk with you, but not here. I know a nice little café around the corner, and I think it's your turn to pay.'

Were it a normal day, Inspector Axel's retort would have been humorous, something like, "It's always my turn to pay", but this was the end of an era, not normal at all.

After the death of John Moss, Claudia's boyfriend, Inspector Axel had tried to talk to her about the event. He'd wanted to support Claudia, offer an opportunity for her to grieve. She was, however, a closed book, and he recalled how she dismissed his concern. "It's always disappointing when an innocent person dies". Despite her responses, the Inspector had recognised her inner pain.

The invitation to take coffee wasn't about Max, he was sure of this. As they walked towards the café in a comfortable silence, as only friends can, Inspector Axel mused on the conversations from Stephen's office and was drawn to the same place: Molly and Samantha Liew. He recalled how Claudia reacted when Stephen hadn't shared her concerns; overly compliant, not like Claudia at all. He suspected she wanted to take matters into her own hands and this is what he expected her to discuss over coffee. She would want his help in whatever scheme she was cooking, but he was quintessentially a policeman who had stumbled into the secret service because of Max and Olivia. He followed rules, liked the rules. Claudia, on the other hand, liked to operate on the fringes.

Claudia sighed as they took a seat, well away from other patrons in a quiet corner of the café. 'Stephen told you about Max?'

Inspector Axel was surprised by Claudia's comment, expecting her to keep his passing private.

'Yes. It's the end of an era and the sad loss of a great man.'

A waiter approached their table. 'Coffees only, or would you also like to see the menu?'

Inspector Axel glanced at Claudia. 'Just coffee for me,' she said.

Inspector Axel looked at the waiter. 'Two flat whites, extra hot please.'

The waiter scurried away. When Claudia was sure they were alone, she said, 'Max and Olivia were a team, an incredible team, who worked together for most of their lives. This will be a difficult time for Olivia, particularly in this COVID environment when she can't give Max a proper burial.'

Inspector Axel pursed his lips and nodded solemnly. 'I agree ... will you speak with Olivia today?'

'Yes.' Claudia hesitated. 'I'm not sure if you were still in the room when I suggested to Stephen that Olivia broker the meeting between me and Monya?'

'Yes, I was. It's a wise suggestion.'

'I also persuaded Stephen to bring Olivia back to the UK, or at least I think I did.'

'I didn't know that, but I'm pleased.'

Claudia rubbed her chin, a sign that she was contemplating what to say next. Inspector Axel recognised the signal, knowing that it was deliberate on her part. She was preparing him for what was coming.

'I was going to ask Max and Olivia to watch over Molly while I was away. That's not possible now. Will you do it?'

Inspector Axel shook his head. 'Sorry, I was given an overseas assignment tracking Linda Orr; we suspect she will soon flee the country.'

Claudia resisted the temptation to ask Inspector Axel what he knew of Linda's whereabouts, particularly after the break in; he may not have been forthcoming. 'Okay. That means I must ask Olivia.'

'Is that wise, given the circumstances?'

'It may be good for her. Occupy her mind during this difficult time. Also, Inspector, in their short time together, Olivia formed a relationship with Samantha and that may prove important.'

'As you did with Molly, Claudia.'

She grinned. 'Yes, we are best friends forever.'

'I understand why you want to protect them, but does Stephen know of your plan?'

'No.'

'I suspected not. Claudia, if something were to happen while we were away, without access to MI6 resources, it will be difficult for Olivia. A challenge for anyone.' He paused, expecting Claudia to respond. When she remained silent, he asked, 'Do Samantha or Richard know you will watch over them?'

'No. The Chinese Ministry of State Security will monitor Samantha and Richard too closely for me to risk contacting them. Besides, who knows where Richard's loyalties lie, the Communist Party or his family? I fear it's the former, Inspector. His family may be a means to an end, as we, in the British Secret Service, have done ourselves.'

'I see. So, that leaves Molly?'

Claudia nodded. 'Before leaving for Rus...' Seeing the waiter approaching, Claudia checked herself. After the coffees had been placed on the table, Claudia said to the waiter, 'Thank you.'

'May I get you anything else?'

'No, thank you.'

Claudia picked up her cup and took a sip. 'Ah, perfect, nice and hot. I do so dislike that lukewarm dishwater some places serve.'

Inspector Axel raised his eyebrows. 'Really. The purist Barista would say you're steaming the milk past its recommended temperature and most likely burning your coffee and dampening your ability to truly taste the delicious brew. I believe sixty degrees is the sweet spot.'

'Why Inspector, I didn't know you were a coffee snob. Wait a minute, didn't you order extra hot too?'

Inspector Axel smiled. 'Fifty, sixty degrees. It's a conspiracy to encourage you to down your coffee and then vamoose out of the café, creating room for another customer.' He took a sip. 'Yes, perfect. Sorry, you were saying Claudia, something you need to do before leaving for Russia.'

'Yes, that's right. I must visit Molly to tell her I'll be watching over her and that she will be safe.'

Inspector Axel scratched his head. 'What do you tell a seven-year-old girl that doesn't send her running home in alarm? Molly's distress would alert her parents and the watching Chinese State Security Service.'

'Molly is eight years old now, Inspector. No longer a young child.'

'No, not such a child... I surmise that you've given this problem some thought?'

'Preliminary Inspector, considering I only learned of the rendition plan last night, and with my imminent departure for Russia, there isn't much time. I would appreciate your input.' Claudia took a breath. 'The first challenge, how would Molly signal

she needed help, because without MI6 resources, she can't be watched twenty-four-hours a day? If I gave her my number or a mobile phone, both could be discovered. I considered, for her own safety, pre-emptively taking her, but doubt she'd come willingly.'

Inspector Axel interrupted. 'Claudia, that would be a criminal act.'

Claudia smiled. 'Kidnapping you mean? I ruled that out. In the end, Inspector, I settled for a simple scheme that requires some MI6 support, albeit small. However, learning that you will be away too has thrown a spanner in the works.'

Inspector Axel grinned. 'You thought I would help.'

Claudia pulled a face. 'Yes, am I wrong?'

'No. I would have offered you my help if I could, and it is within the law.' Inspector Axel glanced around, checking they weren't being overhead. 'Tell me your plan and I will proffer a solution if I can.'

Claudia took a sip of coffee. 'Okay.' From her handbag under the table, Claudia retrieved a blank piece of paper. 'A pen, Inspector, do you have one?' Asking for a pen was a strategy to draw Inspector Axel in; he needed skin in the game.

'Of course.' Inspector Axel fiddled inside of his chest pocket of his suit jacket and produced a ball-point pen, which he handed to Claudia.

'Thank you. Now I want you to use your imagination.'

Inspector Axel thought this a strange request, but remained mute.

'I'm going to tell Molly that if she is in danger and needs me, she should draw a picture of a cat on one side of a piece of paper.'

'A pussy cat like Snowflake? Molly will ask.'

'Yes, that's it, like Snowflake.'

Using the pen, Claudia sketched a crude outline of a cat and held it for Inspector Axel to see.

'I tell her to write on the other side, in capital letters: TO MI6. I will inform her she is writing my address and that there's no need for a postage stamp. This is where I may need some help, Inspector. I require the MI6 office is to act as a Post Master, especially while I'm away... Without Stephen knowing.'

'Hmm, yes. I can see that you may.'

'Then I'll tell Molly that, no matter where she posts the picture, I will come. I may even add something like, this is my solemn vow and promise. Perhaps a little melodramatic, Inspector, but appropriate for an eight-year-old, don't you think?' Claudia stared at Inspector Axel, assessing whether he was still engaged. Satisfied, she continued. 'I imagine Molly might ask me how she knows when she's in danger. It's a tricky question and something I've been grappling with myself. She has a push bike, so I thought I would use it as a metaphor, and say something like this to her.

'Molly, do you have a bicycle?'

'Yes,' she will tell me.

'Have you ever ridden down a hill really, really fast?'

'Yes.'

'Were you scared?'

'Yes.'

'Danger will feel the same, but it won't be fun-scared. I promise Molly that you will know the difference.' Claudia's own childhood had taught her this, and was confident Molly would know.

'Molly will tell me she understands.' Claudia stopped talking and looked at the Inspector. She tilted her head slightly to one side, seeking his opinion.

Inspector Axel took a sip of his coffee while he gathered his thoughts. Hesitation was present in his response. 'It's a plan.'

Claudia pursed her lips. 'But?'

Inspector Axel shook his head. 'No, but's. Um... I wonder if drawing on a piece of paper is the right option, particularly in an emergency.' He rubbed his lip with his finger as he mused, airing his thoughts aloud. 'It needs to be made from something more robust than a scrap of paper which would be easily damaged, or even overlooked by the Post Office. Whatever you use mustn't invoke suspicion, and Molly must be able to use it undetected. A tricky one.' Inspector Axel's eyes lit up.

Seeing his reaction, Claudia asked, 'What is it?'

'A working suggestion, so bear with me. Why not create a deck of playing cards made... say with a picture of a cat on the front in the middle of the distinguishing motifs? The back could be left blank for Molly to write on. She could carry a deck of cards and arouse little suspicion. When the need arises, Molly scribbles on the back *TO MI6* and drops it into a Post Box. Best of all, she has lots of spares.'

Claudia, an edge of excitement in her voice, said, 'Inspector Axel, that is brilliant and exactly what I will do. What about the conundrum of using MI6 as the Post Master?'

Inspector Axel smiled wistfully while shaking his head. 'I can't believe I'm saying this, as Stephen will not like it. We, yes, *we* need to enlist James's services. If a playing card were to arrive, it would be intercepted by his desk first.'

'Excellent, involving James is a good idea. After I've spoken to Olivia, I'll return to the office and ask him.' Claudia grinned. 'I'll use my flirtatious smile and charm. It always works.'

'You know James is gay, or should I say, same sex attracted?'

'That may be so, but he still enjoys a flirtatious smile.'

'I imagine he does, although knowing he's helping Olivia may well be the trump card.'

Claudia fluttered her eyelids. 'Oh, not my charm?' Inspector Axel smiled at Claudia's comment, but he fixed a look of caution on her. 'Is there something else, Inspector?'

'Perhaps. For Molly to keep this secret requires an extraordinary level of trust. I appreciate you were with Molly in trying circumstances and that bonds formed in the face of adversity are strong...' Inspector Axel paused.

'Speak your mind, Inspector.'

'You were the... um ....' Inspector Axel shrugged, unsure how he should continue, '... their precarious predicament was of your doing. You were the evil one. Does that sound harsh? Perhaps the rogue is a better choice?'

Claudia shrugged. 'The evil one has a ring to it. You are right, I was the scoundrel and Molly will want assurance; she'll need to be sure that, if summonsed by her, Olivia or myself will respond. I plan to say something like. Once Molly, a long time ago, when I was not much older than you are now, it was I who was in danger. And do you know who rescued me? She will say, No. It was Max and Olivia and we became Best Friends Forever. Best Friends Forever, Inspector, is a phrase Molly uses in her storytelling. She writes it as BFF. The significance of the phrase won't be lost on her. I will then say,'

'Do you remember, in the dungeon deep below Montserrat Abbey, when I was in danger?'

'Molly will answer, yes.'

'Who was it who came for me?'

'Max and Olivia.'

'Yes, Max and Olivia. And aren't we Best Friends Forever?'

'Yes, she will say. Molly may even add, and Snowflake as well.'

'Both of you, I will answer.'

Inspector Axel was moved by Claudia's play acting. He took a sip of coffee. 'Yes, best friends forever. I'm no psychologist, but using Molly's own language makes it a poignant statement, one to which she will relate.'

'I hope so.' Claudia rubbed her chin in thought.

'What I'm unsure about, Inspector, is how I warn Molly of the peril of travelling to China, a trip which may be presented as a holiday. How do I say she may have to abandon her father? How do you explain these things to a child without terrifying her?'

Inspector Axel waited, wondering if Claudia's questions were rhetorical. In the silence, Claudia fixed her gaze on Inspector Axel, her eyes searching for his wisdom.

Although different, Molly was in danger, as Claudia had been as a child and Inspector Axel wondered if Claudia saw the parallels and was trying to fulfil the role that Max and Olivia had played for her. Alternatively, perhaps the desire to protect Molly was fuelled by guilt. After all, the predicament was of Claudia's making. Whatever the motivation, conscious or unconscious, Inspector Axel was in no doubt. She was willing to die for the girl's safety.

'It will be difficult, Claudia, but children are far more perceptive than we give them credit for.' He took a sip of coffee. 'Molly will not understand that a trip to China would be dangerous but her mother certainly will, Olivia having already warned her of such an occurrence.'

Claudia nodded.

'A mother's protective instincts are difficult to ignore; Molly will sense her mother's unease. As for her father, tell her that the separation is temporary, done for his safety. Hopefully that is the truth.'

'Yes, thank you, Inspector. I also intend making Molly an honorary secret agent.'

'You're turning this into a game for her?'

'Yes. It should build her confidence and keep the plans hush-hush.'

Inspector Axel drained his coffee cup. 'Your scheme is brilliant in its simplicity but, if I may, when Molly posts the card, how will you find her? It could come from anywhere.'

Claudia smiled. 'That's a good question, Inspector. I assumed Molly would still be at home, but the postmark would be my starting place were she not.'

Inspector Axel nodded. 'You can tap into MI6 resources, albeit without Stephen's knowledge, even while you are away. However, were Molly to call on Olivia, Olivia will not have that luxury.'

'Don't underestimate Olivia, Inspector.'

Inspector Axel shook his head. 'I wouldn't, but I suggest you ask Molly to write her whereabouts on the card if she were to post it.'

Claudia finished her drink. 'I will do that.'

Inspector Axel nodded before asking. 'Would you like another drink?'

'No, thank you. As always, Inspector, I've enjoyed our chat and appreciated your wisdom, but it is time I was leaving. There is work to be done before I depart for Russia.' Claudia stood.

'Claudia,' Inspector Axel said. 'Don't put too much stock on Linda's rendition warning because I suspect it was said for her advantage, not yours.'

Resting her hands on the table, Claudia leaned towards the Inspector. 'Best you track her down then, don't you think?'

CHAPTER 6
Pea Soup

With a tinge of impatience decorating her voice, Samantha called from the hallway to her daughter upstairs. 'Come on Molly, or we will be late.' *Again!*

Molly was in her bedroom busying herself doing nothing. 'Where's my school bag?' She called back at the top of her voice.

Samantha shook her head in annoyance. This scene played out identically every school day, Molly's morning routine. That first night at home after becoming a mother, she was overjoyed but also petrified, cradling a newborn in her arm that she was frightened of breaking. "I won't yell at our daughter like my mother did to me," she promised herself and Richard, Molly's father.

As this ritual played out each morning, Samantha realised how like her own mother she had become. Raising her voice but softening her tone, Samantha called back, 'It's where you left it, in the kitchen.' *Like every morning!*

'Oh,' Molly echoed down from upstairs.

I'm sure she does this to test me!

When Molly was younger, not that eight was old, Samantha found the sound of the pitter-patter of Molly's feet rushing down the stairs comforting. Molly would race to greet her father after his long day at work, hold out her arms, utter words enough to make any heart break.

"Cuddle". Molly delivered it with the innocence of unconditional love.

When had "cuddle" become "give your mum and dad a good night hug", and the pitter-patter sound become thud-thud, Samantha couldn't say. The racket of Molly crashing down the staircase reminded Samantha that her precious daughter was growing up. She sighed; it was inevitable.

'We're late. Hurry up!' Samantha yelled; the soft tone forgotten.

Once, Samantha and Richard had been the most important people in Molly's life, Richard more so than Samantha, always a source of annoyance for her, especially as she provided most of the day-to-day care. Samantha hadn't meant to measure her daughter's affections, but it was unavoidable; Molly gave Richard a warmer welcome home than she had given Samantha when she'd returned after a spell away. Richard's return always warranted a hug, whereas Samantha was lucky to receive a greeting. Now, on the unconscious hierarchy of a maturing child, even Richard was being replaced by Molly's friends, though he failed to notice such subtleties.

A wave of sadness washed over Samantha, feeling no longer needed.

The holding hands, hugs, kisses, playing monsters and tickle chasey, an excited Molly, yearning to share every drawing she had done or story she'd written, was passing, and would be left to history. Even the fridge, once the bastion of Molly's creations, was becoming devoid of her artwork.

Molly is growing up too quickly, eight going on eighteen. That wonderful innocence of childhood is being left behind and I won't see it again until I'm a grandmother and then only if Molly has children. My Ms Independence is in a hurry to find her way in the world, as she proved in the tunnels of Montserrat Abbey. I wonder if my mother felt the same about me?

Samantha always wanted to have more than one child; three she'd envisaged. After Molly was born, Richard was insistent that one was enough. After the events of Montserrat, of Claudia, Max, and Olivia, she had changed her mind. Even if Richard relented, knowing of his involvement with the Chinese Ministry of State Security and in espionage, she wanted no more. Samantha glanced at her watch as the approaching thud of Molly's steps brought her back to the present. She groaned. *We will be late again.*

'Come on Molly, get a move on.'

I may not be wanted, but most certainly, I'm needed. I've become your personal slave.

The feeling of sadness and loss was quickly replaced by a sense of being taken for granted. Molly came bounding into view and Samantha recalled Olivia's words of caution when she asked about leaving Richard, a warning that was never far from her mind. "Samantha, nobody can be a hundred percent sure. If you're not an effective team, nothing may happen. More likely, however, the next time Richard travels to China, he will be arrested on trumped-up treason charges, or simply disappear. It could happen to both of you, even Molly. I'm not telling this to scare you, far from it dear, but for you to understand your predicament."

Molly has always been a daddy's girl, and, if I must take her away from him, I wonder if she will ever forgive me? Maybe, perhaps when she's older and understands the danger she was facing.

Samantha realised that her duty was to protect Molly from harm.

For the time being, my precious child, we must be a happy family, until, without anyone noticing, I've squirrelled away enough money for us to be free and, of course, when Olivia tells us it's safe to leave.

I wonder how Max and Olivia are doing? How I wish I could see you again, Olivia. It's so hard not having you to talk to, because this awful secret is such a burden.

'Coming, Mummy.' Thud-thud. Molly jumped the last couple of steps into the hallway.

'What's that in your hand?' Samantha said, peering at a small packet she was grasping.

Molly looked at the pack of playing cards and lifted them so that her mother could see.

Samantha smiled and asked, trying to sound interested rather than inquisitorial, 'How wonderful. Where did they come from?'

Samantha doubted, when Molly became a teenager, that she would fall for such a simple trick. It was all in the tone of her voice.

'Lucy gave them to me for my birthday, even though she doesn't like cats.'

'Who's Lucy?' Samantha said, while holding out her hand.

Molly gave the pack to her mother.

As Molly told her mum that Lucy was her new best friend, Samantha slipped a card from the pack, the Ace of Hearts. When she saw the picture of a cat at its centre, her protective instincts were soothed. She slipped the card back into the deck and returned the pack to Molly.

'I thought Sophie was your best friend?' As she uttered the words, Samantha's memory was drawn to how fickle her own friendships had been at school.

We girls differ from boys.

Molly dropped her gaze and said, 'She used to be... but now it's Lucy and we are best friends forever.'

Samantha listened to the mock regret in Molly's voice as she told her mother about Sophie, replaced immediately with joy as she mentioned Lucy. Then, her eyes were drawn to her watch.

'Quick Molly, fetch your school bag from the kitchen. We are late.'

'What about my lunch?'

'You put it in the bag at breakfast time.'

'Did I? Oh, yes, I remember now.'

Molly ran off to fetch her bag, leaving Samantha to ponder the mistakes she'd made and whether that made her a poor parent.

*** *

Shark Fin restaurant

Richard Liew waited for Samantha in front of the Shark Fin restaurant in Soho, London. It had been Chen Li, Richard's spy boss, who suggested lunch after telling him he and his family were to be stationed in China for twelve months. Chen Li had told Richard that he would break the news to Samantha.

Watching his wife approach, Richard Liew waved and called out, his demeanour betraying nothing. 'Hi, Honey.'

Since returning to the UK, Richard hadn't spoken to Samantha about Spain or his involvement with the Chinese Ministry of State Security. Their sex life had improved and Samantha was behaving as if nothing had happened, a blessing, as Richard knew they were under constant surveillance. Even Molly seemed to have forgotten the events of Montserrat. The forthcoming news would be a shock for Samantha, but he needed the family's behaviour to remain unchanged. The move to China hadn't been posed as a request. It was a directive and there would be dire consequences were Samantha to refuse the assignment. His phone was being monitored, so the text message he'd sent to Samantha had been vague. Unable to prepare her for Chen Li's revelation, he hoped Samantha wouldn't protest. As his wife approached, Richard pondered whether, when they were in Montserrat, Claudia had mentioned the eatery to her. It here, the Shark Fin restaurant, while dining with six of his espionage colleagues, that Richard had first met Claudia. Chen Li had ordered one of those present, Mr Yáyī, an agent known in the service as the Dentist for his methods of torture, to follow Claudia outside. He was about to terminate her, but Claudia turned the tables, pushing a chop stick into his brain, killing him instantly. Claudia had later blamed the men seated around that table for the murder of John Moss, the man she loved. The ills that had befallen his family all started at this restaurant. He hoped, as Samantha waved back, that she didn't know that the Shark Fin was a meeting place for Chinese spies.

Smiling at Samantha, Richard Liew whispered to himself, *Chen Li has set this up to test our loyalty.*

Samantha could smell the restaurant before she saw it, the aroma, a mix of sweet and sour wafting down the street, an enticing greeting to all who approached. With Molly at school, Samantha had rearranged her plans when Richard sent a text to invite her to lunch. Seeing her husband waving and hearing him call out, 'Hi Honey', she raised her arm in reply, a scene to any bystander, more familiar of two lovers, than a married couple of eleven years. Samantha did not know what was in store and couldn't foresee, as their eyes locked, that Molly's future hung on how she reacted to the news she was about to receive.

Richard took his wife's hand and kissing her tenderly on the cheek, whispering, 'Hello, Honey.' Stepping back from their embrace, he saw a welcoming smile on Samantha's face and felt relieved. She knew nothing of the reputation of the Shark Fin Restaurant and even sensed romantic longing radiating from his wife. 'Thanks for coming, Honey. I'm sorry I didn't warn you beforehand.' Richard squeezed her hand before letting it go. 'I hope you didn't have too much else planned for the day.'

Olivia's warning rang out loud in Samantha's mind. Olivia had told Samantha that she and Richard must always seem an effective team, Samantha the obedient doting wife, even in the bedroom. For Molly's sake, it was a role she had embraced with gusto. Samantha grinned lovingly at her husband.

'That's okay, Richard. I was quite pleased to get your text message, although I am curious about the news you have for me.'

'Do you remember, Richard, before Molly came along, we would often meet on a whim for lunch?'

'We did.' Richard recalled, in the early days of their marriage, the liaisons and returning home afterwards, making love to his wife in the middle of the day, always the best time for passion. He grinned. 'Do you know what else I remember?'

Samantha gave a flirtatious giggle. 'Yes, it was always raining.'

Richard released a good-humoured laugh. 'Have you been here before?'

'No, have you?'

That was a stupid question, Richard, now you must lie. That would be another mistake. He would tell the truth.

'Yes, perhaps two or three times, but probably no more than that. I forgot to tell you in my text message that Chen Li, my boss, is joining us. He wants to share some exciting news with you.'

Samantha felt a knot form in the pit of her stomach and, before she could suppress it, her face betrayed her turmoil.

Chen Li!

Exciting news!

Oh, my goodness! Olivia warned me that this could happen. Is this it? Stay calm and play the game.

Richards saw the flash of fear dash across Samantha's eyes. 'You don't mind Chen Li coming, do you?'

He noticed my apprehension. Best not hide it.

Samantha patted her stomach. 'No, not at all. I'm a little nervous at meeting... your boss. Just butterflies, that's all.'

Reassured, Richard smiled at his wife and, in a sympathetic tone, said, 'He's a nice man, Samantha. You have nothing to worry about.' After a moment's pause, he let out a half laugh. Richard looked left then right, checking that they would not be overheard, and beckoned to Samantha, who leaned in towards him.

'Chen Li can be a little intimidating; he doesn't mean to be. We will have butterflies enough to share.' Richard sat back as he said, 'Are you ready?'

'Yes, let's go in.'

Entering the restaurant, Samantha and Richard were greeted by a smartly dressed waiter, wearing black trousers, a white jacket and a black bow tie. 'Good afternoon, Sir and Madam. Do we have a reservation?'

Samantha felt unsettled. There was something in the waiter's manner, and she wondered if he was pretending not to know her husband, a charade for her benefit.

How many times have you been here, Richard? Am I being manipulated, a pawn in some game that I don't understand? I'm sure that I am.

She felt like a betrayed woman slowly unravelling an unfaithful husband's lies, discovering his sordid affairs.

'Yes, the reservation is under the name of Chen Li.'

'Yes Sir, a table for three. If you would kindly follow me.'

Entering the restaurant, they passed a bar to their right. Running down the centre of the room were tables, each with seating for four people. Larger tables, surrounded by semicircular cushioned pods, provided seating for up to ten people were on their left. Tables for two were on their right. The tables were well spaced, a social distancing requirement under the UK's COVID-19 restrictions.

The waiter stopped at a round table in the centre of the room and, pulling back a chair, he invited Samantha to be seated. 'Madam.'

Richard Liew, understanding the restaurant's etiquette, remained standing while Samantha lowered herself into the chair. The waiter came next to him and pulled back his chair as he said, 'Sir.'

With Samantha and Richard seated, the waiter picked up the drinks menu from the table and handed a copy to each of them.

'While you wait for your dining companion, may I interest you in a drink? We pride ourselves on our cellar.'

'Thank you,' Richard said. 'If we might have a moment to consider?'

'Certainly, Sir.'

'Richard!' Samantha whispered in exclamation. 'Have you seen the prices?'

He raised an eyebrow and smiled.

Samantha scanned the drinks list again. 'I can't even pronounce half of these wines, let alone know what to order. Maybe I should stick to water.'

Before Richard could respond, the waiter returned. 'Water Madam?'

'Oh, yes, please.'

'Sparkling or still?'

Not knowing what she should order, Samantha looked to Richard.

'Sparkling,' Richard said.

The waiter filled their glasses and, when he had finished, asked, 'Have you chosen?'

'What would you recommend?' Richard asked.

'Sir, Madam, I find champagne goes with anything. May I suggest, the Perrier-Jouët?'

'Yes, that will do nicely. Thank you.'

As her husband spoke, Samantha ran her finger down the wine list, stopping at the Perrier-Jouët selection. A single glass of the champagne was more than they would normally spend on an entire meal. Her feeling of betrayal grew and, when the waiter left, Richard whispered to her in a reassuring tone, 'It's alright my love, there is no need to fret about the price. Chen Li is picking up the tab.'

As he finished speaking, Richard jumped to his feet. Samantha spotted a man approaching and, by Richard's reaction, guessed it was the head of the Chinese intelligence agency in Britain. Samantha rose gingerly from her chair, causing her knees to catch the edge of the table, sending their glasses of sparkling water flying into the air before depositing the contents across the freshly pressed, starched white linen tablecloth. The waiter, five steps behind Chen Li, a champagne flute in each hand, stopped mid-stride, swivelled on his heals and dashed back towards the bar. With military precision he set down the champagne glasses, about-faced and marched back towards the sodden table. En route, he veered to his right, a trajectory that swept him past a timber sideboard and paused briefly. With the speed and dexterity of a magician's hands, he opened the top draw and selected a replacement table cloth.

Resuming his advance, another smartly dressed waiter fell in behind. As Chen Li arrived at the table and Samantha and Richard surveyed the devastation, the cavalry arrived to rescue them from their embarrassment.

'Did you know Madam,' the waiter smiled, 'these table cloths can retain 15% of their weight in water and don't even feel wet.' As he spoke, the waiter waved to his companion, who swiftly cleared the table and removed the sullied cloth. With the elegance of a ballet dancer, the waiter tossed the new covering into the air and watched as it drifted slowly downwards and fell perfectly into place; an artisan of his craft.

'Madam.' The waiter said, holding her chair, inviting Samantha to sit, a scene he repeated twice more for the men.

'Sir,' he said to Chen Li. 'Champagne? It's on the house.'

With a polite smile and a wave of his hand, Chen Li declined the offer, ordering a bottle of champagne instead. He moved his attention to Samantha. 'Mrs Liew, do you have any dietary requirements?' Samantha, still recovering from her embarrassment, could not find her voice. She shook her head.

'Excellent.' Chen Li reengaged his eye contact with the waiter. 'Our usual, please, for the table.'

The waiter bowed imperceptibly and, after taking a step backwards, scrutinised the new table setting of his colleague. Satisfied, he and his associate departed.

'Mrs Liew,' Chen Li paused. 'May I call you Samantha?'

Having regained her composure, Samantha said, 'Of course, please do.'

'Thank you, Samantha. Ordinarily I would shake your hand but, in these COVID times, such formalities must be forgone. I'm sure Richard has told you we work together or, more accurately, Richard works for me and I asked to meet with you today.'

Samantha smiled and nodded, her heart thumping.

Say something, or you will look like an idiot.

Before she could form a simple response, Chen Li continued.

'I was sorry to hear that you and your lovely daughter Molly became entangled in Richard's work. It was regrettable, and I wanted to apologise to you personally.'

With the apology, Samantha's apprehension receded. Before responding, she stole a glance at Richard. When he smiled, she said to Chen Li, 'Thank you, I appreciate that.'

The long lunch had been pleasant, far from a grilling. Conversation had been engaging, free flowing and often humorous. That changed at dessert.

Despite Olivia's warning, Samantha had been ill prepared for the meeting with Chen Li. Her answers to his questions were unscripted and lubricated by champagne. Samantha recognised that she'd been unwittingly drawn deeper and deeper into the conversation and, at dessert, Chen Li dropped his great surprise. Surprised, Samantha had made the enormous blunder, a serious mistake. Alone in her bedroom, her mind raced through the events of the day.

The meal had been a trap and Richard hadn't helped, not even a kick under the table to stop her from making a fool of herself. Samantha recognised now that an interrogation had occurred, a professional one at that. She was angry with herself, not seen the questions for what they were, or challenged Chen Li enough.

Samantha gasped. She'd divulged her inner feelings, and her words would determine what happened next. As fear washed over

her, she was taken back to the restaurant. Desserts were being served. What had Chen Li said?

'Samantha, you are such enjoyable company. Richard, you are one lucky man... and now, the great news I have for you, the reason we are eating together. We have extended an invitation for Richard to spend twelve-months with us in Beijing, and yourself and Molly are expected to accompany him. No arguments, please.'

Richard heard the words *expected to accompany him* and understood it was a directive. Samantha focused on *the invitation*, as if she had any choice. She'd replied instinctively.

'I don't think so! That will not happen!'

Chen Li's expression hardened, his voice firm as he asked her if there was a problem.

The numbing effects of the champagne were gone and alert to the threat. Olivia's warning beat in her chest, Samantha tried to make amends, frantically searching for a way to undo the mistake, but stumbled over her words. She remembered mentioning as reasons for her reticence, the disruption it would cause to Molly's education, leaving her friends and difficulties with the language. Chen Li had given a dismissive wave of his hand and said, 'Your apprehension for Molly's education is understandable and why we will take care of everything for you. Beijing has a wonderful International School, with students, like Molly, from all over the globe. The education is of the highest standard and its well known that studying abroad boosts career prospects and improves language skills, making it an invaluable experience. We will also find you a place to live and link you with people like yourself. I'm told it doesn't take long to settle in.'

Samantha remembered taking a deep breath to regain her composure, smiling and saying, 'Living in China will be quite an adventure.' Chen Li had ignored her platitude, taken a mouthful of his dessert and said, 'I do so enjoy these egg tarts. It's not something I eat back in China.' An uncomfortable silence had befallen the table and, feeling pressured to speak, Samantha recalled asking,

'Do you have a date in mind?'

It wasn't Chen Li who replied, but her husband. They had four weeks to sort out their affairs.

'Four weeks.' Samantha placed her head in her hands and wept.

CHAPTER 7
Federal Security Service

Claudia's plane began its final approach, lowering its wheels in preparation to touch down at Sheremetyevo International Airport, one of four international airports that serve Moscow and the fifth-busiest airport in Europe. Claudia checked her seat was in the upright position and gave a slight tug on the lap seat belt.

I'm feeling a little melancholy. Hmm, I wonder where that has come from? Why has the simple act of landing at an airport triggered such an emotion?

She breathed out heavily in recognition.

Oh, that's it.

The last time Claudia had been to Moscow, she had stayed at her billionaire lover's mansion, accompanied by Max—the very man Monya Mogilevick had tasked her to kill.

'I dreaded creating a martyr by killing him,' she had told Monya, to justify bringing him to Moscow with her, but the truth was more bizarre. With her pistol pointed between his eyes, she recognised Max for who he was: the man who saved her as a fourteen-year-old from child sex slavery. Despite being the boss's mistress, had her mission to the UK not delivered a substantial financial windfall for the Mafia, Monya would have eliminated Max himself. Instead, he allowed Claudia to take Max on assignment to Dubrovnik as her prisoner. Claudia hadn't expected octogenarian Olivia, Max's wife, to come to his rescue. In a few days, Claudia's life had been turned upside down. By choosing to protect Max and Olivia over the orders of the Mafia, she was forced into the service of MI6 and, for a time, a woman with a Mafia price on her head. Claudia wondered when she had stopped fighting and let Max and Olivia into her hitherto icy heart.

'Max,' Claudia whispered to herself. 'I miss you.'

Thump. The wheels hit the runway, followed by the screech of brakes and the roar of the jet engines in reverse as the plane slowed before taxiing toward the airport terminal. There was more to Claudia's feelings than her memory of Max. She was accompanied by a sense of nostalgia. Russia, Moscow, had been home when she lived with Monya Mogilevick.

When she defected to MI6, Claudia hadn't expected to set foot on Russian soil again, let alone have the Mafia pick her up from the airport and be invited to stay at Monya's mansion. They say that life turns on a dime, and it had. All was forgiven when Max and Olivia stole, from Melk Abbey, a hidden copy of the Gutenberg bible for Monya. A bibliophilic lover of books, Monya's eternal gratitude was bestowed upon them.

'Comrade Max and Olivia,' Monya had said. 'You are my friends and the Brotherhood will be your protector. I will even free Claudia and spare her life.' Monya Mogilevick honoured his words and, in Spain, when Max and Olivia were in grave peril, he came to their rescue.

Having collected her luggage and passed through customs, Claudia entered the arrival hall and scanned the awaiting crowd of people. Drivers held up signs in multiple languages, emblazoned with the name of the person they were expecting. Children, with unused energy, dashed up and down, seeking their returning mother, father, babushka and dedushka, while others waved enthusiastically, hoping to attract the attention of their loved ones. People in motion, meeting the returned travellers, business people, holiday makers and family. Claudia lifted herself onto her tiptoes and peered over the sea of swarming people.

Oh no! It had to be you two.

Claudia spotted the heads of Vladimir and Semyon, Mafia ex-accomplices, looking disinterested, standing at the back of the arrival hall. She'd been their lieutenant and Claudia recalled they were not the brightest or most enthusiastic of her crew. When Monya, despite her reservations, assigned Vladimir and Semyon to her, she knew better than to argue. It must have been a family connection, Claudia had concluded, because their position in the Mafia wasn't based on merit. Family connection or not, this had not stopped Claudia from treating both harshly, even instructing them how to dress.

'While you are working with me,' Claudia had said, 'You don't wear ill-fitting rags as suits. Do your buttons up! No one wants to see either of your fat bellies poking through your shirts.'

She improved their attire but was never confident in their abilities, rarely sending them on assignments and on the occasions that she relented, the missions rarely went to plan. They were no better than lackies.

Shall I be passive or aggressive? They will want payback, so it's best not to give them an inch. Behave as if you are still their boss.

Making her way towards Vladimir and Semyon, Claudia noticed they had reverted to their dishevelled ways. Appearing in front of them, she looked them up and down before shaking her head disapprovingly. 'If it isn't my old friends Curley and Moe,' a reference to The Three Stooges, members of an old American comedy team. The comment was intended as a putdown, but it missed the mark as they stared blankly back at her, their expressions suggesting that they thought Claudia had forgotten their names.

'Well, that was a waste of time,' Claudia mumbled and then said, a smile spreading across her face, 'Hello, Semyon and Vladimir.'

Despite Claudia's frosty tone, she beamed a smile, and the gesture confused the men.

It wasn't the Russians she was smiling at. Her use of the name "Vladimir" brought back fond memories of Daniel Tinkov, Saint Vladimir, the man MI6 sent her to protect from Sergey Rutskoy. It had been thoughts of him that caused her to smile.

'Hello, Claudia,' Vladimir and Semyon replied in unison.

Claudia dropped her suitcase at their feet. 'Which of you two comrades is going to carry that for me?' They peered at each other in disbelief and, as Semyon was about to deliver a sarcastic reply, Claudia picked up her bag, and chirpily said, 'Just joking. Lighten up boys and lead on.'

Claudia's incongruous behaviour had the desired effect, causing Vladimir and Semyon to feel unsettled, unsure how to respond, so they walked to the car in silence. When they arrived, Claudia was tempted to try another quip. *"Which of you is going to open the door for me?"* but thought better of it; she wanted to pump them for information on the way to Monya's mansion. She was fearful that her flippancy may have shut them down completely.

Come on, boys. It's time for you to speak up.

Inside the car, Vladimir and Semyon sat in the front, while Claudia occupied the rear seat. The men's confidence surged as they exchanged pointed remarks about her, laughing at their own humour, fully aware that she could hear every word.

Claudia fought back an urge to provoke them, and she bit her tongue.

Boys, you are pathetic. Let them rant, Claudia. Slowly, slowly, catchy monkey.

Buoyed by Claudia's silence, Vladimir called over his shoulder, 'The Brotherhood is not fond of traitors. It's against the code. Who knows what will happen while you are in Russia?'

Semyon, who was driving, smiled at Vladimir's veiled threat, glancing in the rear-view mirror to gauge Claudia's reaction. She remained stone faced and said, 'It's just as well that I have you two to protect me. Remember, they are Monya's instructions!'

Semyon retorted. 'For now.'

Hmm. I will see Monya, but withdrawing and returning to London may be more difficult, a more complicated matter. How interesting. It's fortunate I love my work.

Vladimir addressed Semyon, 'It's not the Brotherhood I'd be worried about if I were Claudia. Alexandria will rip her eyes out.' He made a cat's claw with his hand and, with a swiping motion in the air, said, 'ME-OW.'

Claudia didn't recognise the woman's name, but the inference was that she was Monya's lover.

Well, at least I don't have to sleep with him, or do I? Um, that would certainly set the cat among the pigeons. Okay, girly, let's see what you can find out about this Alexandria.

Claudia laughed and said dismissively. 'That old cow. I thought she'd have been sent to the knackers by now, Vladimir.'

'Old cow? She's younger than you.'

Damn!

Claudia had hoped to hide her ignorance from Vladimir and Semyon.

Okay, I now know Alexandria is younger than me, but how do I recover from that faux pas?

With humour decorating her voice, Claudia said, 'No wonder you're not married, Vladimir. I meant her character, not her age.'

Semyon laughed as he responded, 'That's right, she is a real bitch.'

Nailed it!

'Semyon, we call girls like Alexandria high maintenance.'

'High maintenance, that's Alexandria, alright. She must have the most expensive urine in all of Russia. You should see those...' Semyon mimicked a cultured Russian voice. 'N... natural health pills that she pops.'

Vladimir swivelled his head and shoulders and stole a glance at Claudia. 'You should have heard her when she knew you were staying. Went right off the rails. I was surprised the boss didn't slap her across the face.'

Be careful what you say next, Claudia. Never undermine Monya, especially as the boys will use it against you.

'Monya understands that this is purely a professional visit. Alexandria is a young thing, not attuned to the ways of the Brotherhood.' Claudia saw, from the expression on Semyon's face, reflected in the driver's mirror, that she had made another mistake.

Damn!

Claudia held her breath, wishing Vladimir or Semyon would drop a hint that would help her correct her course. If her next words were off, they would see that she had little knowledge of Alexandria. In that moment, silence was her best—and only—strategy.

'She's Sergei's daughter,' Vladimir said.

Claudia recognised the name immediately. Sergei Popov was a Pakhan, the head of one of the Mafia families in Monya's Brotherhood empire. She seized the opportunity. 'Exactly Vladimir, Alexandria has been spoilt.'

Vladimir and Semyon nodded in unison, believing Claudia knew Alexandria well. In their minds, Alexandria *was* spoilt, rich, and prone to hissy fits. Semyon knew that Sergei Popov held Claudia in disdain and wondered if Claudia realised how treacherous Alexandria could be? She was a daddy's girl.

Unbeknown to Semyon, Claudia was having similar thoughts.

Alexandria is a dangerous woman. Vladimir and Semyon have already told me that the Brotherhood isn't happy with my presence. One word in daddy's ear from Alexandria and Sergei will take matters into his own hands. His daughter may give Sergei the excuse he needs to strike against me. It would be wise not to antagonise her.

Claudia pondered as she looked out of the side window and watched the traffic and city rush past.

Is Monya losing his grip on power?

Dismissing the thought, Claudia refocused her eyes inside the car. A moment later, her attention was drawn to Semyon when, three times in quick succession, he glanced in the driver's rear-view mirror. Claudia turned her head and glanced out of the window. They were driving in heavy but free moving traffic. If they were being followed, she couldn't tell. 'What do you see?'

Semyon glanced in the mirror again. 'Two cars back, a black Mercedes has been with us for a while. I'm going to up our pace and see if it follows.'

Semyon leaned on the accelerator pedal. The exhaust growled and their four-door AMG Mercedes V8 sedan responded, springing them effortlessly forward. Indicating left, he overtook the car in front, then moved right again to pass a slower vehicle, before swerving back and increasing his speed. Claudia resisted the urge to peer out of the rear window. If a car was following, she didn't want to telegraph that they were onto them, but she need not have worried. Her curiosity was soon answered. Passing a freeway exit, without warning, Semyon swerved right. His manoeuvre cut in front of a light truck which jumped on its brakes. As the AMG raced onto the off ramp, Claudia was pushed back into her seat as Semyon increased speed aggressively before decelerating, braking heavily with equal vigour, to manoeuvre through a long sweeping curve. Semyon negotiated the corner awkwardly, giving a series of jerky movements of the steering wheel accompanied by erratic throttle control. The stability and traction control warning lights flashed on and off on the AMG's dashboard, the car's electronic driver's aid compensating for Semyon's lack of finesse.

If we get into a serious car chase, this will not end well. Semyon has the car control of a baboon.

Hiding her qualms, Claudia said, her voice controlled, 'Have you lost them?'

Semyon raised his eyes from the road and glanced back, using his mirror. A smile spread across his face. 'Of course,' he answered, oozing confidence.

Vladimir looked across at Semyon and gave him a nod of approval. 'You're the master.'

Claudia bit her lip and resisting the urge to shake her head in despair.

I'm travelling with Laurel and Hardy.

Claudia stole a look out of the rear window. 'Did you say it was a black Mercedes that was following?'

Semyon checked the mirror again, while Vladimir swivelled in his seat, staring past Claudia and out the window to watch a black Mercedes gaining on them. Semyon punched the accelerator to the floor, triggering a Christmas tree of warning lights on the dashboard as the AMG tried to prevent its rear wheels from spinning, while transferring all of its power to the ground. Claudia felt the rear of the car lurch left, then right, as the computer fought to keep the AMG in a straight line. Again, as it had done on the freeway exit, the vehicle's cleverness compensated for Semyon's lack of proficiency. As the car rocketed up the road, Claudia saw Semyon clasp the steering wheel ever tighter, his knuckles turning white. She wanted to say, *relax your grip*, but remained silent.

Within a matter of seconds, the AMG was snarled up in slower traffic. If they were to evade their pursuer, navigating through the vehicles in front had to be negotiated with the care and skill of threading the eye of a needle. In preparation, Semyon shifted his driving position, sitting upright, stiff in the seat. His arms and hands were rigid, contrary to a relaxed touch needed to manoeuvre in and out of the obstacles in front that would slow their escape. With all the finesse of a bull in a china shop, Semyon leaned his body and shoulders in the direction he wanted the car to go, the AMG's steering wheel turning, causing the car to respond with sharp directional changes. Claudia knew that those trailing would see that Semyon was a clumsy getaway driver. To bring about their demise, all they needed to do was to pressure him into a driving mistake and cause a fatal crash. Easy, they needn't even risk a gun fight.

Claudia shrugged her shoulders at Vladimir and Semyon, who seemed oblivious to their own ineptness. She called from the backseat, 'They may be difficult to outrun,' wanting to encourage them to stop and fight, but her words fell on deaf ears.

Semyon stole a glance in the rear-view mirror. 'Damn, they must have a faster car because they are still with us.' He paused, before saying to Vladimir, 'I think we should lead them into the side streets, where I can out-drive them.'

'That's a good idea,' Vladimir replied.

Claudia rolled her eyes. 'I believe Semyon is asking you to navigate, Vladimir–though I accept the request was... somewhat vague.'

'Yeah, that's right,' Semyon said.

'I knew that.' Vladimir fiddled in his pocket for his smart phone. Once it was in hand, he said, 'Gees, Semyon, can't you hold the car steady so I can open the maps? Damn! I said, hold the car steady!' After a couple of failed attempts, speaking rapidly, he said, 'Okay, I have us. Alright, coming up in front, take the next right.' He pointed... 'there!'

Vladimir's instructions came too late, and they were travelling at high speed in the outside lane. Even a person of Semyon's ineptitude knew not to attempt the turn or even jump on the brakes.

Claudia asked calmly, 'Vladimir, how far to the next turn?'

'Hang on while I check. Yep, I can see it now. Err, it's one mile. Did you hear that, Semyon? I said, one mile.'

Raising her voice to take command, Claudia said. 'That's excellent. Listen Semyon. I want you to move across to the right. Do it nice and gently, so slow down. We don't want to roll.'

An edge of unease was present in his voice, Semyon said. 'Slow down? What about the black Mercedes?'

'For the time being, I don't want you to worry about the black Mercedes.'

In making the manoeuvre, Claudia watched Semyon move his head and body to the right. The steering wheel and car followed.

'Well done, Semyon.' Claudia said, 'Now Vladimir, once we come off the motorway, I want you to direct Semyon to a nice quiet street, so we can lure them into a trap. Are you both armed?'

'Yes,' they answered in unison.

'Excellent. Do you have a spare pistol for me?'

Semyon and Vladimir shook their heads.

Vladimir pointed. 'There... turn right.'

As they negotiated the next exit, Claudia said, her voice steady, 'Good. Now Vladimir, tell Semyon what he will see next ... and before he gets there.'

Vladimir grimaced, angry at Claudia's patronising style. He glanced at his phone, his voice betraying his vexation. 'It's a T-junction.'

Claudia rolled her eyes. 'And what does Semyon do at this T-junction?'

'Sorry, Semyon, you turn right. It will take us back to a divided road, but it won't be for long. From there, I have a plan to lose them.'

Claudia rubbed her chin. 'Excellent, Vladimir. Now I'm wondering, how far away would this T-junction be? The one where Semyon will turn right?'

Vladimir snapped, 'Half a mile.'

'Settle Vladimir,' Claudia said. 'I'm playing with you.'

'Stop the bickering you two,' Semyon said. The AMG rocked left then right as he overtook a slower car. Glancing in the mirror, Semyon added, 'They are still with us.'

Claudia looked behind her. 'Excellent Semyon, this is just what we want.' Claudia paused. 'Gentleman, shooting people is what I'm good at, so which one of you would like to lend me your pistol? Or if you prefer, try to take them yourselves?'

Vladimir looked at Semyon with a disbelieving expression. Semyon, keeping his eyes on the road, shrugged his shoulders, which inadvertently turned the steering wheel, causing the car to move. Oblivious to the cause or the deviation, he corrected the car with a lean to the left.

Claudia had expected that they would willingly shed their weapons to let her do the killing. She might have been wrong.

That was a stupid question, Claudia. Neither Semyon nor Vladimir have a clue and they don't realise how incompetent they are. Should I use charm or intimidation? After my belittling of Vladimir, I'll try some charm.

In her most alluring tone, Claudia said, repeating part of her previous statement, 'Gentleman, it is what I'm good at! If you remember, when it comes to killing, I'm better than very good.'

In readiness for the T-junction, Semyon braked heavily.

BANG!

The black Mercedes tapped the rear of their car, trying to force the AMG to spin while it was off balance, making the right turn.

'Well, gentleman? I need a decision. Now would be a good time.'

Vladimir nodded, 'Okay, if we can't lose them... turn here Semyon, here.' Vladimir stretched his arm in front of Semyon's face, pointing with his finger. 'Turn left.'

'Where, Vladimir? I can't see it.'

'There, Semyon! It's on your left!'

'What? The other side of the medium strip?'

'Yes, Semyon. Brake! Brake now or you'll miss it.'

Following Vladimir's instruction and ignoring oncoming vehicles, Semyon threw the AMG left, sending it crashing through the central reservation separating traffic on the divided road. The erratic manoeuvre forced a heavily laden truck to brake, sending its tray sliding left and then right in a plume of burning rubber, triggering a chain reaction as vehicles swerved and braked to avoid a collision. The occupants of the AMG were now on the other side of the road and, for a moment, travelling in the wrong direction until they made the turn. Entering the side road, they were oblivious to the chaos unfolding behind them. The tactic, Claudia admitted to herself, was inspired, a test for even the most seasoned getaway driver, a task that Semyon masterfully executed.

Go figure, Claudia thought. *How did he do that when he's such a buffoon?* 'Semyon, that was a nice bit of driving.'

Semyon checked the rear-view mirrors, relaxed his vice like grip on the steering wheel as blood returned to his fingers. He gently eased on the brakes and slowed the AMG to a crawl. In a tone dripping with confidence after Claudia's praise, he said. 'Vladimir, that was a good choice and excellent navigating. We've given them the shake.'

Vladimir smiled. 'We are still the best team!'

'Yes. The A Team.'

Vladimir, his voice dripping with praise, said, 'That was inspired driving Semyon.'

Unbelievable! Claudia whispered to herself.

Semyon glanced at Vladimir. 'Where are we?'

Vladimir looked at the map on his phone. 'We are near Gorky Park. I'm hoping... oh, great, that's what I wanted. See Semyon, the park gates are open.'

'No.'

'Look, there! It's coming up on your left.'

'Yep, got it.'

'Excellent. Drive in, but watch out for the pedestrians. The path will take us to the service roads that crisscross the park.'

Semyon manoeuvred the AMG through the wrought-iron gates while Vladimir studied the map. Glancing up from his phone, Vladimir said, 'I want you to follow this path down towards the Moskva River. From there we'll cross under the motorway and come out near the ring road.' He let out a chuckle. 'They will never find us here.'

The Gorky Central Park of Culture and Leisure as it was officially named, though it was usually known as Gorky Park, named after Soviet writer Maxim Gorky, was loved by the Muscovites. Today wasn't busy, but there were still plenty of people leisurely walking or riding bicycles along the roadway. To Claudia's surprise, no one paid any attention as Semyon drove among the sightseers, individuals, couples, and families out for a relaxing stroll. Nearing the Bather's Fountain, a sculpture of a bather below which are a series of steps through which water flows to the Moskva River from the Yekaterininsky pond, Semyon stopped suddenly.

'What is it?' Vladimir asked.

'Over there, through the trees. I thought I saw another car.'

Claudia and Vladimir both looked, arriving at different conclusions.

'It's them!' Vladimir said.

Before Claudia could contradict Semyon, seeing the flight of steps leading down to the river, he chose the descent as his escape route. Turning the steering wheel and stepping on the accelerator, the AMG sprang to life. Racing down a flight of steps to evade capture, as they do in the movies, is seldom as easy in real life. Had Semyon eased the car down, perhaps he could have positioned it the correctly to make the right-angle turn at the first landing and avoided the Yekaterininsky pond below. But he did not.

CRASH.

BANG.

SPLASH.

The AMG came to rest in the pond.

Claudia felt her blood boil.

They are both clowns.

She opened the door and, to the bemusement of the gathered spectators, waded through the water to reach the river bank. She couldn't recall if the AMG wheels had even touched the stone staircase. More likely was that Semyon had launched them from the top with such vigour that they had jumped all the steps, crashed through the marble barrier and ended up in the pond. Had Semyon really seen their pursuers, they would now be in trouble.

Claudia, still in the pond, stopped and waited for Vladimir and Semyon to extract themselves from the vehicle. As they caught up, she mouthed but did not speak aloud, 'You imbeciles. That was not the pursuit vehicle, it was one from the Parks and Garden administration.' She stopped herself, and pointed back to the AMG and, before turning and walking away, said, 'Don't forget my bags.'

'Where are you going?' Vladimir called.

Claudia turned and faced him and, to her surprise, her anger had faded and she felt in good humour, amused by their antics. 'I'll find my own way from here. It will be safer for ... all of us.' Claudia stepped from the pond, her wet feet squelching as she strode along the footpath.

Whatever family connections keep you gentlemen in Monya's service, this debacle must surely test it.

Looking about her, Claudia smiled as she said to onlookers, 'It's a nice day for a walk, although a new pair of shoes is in order.'

She followed the river, passing under the ring road and exiting the park when she reached the Akademicheskiy Universitet Gumanitarnykh Nauk, The State Academic University of the Humanities. Using the footbridge, she crossed the Moskva River. Nearing the other side, she noticed a parked car, vapour drifting from the exhaust, a telltale sign its engine was idling. For a moment, Claudia considered backtracking but dismissed the thought and continued on. Without moving her head, eyes straight ahead, she kept a careful watch on the car, pretending not to have noticed it, while assessing the risk.

A single occupant, male, well-dressed and, from his profile, I would estimate in his mid to late fifties. Maybe Claudia, you're

The man walked briskly towards Claudia, adjusting his angle for their paths to intercept. Claudia slowed her pace as the man raised his hand, showing he wanted to talk. She stopped.

A shortness of breath was present in his voice as he called out, 'Ah, Claudia.' The brief dash from the car weighed on his lungs. He smiled. 'I should have given up smoking years ago.'

Claudia didn't reply, however, he observed from her facial expression and physical stance that she was saying. *What do you want?*

The humour gone, the man said in an uncompromising voice oozing with authority, 'Andrei Gorbachev would like a word.'

Claudia hadn't met Andrei Gorbachev as he was above her pay scale, however she immediately recognised the name as the Director of the Federal Security Service of the Russian Federation, the FSB, as it was known, the principal security agency of Russia and the successor to the USSR's KGB. Its headquarters were in Lubyanka Square, 900 metres north-east of Moscow's Red Square, in the main building of the former KGB. It was Andrei Gorbachev who is credited with calling her ex-lover and boss, Monya Mogilevick, the *President's Gardener*, because one of Monya's companies provided gardening services to the Kremlin. However, it was through Keiser, another of Monya's companies, that they were really connected. Keiser provided services to the Kremlin when the Russian Government wanted to deny any involvement in an operation. Monya had provided mercenaries for Russia's activities in Eastern Ukraine, Syria and elsewhere. Keiser was also behind opinion-forming operations on social media that were in the

Russian States interest, fake news as it became better known, as well as a string of sophisticated cyber-attacks. It was Monya's connections within the FSB and the Kremlin that kept him the undisputed head of the Russian Mafia crime families.

"Andrei Gorbachev, would like a word", wasn't a request. Claudia understood; it was a command and one that couldn't be refused. As if checking her appearance for such an important meeting, Claudia straightened her suit jacket and looked at her feet. 'Um, is there a chance of procuring dry shoes before our chat? I find soggy feet most unbecoming... and most uncomfortable.'

'I watched your misadventure with keen interest. Unfortunately, Mr Gorbachev is waiting, so a change of clothing will have to wait. Perhaps, on the way to see Monya Mogilevick, we can pick up some shoes for you?'

That's promising. Perhaps not about to be detained.

'This way,' the man said, pointing towards the car. When they arrived at the vehicle, Claudia went to open the rear door, but the man insisted that she join him in the front. He knew better than to have a killer such as Claudia behind him, not that being with him in the front could stop her; it was his position in the FSB that saw to that. Claudia expected to be taken to the FSB headquarters, close to where they were, but they left the main roads and drove along the back streets. She was tempted to ask him if he was lost, but chose silence. The car stopped at the front of an old Stalinist building.

'We are here,' the man said.

Behind the plain front entrance was a staircase leading down to the basement.

Am I allowing myself to be passively guided to an interrogation and torture room?

Half way down the stairs, Claudia heard the clatter of cups, cutlery and plates, and people enjoying themselves. It was a café.

Inside, the man pointed Claudia towards a private table at the corner of the restaurant. She recognised Andrei Gorbachev from pictures she'd seen of him. An older man, probably in his mid-seventies, dressed in a dark pinstriped suit, wearing a white shirt and red tie. He had the look of a relic, a throwback to the days of the USSR, and not the man at the helm of the FSB, an agency which was more than an ordinary security service. It combined the functions of an elite police force with those of a spy agency, although not foreign spies, and wielded immense power and influence. As Claudia approached, Andrei Gorbachev stood, splaying his arms as he spoke.

'What do you think of my hidden gem? It's good, no?'

Claudia looked around her. 'It's a surprise, yes'

'Alas, the young people have discovered it now, hipsters. I think they call them in the West. I suppose nothing stays the same.' Glancing at Claudia's wet feet and legs, Andrei said. 'Trouble seems to follow you. Please, my dear, sit.' Andrei Gorbachev turned to the man who had accompanied Claudia and said, 'Wait in the car.'

Andrei, as if it were a great effort, lowered himself back into his chair. On the table in front of him was a striking rectangular serving tray crafted in white porcelain on which sat a matching white glazed cup and a copper Turka of strong brewed coffee. As he poured from the Turka into the cup, he said, 'I am told that this is a tradition developed by Peter the Great and that it came from the Ottoman Empire. The Persians and Turks drank brewed coffee after dinner. It was also a medicine, used to prevent bloating, runny noses, and headaches. There's an old Turkish proverb which perfectly describes the intensity and passion behind traditional

Turkish coffee. *Coffee should be black as hell, strong as death, and sweet as love.*' Staring at Claudia, he took the cup between his finger and thumb, lifting the rim to his mouth. After taking a sip, he let the cup linger in the air and silence fall between them. Gaze still firmly fixed on Claudia, he took another sip of coffee and put the cup back on the serving tray before he spoke.

'Now, my dear Claudia, what brings you to Russia?'

'A social visit. Nothing more.'

'Monya?'

'Yes.'

Andrei Gorbachev nodded disbelievingly. 'Claudia, you're an MI6 agent. Why shouldn't I have you arrested?'

Claudia raised both hands, a gesture suggesting that she did not know, before she said, 'Such things start tit-for-tat reactions. The Americans and British arrest one of yours in retaliation, an unnecessary outcome for a mere social visit.'

'Really... and you're saying the Americans know you are here?'

You wily old dog. I said no such thing.

Claudia ignored Andrei's comment. 'I'll have left Russia in two or three days.'

Andrei took another sip of his coffee. 'You know Monya is afforded a special relationship with the Kremlin and that this cements his position as head of the Brotherhood. Innocent as you say your visit is, an MI6 agent with Monya can undermine the trust our government gives him.' Andrei paused and took a breath, as if searching for the right words. 'A woman of your reputation can have an unsettling influence, even for Monya, and I don't want to see a repeat of the events of Gorky Park. It's not in anyone's interest for a turf war to breakout within the Brotherhood, Claudia. A woman such as you can spark such things.'

The rebellious side of Claudia wanted to say that she was flattered, but she nodded her agreement.

Andrei waited, his eyes fixed on Claudia, the silence tangible. When she remained mute, he dropped his gaze and poured more coffee from the Turka into his cup. When he regained his stare, his demeanour had changed. 'How rude of me,' he said, smiling. 'Would you like one?' With his free hand, Andrei gestured towards a spare cup.

'That's most kind. But no thank you.'

Here we go. I'm about to find out what he really wants.

'MI6 had dealings with Azim Singh, the CEO of an Indian company based in London, H1 Technologies?'

What does he know? Is this an interrogation? I can't help but wonder.

'I've heard the name but have had no personal dealings with Mr Singh.' Claudia's answer was partially true but deliberately omitted details, a play that Andrei Gorbachev would be expecting. Her response alerted the FSB boss to the fact that Claudia was curious. They both wanted each other's secrets, while revealing as little as possible of their own.

Andrei Gorbachev said, 'A little cat told me that H1 Technologies gave you the runaround in Spain.'

Claudia recognised Gorbachev's play on the phrase, "A little Birdie Told Me". He was telling her he knew of Snowflake, the cat, and therefore the Liew's.

Andrei Gorbachev is well informed, which is no surprise, although he may not know that Azim Singh is Davros, so choose your words carefully.

'And this interests the FSB?' Claudia asked.

Andrei Gorbachev took a sip of his coffee. 'Let me be more forthcoming. H1 Technologies tentacles have reached Russia and we suspect the company is engaged in organised crime activities.'

Claudia shrugged. 'I don't mean to be disrespectful, Sir, but even if that were true, why would it concern MI6?'

Andrei Gorbachev put his cup down and stared into Claudia's eyes. 'Let me be blunt. H1 Technologies is fast becoming a dominant world corporation. From our investigations into its activities, we suspect the company acts as a front for an international criminal and terrorist organisation, one that is pursuing a strategy for geopolitical advantage and is a threat to national security and sovereignty, not only here in Russia, but to Britain and the United States. It's a threat to our collective security.'

Andrei Gorbachev's candour caught Claudia by surprise. Her expression however, remained poker faced.

I wonder, does he know of The Firm? How should I respond? Carefully, and by keeping your cards close to your chest.

'I see ... please, Mr Gorbachev, I hope you appreciate I am not authorised to speak on such matters.'

Andrei nodded. 'I do, Claudia, but I seek your unofficial opinion on H1 Technologies and you are in Russia now. Always remember that.'

Claudia rubbed her chin, contemplating how to reply.

To stay in the game, I need to share something—and he's right; he holds all the cards.

'I do not believe that MI6 shares your concerns. The United Kingdom's involvement with Mr Singh is as a supplier of equipment for the 5G Network. He's not on the security services radar.'

Andrei Gorbachev gave Claudia a sideways look. 'Come now Claudia, that is difficult to believe. While assessing H1 Technologies suitability to provide sensitive telecommunication equipment to the UK, MI6 would have uncovered its links to organised crime. Of that, I'm in no doubt.'

He's calling your bluff girly. Best give him some more line, or you risk him shutting down.

Claudia gave Andrei Gorbachev a respectful smile, one that acknowledged his wisdom. 'It is fair to say, we know he's not squeaky clean, but there is nothing to suggest he's a national or international threat. If that were the case, the UK would not be dealing with him.'

Andrei Gorbachev weighed up Claudia's words and picked up his cup, taking another sip of coffee. After replacing it, he rubbed his chin before he spoke.

'I understand, Claudia, that Britain wants to strengthen its military ties with the emerging power of India, and Azim Singh is an influential figure within that country's politics. Good relations with Azim Singh are beneficial for Britain, so he will be of strategic importance. I appreciate this... however, there is more to H1 Technologies than perhaps the British realise. India has relied on Russia as its biggest weapons supplier and tacitly supported our annexation of Crimea. It has brokered its own trilateral arrangements with Moscow and Tokyo, in part to assuage Russian concern about the Quadrilateral Security Dialogue between the United States, Japan, Australia and India. India is strategically important to Russia too, as I am sure you are aware, Claudia. So, why do you question my motives?' Andrei Gorbachev breathed out heavily as he considered what he was willing to share. 'H1 Technologies has a secret division headed by a person called Sun-Tzu.' He peered at Claudia, searching for signs of recognition. Seeing none, he continued. 'Sun-Tzu is weaponizing the company's technologies for the five warfare domains–land, sea, air, information/cyber and space. We suspect that they already have a functioning Direct Energy Weapon and that Sun-Tzu has created a private military.' Andrei Gorbachev waited, hoping Claudia would speak. When she remained silent, he continued.

'This is a serious matter and, having been more than liberal with our intelligence, I ask you this: have you heard of, or come across Sun-Tzu?'

Sun-Tzu! Could this be another piece of the puzzle involving The Firm? Yes, that would make more sense than a division of H1 Technologies. Sun-Tzu is the avatar name of another member of the SEVEN. It's not as the FSB believes; The Firm poses a genuine threat to national security and sovereignty. This is serious. I need to keep probing and see what else Andrei Gorbachev is willing to share. But what can I offer? Should I mention Cozy Bear? No, Claudia, that would raise alarms about your purpose in Russia, and the FSB would quickly deduce that MI6 is trying to recruit Monya's assistance. Should I reveal anything about The Firm? No, not unless absolutely necessary.

Claudia shook her head. 'No, except for Sun-Tzu, the revered 5th century Chinese general credited as the author of *The Art of War*.' A book from memory that discussed military manoeuvres and the effect of terrain on the outcome of battle. It also stressed the importance of accurate information on the enemy's forces, disposition, deployments, and movements. Sun-Tzu wrote about the use of spies as an alternative to war itself and the making and keeping of alliances, even the use of deceit. *The Art of War* has influenced not only Western and Asian military thinking, it's had a much wider impact.'

Andrei nodded. 'Without a doubt, Sun-Tze is an aptly named person for H1 Technologies.'

Claudia was struck by a realisation, a memory triggered by the mention of *The Art of War*.

That's where I've heard it before, at the Windsor Castle pub, when Linda told me that opportunities multiply as they are seized. That's a quote from The Art of War. A coincidence? I think not. I don't believe in coincidences.

Andrei Gorbachev picked up on Claudia's micro-facial movement. 'What is it?'

'A quote by a friend with links to H1 Technologies. I realise now that it came from *The Art of War*. Perhaps a coincidence, but I doubt it.' Claudia shrugged. 'Besides, whether an individual by the name of Sun-Tzu existed at all is disputed by scholars and historians.'

A wry grin formed around Andrei Gorbachev's lips. 'This is something where we need further investigation.'

'With respect, a matter of this seriousness should be raised directly with Stephen Walls, or at higher levels between our governments.'

'Normally yes but, with Anglo-Soviet relations marred by distrust and contention, the UK may be close-minded to such an approach even if the evidence is compelling. May I be blunt with you, Claudia? Azim Singh and Sun-Tzu are amassing economic, technological, political and military capacity, all capable of threatening our nations and others.'

Claudia nodded. 'Sir, have you sent your own agents to find Sun-Tzu?' She watched Andrei Gorbachev hesitate, unsure if he should tell her.

'Yes.'

Claudia didn't respond, letting the silence encourage him to continue.

Andrei Gorbachev took a sip of his coffee, extending the quiet between them. 'Our intelligence led us to Turkey and we've sent five of our best agents; none returned.'

The mention of Turkey piqued Claudia's interest, Altindere Vadisi and Sumela Monastery, the place Tomoe had invited her to visit was in Turkey. 'Turkey is a big country Sir, are you willing to be more specific?'

Sensing that Turkey meant something to Claudia, Andrei Gorbachev said, 'Are you?'

Claudia thought for a moment, calculating what she could say without mentioning the Sumela Monastery. 'We are looking into a person who goes by the name of Tomoe, originally a twelfth century female Samurai warrior. You will appreciate I'm not authorised to say any more. However, surprisingly, our trail has taken us to Turkey, not Japan as you might expect, and to a city on the Black Sea.'

'To Trabzon?' Andrei Gorbachev questioned.

'Yes. Trabzon.'

'It would seem, Claudia, that our Sun-Tzu and your Tomoe are linked. The choice of name alone tells us this.' Andrei

Gorbachev stroked his chin and, after a brief pause, said, 'Russia has a complex relationship with the United Kingdom and our interests don't always align perfectly. With Azim Singh, Tomoe, and Sun-Tzu, our collective interests demand that we work together. That is the message I want you to take to Stephen Walls. MI6 needs to listen with an open mind.'

Claudia gave an understanding nod of her head. 'I'm no diplomat, Mr Gorbachev, but, following the poisoning and imprisonment of a Russian Opposition Leader, Alexei Navalny and the Russian statement in response to the proposed EU sanctions, "If you want peace, you must prepare for war". The trust between our two nations is, how may I put this? Strained.'

'That may be so, Claudia. Russia will, as it always has... Andrei Gorbachev paused. He stroked his chin. 'Russia has always engaged in mutually beneficial cooperation. I ask that you remind Stephen of this axiom.'

'Please accept my apology, Sir. It was not my place to represent potential views of the British establishment. I will, of course, pass your message to Stephen when I next speak to him.'

'Good, good.' Andrei Gorbachev waved his hand towards a woman in her mid-thirties seated on the other side of the café. The woman stood and strolled towards their table. As she approached, Andrei said to Claudia, 'Katina will walk you to the car, then Victor will drive you to Monya's mansion as we wouldn't want you having another accident, or was it a swim?' He chuckled. Being escorted by the FSB was a subliminal message for Monya that the FSB was watching him.

Claudia smiled at his attempted joke and stood to leave.

Andrei Gorbachev looked Claudia up and down before speaking to Katina. 'Instruct Victor to take Claudia shopping. We can't have her catching a cold.'

CHAPTER 8
Tears

Samantha was in the ensuite, the only place she thought she was safe from Chinese Security Service prying eyes, using the toilet pan as a chair. Richard had left for work and, with Molly readying herself for school, she had a moment to herself. She buried her face in her hands and sobbed. The previous night, after the revelation at the Shark Fin restaurant, she and Richard had broken the news to Molly of their impending move to Beijing. Secretly, Samantha hoped her daughter would object, telling her father all the things that she was too frightened to say. In retrospect, this was unfair—after all, Molly was merely a child. After her initial surprise, Molly accepted the move with little fuss, especially when Richard reassured her that Snowflake could come too. Olivia's words weighed heavily and, as she watched the warning becoming reality, with only four weeks, she was helpless. How could she save her daughter?

Continuing her daily routine, Molly cried out from her bedroom, asking the usual question about the whereabouts of her schoolbag. Samantha didn't reply as she would normally have done, so Molly put her hands on her hips in frustration. She rolled her eyes and uttered a low growling noise, 'Grrrrrr'. Molly called again, this time with increased vigour, but Samantha did not respond, lost in her own sorrows.

Where can we go?

Molly stomped out of the bedroom seeking her mother. When she heard Samantha's sobs, Molly's tantrum faded.

'What's wrong Mummy?' When Samantha didn't look up, Molly placed her hand on her mother's arm and whispered, 'What's wrong Mummy? Tell me.'

Molly's touch and soft words caught Samantha by surprise. She looked up and, wiping her eyes, said, 'Nothing love, nothing. Just a little headache, that's all.' She smiled, trying to hide her fears as she attempted to project a more upbeat tone and continued, 'Are you ready for school?'

'It's about moving to China, isn't it Mummy? We mustn't go, it's not safe for us.'

Samantha marvelled at the wisdom of Molly's innocence. Her daughter didn't judge her parents yet displayed a depth of understanding and courage that was beyond her years. As her mother, Samantha wanted to be a tower of strength but, when Molly uttered those words, Samantha broke down and, for the first time since returning from Spain, she wept, not in secret but openly.

Pull yourself together, Samantha.

Wiping her eyes, Samantha said, her voice controlled, hiding her fears, 'It's not safe to cry either, Molly.'

'It's okay Mummy, they can't hear us in here.'

Samantha's eyes opened wide in surprise. She stared at Molly.

Does she know we are being watched? How could that be possible? She's only eight and still a child?

'Who can't hear us, Honey?'

'The bad people. The men Daddy works for.'

Realisation dawned; Molly was alert, in tune with what was going on around her, certainly more than she had given her credit for. There was little point in concealing the truth anymore. 'We can't stay in here too long Molly, in case they become suspicious and we mustn't ever talk about this in the car.'

How on earth are we ever going to work this out?

She wiped the remaining teardrop away as Molly grinned.

'What is it, Molly?'

'They're not listening at school, Mummy.'

'What? How do you know this, Molly?'

Molly ignored her mother's question because it was Claudia who told her, a person her mother didn't trust. 'At school today, I will have a tummy ache. When they call you to fetch me, we can talk in the Sick Bay. They won't hear us in there.'

For the second time in a matter of minutes, Samantha looked wide eyed at her daughter, seeing her anew.

Oh, my goodness. What's happening?

She opened her mouth to speak but, finding herself lost for words, closed it again in a fashion befitting a goldfish gulping for air. A giggle escape Molly's lips.

'Don't you worry, Mummy, I have a plan. Come on, it's time for school.'

Samantha tried to speak.

WOOSH.

Molly raced from the ensuite as Samantha shook her head in disbelief.

What just happened? Pull yourself together, woman!

She straightened her dress and checked her appearance in the bathroom mirror.

You look awful.

After wiping her eyes, Samantha hastily applied some makeup and, stepping back from the mirror, examined her artistry, telling herself that she would have to do. She descended the stairs, but Molly was nowhere to be seen.

Where are you?

Samantha glanced at her watch and, right on cue, she heard a familiar shout.

'Mummy, where's my school bag?'

***

Samantha had barely returned home from the school run when her phone rang. It was the school nurse who told her that Molly was unwell, vomiting and asked that she return immediately to collect her daughter. 'Molly is waiting for you in the Sick Bay.'

I suspect Molly put her fingers down the throat to make herself sick. She is a resourceful little thing.

The plan almost immediately came undone when the nurse accompanied Samantha into the Sick Bay and seemed set to stay until they left for home. Samantha was stressed at the thought of the deception, but it was her resourcefulness that resolved the situation. Molly was lying on the bed, looking pale. Her mother placed her hand on the child's forehead and said to the nurse, 'Would you mind if I stay with Molly for a while before putting her in the car? I want to be sure her tummy is settled.' A reasonable request had Samantha stopped there, but her nerves overtook her and she added, 'I wouldn't want her to vomit in the car. It's an awful lingering odour.'

The nurse stared at Samantha, displeased.

'I meant the smell of vomit... from the car.'

Her annoyance on display, the nurse snapped, 'No, Mrs Liew, I suppose you can't. I will leave you alone for a few moments.'

The nurse left and, the moment the sick bay door closed behind her, Samantha let out a sigh of relief and plopped herself down on the end of the bed. Molly, pleased with her cunning, sprang upright and beamed at her mother. Molly's smile was misinterpreted by Samantha as one of joy; anger washed over Samantha and she wanted to tell her daughter how much danger they were in. Instead, she held her tongue and an awkward silence spread across the room. Molly fiddled with the box of cards she was holding until Samantha finally spoke, her voice filled with misgiving. 'Oh, Molly. What are we going to do?'

'Mommy, I told you, I have a plan.'

Molly had searched her memory of spy stories she had read or seen on films and it had influenced her plan, even fantasising booby trapping their house, like they did in the movies, especially Home Alone. She dismissed the proposition as childish and silly. Claudia had told Molly that, for secret spy reasons, when they had to leave, they couldn't tell Richard, her father. Molly had been concerned by this revelation, but Claudia had promised that he could return later, when it was safe. Claudia or Olivia would come to their rescue. Claudia had been insistent.

Half listening and her mind elsewhere, Samantha nodded.

Molly straightened herself. 'We will tell Daddy that there's a school camp, and it is my last chance to be with my friends before leaving for China. I will tell him he must let me go. I can be very persuasive, Mummy. Do you remember the camp last year?' A statement not a question, so Molly continued, 'Parents were asked to be volunteers. You were too busy to help, but not this year. We both pack and you drive me to camp where you will be a helper.'

Her mind focusing on the last part of the conversation, Samantha said, 'Is there a camp?'

Molly put her hands on her hips in mock frustration. 'No, of course not!'

'I see, a trick. I knew that. Um... when is it to be?'

'It's next week, and I was thinking of Tuesday until Friday. Of course, you must find somewhere for us to stay.' As she was speaking, Molly remembered that, with Claudia overseas, it would be Olivia who would come.

Mummy really likes Olivia. It would be easier to confide in her about the secret, but no. If she found out that the playing cards were Claudia's idea, she would take them away from me. When should I signal to Olivia that we need help? If I wait until we reach the hideout, Olivia will know where to find us.

A feeling of panic washed over Samantha, which set her mind racing.

Molly doesn't realise how complicated this really is. Once we run, there's no going back, and she may never see her father again. The deception of the camp gives us a three-day head start before Richard and the Chinese begin their search, and that's not nearly long enough.

Samantha had siphoned cash from the bank but, with everything happening so soon, it was hardly enough.

I'll have to risk withdrawing a lump sum, just in case Richard realises we're gone and closes the account. But what if he actually wants to be with us and is just playacting for the Chinese to ensure our safety? How can I ask him without raising his suspicion, and would he even tell me the truth? So many questions, Samantha. If only I could talk to Olivia—she would know what to do. And what about the Chinese Security Service? If they decide to track us down, how can we possibly hide from them? We simply can't. What choice do we have? None. So maybe our best option is to go to China.

Samantha's attention was brought back by Molly's voice requesting her attention.

'Sorry, darling, what was the question again?'

'I asked you if you can find us somewhere to stay.'

With a tone of vagueness garnishing her reply, Samantha said, 'Yes.'

Molly, hearing her mother's hesitation, said, 'We have to be brave Mummy.'

Samantha was annoyed at herself, but proud of her daughter. She so wanted to be a pillar of strength and not for Molly to take the lead. Stuttering, she said, 'Um, err, the thing is, Molly, err, it's not that easy, not if we are to get away safely.' Samantha racked her brain for a concrete example that would pass her daughter's muster and remembered a phone app that she and Richard had downloaded. When they opened Google maps, the app displayed the location of their car; useful when parked in a large shopping centre or at a sporting event. The app would now give them away. Her heart missed a beat, knowing if they took the car, Richard would know their location. 'We can't take the car dear; your school camp scam won't work.'

'Can't we? Why not?'

Samantha wanted to keep Richard out of her response, and nor did she wish to explain a convoluted tale of apps and maps.

'Do you remember when you told me we couldn't talk in the car because bad people were listening?' Molly hadn't brought up the subject; Samantha had. She hoped Molly wouldn't remember.

Molly nodded.

'If they are listening, they will also be watching. Somewhere, hidden in the car so that we can't find it, is a tracking device, like in the spy movies.'

Molly put her hand over her mouth and grasped, 'I hadn't thought of that.'

Frustrated at missing something so obvious, Molly's mind went into overdrive and, seconds later, she said, 'Mommy, I have an idea. Sometimes, before you drop me at school, you take the car in for a service and the garage gives you a courtesy car. On the day of the camp, book our car in for a service and tell the garage that we will be away for three days.'

In Molly's view, everything would be okay once Olivia arrived; three days would be enough.

If I post the emergency alert card when we arrive, wherever that is, it will take another day to reach MI6, and Olivia will come the next.

The temptation to tell her mother surfaced again, but she pushed it aside.

This must be kept top secret, Molly, top secret. Three days, that is all.

Samantha, while mulling over Molly's plan, inadvertently muttered, 'The car isn't due for a service.'

Even though Molly was seated on the bed, she thrust her hands on to her hips again, a mirror image of her mother when irritated by Richard. She even managed the same annoyed tone.

'Mummy! It doesn't have to be a service. Tell Daddy the engine is making a funny noise and you've booked it in to be checked. He won't know, and I've heard you mention many times that he's useless at fixing things.'

'I'm not sure that I've called your father useless.'

'Yes, you did. You told Jenny's mother that Richard was useless at fixing anything. "When something needs repairing, I have to call for a man."'

'Err, well, if I said that... I'm sorry. It was supposed to be funny, but it was wrong of me to say that about your father. Your suggestion is excellent, but I think we should hire a car rather than taking a courtesy vehicle. If we're late returning it to the garage, they may think we've stolen it and report it missing to the police. You understand Molly that, for a while at least, we won't be able to return to the house and we can't tell Daddy where we are because it's safer for him if he doesn't know.'

Molly felt scared but, remembering that Olivia was coming, she nodded, knowing everything was going to be alright.

Samantha gave her daughter a reassuring smile. 'Honey, it's time we were leaving. Are you ready?'

Molly swung her feet off the bed before halting. 'If we are not coming back, what about Snowflake? We can't leave Snowflake behind!'

Samantha had overlooked the cat, and the mention of its name made her feel inadequate.

Don't let your failings show!

Samantha breathed out loudly. 'Molly! And I suppose you think I forgot about Snowflake. Well, I never.' Not knowing what to say next, Samantha blurted out the first thing that came to her. 'A cattery, Molly, a cattery.'

'What?' Molly said, shaking her head. 'Snowflake hates boarding kennels. She can't go there.'

It was Samantha's turn to put her hands on her hips, imitating her daughter's oft performed gesture. 'Who said anything about leaving Snowflake at the cattery?'

Molly grinned excitedly, waiting to hear what her mother had to say, but Samantha hoped that she'd said enough. When Samantha remained mute, Molly said, 'Go on Mummy. Tell me your plan.'

Samantha stalled, playing for time to think. 'It's only for one night.'

'One night?'

'Oh, definitely—just one night. Um... the day before we leave... when Daddy is at work... I'll take Snowflake to the cattery. I'll say she's at the vet's and that you and I are picking her up after the school camp.'

'Mummy, why would Snowflake be at the Vets?'

To camouflage her impromptu plan, Samantha huffed. 'Molly... I will make something up. After all, that's what you would do.'

Molly beamed with a new idea. 'I know, say Snowflake was attacked by the neighbour's dog.'

'Who, Edgar? The affectionate, silky, long coated, drop eared and pushed in nose, English Toy Spaniel. The poor timid creature that Snowflake menaces at every opportunity?' Samantha shook her head, feigning disbelief. 'Even Daddy would be suspicious of that.'

'What about a broken leg, then?'

'Maybe, although I was thinking of something less dramatic, perhaps pus in the eye.'

Molly nodded before saying, 'Oooh, how gross!'

***

Since discovering her husband was a foreign agent, Samantha and Richard had not spoken of it. Samantha's silence resulted from Olivia's warning, but Richard's was a total mystery to her. Following Chen Li's revelation, and having plotted the escape plan with Molly, Samantha had, on three occasions, joined Richard in the ensuite, the only place safe to converse without being overheard. She'd hoped that he would talk about moving to Beijing so that she could gauge his true loyalty- the Chinese Ministry of State Security or his family. Each time, he'd been silent on the topic and their conversation was polite chatter.

On the fourth occasion, fearing that there was nothing to lose, Samantha asked him bluntly, 'Will we be safe in Beijing?' She was taken aback by Richard's response, or lack of it.

In a dismissive tone, he replied, 'Of course dear,' and kissed her gently on the cheek, immediately changing the topic, 'What are your plans for the rest of the day?'

Reflecting on it now, as Samantha walked the high street, she regretted having not confronted him, telling Richard that his answer was insufficient. In her heart of hearts, she'd hoped that he would confirm his commitment to them by keeping her and Molly safe. She knew now that the moment to challenge had passed.

With trepidation, Samantha had told Richard about Molly's camp and that she was going along as a parent leader. She'd fully expected him to object. To her surprise, Richard barely gave the school camp a second thought.

His silence was telling.

She pretended to examine a green and white designer print, contemporary boat-neck kick-flare skirt with three-quarter-length sleeves, on display in the shop window.

What to make of Richard's disinterest...? I don't know.

She sighed as a teardrop formed in the corner of her eye and trickled down her cheek. Discovering that your husband lived a life of secrets was like finding out that he was unfaithful. She believed that his involvement in espionage was something from her husband's past, but wondered if their marriage was part of the same game. Her emotions were complicated, and she needed to sort through them before she could move forward. Since Spain, her life had been a roller coaster, with feelings of anger, shock, depression, fear, confusion, and mistrust surfacing at different times. Their marriage had changed, never to return to where it once was. For Molly's sake, Samantha behaved as if nothing had happened. She moved to the next window admiring an elegant red oak Leopard pop, loose jersey dress with gently puffed sleeves finished with neat cuffs. Suspecting that this was the beginning of the end of her marriage, Samantha realised she had to give thought to practical matters, particularly where and how they would live after the imagined three-day camp.

We can't go to family. That's the first place anyone would look.

Samantha sighed again.

When did I stop loving him?

A reflection in the shop window caught Samantha's attention. A silver BMW SUV was parked on the opposite side of the road. It could have been any silver BMW SUV because they were a common enough car, except that Samantha knew she'd seen this one before, and more than once. She remembered the roof rails because she was contemplating fitting them on their own BMW. Samantha tried to recall when she first noticed the vehicle and the revelation shocked her.

It is since the Shark Fin restaurant and only when I'm a pedestrian. Oh, my. I'm being followed!

With her heart pounding, Samantha turned from the window and continued her journey down the street. Reaching a set of traffic lights, she turned right and followed another main road. About two-hundred and fifty yards down the street, she spotted another woman's fashion shop. In keeping with her ploy, Samantha faced the window, ignoring the goods on display, instead concentrating on the reflection in the glass. Adjusting the angle of her head to look back in the direction she'd walked, Samantha watched as the BMW SUV pulled up and parked on the opposite side of the road. Her mind raced.

Do they know that Molly and I are about to run? Don't be silly, Samantha, how can they? Should I try to lose them by dashing into an alleyway or somewhere a car can't follow like they do in the movie? Stupid woman. That would raise their suspicions. What do I do? I don't normally window shop and they will guess something is unusual. You should buy something. Go into the shop. That way, everything seems normal. Then stroll home with your newly purchased wares as if you don't have a care in the world.

Samantha changed her focus from the reflection in the glass to the items on display.

Oh damn! That's about the last thing I want. Bloody sexy women's lingerie. I'm not buying a thong! How anybody wears one of those is beyond me.

Samantha huffed.

Well, I suppose with the Chinese spying on us, I'll have to give Richard a fashion parade. What's it to be then, the black Brazilian knickers and bra with floral lace or the pink champagne mesh and lace Teddy?

Samantha strolled into the store and pretended to examine the variety of undergarments on display before making her purchase. She mulled over how they could lose the surveillance when Molly and she made their bid for freedom.

A disguise, Samantha. You and Molly will need a disguise of some sort.

Samantha realised that her trip to town was the perfect time to find what she needed.

Sun glasses and a baseball hat for Molly and a wig for me, a red one, perhaps. A pharmacy should have those. I'll walk past one on the way home. Perfect.

Pleased with her plan, the momentary feeling of satisfaction vanished as she ordered the Brazilian knickers and matching floral lace bra.

'Would Madam like a bag?' the middle-aged shop assistant asked.

No, I thought I'd wear them home over the top of my clothes. What a silly question.

'Yes. That would be perfect, thank you.'

Leaving the lingerie shop, Samantha paused on the footpath and glanced inside the shopping bag, smiling to give the appearance to her watchers that she was pleased with her purchase. A spring in her step, Samantha turned back the way she'd come and dashed towards the pharmacy. Pretending not to notice her, the SUV was still parked on the opposite side of the road. The constant stream of traffic moving through the street and Samantha's hesitancy made it difficult for her to see the occupants.

Two Asian men, but I can't see in the back. There could be more.

Passing the front of the BMW, her eyes turned towards the vehicle like adaptive headlights illuminating around corners. With its heavily tinted windows, if there were occupants in the back, they were shielded from prying eyes. Two steps forward and the BMW drifted from her peripheral vision. At the pharmacy, Samantha entered and allowed herself a deep breath, feeling immediately safer. Starting the search, Samantha located the sunglasses picking those with yellow lenses, thinking that they would make Molly look older. Next was a black baseball hat, which she found easily, leaving Samantha to seek the last item, pacing the aisles to no avail.

Damn, where are you?

'May I help you?' A voice said from behind.

Turning, Samantha opened her mouth, ready to ask the assistant where they kept wigs. She quickly closed it again, conscious of not giving away her plan.

'I'm just looking, thank you.'

Well, that was stupid because you still have to pay for the wig at the checkout.

At the far end of the accessory aisle, she finally caught up with the salesperson—a young woman, no older than twenty-three, who likely juggled her retail job with university studies.

'Sorry, excuse me. Wigs. Do you have them?'

'Not on the shelves, Madam, but we have a wig clinic. I can make an appointment for you if you wish.'

'No, thank you. It's ... Er ... not a medical matter. Fancy dress really ... I'm hoping to go as red head.'

The young woman nodded. 'We have a selection of brilliant hair dye, even some single use ones that wash out easily. I know people use them for parties, and they are inexpensive. They'll save you a trip to the hairdressers.'

Before she could decline, the woman moved away, expecting Samantha to follow. Stopping at the hair dye shelves, the assistant ran her finger along the array of products, saying aloud as she did, 'Red... Red... I know you are here somewhere, ah, there you are.' Reading from the label, she said, 'It says here that it's a temporary colour.' She turned the package for Samantha to see before offering it.

'Thank you,' Samantha said, taking the proffered package.

'Is there anything else I can assist you with?'

'No, thank you, but I'd like to browse for a while. Thank you for your help.'

'You're most welcome, all part of our service.' The young woman turned to leave.

'Wait, just a second.'

'Yes.'

'Scrunchies. Where are they?'

The shop assistant smiled before pointing to a shelf next to where Samantha was standing. 'We have a nice selection. Personally, I adore the brightly coloured ones.' The young woman walked across to the shelf and touched the scrunchies as she spoke. 'Like this bright red one, or this blush pink. My favourite is yellow with brown spots. It would suit you perfectly.'

Samantha grinned. 'You're quite the sales woman. Yes, I'll take it.'

'Why thank you Madam. Is there anything else?'

'No, you have been more than helpful.' Once more alone, Samantha lingered in the product aisles, picking up and examining items for no real purpose. The distraction the sales lady provided faded and, like in the lingerie shop, her mind was filled with their plan to escape. Her eyes were drawn to a bright pink sun hat.

Maybe I should pick that up? How I will use it is a mystery.

With the assortment of purchases in hand, Samantha proceeded to the checkout, where, next to the cash register, she spotted a range of designer face masks. Face masks, although not compulsory, many people were using them. They *were* mandatory on public transport, Samantha recalled. She fingered through the collection, stopping at a light green mask decorated with printed yellow flowers.

'I'll take this one, I think.' Samantha said, adding it to her items.

The cashier scanned the face mask and, as Samantha was about to pay for her purchases, she said. 'Oh, you had better let me have a box of disposable masks, too.'

Samantha felt confident when she was leaving the underwear shop but, as she exited the pharmacy for the walk home, she was consumed by panic. It wasn't being followed that troubled her; it was the dawning realisation that the plan she and Molly had devised was likely to fail. Laying out the scheme in her mind, she realised there were too many coincidences for Richard to overlook: Snowflake hospitalised at the vet, the car in the shop for repairs, and both her and Molly away at camp.

Too many, for sure.

It's the bloody cat that is the problem. Surely Molly will understand if we don't take Snowflake?

Samantha sighed.

No, she will never forgive me. You need to be brave Samantha; leave the cat, Molly will get over it. Okay, what's next...

Samantha took a deep breath.

Money? I've already considered that. How much should I withdraw? At least ten thousand pounds should keep us afloat while I figure things out. As for when? Before we leave, of course. But if I take the money and Richard checks our account, he'll realise we've made a run for it. I need to wait until Friday. But wait—I can't risk him closing the account. If he does, I'll be left with nothing.

Samantha's ruminating had turned full circle. She breathed slowly and increased her stride, huffing in frustration as she walked.

I can't leave Snowflake behind. It won't work.

She knew that searching the internet for a cattery could wait but, in her anxious state she felt compelled to look. With her free hand, Samantha took her phone from her pocket and tried one handed to enter the password, but she was all fingers and thumbs.

She slowed to allow her to use both hands, her knees knocking against the shopping bag. Samantha tried to enter the phrase *Cattery near Dalston* into the search engine. Her first attempt was impeded by her body and hands swaying to the rhythm of her footsteps and glanced at what she'd typed.

Catreey neae dalton.

Seeing the gobbledygook, Samantha grumbled in annoyance before trying again.

Cattwry neae salaron.

Irritated, Samantha paused for a moment, then remembered she was being followed and began moving again. A café caught her eye, and she let out a frustrated sigh, murmuring under her breath.

Slow down, Samantha, and have a coffee. Visiting a café isn't suspicious. There you can look for a place for Snowflake. Now, Samantha, you're thinking like a spy.

The thought brought a smile to her face, easing the tension.

Samantha chose a table with a view from the window up the high street. She used her smart phone to seek the cattery again and, to her surprise and delight, twenty minutes from where they lived, in Finsbury Park, was Holloway Vets and Cattery.

A Vet and a Cattery, all in one! How perfect is that? Even if my movements are being tracked, taking Snowflake there will match the story about the cat's condition - pus in her eye. This is good, Samantha, very good indeed.

She placed the phone on the table in front of her and forced herself to relax, deciding to finish the coffee before booking Snowflake in for a night's stay. Having drained the last drops of her beverage, Samantha called the cattery and was all but finished making the arrangements when the silver BMW SUV with its roof racks parked directly opposite, in front of the window. Samantha's heart started raced as one of the men stared at her.

The cattery receptionist, noticing a change in Samantha's voice, asked, 'Is everything okay?'

'What? Oh, yes ... sorry. I was ...' Samantha stopped mid-sentence and changed what she was going to say. 'Um, sorry, this is the first time Snowflake's been away. It sounds silly, I know.'

'Not at all, Mrs Liew. I totally understand and promise that we will take good care of Snowflake.'

Samantha's thoughts were elsewhere, on the SUV.

Bastards. They're intimidating me, not even trying to conceal themselves.

'Madam?'

Samantha realised the receptionist was trying to get her attention. 'Oh, please excuse my nervousness. I'm sure you will look after Snowflake.'

'Mrs Liew, we will see you at ten-thirty this coming Monday.'

'Yes, ten-thirty. I will be there... and Snowflake, of course. Thank you.'

Hanging up the phone, Samantha's eyes were drawn to the BMW. The man was still staring at her.

They want me to know I'm being followed.

She averted her gaze and raised her coffee cup to her lips, only to realise it was empty. Undeterred, she pretended to sip from it. As she fought to suppress her rising anxiety, various scenarios played out in her mind. She remembered a scene from a movie—

though the title escaped her—where the person being followed ordered coffees for her watchers.

That would show them I will not be pressurised.

In another film, she recalled a person sneaking out of the back door to avoid surveillance. She shook her head.

No. They would watch me more closely in the future. The best strategy is to pretend you haven't noticed them.

Samantha took another sip from her empty cup as her pulse slowed until her mind raced with irrational thoughts.

Why now? They must know! They know I'm planning something. Calm down, Samantha, you're being silly. I've done nothing yet. It's all a coincidence or they've been following me for a while and I haven't noticed. It's time to go home, so take a deep breath.

Good.

Now another.

Okay. What did I say? Pretend not to have seen them. What if they get out of the car?

Stop it! I'm worrying unnecessarily. Play dumb, I'm good at that.

Finishing the remains of her make-believe drink, with her shopping in hand, Samantha stood and drifted from the café. Resisting the urge, she walked home without looking behind; if they followed her, Samantha wasn't aware. When Richard returned from work, she pondered whether she should tell him of the surveillance.

True to form, Richard asked Samantha what she'd done with her day and Samantha opened the lingerie bag and, holding the underwear for him to see, said, 'I brought us a little going away gift.'

Richard smiled and said, 'Very classy,' while inside, he thought.

What's going on?

His suspicions were raised.

CHAPTER 9
Crunch

Monday Morning

It was Monday morning and, with everything at stake, Samantha thought Molly would be on time for once. With an edge of impatience in her voice, Samantha called from the hallway, 'Come on Molly or we will be late.'

'Where's my school bag?'

'Where do you think? It's where you always leave it. In the kitchen.'

'What?'

Samantha yelled louder. 'It's in the kitchen.'

'Don't yell Mummy. The neighbours will hear.'

Infuriated by her daughter, the anxiety Samantha was experiencing since deciding to leave Richard, temporarily faded, forgotten in the daily battle of leaving on time for Molly's school.

Molly popped her head over the banisters, saying in a moderated tone. 'Mummy, I don't think Snowflake is well.'

The unscripted play from Molly caught Samantha by surprise and, for a second, she wondered if Snowflake was truly unwell.

Molly's more grown up than I give her credit for.

Moving to the foot of the stairs, Samantha said in a concerned voice, 'Oh dear. I'm coming up.'

Upstairs, to the bemusement of the cat who would have preferred to be left alone to sleep at the bottom of Molly's bed, mother and daughter fussed over it in a pantomime of concern for the benefit of the Chinese State Security watchers.

Samantha gave Molly Snowflake to hold while she examined the cat. 'I think you're right, Molly. Snowflake has an infected eye. Maybe something is in it.'

Stroking the cat's head, Molly said, 'Oh, poor sick Snowflake. We must take her to the Vet right away!'

Samantha bit her lip, trying not to grin.

You're not getting out of school that easily.

She nodded. 'Yes, once I've dropped you at school, I'll head straight to the Vets.'

Snowflake, behaving as if she understood the word vet, jumped free of Molly's grasp, depositing herself under the bed and out of sight.

Molly shook her head vehemently in disagreement with her mother. 'Snowflake is scared, so I need to come with you.' Molly dropped to one knee in search of the cat, calling, 'Snowflake, Snowflake, come here.'

Using her displeased mother's voice, Samantha said, 'You, young lady, need to fetch your school bag from the kitchen and get yourself into the car. I will find the cat. We are late... again.'

'But mum!'

'No buts. Now move!' Samantha softened her tone. 'I'll look after Snowflake and, as I have said, once I've dropped you at school, I will take her to the Vets.'

'Promise?'

'Yes. Promise.'

Molly reached under the bed and retrieved Snowflake.

Samantha shook her head in frustration. 'What on earth are you doing now?'

Molly stared at her mother wide-eyed, as if to say, *what do you mean?* 'I'm taking Snowflake to the car. You told me you'll take her to the Vets once you've dropped me off.'

Samantha breathed out heavily.

She's taking this play acting too far.

'I'll come home first. Now get your bag.'

'Where's my school bag?'

'You and I, young lady, are going to have a falling out. It's in the kitchen. Now go!'

***

On the drive to Holloway Vets and Cattery, Samantha kept a watchful eye for the Silver BMW SUV in the mirrors. Seeing nothing, she was hopeful the hoax had worked and felt surprisingly relaxed and ready for her return trip home. As she left Snowflake at the cattery, the cat's behaviour having made her smile. Snowflake, annoyed at the indignation of being left, had flicked her tail at Samantha and, with feline aloofness, walked nonchalantly to the attendant. *Leave me, will you? See if I care.*

Preparing to leave the car park and enter the main road, Samantha pushed on the left indicator while turning her head to the right, checking for approaching vehicles by looking out through the side window. A knot formed in her stomach as a Silver BMW filled her vision but it drove past, paying no attention to her.

No roof racks, you silly thing. They've certainly got me jumping at shadows.

Entering the roadway, Samantha's mind turned to the next deception. Without Richard becoming suspicious, how to dispose of the car?

Richard! I should have rung Richard about Snowflake.

'Call Richard Liew,' Samantha said to her car's voice activated media unit. The car radio, which had until then been playing music, fell silent. Two seconds later, she heard Richard's phone ringing.

'Hi Honey.'

Samantha slowed, stopping at a set of traffic lights and checking the mirrors. Plenty of traffic, but no Silver SUV with roof racks.'

'I'm just leaving the Vets, Richard.'

'The Vets. What happened?'

Samantha began spinning the story of Snowflake's infected eye. She was still talking as the lights turned green and she moved off. Two-hundred yards later, when Samantha checked in her mirrors again, they were filled with the grill of a light delivery truck.

She growled, 'Back off!'

'What is it, Honey?'

'A stupid driver is right up my backside.'

That's it.

A plan suddenly forming in Samantha's mind.

Knowing Richard would hear, Samantha released a startled scream before slamming her foot on the brakes. She gripped the steering wheel as hard as she could and braced for the impact.

SMASH!

The sound of the collision as the light truck impacted the back of Samantha's car was unmistakable to Richard.

'Honey? Samantha, are you alright?'

'Oh, my gosh!' Samantha exclaimed as her BMW was pushed into the rear of the car in front.

CRUNCH!

Panic filling his voice, Richard repeated. 'Honey, Samantha, are you alright?'

Feigning sobbing, Samantha said, 'Oh, Richard, I'm so sorry. I've crashed the car. That truck hit me from behind and...' Richard interrupted.

'Don't worry about the car. Are you okay?'

Samantha nodded, even though there was no one there to see the gesture. 'Yes, shaken, that's all.'

'Good,' Richard said. 'Now, tell me where you are and I'll catch a taxi.'

'No!' Samantha exclaimed in alarm. The moment the word slipped from her lips; she realised it sounded overly enthusiastic. In a softer manner, she said, 'That's so thoughtful, Richard; but there's no point. I'm fine, it's just an accident. I have the insurance company's number in my phone...' Samantha was interrupted by a stocky middle-aged woman with red tips in her hair tapping on the driver door window. In a broad Liverpool scouse accent she said, 'Are you alright, Love?'

'Yes. Thank you.' Samantha opened her door.

'What's happening?' Richard asked.

'Sorry Richard, I must go. I'll talk to you tonight.'

She ended the call without waiting for his reply.

Samantha stepped from her damaged BMW into the midst of a small crowd gathering at the scene of the three-vehicle pileup. A dark-haired man in his early thirties, sporting a black neatly cropped beard, wearing blue jeans, red shirt and a yellow high-vis safety jacket, the delivery driver, confronted Samantha.

Invading her personal space, he waved his finger at her and sneered, 'You stupid woman. What the bloody hell were you doing by slamming the brakes on?'

It was an accusation, not a question.

Samantha pushed her shoulders back, puffed out her chest and, her tone dripping with scorn, said, 'Don't you dare, stupid woman me! And you can put that finger away too!' Samantha was aware of the presence of another person, when the lady with the red tips pushed her shoulder against Samantha's. The two women joined forces, creating a formidable pair. The man didn't stand a chance. He took half a pace back.

His demeanour softened as he said, 'My bad.'

My Bad! What kind of statement is that?

Samantha was about to give the driver another mouthful when, from the corner of her eye, she saw a bystander, hoping for a fiery exchange in the belief that they were a social activist, filming on her smart phone. Samantha knew that, if she wasn't careful and the footage was uploaded, later that day, her more outspoken social media friends would comment on the encounter, something she would regret. Relaxing her stance, and in a matter-of-fact voice, Samantha said, 'It's a requirement that we exchange insurance details.'

The delivery man nodded as the lady with the red tips left Samantha's side without a word and melted into the background. Samantha wanted to thank her. In the vain hope of spotting her, she scanned the road, but the woman had vanished. What Samantha saw, its rear lights barely visible in a side street, was the back end of a silver BMW SUV with its telltale roof racks.

CHAPTER 10
Monya

Compliments of the Russian Federal Security Service, Claudia, dressed in a new and dry outfit, travelled the final thirty minutes to Monya's compound in the back seat of the car. She'd chosen a modern, petite black single buttoned suit jacket with matching pants, a white top, and black flat-soled shoes. Her new suit looked like the wool blend one lost to moisture, although it was polyester and viscose, Claudia having chosen time and convenience over quality.

Arriving at the security gates of Monya's mansion, Victor wound down the driver's side window and pressed the intercom button. Without words being exchanged, the automatic gates opened and Victor eased the vehicle into the driveway. Claudia peered out of the windows as they drove the short distance to the mansion's main entrance. Behind the fortified fence, Claudia was accustomed to seeing heavily armed sentries, but this time there were none. It wasn't until she stepped out of the car that she noticed the "Robotic Dogs"—semi-autonomous, all-terrain quadrupedal unmanned ground vehicles—watching her. About the size of a medium-weight dog, one of the headless robots approached her.

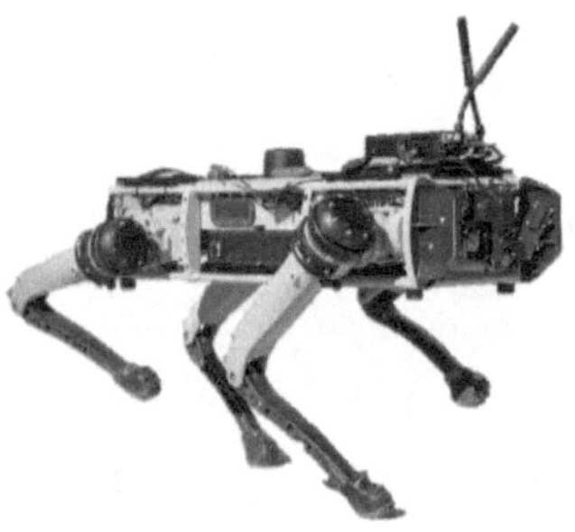

A person speaking through the radio activated speaker attached to the dog said, 'Welcome, Claudia. Monya is expecting you, so please proceed to the front door where his secretary is waiting.'

'Thank you.' Claudia replied, not perturbed by speaking to a machine. She turned to close the car door.

Victor, who had already witnessed the robotic animal, said, 'This is the beginning of a new era.'

Claudia acknowledged with a nod of her head, before saying, 'Have you seen the big ones?'

'No.'

'They weigh one hundred and ten kilos, are the size of a small mule and can even stand upright. It's a scary-looking bugger... thanks for the ride.' Claudia pushed the door shut and began walking. From her peripheral vision she spotted two more robotic-dogs patrolling the grounds. Claudia paused and scanned the area. There were no other people. She said to herself,

I wonder if one day I'll find myself side-lined because of technology. It's happened throughout history, so why would my profession be any different? Although, a lot of my work is about relationships, even if they can be deceptive. Relationships are something robots don't do well, if at all. The boffins tell us that these new technologies, like electronic warfare and drones, mean that greater impact can be delivered with fewer people. In this context, you must love the use of the term productivity; in truth, it's code for cheaper and more effective ways to kill. Here's a philosophical question for you, Claudia. Are robotic-K-9's drones? Yes, but I suppose we need a way of differentiating those flying from those walking. Robotic soldiers can't be that far away. Science fiction is here. Ha, Claudia, you're sounding like a has-been, not the modern-day creature you claim to be. Perhaps the world is moving too fast, even for me? If Andrei Gorbachev is to be believed,

Sun-Tzu, in technological terms, is ahead of the game. The race for superiority in autonomous weapons has begun.

As Claudia approached Monya's mansion, the front door opened. Waiting to greet her was a man in his mid-to-late-fifties. Claudia smiled; she was half expecting another robot.

Without introducing himself, the man said, his manner polite, 'Ordinarily Claudia, you would be shown to your room to freshen up first before you meet Monya. As your luggage has been delayed, and I see you are no longer sodden, that won't be necessary.'

'News travels fast.'

The man ignored Claudia's remark and said, 'If you would kindly follow me, Monya is waiting for you in his study.'

As Monya's lover, Claudia had lived in this mansion. Stepping through the front door, the stamp of a new mistress was obvious.

Tacky.

Claudia scanned the graffiti art that now hung from the walls. She preferred the old décor. Works of Raphael, Michelangelo, Leonardo da Vinci, and Giulio Romano. She loved art from the Renaissance period and thought Monya had as well. First robotic K-9's and now a fresh taste in art.

What does this say about you, Claudia? Am I fast becoming a dinosaur? No. Alexandria is a young twat!

Monya's study used to be to the left at the back of the house with views through the bay windows out over the gardens. Claudia was surprised when she was taken into the centre of the house, to what was once the dining room. The man stopped in front of large wooden double doors and knocked. Without waiting for an invitation, he opened them. On her left, Claudia noticed two LED lights on the wall beside the doors, one green and one red. The green was illuminated, meaning they could enter. The man took a couple of steps inside the room and stopped. Claudia followed. Inside, music was playing. She scanned the room, finding it smaller than she remembered. The elegant table that once graced the dining area was conspicuously absent. This had been her favourite room in the house.

Even this has changed.

Monya was seated in a high-backed charcoal coloured Italian leather chair, his attention on papers placed on an art déco glass-topped desk supported by curved polished black timber and gold-plated steel legs. A traditional table lamp, featuring an antique brass and clear glass column base complete with cream shade, was at one end of his desk. Claudia thought his workspace looked out of place, as did the floor to ceiling mahogany book case. Its shelves were filled with Monya's passion, rare editions of collectable books. She wondered where he stored his Gutenberg Bible, one of only a handful of complete copies. Claudia's eyes were drawn back to where Monya was seated.

Monya raised his head. 'Thank you, Fabian. If you would relieve our guest of her mobile phone.'

Our guest! He's not calling me by my name. It seems I have some bridges to mend.

The man Claudia now knew as Fabian turned towards her and held out his hand.

Claudia removed the phone from her pocket and passed it to him. 'The last time I gave someone my phone, it didn't end well... For me! Will I find traces of a Pegasus infection when I get it back?'

Monya chuckled. 'That may be so for the last time. Fear not, we will keep it safe for the duration of your visit and we won't tamper with it. Never-the-less, I imagine you will want to replace it. One can't be too careful. Please give Fabian your watch, too.'

Claudia undid the strap on her watch. 'It's an analogue, no secret gimmicks.'

'Ah, analogue. There are some things that the technological revolution doesn't do as well, and never will. I love the aesthetics of a high-quality analogue movement.'

Claudia noticed Monya was still wearing the watch she'd bought him as a present. She smiled and held her identical watch for Monya to see. They were purchased as a matching pair. 'It's an old favourite. Will I need to replace this as well?'

She handed the watch to Fabian.

'No,' Monya said, his distant tone showing he was unmoved by her attempt at sentimentality. He looked at Fabian. 'Run the sweep over her.'

Without responding, Fabian placed Claudia's phone and watch into a small basket that was on a table beside the entrance. Next to the basket was a scanning device used to detect electronic bugs, listening devices, hidden cameras, laser microphones, burst transmitters, and other similar eavesdropping devices. Picking it up, he meticulously waved it across her body, even requesting that Claudia raise her feet so that he could check her shoes.

Fabian said, 'She's clean, Sir,'

'Thank you, Fabian. I don't wish to be disturbed. You may go.'

Fabian bowed his head. 'Sir, will your guest be joining you and Alexandria for dinner tonight?'

Monya nodded.

'Very well, Sir. I will tell the chef.' Fabian left the room, closing the door behind him.

As Claudia walked towards the vacant chair in front of Monya's desk, she opened her mouth, intending to say, 'I'm pleased to see that you still have a dining room.' She stopped herself. Her off handed comments would once have been received as intended–humour, however under the circumstances, she needed to moderate her familiarity. This was a professional visit... but she was still Monya's ex-mistress. It was necessary, if she were to win his trust, to acknowledge that everything had changed. It would be a delicate balancing act. She stopped beside the vacant chair and waited for Monya's permission to sit.

'Please,' Monya said, indicating with his hand for her to be seated.

'Thank you.'

To help break the ice, I need to say something serious but with a touch of humour.

'The new K-9's, they're impressive.' Claudia paused before adding, 'And they will be cheaper to feed.'

'Ha. Yes, and they don't complain about the cold or fall asleep on the job. These are exhilarating times, Claudia.'

Good, Monya used my name.

'I've heard this period described as the fourth industrial revolution, Claudia, the second machine age and the fourth era of technologies. Whatever term is used, it will be marked by breakthroughs in technologies like robotics, artificial intelligence, nanotechnology, quantum computing, biotechnology, autonomous vehicles and other gadgets I'm probably not aware of. The four-legged K-9 guards perform random or programmed patrols and alert their human overseers when they detect anything untoward. They can also be directed by personnel wearing virtual-reality headsets; they see exactly what robot does. The K-9's carry an array of cameras and sensor platforms like tactical radar, thermal imaging and infra-red. I'm sure you heard when you came in, we can issue verbal commands via a radio attached to them. Ours here are powered by fuel cell technology, more advanced than lithium battery, the ones the American military has. They're versatile and they can even swim, though I haven't seen that yet.' Monya shrugged his shoulders. 'Some kind of inflatable bladder, apparently.'

'Do you plan to weaponise them?'

'If you mean attach guns. No, not these anyway. The bigger ones, yes.'

'You have the alpha dogs?'

Monya chuckled. 'You're not expecting me to share all my trade secrets with you, surely.'

He's softening. It's time to acknowledge our shared loss, the passing of Max.

Claudia shook her head. 'No, of course not.' She curled her lips, a sign she was thinking about what to say next. Monya waited. Claudia breathed out heavily. 'Looking at the wonderful collection of books behind you reminds me of Max. I'm saddened that he had to die alone. If it had been possible, I know you would have been there for him, as would I.'

Monya stroked his chin. His features hardened.

I may have made a mistake.

Monya pursed his lips. 'Have you considered that, in seeking retribution for the death of John Moss, you contributed to Max's passing? He and Olivia left the security of my safe house in Barcelona for you.'

Claudia dropped her eyes. In contrition, 'Yes, I feel some responsibility for his death and guilt weighs heavily on me. Olivia doesn't attribute blame, which says much about her.'

Monya considered Claudia's response. 'I spoke at length to Olivia when she called to arrange this meeting. You're right, she harbours no ill will against you and, were Max alive, he wouldn't either. In deference to them, Claudia, neither shall I.'

'Thank you.'

Monya sighed. 'It's important for you to understand that I agreed to meet you solely because Olivia asked me to.'

'Yes, I understand that.'

'Good. While you're here, Claudia, you will be offered the hospitality I reserve for Max and Olivia. In return, I expect you to respect my position and privacy. No spying. Do you agree?'

'Yes.'

'Excellent, then we understand each other.'

'Yes.'

'Good. Let me apologise for the trouble you experienced on the way here. Some in the Brotherhood are not as forgiving as myself. However, the incident won't be repeated while you're my guest.' From the inside pocket of his suit jacket, Monya removed his mobile phone and then opened the top draw of his desk. After putting the phone inside, he closed it again. 'We shall move to a secure location to discuss the reason for your visit.'

Monya's statement caused Claudia to raise an eyebrow. She would have expected Monya's office to be secure.

'The technological revolution, Claudia, has its downsides. You can trust nothing with a micro-chip or any device connected to the internet.' Monya glanced around him. 'This room has no windows but, as you know, a laser microphone can hear conversations through walls, whether they are made from brick, concrete or anything else.' Monya stood. 'If you would follow me.'

Monya turned and took two paces towards the bookcase, activated a hidden latch to open a secret door built into the structure. Glancing through the gap, Claudia spotted an elevator, its door open. 'After you, Claudia,' Monya said, gesturing with his hand for her to enter. He waited until Claudia was inside before joining her, and they both turned to face the front. To the right was the control panel with five buttons.

This lift is like something from a nineteen fifties movie.

Monya, as if hearing Claudia's thoughts, said, 'There are no digital electronics in here. I find it cathartic, taking the elevator ride, its slower pace a temporary respite from the overbearing modern world.'

Monya pushed the down button and, three seconds later, the doors clattered closed. After another two second delay, the elevator began descending.

Claudia looked about the lift. 'I love it. All that's missing is the elevator music.'

Monya didn't respond but, moments later with a bit of a jerk, they came to a stop. As the doors rattled open, Monya said, 'This was the oldest I could find–nothing remotely modern about it, which was the plan.'

The lift opened into an underground lightly decorated room. In front to Claudia's right was an Italian red Chesterfield lounge suite, three-seater, with dual two seaters creating a horseshoe shape.

A large brown rug covered the floor and played host to an elegant glass coffee table. Directly in front at the far end of the room was Monya's desk, an extravagant solid, dark wooded masterpiece. The room was more in tune with the Monya that Claudia remembered, with less fine art.

The room has been spared Alexandria's tentacles.

'Welcome to the Zmei Cave. Please take a seat,' Monya said, pointing towards the lounge suite.

As they approached the Chesterfields, Claudia spotted a computer and old fashion phone on Monya's desk. She gestured towards the PC. 'I thought you told me that there was nothing with a microchip down here.'

Monya grinned. 'Almost. You will see the computer isn't connected to the internet, nor has it Bluetooth, or anything like it. Unfortunately, there are some things I can't manage without and the computer is one.' Monya stopped and scanned the room. 'This is about as secure as I can make it. The phone is connected by wire to the twin on Fabian's desk.'

'I hope you don't mind me asking, but how did you get the furniture here? That lift we arrived in is only large enough for us, let alone such a beautiful table.' Claudia looked towards Monya's desk as she stroked her hand down one of the two-seaters. 'And this lounge suite.'

Monya sat on the three-seater Chesterfield. 'During the construction phase, Claudia. They're here for life and will see me out.'

Claudia nodded. 'Things have changed since I left. I hope you don't mind me asking, but you'd struggle to accommodate a meeting of the Brotherhood down here.'

Monya chuckled. 'Still nosy, I see... no harm in answering, I suppose. Yes, they have changed, as they do Claudia. It is my fellow compatriots' prying eyes I'm concerned about. The Brotherhood meets upstairs...' Monya hesitated before he chuckled. 'We have a lift, so technically it's not upstairs or am I misunderstanding the English language?'

Claudia grinned. 'It's often said that English is one of the hardest languages to learn. Uplift doesn't quite have the same ring to it as upstairs. It's one of those things in English that makes no sense, like there is no ham in hamburger, so you don't need a staircase to go upstairs. English is full of contradictions.'

Monya nodded. 'Well, you've mastered English well, Claudia, but enough of this small talk. What brings you to my doorstep?'

'Cosy Bear!'

Monya tilted his head to one side, wondering if he'd heard her correctly. 'Cozy Bear?'

'MI6 believe Cosy Bear, spelt with an "S" and not "Z", another English language quirk as they are pronounced the same, is the code name for a rogue operation in Russia's own hacking group. MI6 believe the FSB knows nothing about Cosy Bear, yet it operates from within their outfit.'

Monya crossed his legs and folded his arms. From experience of his body language, Claudia knew he was closed to the coming discussion. His tone was unfriendly, as Monya asked, 'What leads you to that conclusion?'

'The group is engaging in cyber extortion and ransomware, normally your domain.'

Monya shrugged his shoulders, as if to say 'so what'. After a brief pause, he asked. 'Did you share your belief with Andrei Gorbachev?'

'No.'

Monya tilted his head to one side. 'Yet you're here to seek my help, knowing my connections with Andrei Gorbachev and the State?'

You need to think quickly, Claudia, as Monya is close to shutting down this conversation. Take a gamble on Monya knowing the existence of The Firm.

'I respect your concern, Monya. Let me assure you that this was not dismissed by MI6. Cosy Bear with an S, is part of a new international criminal organisation called The Firm.' Claudia saw a flicker of recognition in Monya's eyes. 'It would be a surprise to MI6 if the leader of The Firm, the Principal, wasn't already on your radar. The Firm seeks global dominance of the underworld. Your Brotherhood, with its international footprint, is a threat to their plans. If The Firm hasn't already done so, it will issue you an ultimatum. Join them, or face extinction.' Claudia lifted her hands, revealing her palms, suggesting that she was telling the truth. 'MI6 believe we face a mutual enemy and that's why I was sent.' Pleased with herself, Claudia paused, expecting Monya to respond, but he remained silent, his facial expression neutral.

Monya hadn't outright rejected the proposition yet, but he needed further convincing before he agrees to cross the line. What could persuade him? A touch of theatrics, perhaps—something to add urgency to the moment. Think, girl, think.

From deep within her subconsciousness, an image of Molly flashed into Claudia's mind, triggering an idea.

Yes, that will do.

'During the 2003 invasion of Iraq, the U.S. Defence Intelligence Agency developed a set of playing cards to help troops identify the most-wanted members of Saddam Hussein's government. The cards were named the "personality identification playing cards". Each card contained the wanted person's details, with the ace of spades being Saddam Hussein. MI6 is doing this for The Firm and *our* ace of spades is The Principal. The King of Spades is Cosy Bear... with an S.'

Monya unfolded his arms, but remained mute. Claudia knew that the next move was his, and she let the silence build between them. After a protracted thirty seconds, Monya spoke.

'The most-wanted Iraqi playing cards contained.... the wanted person's photo, address and job? Do you have this for Cosy Bear and members of The Firm?'

Claudia shook her head.

Monya said bluntly. 'MI6 doesn't know the identity of Cosy Bear?' Making the sign of quotations marks with his fingers. 'With an S... that's what you're telling me?'

'I am.'

Monya scrunched up his face. 'Seriously Claudia? MI6 want me to take down a cyber-warfare department of the Kremlin to eliminate this Cosy Bear of yours?'

Think quickly girly.

'No.'

'What then?'

What are you going to say, Claudia?

'We want you to put a name to the avatar. MI6 wants to know the identity of Cosy Bear inside the Kremlin.'

Monya folded his arms, annoyance present in his voice. 'Just call them S and Z, Claudia, but you're grasping at straws. The two are inseparable, probably one and the same. You know that. What about the other members of The Firm?'

To secure his cooperation, I must give him more.

Claudia sighed. 'We believe that, besides the Principal, there are seven other avatars of which we know five: Davros, Jasper, Cosy Bear, Sun-Tzu and Tomoe.'

'The assumption, Monya, is that each member brings a particular skill to The Firm. Jasper is the banker, Cosy Bear - cyber warfare and ransomware, Sun-Tzu - military, Davros - Information Technology and, as for Tomoe, we are still to discover. We are yet to attribute identities to the avatars.' Claudia's statement was an exaggeration of the truth, and she hoped Monya wouldn't detect the deception.

Monya pursed his lips as he pondered, then unfolded his arms and legs before pushing himself back into the Chesterfield. Having considered Claudia's revelations, Monya assessed she was telling mostly the truth, enough for him to consider cooperating.

'I have a sixth member for you to add to your list Claudia: Taipan. The...' Monya paused, trying to recall Claudia's depiction. 'The... Avatar is that of a snake's head.' He gave Claudia an inquisitive look. 'Do you know of this?'

Claudia shook her head from side to side, showing the name was new to her.

The game of chess continued and Claudia knew it was her move, the outcome dependent on what she told him. She surmised Taipan was Monya's adversary and knew if she pried, he would shut down the discussion and any chance of a deal. Claudia shifted her position on the sofa and clasped her hands together. She said,

'You understand the seriousness of The Firm. I wouldn't make a trip like this if it wasn't necessary.'

Monya's head moved imperceptibly, which Claudia interpreted as cautious agreement.

It's now or never. Be direct.

'We have a mutual threat to discuss.'

Claudia watched Monya weighing up his response. Ten seconds later, he said, 'In four days' time there is a meeting of the Brotherhood. I will table your unusual request for their consideration and, if they agree to it, we'll expect a quid pro quo.'

Monya was taken by surprise when Claudia shook her head. He tilted his head and hardened his expression.

You try my patience!

Claudia interlocked her fingers and rested her hands on her lap. She knew the outcome depended on each side's leverage. Sensing an advantage, Claudia wanted to take a powerful position from which she could make concessions. 'The Intelligence Agencies will dismantle the Principal's empire, Taipan and the others. This is financially and strategically to your benefit, which should be payment enough.'

Monya recognised the ploy. He smiled, waving his hand at Claudia dismissively. 'This is a matter for the Brotherhood. Until then, Claudia, you will remain here as my guest.'

Recognising that the discussion was over, Claudia relaxed into the sofa. 'May I ring the office?'

Monya shook his head. 'I cannot permit communications until after the meeting of the Brotherhood. In the meantime, you are restricted to the grounds. If you disobey me, our dialogue is over. Do we understand each other?'

'We do.'

'Good.' Monya stood and Claudia followed. 'Dinner is at 7.30pm. You will join Alexandria and myself.'

'Thank you,' Claudia said.

I wonder if that is wise?

CHAPTER 11
Unicorns

The Liew family's car insurance policy included coverage for a hire car while their own vehicle was being repaired. After the accident, Samantha organised to pick up the replacement vehicle at nine-thirty the following morning from Thrifty Car and Van Rentals, just a short walk from Hackney Wick railway station. That night, when Richard inquired about the arrangements, Samantha simply told him that the insurance company would call in the morning. She didn't want to disclose any details.

'Will you have the car in time to drive Molly to the camp?'

'They know I'm going on a trip and promised to call by nine tomorrow morning.'

'Will you have enough time?'

'Plenty. Molly and I don't have to be there until early afternoon.'

'Will you take a taxi to the car rental?'

'Most likely. We'll walk to the taxi rank at the railway station in the morning.'

Richard gave Samantha a curious look. 'With your bags? Why not call from here?'

Taking a taxi to the car rental site was the sensible option, but Samantha knew that the Chinese Security Service would follow it, rendering her deception useless. To escape without being shadowed, she and Molly needed to pick up the vehicle in secret. Telling Richard that they were going to take a taxi was part of Samantha's subterfuge, a trick to place her near the railway station.

Her new challenge was to explain why she couldn't have the taxi come to the house.

'No, honey. Look, you walk to the station every day, so I'm sure Molly and I can manage. Anyway, we all have...' Samantha wanted to mention wheelie-rucksacks but, not wanting surveillance to know, she said instead, 'Trolly luggage. It will pull along easily behind us. Besides, walking will make my life a lot easier. You know what it's like getting our daughter into the car every morning, a nightmare. The last thing I need tomorrow is the pressure of a taxi waiting outside while I'm trying to coax Molly from the house. There's always a taxi near the station. No hassle, stress free.'

Richard smiled. 'Yes, mornings with Molly are a trial. Why don't I go into work late and come with you, help with Molly and the luggage?'

A feeling of panic surged through Samantha.

How am I going to talk my way out of this one?

'You're a lovely man, but don't be silly. Molly and I will be just fine.'

'Are you sure?'

'Yes, I survive Molly, the whirlwind, every school morning, so tomorrow will be no different.'

Damn, that sounded like a criticism of Richard.

She saw in his eyes that he had noticed the slight.

Maybe that's not such a bad thing?

Capitalising on the lull in the conversation, Samantha said, as she left the room, 'I best supervise Molly's packing.'

Well done, Samantha, you closed that out well. Be nice to him tonight and, by morning, he will have forgotten. This is like being a teenager all over again. At least this time, I know I'm being manipulative. Oh, if Molly is anything like I was, we're in for trouble.

The morning of the camp.

Samantha joined Richard in the kitchen. He was finishing his breakfast before heading to work. Richard smiled as she entered and said, his voice cheerful, 'You're wearing your red hat and it suits the green dress, which surprises me.'

No!

Did Richard just give a detailed description of what I'm wearing for our watchers?

Am I being silly? Could it be a coincidence?

Richard wouldn't do that, would he?

I'm jumping at shadows but it's better to be safe than sorry. Perhaps I can use this to my advantage.

'Richard!' Samantha said, feigning frustration. 'It's burgundy, not red.'

'I know.'

Samantha swirled, flaring her dress in the motion and in a jovial voice said, 'You're not totally colour blind. It is a green dress. I thought I could do with some cheering up, especially after the accident. What is it they say? Clothes maketh the person. This person is bright and cheery.' From her closed hand, Samantha revealed a face mask, holding it over her nose and mouth for Richard to see.

If he doesn't describe it, I will.

'Who would have thought a light green and yellow flowered face mask would be so becoming? You will be the prettiest woman at the camp.'

He did it again! I'm sure of it.

Samantha's suspicion bubbled. She had wanted him to describe it, but now she knew he was betraying her with his employers. It made what she had to do easier.

Richard bit into his toast and took a sip of his coffee, glancing at his watch. 'Sorry, Honey, but I have to go. I hope the car they give you is suitable, and that you and Molly have a wonderful couple of days. I'll call you this evening.' As he left the kitchen, Richard paused and gave Samantha a quick kiss on the lips.

Samantha hid her feelings of mistrust.

We are an effective team.

'I'll see you on Friday.'

Samantha waited for the sound of the front door closing before she said aloud, 'Right now to get Molly organised.'

The evening before, she had packed Molly's travel bag and laid out her clothes. Samantha knew the house was bugged, so hadn't involved Molly in the choice of outfits. She feared Molly would object to her selection. Molly loved pink in her bedroom but had stopped wearing it as a fashion colour. If Miss Independence protested, the plan could end up a train wreck before it had even started. To blend into the surroundings, natural and neutral colours worked best with nothing too fashionable or out of fashion. Ordinary wear, the kind of person people ignore. However, Samantha knew they were going to be followed, so chose exaggerated colours, to stand out in the crowd, not in an unsophisticated manner, but as an in-vogue mother and child.

Samantha knocked before she opened Molly's bedroom door. Her daughter was already up and seated on the bed, dressed in the clothes that had been placed out for her. 'Are you ready for your breakfast?'

Molly jumped up and brushed down her pink dress, her mouth silent but eyes shouting, 'I hope you have a good reason for this!'

'Would you like me to carry your bag down for you?'

'I'm not a child, I can manage.' As Molly picked up her luggage, she noticed the sticker of a unicorn attached to its back. The penny dropped on her mother's ploy. 'Oh Mummy, it's too heavy for me. Will you carry it down the steps?'

After breakfast, like every other morning, Molly vanished upstairs. After cleaning away the dishes, Samantha looked at her watch.

Eight-thirty, time to go.

Samantha moved into the hallway and called in a loud voice, 'Come on Molly, it's time to go.'

Molly shouted back, 'Where's my bag?'

Normally, this daily ritual irritated Samantha, but she knew Molly was acting out their routine for the benefit of their spectators.

Molly's more grown up than I sometimes give her credit for.

On the walk to the railway station, believing they were free of prying ears, Molly asked, 'Where did you find the Unicorn sticker?'

Samantha grinned. 'I thought you liked Unicorns.'

'I do, but it's just not cool to like them anymore.'

Molly's answer surprised Samantha, for she would never have been so honest with her own mother. She hesitated a moment before saying, 'Oh, that's sad.'

'It's called growing up, Mummy.'

'I know, but it's still sad.'

'Still, I would like to know where you found the sticker? I thought I'd thrown them all away.'

Samantha sighed. 'In my bedroom cupboard there's a box full of your kindergarten drawings, stories you've written, the things we used to pin on the fridge. I found the Unicorns in there. It's wonderful that you're growing up, but as a parent, there's something special about childhood. The games, fantasies, playing. You've started caring less now about what used to matter most to you, like Unicorns. I'm not criticising. That's the truth of ageing. We are both moving into the great unknowns of you growing up. Molly, perhaps one day, when you're as old as I am now, the box of your childhood things may be important to you. My mother threw everything out... I wish she hadn't.'

'Sometimes Mummy, I don't want to grow up.' Molly slipped her free hand into her mother's and walked beside her in silence. After around three minutes, Molly said, 'Do you think they're following us?'

'I'm sure of it.'

'Are you scared?'

Samantha was stunned by the forthrightness of her daughter's question.

Should I lie and tell her I'm not, or do I tell the truth?

'Yes, I am. Are you scared Molly?'

Molly smiled. She knew that, once the card was posted, Olivia would come and they would be safe. There was nothing to fear.

She lied. 'Yes. But Snowflake won't be.'

I hadn't noticed that before. Snowflake is Molly's connection to her childhood years.

Samantha halted, panic rippling through her body. On the opposite side of the street, parked in Ridley Road, facing the railway station, was the silver BMW SUV.

'Do you see them, Molly?'

'Who Mummy?'

'I'm sorry, Honey, but don't stare. Do you see the Silver SUV? It's following us.'

'How do you know?'

'I just do.' Taking a deep breath, Samantha said, 'Here we go, Molly. I want you to follow my lead. Do you see the 149 bus to Edmonton Green coming up the road?'

'Yes.'

'Let's start walking towards the bus stop as if we intend on catching it.'

'What about the taxi?'

'Can you see one?'

'No.'

'We are improvising, Molly. Keep holding my hand because things may change quickly.'

Michael Tan and Kang Long, from the Chinese Ministry of State Security, watched their targets approach.

The driver, Kang Long said, 'It looks as though they are going to catch that bus. You better get out and follow them.'

'Okay. This is a lot of fuss over nothing. She's not a British agent.'

'Perhaps. You won't have any trouble following her then, will you?'

'Ha ha.'

Michael Tan opened the car door and stood on the pavement as Kang Long called, 'We should check the radio. Testing, one, two, three.'

Michael Tan touched his earpiece. 'Yep.' He then whispered into his lapel mike. 'Testing, one, two, three.'

Kang Long said, 'Loud and clear. They are all yours.'

Michael Tan put his head inside the open car door. 'Chen Li should track her phone. That would be easier and cheaper than us tailing her.'

'Chen Li wants to pressure Samantha, to make sure that she isn't a British spy. If she is, who knows what she's learnt already?'

'Look at her in that getup. You can spot her from half a mile away. She's no agent.'

Kang Long smiled, 'Ten pounds on Samantha and her daughter giving you the slip.'

Michael Tan rolled his eyes. 'You're on.'

'Best hurry, the bus is stopping.'

As Samantha and Molly reached the railway station bus stop, the 149 was pulling in. There were five other people in front of them, waiting to catch the bus.

Michael Tan dashed across the road, the slowing bus blocking his view of Samantha and Molly.

As the bus came to a halt, Samantha pulled Molly along with her as she said, 'Quick Molly, change of plan, we're taking the train.'

The wrench from her mother momentarily wrong-footed Molly. Recovering and dragging her bag with her, Molly said. 'Which one?'

'It doesn't matter, whatever is on the platform.'

The 149 stopped and passengers disembarked. Michael Tan scanned the people waiting. 'Shivers,' he said into the mike. 'They are not here.'

'Check the railway station,' came the cool reply.

Michael Tan sprinted to the station entrance. Inside, he looked about urgently, spotting the back of a pink top worn by a black-haired girl dragging trolley luggage. In front was a woman in a green dress with a red hat and they were about to board a train. He whispered into his mike. 'I've got them. They're taking the train.'

Wanting to follow in the car, Kang Long asked, 'Where's it heading?'

'Hang on.' Michael Tan rushed onto the platform and, from the overhead monitor, he relayed to Kang Long, 'East Hackney Central, then Homerton.'

Over the railway station PA system, Michael Tan heard. 'Train now departing. Stand clear, please. Stand clear!'

Michael Tan reached the automated doors as they were closing. He thrust his hands between them and leveraged them apart before stepping on board. The doors shut behind him with a whoosh. He rocked on the balls of his feet as the train left the platform and grabbed one of the hanging straps available for standing passengers.

'I'm in,' He relayed to his partner.

Concentrating on the traffic, there was a slight delay before Kang Long replied to his colleague. 'Do you have visual?'

Conscious of the other passengers, Michael Tan whispered, 'Negative. They're two carriages down. I'll make my way towards them.'

Samantha, watching from the train as it was about to depart, saw a man of Asian origin wearing a suit acting suspiciously on the platform. He'd jumped onto the train at the last moment. As they pulled away from the platform, Samantha said to Molly, 'We have to move.' They travelled through to the next carriage and found two vacant seats halfway along.

'Sit,' she directed Molly before joining her and peering around a standing passenger to scan back the way they'd come. Through the windows in the doors that separated the carriages, Samantha watched as the Asian man moved in their direction. Ignoring the other passengers, she took a deep breath and opened her travel bag to remove a pair of blue jeans for Molly and the same for herself. In her rush, Snowflake's collar and lead fell on the floor, pulled out with the clothes. Samantha held the jeans towards Molly. 'Put these on over your dress.'

Molly nodded.

'Good girl, as quick as you can, then tuck your dress inside the pants.' While still seated, Samantha slipped into her own jeans and watched as Molly finished dressing. She checked for their pursuer and whether he'd seen them. Satisfied that they had not been noticed, she removed more items from the bag.

'Okay, Molly. Now, I want you to put on this white t-shirt over your pink one.' She waited while Molly did as she was told. 'Right. Here's a baseball cap and sunglasses for you to wear. Now, put on this surgical mask... Perfect, even I don't recognise you.'

Samantha stole a glance towards the end of the carriage and watched as the Asian man neared the door which joined their carriage. The train slowed for the next station. From her bag, with heart racing, Samantha removed a grey cardigan which she donned over her dress. Next, she removed her burgundy hat, replacing it with a straw-coloured fedora crown and short brim hat. She stuffed the old hat into her travel bag and zipped it closed.

The train was on the verge of stopping.

'Mummy. Snowflake's lead!'

In one flowing motion, Samantha reached down, swooped up Snowflake's accessories, unzipped her bag, and stuffed them inside. She stole another glance at the man who had stopped advancing.

He is waiting to see if we leave at this station before continuing.

'Listen carefully, Honey,' Samantha said to Molly. 'You are no longer eight. You are fourteen and I want you to behave like it. Stand up. I'm going to put the bag on your back so that you wear it like a rucksack.' Samantha undid the zips which housed the straps and then stood to hoist the bag onto Molly's back, removing the Unicorn sticker at the same time. 'Good girl.' Taking hold of Molly, she turned her so they were facing each other. 'I want you to go to the exit at the far end of the carriage and leave when the train comes to a stop. Got it?'

Molly nodded.

'Do you remember the coffee shop that we've been to? The one near the station?'

'Yes, the Black Sheep.'

'Can you find it?'

'Of course I can. I'm fourteen, you know.'

Samantha grinned. 'Okay, meet me inside. Say you're waiting for your mum and don't say Mummy.'

Before Molly could answer, Samantha said, 'Go now.'

The train came to a halt, and after a brief pause, the automatic doors slid open. From her jeans' pocket, Samantha took a surgical face mask to replace her light green with yellow flowers mask. Picking up her travel bag by the handles to carry it like a suitcase, she moved toward the carriage door. She tried to stuff the discarded face mask and Unicorn sticker into her jeans pocket, but unbeknown to her, they fell to the carriage floor. On leaving the train, Samantha moved to the back of the platform and strolled towards the exit.

Michael Tan stepped from the carriage and watch the people leaving the train. The PA system announced, 'Train now departing. Stand clear, please. Stand clear!' He stepped back inside, satisfied that his targets were on board, saying into his radio, 'Drive to the next station.' As the train moved off, Michael Tan opened the door separating him from the carriage, where he knew Samantha and Molly were seated. He'd seen them move there and he couldn't have been mistaken.

Where are you?

He walked down the aisle.

You must be here; I would have noticed if you'd moved.

Michael Tan made his way through the carriage and, halfway along, his eyes were drawn to a decorative face mask on the floor. He picked it up and spotted the yellow flowers and, next to it, a crumpled unicorn.

He shook his head.

This is what Samantha was wearing! The bitch!

He tried to recall the identity of the passengers who had left the train at the last stop. Nothing unusual jumped out at him.

They must be still on board.

He moved into the last carriage and continued the search, reaching the end as the train pulled into Homerton Station. As Michael Tan stepped clear of the train, he said into his lapel mike. 'I've lost them.'

'How so?' came the reply.

'They changed their appearance and slipped past me.'

'To avoid you?'

'I can see no other reason. Looks like I owe you ten pounds.'

Kang Long laughed, then in a serious voice said, 'The boss will be displeased.'

'Perhaps she is an agent and Chen Li will make the arrangements to have her phone tracked now?'

Kang Long thought for a moment before answering. 'I don't agree. If Samantha Liew worked for MI6, they would have taken her in. I think it was our obvious presence that made her run.'

'Are you going to say that to Chen Li?'

'Ha, ha. How does that western saying go? "Mine is not to reason why..."'

Michael Tan left the railway station and stood on the footpath to search the road for his partner. As the car approached, he raised his hand and waved. Inside, he continued the conversation he'd been having over the radio. 'Do you think Richard Liew knows that his wife and child have done a runner?'

'Who can tell? Pity we can't simply kill them. It would save all of this mucking around.'

Michael Tan shrugged his shoulders. 'It's not that easy in a foreign country. Once they are in China, well, that is a different matter entirely.'

CHAPTER 12
Olivia

Olivia rubbed her ears that were painful after the descent, though not preventing a welling of emotion as she gazed out of the aeroplane window now approaching Heathrow Airport, United Kingdom, from Barcelona, Spain. The plane rumbled and shook as its landing gear extended, engaging with a loud thud. Following the Gutenberg Bible incident, when she and Max had accepted self-imposed exile, Olivia thought she'd never see Britain again. Her joy was tinged with sadness; it was a homecoming without her beloved Max. There was a jolt and Olivia rocked in her seat as the wheels touched down on the runway. As the brakes were applied and the engines roared, Olivia was tilted slightly forward, her thoughts interrupted by the landing. The plane taxied to the terminal and stopped. The *bing* of the seat-belt light being extinguished caused passengers to leap from their seat in a race to queue in the aisle. Occupying a window seat, Olivia was no obstacle to her fellow travellers, so she closed her eyes and relaxed into her seat as those about her jostled for their aisle position. When she had waited for her turn to exit on prior occasions, she'd hold Max's hand, but he was gone. Even when Max had been kidnapped, she'd travelled with Inspector Axel. As far back as Olivia could remember, this was the first time that she'd journeyed alone.

Olivia sighed.

It won't be long before I'm with you, my love.

Even though Olivia and Max held their faith, Olivia wasn't referring to the afterlife, they'd long ago ceased believing in a heaven or hell. She thought of death, which Max had described as being the space between dreams, a place visited every night devoid of time and memories. Discounting the truth of a resurrection hadn't been at the expense of a strong moral and spiritual code. They had tried to live good lives, to not pursue only personal happiness, but to strive for a greater good in the service of their country. For Olivia and Max, this was what Jesus taught.

Other than a day-pack, one she could carry on her shoulders, containing essentials, and particularly an ancient black British umbrella belonging to Max that she used to support her, Olivia travelled to the UK without luggage. At her age, a suitcase was a hindrance, an unnecessary burden to mobility, its weight insurmountable. She'd told herself before leaving that there was nothing she needed that couldn't be purchased. The umbrella was her connection to Max, something she could hold that reminded her of his eccentricities, though his love of English brollies had been a point of difference between them.

Clearing passport control and customs, Olivia entered the arrival hall. She knew that Claudia and Inspector Axel were both on MI6 missions overseas, but she hoped they had arranged for someone to meet her. In a vain hope, Olivia lingered for a moment, looking this way and that. She glanced at her watch; it was eight in the morning.

I'm too old for these early flights.

Olivia yawned, then rubbed her eyes. A man in his thirties, dressed in a smart suit, approached her. She didn't recognise him, but watched his advance in anticipation.

His voice was kind as he said, 'Excuse me, Madam. John Loch at your service. You seem lost. May I be of help?'

Olivia released a deep sigh. 'That's most kind of you, Mr Loch. I was taking in the changes since I was last here. Time seems to run away from one.'

John looked at Olivia, but he doubted the elderly woman's statement and his qualms were betrayed by his eyes. 'Is someone meeting you?'

What do I say?

Is John Loch a concerned and generous citizen or a foreign agent seeking to discover where I'm going and why I'm here?

If I say I'm on my own, will he offer to walk me to a taxi, perhaps even suggest a ride share? Is Mr Loch a friend or foe?

A lifetime of secrets, seeing the world through the prism of mistrust, had rendered acts of kindness from strangers suspicious. Pondering her response, Olivia wondered if their life in espionage was to blame for their detached relationship with their adult children, Melissa and Gordon. Parents often formed friendships with other parents through child care, kindergarten, and school. Unable to let their guard down, she and Max had remained aloof, wanting amity. Even Max's cover as a spy, an eccentric Anglican Parish Priest, had dissuaded relationships. Personal boundaries were sacrosanct; this had played out at home and with their children. In later years, when she and Max reflected on the missed opportunities with Melissa and Gordon, they vowed to make amends when grandchildren came along. Granddaughter Penny had grown to become a trusted confidant. Their love for her had placed Penny in harm's way and she'd been kidnapped one time. Olivia lamented that, as spies, love and friendships could be used as a weapon against one.

Olivia whispered to herself, inadvertently loud enough for John Loch to hear, 'I can't trust anyone!'

John Loch spoke, concern written across his face. 'Are you alright?'

Realising that she'd allowed her mind to drift and her tongue to wag, she was annoyed at herself.

He will think I'm nuts.

Looking John Loch straight in the eyes, she said decisively, her voice betraying irritation, 'Yes! Absolutely! I'm alright and no, I am not lost!'

John Loch smiled reassuringly. 'Is someone meeting you?'

Choosing the voice of a character she'd used to great effect in the past, Lady Olivia Suzanne Elizabeth Huggins, Olivia said resolutely, 'Meeting me! Oh, my goodness, young man. No! I'm fiercely protective of my independence. I wouldn't hear of it. At my age, people look at you and assume you're senile.'

John Loch grimaced. 'I'm sorry to have disturbed you, Madam, and hope you have a pleasant day.'

She instantly regretted her harsh words.

It's time to stop treating strangers as if they are all hostile agents. From here on, no more.

Olivia placed a hand on John Loch's arm and, her voice reassuring, said, 'Kind Sir, I am touched by your concern. Thank you.'

Reinvigorated by Olivia's words, John Loch's spirits were raised and he departed, a good Samaritan for another day.

Outside of the airport terminal, Olivia queued at the rank for a taxi and, with the line moving quickly, she soon had her ride.

'Where to M'lady?' The taxi driver asked.

M'lady is what Max would call Olivia. When she heard the phrase, emotion welled up from nowhere. Fighting back tears,

Olivia gave the driver an address in Croydon, walking distance to the shop where Claudia had left the key to her apartment with an MI6 colleague. The old fashion key was part of Claudia's security upgrades since her intruder incident. From Croydon, Olivia planned to take another taxi into London.

The gentle motion of the taxi and the hum of its tyres invited sleep. As Olivia dozed, she was transported back to when she first met her beloved husband at the top-secret headquarters of the Agency, a covert Second World War organisation, based out of a private house in the small Cornish village of Cliff. She was an officer, a Wren, working from Cliff, coordinating special operations. There was a knock at her front door, and expecting a recruit, she answered. A young man in his teens and dressed, like everybody working from Cliff, in civilian clothing, looked at her nervously.

'Can I help you?' she'd asked.

The young man spoke the password. 'I'm looking for Robin.'

It had been love at first sight for Olivia. Max was a handsome young man, a rating in the Royal Navy, a novice joining seasoned men performing dangerous and clandestine missions for which no records were kept. The affection they felt for each other, like the duties they performed, were kept secret. In those days, enlisted men couldn't date officers, so their love remained hidden until hostilities ended. Olivia recalled the anguish she felt when she sent him away on missions where he was unlikely to survive. Never once did she allow her feelings for Max to distract her from her responsibilities. In the line of duty, she awarded Max no favours. Of his operations group, Max was the only one to survive the war. The others were killed in the service of their country. Even in her sleep, the memory of the loss of those brave souls caused a pain in the pit of her stomach. One after another, the faces of the men who had perished visited her dreams. She remembered their names and heard their voices and laughter. It had been part of Olivia's role to type the letters, signed by the Commanding Officer, to grieving families. Each was personal, individual to the relative, but they all contained the same lie. They told of their loved one being killed in action and their body lost to the savage sea. The true circumstance of their death were committed only to the memories of those connected with the operation. The dream changed and the mist of sadness lifted as a smile rippled across Olivia's face: her wedding day. Max, like the first day she saw him, was young and handsome, but he carried a toughness born of war, as she herself did. In just a matter of minutes, their life together unfolded before her eyes. Now eighty-five years old and in Poland, they had been sent to retrieve the Janus Key from the tunnels near Walbrzych. Even in her sleep, Olivia felt a stabbing pain as memories of the motorbike and sidecar accident replayed in her mind—an attempt on their lives that had left them seriously injured and presumed dead. She watched as their independence crumbled; in the blink of an eye, they had become forgotten, sent to God's waiting room—a nursing home where they awaited their last moments. Olivia remembered how Max had described it. *Our, Club Med...ication*, our, *La Abattoir*. Each second that they were there, they withered and died a little more.

In the space between awake and sleep, Olivia recalled how their lives were rekindled when Max found a coded message in the newspaper. In a matter of days, they'd escaped from the nursing home and travelled to London, back into the service of Her Majesty's Government where a new world of espionage and adventures beckoned them. Over the last couple of years, she and Max had been reunited with Claudia, a girl who, when fourteen, they'd rescued from child sex slavery. They'd criss-crossed the globe in pursuit of foreign adversaries, formed an unlikely alliance with the Russian Mafia boss, Monya Mogilevick, and, in her last mission with Max before his passing, rescued Claudia from the dungeons deep below Montserrat Abbey.

The dream changed and Olivia was grief stricken as she recalled how COVID-19 had taken Max's life. She forced the thought from her mind and was transported back to their wedding day, saying aloud as a teardrop formed in the corner of her eye, 'I've never regretted a moment.'

And neither have I, my love.

Hearing Max's voice in her mind, Olivia unconsciously reached out across the seat to hold the hand of the man she loved. The space was empty, occupied only by his umbrella, yet she felt his fingers wrap around hers. The sensation startled Olivia, and she awoke with a noisy snort. Aware of the sound she'd made, Olivia raised her eyes and saw the taxi driver watching her in the mirror.

Mortified by the undignified sound she'd made, Olivia said, 'Oh dear, please excuse me. How embarrassing, I must have drifted off.'

'Welcome back M'lady.' The taxi driver raised his head so that, in the reflection, Olivia could see him smile–a genuine smile.

'I would like to say that you slept like a baby but, sadly, M'lady, you have the appearance of a woman who has recently experienced a significant loss.'

Olivia noticed her arm was still outstretched, her hand reaching for the invisible man to grasp. Feeling incomplete in the absence of Max, but remembering her recent promise not to treat people as enemy agents, she said, 'I was married for sixty-eight years to the same man and have never regretted a moment. Max, my husband, died recently.'

'I'm truly sorry for your loss, M'lady.'

'Thank you.' Olivia said as she raised her arm, showing her palm to the mirror. 'Out of habit, I was reaching for his hand; for so many years I always have. It's difficult to accept that he's not here and will never be again. I shouldn't complain; we shared a lifetime together and how many people can say that? We were complete, seeing the world through each other's eyes. It didn't start out that way. Yes, we loved each other, but the conjoining of mind and spirit happens on the life journey together, until two become as one. In the silence of my soul, I scan for him and wonder if he seeks me. I hold out my hand for him to take; should I resist the urge for fear of appearing senile? Perhaps I am becoming enfeebled, as I feel his presence often.'

Olivia sighed and took a deep breath. 'Max and I met in a time of war, mere children in the guise of adults. For the freedoms we now take for granted, I ordered many men to an early grave. I loved Max at first sight but the promise, made at the altar, to surrender a version of ourselves to each other and be of good heart came from a desire to honour those who perished to give us life.'

'Max and I were married in a quintessential Cornish village church, surrounded by its rich history, stone walls, and a view of the ocean. Because we served in the Royal Navy, it was imperative to us that the sea, with its war memories, witness the promise we made to each other. Hand in hand, we left the church and paused outside, straining to listen for the sound of the waves. The friends that we lost to the deep called out to us that day, freeing us from the past to heal our wounds.'

'Is it true there is a soul mate for each of us, or is that laughable? For Max and I, our dreams did come true, not the cheap, insincere love of Hollywood, nor steamy romance books or glossy magazines. Ours was a love born from a life of commitment, hard work, and mutual respect. I can't think what my life would have been like without him. I shared with Max what most people only dream about. How wonderful that, in his absence and when the loss weighs heavy on my heart, I reach out for the man I still love. Our time together was blessed; if I'm going senile, then so be it. I so want to be with him.'

The taxi driver glanced at Olivia in the mirror as she spoke while keeping a watchful eye on the road. When she fell silent, he looked up, saying. 'I read somewhere that dreams can't come true if you don't put in the work to make it so.'

Olivia laughed. 'Max was sometimes infuriating.'

The taxi driver nodded, and after a momentary pause, said. 'What will you do now?'

Olivia, despite her melancholic mood, laughed at her own thoughts.

You wouldn't believe me if I told you. I need to protect a wonderful woman named Samantha and her beautiful daughter Molly from being taken by agents of the Chinese Ministry of State Security.

Thinking of the Liew's and Snowflake reminded Olivia of why she'd come to the United Kingdom.

If Max was wallowing in his own self-pity, as I am now, I would have grumbled and given him the sharp edge of my tongue.

She remembered that when the fog, the black dog of old age, had suckled on the remnant of Max's energy, like Sirens perched on jagged rocks singing beautifully, luring passing sailors to their death, it was she who had sounded the reveille, demanding that he wake and step back from the abyss. That stubborn resolve she'd demanded of Max was needed by herself.

Determined to throw off her malaise and break free of the melancholy, Olivia shook her head, a symbolic gesture of clearing her mind. Repeating the taxi driver's question, Olivia said, 'What will I do now? That's a good question. Well, I'm...'

She was interrupted by her phone ringing and looked at the screen, deciding whether to answer it. The caller ID read James MIT - MIT was used in Olivia's address book to designate MI6.

Olivia's newly found trust in strangers didn't extend to business, however, she knew MI6 wouldn't call unless it was important. Urgent even.

'Please excuse me, I need to take this one.'

'No problem, Love.'

Swiping right and lifting the phone to her ear, Olivia said. 'Hello, James.'

'Olivia. I hope you've made it safely to the UK?'

'Indeed, I have.'

'Excellent. A pleasant flight, I hope.' Before Olivia could reply, James continued, 'Where are you?'

'In a taxi, en route to London.'

'Are you free to talk?'

'No, not presently.'

There was a pause while James considered what to do next. 'Can you listen?'

'That's much better. I can hear you now.'

'Excellent. We've just received a Snowflake, the cat, playing card. Two actually.'

The news took Olivia by surprise as she hoped nothing would happen while Claudia and Inspector Axel were away. Her heart skipped a beat in anticipation. 'Do you want me to come to you?'

An edge of alarm decorated his voice as James said, 'Don't do that! Stephen will have my guts for garters. You understand that this isn't sanctioned?'

Olivia chuckled.

'You may well laugh, Olivia. I'm a long way from retirement.'

'You hope.'

'Ha ha. If you would kindly listen. It seems Samantha and Molly Liew are on the move. The cards were both posted yesterday; one was from the Beaconsfield Services Centre on the M40 and the other at the Knutsford Service Centre on the M6. Knutsford is on the way to Liverpool and Manchester. Neither card contained an address, so I can only speculate that Molly doesn't know where they are going. What she is telling us is that they are travelling north. Best get yourself to... Manchester. That is as good a place as any to start.'

Questions for James flooded into Olivia's mind, ones she couldn't ask while in the taxi.

Had Molly been taken by the Chinese, or was she with Samantha, Richard, perhaps both?

Has MI6 put a trace on Richard and Samantha's phones?

Is there CCTV footage to provide a picture of what was happening?

Had James spoken to Claudia about the cards?

In keeping with the subterfuge, Olivia said, 'Sure, I can take a train to Oxford.' She gazed out of the taxi window and gauged their location. 'We're not far from Woking. I will have the taxi drop me at the station.' She paused, as if listening to a reply. 'I'll call you when I'm about thirty minutes out of Oxford.'

'Okay. When you're free to talk, call me. There's not much more I can tell you so, bye for now.'

'Goodbye.'

Olivia looked in the driver's mirror to see if the taxi driver had been listening. His eyes were focused on the road ahead.

'There's been a change of plans.'

Olivia watched as the driver glanced at her in the mirror, which she took as his acknowledgement of a pending instruction. 'Take the Woking turn off and drop me at the railway station, please.'

The driver gave a slight nod of his head.

Before leaving Spain, Claudia had told Olivia that, to protect Samantha and Molly, they were operating outside of normal MI6 procedures. Given an address, Olivia was confident that she could secure their safety but, without one, it would be like seeking a needle in a haystack. The taxi slowed and Olivia peered out of the window. They were in bumper-to-bumper traffic and approaching her exit.

Good.

Her thoughts returned to finding Molly and Samantha, and she felt a knot in her stomach.

Not much more James can tell me, that isn't promising. How can I do this alone? I need more information from Molly.

The taxi rocked to a stop and Olivia glanced from the window again. The M5 was living up to its reputation as a car park where traffic congestion dominated long stretches.

Her mind returned to Molly.

Hang on, we've missed the turnoff.

'Excuse me driver, you've missed my exit.' The man remained silent. 'My good man, did you not hear me? You've missed my exit!'

The taxi driver raised his eyes so that Olivia could see them in the mirror. 'You might as well sit back and relax... Olivia.'

He knows my name!

'Do you know that my conversation with you was the first time I've trusted a stranger for a long time? Look what you've done, shattered my faith in humanity. Tell me who you are and where we are going. While you're at it, what do you want of me?'

While Olivia was speaking, she surreptitiously depressed the electric window wider, hoping to attract the attention of one of the stationary drivers to her plight by screaming for help. As she feared, the windows were deactivated.

Damn.

Olivia considered banging her fist on the window and waving for help, but guessed that the attempt would end in failure. Having been in situations like this before, Olivia knew that there was one chance of escape, and it had to be chosen wisely.

Don't try the car door–it will be locked–or do anything to unsettle the driver. Best to play the compliant old lady and lull him into a false sense of security. Max, I wish you were here.

I'll always be beside you, my love.

Olivia tilted her head slightly to one side, a confused expression momentarily appearing on her face before she pushed it away. She'd heard Max speak as if he was seated beside her, and she was *certain* of it. Ordinarily, Olivia would have been wary that she was losing her mind, but not today. With her life hanging in the balance, Max's reassuring words were welcome.

Thank you.

Before embarking on the mission, the taxi driver had been warned by Miss Adele that Olivia was not as harmless as she appeared. However, with Max's death and Olivia unarmed, having come through airport security, Miss Adele didn't envisage Olivia would pose a threat to him, providing he stayed alert.

Miss Adele had said to the driver, 'I have a special end planned for Olivia. However, if she plays up, do whatever is necessary.'

'Including eliminating?'

'Yes, but a word of caution. If you decide to kill her, do not hesitate. There are those before you who did. They did not live to tell the tale.'

The driver removed his hand from the steering wheel and felt for his silenced pistol concealed next to him. Satisfied that it was within easy reach, he smiled and returned his hand to the wheel.

'Who I am is of no concern to yours. As for where we are going?' The driver laughed, 'For a ride, courtesy of Miss Adele. I heard you say that you want to be with your beloved Max. Oh, I know who I am. An angel sent to grant your wish. Ha, ha ha.' The traffic in front started moving, and the man eased his foot off the brake, causing the car to roll forward. 'If you try anything funny, I won't hesitate in shooting you. Do we understand each other?'

'Perfectly.'

'Good. Now Olivia, we wouldn't want you ringing a friend, so toss the mobile phone onto the seat next to me.' Following the instruction, Olivia slumped back into the seat and closed her eyes.

Think Olivia! If only Max were here.

Olivia reached out to take the invisible hand of Max, causing her fingers to brush against the umbrella lying where he should have been.

Thank you.

We've used the brolly as a weapon before, but how can I activate it in this situation?

Choking him by hooking the handle around his neck and yanking?

No, that won't work. I can't pull a luggage trolley, let alone summon up the strength to strangle someone. He would quickly overpower me.

Okay.

How about knocking him unconscious by hitting him over the head? No, with my muscles, it will be like him being slapped by a wet fish.

Think, Olivia.

I know I'll smash the window with its steel point and wave frantically for help? Even I could break the window, I'm sure of it.

Olivia began lifting the umbrella.

Stop!

What on earth am I doing? This man is a professional and will shoot me before anyone realises what is going on. I need to think fast before the traffic flows freely. By then, it will be too late.

Olivia peered out from behind her semi-closed eyes and scanned the taxi for other means of escape. Not discovering any, her mind returned to the only weapon at hand, the umbrella.

The driver is seated directly in front of me and is obviously unconcerned by my presence, which is to my advantage.

Okay.

Olivia, what else do I see?

The driver's seat has an adjustable height, detachable headrest. I can see his neck through it. I could, if I can summon up enough strength, kill him by stabbing the steel point of the umbrella through the gap in the headrest and into the back of his neck. It's my only option and best done when the car is stationary.

Discretely, Olivia pulled the umbrella towards her, placing its point between her feet and on the floor. To her dismay, the handle reached halfway up her torso, its size, and the cramped conditions of the back seat, preventing it from being wielded as a weapon. Despondently, Olivia breathed out heavily and opened her eyes. The driver glanced at her in the mirror, then returned his eyes to the road, concentrating as he nudged the taxi forward in the heavy traffic. Olivia glanced out her side window. A car in the next lane was travelling at the same pace, rolling alongside. A woman in the passenger seat turned her head and met Olivia's gaze. Expecting her cry to go unnoticed, Olivia mouthed, 'Help me.'

'Are you alright?' the woman mimed back.

'No. HELP!'

The woman nodded. 'Hang on.'

The taxi came to another stop and the vehicle, which had been next to them, pulled back, halting out of Olivia's view. When the traffic moved again, Olivia knew she needed to keep her gaze to the front for fear of alerting her assailant.

Oh please, be ringing the police.

'At last,' the driver said loudly, as he gained speed, the congestion easing. Olivia, peering through the windscreen, felt despondent, knowing that her one chance at freedom was fading. Thirty seconds up the road, the traffic came to an abrupt halt and the driver hit the brakes hard to avoid a collision with the car in front.

CRUNCH!

Olivia's body was restrained by the seat belt, but her head rocked forward with the force of the impact from behind and again when the taxi was shunted into the vehicle in front. Fitted with impact sensing doors, Olivia heard her door automatically unlock after the collision. The taxi had barely stopped moving when she pushed open her door and, grabbing the umbrella, stepped out onto the motorway. The traffic in her lane was at a standstill, but was still moving in the lane next to her. Using the umbrella as a STOP sign and intent on following it, Olivia thrust the brolly into the line of traffic. The brolly was ripped from her hand by a car travelling too quickly to stop and she stumbled into the path of the vehicle behind. Fortunately, it had already slowed and avoided colliding with Olivia as it halted, its bonnet resting against her leg.

Olivia turned and pointed her finger at the taxi, yelling at the top of her voice, 'HELP! That man is trying to kidnap me! HELP!'

Olivia heard an electric motor as a window was wound down on the car that almost hit her.

She called out again, 'He tried to kidnap me! HELP!'

Enraged, the taxi driver hit the steering wheel, 'The Bitch,' he said angrily while fumbling for the pistol. With gun in hand, he exited the taxi, intent on finishing Olivia off. He raised the gun and took aim.

BEEP, BEEP, BEEP.

The sounds of car horns rang out in unison as Olivia turned away from the taxi driver and hurried up the motorway, calling like a madwoman, 'He tried to kidnap me. Help.'

The taxi driver, distracted by the car horns, scanned about him to identify the source of the noise. When he glanced back, ready to pull the trigger, Olivia was gone. He shook his head in disbelief.

How did the bitch do that? Vanished into the traffic. I'm not looking forward to telling Miss Adele. She won't be pleased.

Tucking the pistol into the top of his pants and angry at himself, the taxi driver slapped his leg with his hand before calmly walking away.

After the collision, the M25 came to a standstill. Car doors opened, people left their vehicles and milled around. Olivia stopped to catch her breath, now confident that she was free.

'Are you alright?' Olivia heard a woman's voice say, and she turned to look at the speaker; it was the lady she'd implored to help her.

Olivia placed her hand on the woman's arm. 'Was it you, Love, who rammed us from behind?'

'Yes.'

'Thank you. I truly thought I was a goner.'

The woman smiled. 'I told my husband to smash into the bastard and, for once, he did as he was told.'

'How fortunate I was that it was you who spotted me and not someone else. You are wonderful people and I owe you my life.'

The woman smiled.

'If I could ask another favour. Would you be a dear and help me back to the taxi to find my phone? It should be on the floor. I need to ring the office.'

The woman gave Olivia a look of surprise. She wasn't expecting a woman of Olivia's age to have an office, let alone contact one.

***

Despite Olivia's objections, she had been persuaded by the ambulance to accompany them to the emergency department of the nearby hospital. 'Madam. You've been involved in a serious car accident.'

Stephen Walls, head of MI6, and Superintendent of Police, Evelyn Watts, were waiting in the Royal Surrey Hospital emergency department for Olivia to arrive. The Superintendent was bristling at the intelligence services interference. They had claimed jurisdictional authority over what she considered a criminal matter, an attempted kidnapping.

'Mr Walls,' Superintendent Evelyn Watts said, 'I'm told that Olivia is an elderly woman, in her late eighties, possibly nineties. I needn't remind you that retired agents are ordinary citizens and fall under the gamut of the Police Department.'

Inwardly, Stephen Walls smiled, but his face remained neutral.

Needn't remind me? It seems you just have.

He hadn't met Evelyn Watts before and imagined that this was her first encounter with the Secret Intelligence Service, MI6.

Because of counter-terrorism operations, she would have been familiar with MI5, but not MI6.

Before Stephen Walls could reply, Olivia was wheeled into the emergency department on a trolley. He and Superintendent Watts followed the accompanying staff into a medical cubical where they watched Olivia being transferred from the ambulance trolley onto a bed. The medical personnel left, except for a male nurse. The nurse adjusted Olivia's bed to allow her to sit up.

'Hi Olivia, my name is Peter and I'm going to check your blood pressure and heart rate. Is that okay?'

'Yes.'

Nurse Peter rolled Olivia's sleeve up, wrapping the pressure cuff of the digital blood pressure monitor around her bare arm. Olivia felt the cuff tighten, then loosen again. Gazing at the results, Peter said, 'Your blood pressure is a little high but, considering the scare you've had, that's understandable. Nothing to worry about. We will keep an eye on it. Are you comfortable?'

'Yes.'

'That's good. The Doctor will be in to see you shortly.' Peter unclipped the nurse call button from behind Olivia's head and placed it on the bed next to her. 'I'll put this here in easy reach and, if you experience any problems, just push the buzzer.'

'Thanks,' Olivia replied.

Nurse Peter acknowledged Stephen Walls and Evelyn Watts with a bow of his head before he left the cubical and pulled the curtain closed behind him.

Stephen Walls said with a smile, 'Superintendent Watts, this is the famous Olivia.' He touched Olivia's arm. 'Why she insists on frightening us in this way, I'm none too sure. I'm sorry that this had to happen to you, Olivia. If we knew you were in danger, I would have had someone meet you at the airport.'

Olivia gave a slight shrugged of her shoulders. 'It seems I've made some enemies in the service to this country, Stephen.'

'Indeed.'

The Chief Inspector spoke, surprise adding a shrill tone to her voice. 'You're an active agent, still?'

Surmising the presence of a senior police officer signified a jurisdictional dispute, Olivia hesitated, unsure of a diplomatically correct answer. She glanced at Stephen, who nodded.

'Yes, a serving agent and quite a long-standing one, actually.'

Superintendent Watts was not taken in by the façade, her tone betraying her disquiet as she said, 'I see.'

Stephen Walls, ignoring the Superintendent's consternation, said, 'This is, as you were informed, Superintendent, a matter for the Secret Intelligence Service. I will keep you posted on developments, of course.'

Superintendent Watts was not easily dissuaded. 'That may be so, Mr Walls, but Olivia is still required to make a statement. Did you know the man who was driving the taxi?'

Before Olivia could bat away the question, the curtain opened with a whoosh and a nurse, of stern appearance, a throwback to the days of the matron who would brood no argument, stood on the cubicle's precipice. Noticing a Police Officer questioning her patient, she said, her voice strident in its resolve, 'Are either of you family?'

'No.'

'Then, out you go, both of you, and wait outside.'

Olivia half raised her hand, akin to a school child seeking permission from the headmistress to speak.

Matron's face warmed; her tone softened. 'Yes, dear?'

'Might Stephen stay, please?'

'Oh, of course.' The severe voice returned as Matron said, 'Which of you is Stephen?'

Olivia thought the question strange given the obvious gender difference between Stephen and Superintendent Evelyn Watts. She decided it must be part of the nurse's gender-neutral training.

Stephen said, his voice verging on timid, causing Olivia to smile, 'Ah, that would be me.'

'Okay, seat yourself over there. Now as for you, Ma'am, it's out!' To ensure that there was no misunderstanding, Matron accompanied the Superintendent, pointing to the exit.

'I'll ring,' Stephen Walls called out as the Superintendent left.

The Superintendent turned and smiled, a paradox to the vexation decorating her eyes. 'I look forward to it, Mr Walls.'

***

Stephen waited patiently as Olivia underwent her medical examination and, at its completion, the Doctor recommended she remain in the emergency room while her blood pressure settled. They would continue monitoring her over the next hour or so and, if it didn't come down, she would be transferred to a ward. With the events pushing Molly from her mind, Olivia agreed. When they were alone, Stephen said, 'Do you have any idea who was behind the kidnap attempt?'

'Yes, Stephen. Miss Adele—the woman Inspector Axel had a confrontation with. The driver mentioned I would join Max, implying that Miss Adele wasn't considering a ransom; rather, it was more about payback for Spain. Her knowledge of my arrival in the UK and the flight I was taking reveals just how sophisticated the intelligence the Firm has at its disposal.'

Stephen, thinking, bit his top lip before saying, 'This won't be the last we hear of Miss Adele. For the time being, your safety is paramount. Before leaving the UK, Claudia mentioned you would stay in her apartment. Is that right?'

'Yes. Until I can find a place of my own.'

'With Claudia away, without security, it is unwise to stay there on your own. I'll have James organise twenty-four-hour protection for you until Claudia returns. In the meantime, I'll stay here until you're discharged, then drive you to the apartment myself. We have little evidence against Miss Adele that would stand up in court. Not yet.'

Olivia started to nod in agreement when she remembered Molly's plight and the need to be in Manchester.

Stephen saw her hesitation. 'Is something wrong?'

Olivia faced a dilemma. Did she deceive Stephen or tell the truth and expose Claudia's scheme, a plan that involved MI6 without his knowledge? The course of action was clear to her; she had little choice.

'Claudia asked me to watch over Molly while she is away.'

'Did she indeed, and is there a reason this can't be done from Claudia's apartment?'

'It appears...' Olivia stopped herself, unsure how to continue, '... that Molly is on the run.'

'On the run?'

'Yes. Molly has called for help.'

'Do you know where she is?'

Olivia shrugged her shoulders. 'Not exactly.'

Stephen shook his head, guessing that Claudia had put some elaborate plot in place before leaving for Russia, of which Olivia was a part. Annoyed and wanting to uncover MI6's level of involvement, Stephen went on a proverbial fishing expedition with his next question. 'I see. I take it that neither Molly nor Samantha has phoned you for help?'

'Not exactly. Sorry Stephen, this sounds deceptive and I promise that is not my intention. Claudia gave Molly a deck of playing cards, telling her that if she needed help, she was to post one. Molly sent two yesterday. We know where they were posted from, but nothing else. She's heading north, so I was heading for Manchester to stay until the next card arrives.'

'Forgive me, Olivia, to where are these cards being sent?' Before Olivia could answer, Stephen put his hand up. 'No, forget it. The answer is obvious. Molly is posting them to MI6.' Stephen shook his head in irritation. 'I also won't ask to whom, not yet anyway. I take it you don't have Samantha's mobile phone number or you would have called her?'

Olivia nodded her head. 'That's correct, I don't.'

Stephen folded his arms. 'I would have thought Claudia would have given that to you before she left.'

Olivia sighed. 'Claudia was under the assumption I had it and I forgot to ask, which is my mistake.'

Stephen gave a reassuring smile, his demeanour softening. 'Given all that's happened, Olivia, don't be too harsh on yourself.

Other than knowing a card has arrived, are you getting any other help from MI6?'

'No, only the location of where the card was posted.'

Stephen paused to think. He believed Claudia had gone against his express wishes and instigated an elaborate plan involving MI6. It sounded like James was involved, but that was all. His irritation settled. 'Is it possible, Olivia, that today's incident in the taxi and your search for Molly are linked?'

Olivia shook her head. 'No, I wouldn't think so, Stephen.'

Stephen rubbed his chin. 'Okay. While you rest, I'll ask James to find Samantha's number for you.'

Olivia gave a pleading look. 'Could you, by the location of her phone, find out where she and Molly are?'

'I have that power, but under UK law, to exercise it, it must be deemed necessary, and this is not one of those occasions. I'm sure Claudia's and my opinion would differ.'

'Whilst I appreciate and welcome the privacy safeguards, Stephen; the Chinese will have no such qualms, as you know.'

'That may be so, Olivia, but the Chinese don't have an oversight committee looking over their shoulders.'

'I'm not asking that we listen in on her conversations.' Olivia paused, not wanting to put Stephen in a difficult position. 'Perhaps you could consider a mobile phone tower ping at the least? It would narrow the search.'

'Let me think about it. In the meantime, get some rest while I organise your protection.'

'Thank you, Stephen, but that won't be necessary.'

'No?'

'No,' Olivia repeated. 'I made a promise to watch over Molly and that means that I must leave immediately. I have a train to Manchester to catch.'

'What about your blood pressure?'

'I must look after Molly and if I don't honour my promise, my blood pressure will enter the record books.'

Stephen knew there was little point in arguing and a look of reluctant acceptance crept across his face. 'Okay, Olivia, you win. Get your things together and I'll drive you to the station. I'll call James on the way.'

As Stephen watched Olivia disconnect her monitoring equipment, he wondered if Claudia had spoken to her about Tomoe. After all, Olivia was supposed to be staying in Claudia's apartment.

'Olivia, did Claudia mentioned Tomoe to you?'

'Yes. I'm sceptical of the invitation to Altindere Vadisi.'

'Are there no national secrets?'

Olivia smiled. 'It was you, Stephen, who told Superintendent Watts that I was an active agent.'

'Indeed.'

Olivia sat up, swung her legs over the bed, grinned and said, 'What about Matron? You know Stephen, I'm more frightened of her than the man who tried to kidnap me and Miss Adele.'

'I'll say we have to move you for your own safety, into police protection or something like that.'

Olivia smiled. 'Matron should accept that.'

'Let's hope so.' Stephen offered Olivia his arm to help her balance as she stood up. 'You leaving the hospital is against my better judgement.'

'I understand.'

Stephen sighed. 'I'll do this for you, Olivia, but you must promise me that, if you feel unwell, you will call an ambulance.'

Olivia met his concerned gaze and, speaking with sincerity, said, 'Of course I will, Stephen. I'm no help to anyone if I'm poorly.'

***

Stephen waited with Olivia at Guildford Station for the twelve thirty-seven train to arrive. The journey to Manchester would take Olivia three hours and fifty-one minutes with two changes, the first at Vauxhall and the second, London Euston. As the train pulled into Guildford, Stephen said, 'I've told James to call you with Samantha's number.'

'No ping?' Olivia asked, giving a sly grin.

'Try ringing her first. If you have no joy, then we shall see.'

Olivia had been travelling on the train for ten minutes when her phone rang. Conscious of public transport etiquette, not that others were, and of being overheard, Olivia asked James to hold while she found a private space away from fellow travellers. Olivia prided herself on an excellent memory, an essential trait for any spy, but when James read out Samantha's phone number, she realised she couldn't remember it. With no pen and paper to jot it down, Olivia asked James to repeat the number. Again, the numbers wouldn't stick and she flushed with embarrassment, even though James couldn't see her.

'I'm so sorry, James but, since the death of Max, my mind has become a bit of a sieve. Would you be a dear and text it to me?' If James had any concerns about her abilities, Olivia couldn't tell so from his manner and, while she was still talking, her phone beeped, telling her of an incoming message.

'You should have it now,' James said.

Even though Olivia could see the number on her screen, she still had to repeat it four times to herself before it lodged in her memory, enabling her to place a call. As she tapped in the number and pressed the green call button, she wondered what to say to Samantha. The phone rang, disconnecting after the third ring.

Olivia, fearing the worst, contemplated what to do next.

Perhaps Samantha ended the call because she didn't know who was dialling. Yes, that is a possibility. Try sending a text message with something only you and Samantha share: "When Harry met Sally".

CHAPTER 13
Wait And See

Sending eight-year-old Molly on her own to meet her at The Black Sheep Café had been a tough decision for Samantha. The chances of escaping if they stayed together made the risk a necessity, nevertheless, it made the judgment no less difficult. Samantha knew because of Molly's age; evading spies was simply a game; as a child, she didn't appreciate the consequences of being caught. Entering the café, Samantha scanned the patrons. Seeing Molly seated at a table wearing a baseball cap and sporting yellow sunglasses, she breathed a sigh of relief, resisting the maternal instinct to rush over and hug her daughter. Instead, Samantha gave Molly the measured wave of a mother meeting a teenage daughter for coffee.

Joining Molly at the table, Samantha asked, 'Did anyone in the café ask where your mother was?'

Molly shook her head. 'No.'

'Oh!' Though this was the outcome Samantha had hoped for, she couldn't hide her disappointment. Her daughter had already grown up. 'Any problems evading our tail?'

'No,' Molly said matter-of-factly, as if evading foreign agents was an everyday occurrence.

'Good morning, ladies,' said the waiter, who approached the table while they were chatting. 'Would you like to see the breakfast menu?'

Samantha looked up. 'No, thank you, we're just having drinks.'

'No problem, and do you know what you're having?'

Samantha opened her mouth, ready to order as she'd done on many occasions: *a Latte for herself and a hot chocolate for Molly.* Then she recalled Molly's teenage disguise. Teenagers always ordered for themselves. 'I'll have a latte. What would you like?'

A smile crept across Molly's face as she recognised her mother's dilemma. 'I've already had coffee this morning... perhaps a hot chocolate with no marshmallow please.'

Samantha was relieved, a silly reaction considering the dangers they were facing.

*

After leaving the café, Samantha and Molly picked up the hire car and drove to the cattery for Snowflake, who, with a flick of her tail, registered her displeasure at having been imprisoned for the night. The events went smoothly, but took longer than Samantha had expected. She had planned to drive the six hours to Carlisle, seven and half allowing for stops and traffic, then onto Scotland the following day and the hideout in Inverness. Mid-day was already behind them when Samantha, Molly and Snowflake left the London outskirts and started their journey north.

In the front seat of the car, Molly fingered the playing cards given to her by Claudia, pondering when and how to send her message for help. She'd already asked Samantha three times where they were staying, each request deflected by wait-and-see. Judging by her mother's persistent checking of the time, Molly guessed the destination was some distance and that they were running behind schedule. Molly pulled the two of diamonds from the deck and, turning it over in her hand, mulled over her thoughts. She returned it to the deck.

If I wait to post the card, it may be too late. But without an address, how will Olivia know where to find us?

One of her favourite bedtime fairy-tales popped into her mind, the story of Hansel and Gretel. Of course, the situation was different to the tale because her mother didn't want rid of her, but the children left a trail to find their way home, first with pebbles and then with bread crumbs.

If I lay a path for Olivia to follow, that might work?

Molly smiled as a plan took shape in her mind. To keep her occupied on the long drive, Samantha had packed a colouring book and pencil case in to her day pack. She would hide one card in the colouring book and secretly address it to MI6 as they drove. When they stopped, she'd post it as the first of the breadcrumbs.

No, it's a stone because, in the fairy tale, the birds ate the bread.

The day pack was between her legs on the floor, so she told Samantha that she would do some art work before retrieving the book and pencils, placing them on her lap as she shifted her thoughts to how she would get her mother to stop.

Molly chose a whining tone when she spoke. 'I'm hunnnngrrry. When are we going to stop?'

Samantha glanced at her watch and felt torn. She desperately wanted to push on, but it was well past lunchtime.

I should have packed something

'Not yet.'

Well, that didn't work, Molly thought. *I need another trick.*

A minute later, she remembered something that had never failed when they were on a road trip. Grinning, she decided to wait before using the ruse, giving her time to prepare and to allay any suspicions her mother may have. Molly again removed the two of diamonds from the deck, placed it face down inside the colouring book and, after writing *TO MI6* on the back, slipped it into her pocket. With her actions unnoticed, Molly addressed two more cards in preparation. These she returned to the deck before placing the deck in the daypack.

Well done, Molly! She muttered to herself.

She started colouring again and allowed five minutes to pass before deciding that it was time. 'Mummy! I need to go to the toilet.'

'Can you hold on?'

Ham it up, Molly. She'll tell you off, but it's sure to work.

'No, I'm desperate. I'm going to pee my pants!'

'Molly! There is no need to say that.'

'Say what, Mummy?'

'You know exactly what I mean, young lady.'

'Sorry, Mummy. I must go! Really, I do.'

Samantha sighed. 'Okay. I'll stop at the next service centre.'

Contented, Molly placed the colouring book and pencils back into her day pack. She bit her lip, trying not to smile. *The toilet trick always works, even at school.*

Ten minutes further up the road, the drive accompanied by Molly's frequent grunts, crossing, and uncrossing of her legs while pretending to be desperately holding on, Samantha spotted a blue sign on the M40 motorway: "Beaconsfield Services Centre 2 Miles". Molly felt inside her pocket for the two of diamonds and though she'd not been out of the car, was relieved that it was still there. Her heart skipped a beat as she wondered how she would post it without her mother noticing. Samantha decelerated and turned off the motorway, ready to enter the service centre. Molly knew that, once out of the car, it would be difficult to get away from her mother. Samantha would even accompany her to the toilet, wait and they would walk to the café together. This is what always happened. As the car slowed, Molly saw the petrol pumps, sparking an idea. 'Are you going to fill up with fuel, Mummy?'

Samantha peered at the petrol gauge.

'No honey, I still have over half a tank.'

'Daddy always does. If you're going to stop at a service centre, might as well top up, that's what he says.'

Samantha turned her head, looked at Molly and made a face that said, "really", before returning her eyes to the road. 'Does he? I don't remember him saying that!'

'It makes sense, Mummy. Who knows when we will have the chance to stop again?'

Samantha shrugged.

Molly held her breath and, as she thought her mother was going to pass the petrol station, Samantha turned right, driving in and stopping at a pump.

Here's my chance.

As Samantha opened the car door and left, Molly jumped out, too. Molly waited for Samantha to remove the nozzle from the petrol pump and insert it into the car. Knowing Samantha could not object, Molly said, 'I'll meet you inside.'

'Where are you going?'

'To the toilet. I'm busting, remember.'

'Oh, alright. What about Snowflake?'

Molly dashed away, pretending not to hear her mother.

'That little imp. I suppose now I'll have to find somewhere for Snowflake to relieve herself. Still holding the petrol pump, Samantha scanned about for a garden bed.'

***

Molly had left her first pebble and was feeling pleased with herself as they departed the Beaconsfield Services Centre to re-join the motorway, knowing that Olivia would soon be on her way. Under the guise of searching for her colouring book and pencils, Molly opened her day pack and fiddled inside, feeling again for the deck of cards. She opened the packet and removed the next one she'd send, sliding it inside the book. After replacing the bag back on the floor, Molly busied herself colouring while seeking an opportunity to hide it on her person. When Samantha indicated to overtake a slower vehicle, Molly waited for her mother to look in the mirror before slipping the card from between the pages and concealing it in her pocket. She was ready for the next drop as they continued the journey north. With the radio playing in the background, Samantha and Molly travelled in silence, each consumed by thoughts that they were unwilling to share. Samantha wrestled with her fears and trepidation, not only about their immediate safety but also the future and how they would manage on their own. Molly was frightened to speak in case she revealed Claudia's plan, one she knew her mother would reject. She comforted herself, however, with the thought that once her mother saw Olivia, everything would be alright. Molly turned the page of her book. With the warmth and rocking motion of the car, her head drooped and the colouring pencil slipped from her fingers as she drifted into a deep sleep, waking only when Samantha gently shook her. Yawning and wiping the sleep from her eyes, Molly asked, 'Where are we?'

'The Knutsford Service Centre.'

Molly yawned again. 'Where's that?'

'The M6, between Liverpool and Manchester.'

Hoping to learn their final destination, Molly became fully alert. 'Is that where we are heading, Liverpool or Manchester?'

'No. It's late and I'm tired, so I thought we would stop for a drink and to find a place for us to stay for the night. Come on, sleepyhead. I'll buy you a milkshake.'

Snowflake, seeking affection, jumped from the rear seat of the car onto Molly's lap, purring.

'What about Snowflake?' Molly asked.

'Snowflake can look after the car.'

'Okay.'

When Molly attempted to move Snowflake to the back seat, the cat resisted, clinging to her clothes in a statement of defiance. *Why should I have to stay in the car? They forget who is the boss.*

***

Inside the bustling eating hall, Samantha collected their drinks and found a table for two, tucked in the corner away from noise, a spot where she could concentrate on finding overnight accommodation. Using her smart phone, Samantha searched for places to stay, mumbling to herself as she scrolled through the options. While her mother was engrossed, Molly saw an opportunity to drop another stone for Olivia to follow.

'Mummy, can I go to the toilet?'

Samantha looked up. 'Will you be alright on your own?'

Molly put her hands on her hips, 'Of course I will. I'm not a child.'

'Alright, alright. I was just asking. Don't be long.'

Samantha watched Molly leave and then returned her eyes to the screen, muttering to herself, 'Liverpool and Manchester are both within easy driving distance, with an abundance of places to stay. Neither feels right. I think, to be on the safe side, we should stay clear of the major centres.' She closed the accommodation App and opened a map, zooming in and out, seeking somewhere secluded, not too far from the motorway and from where they were. She spotted the village of Croft in the parish of Warrington.

If I can find a B&B there, Croft will do nicely.

Unlike Beaconsfield, finding a post box proved a greater challenge for Molly, who had to ask three people, the last one pointing her in the right direction. As she walked back towards the café table, Molly rehearsed excuses she could use for her long absence, settling on, 'I thought I would check on Snowflake which was silly, Mummy, because I didn't have the key.' Molly hoped the senselessness of the trip would prove a distraction from her absence.

Engrossed in finding and booking a place to stay, Samantha hadn't noticed Molly's absence and simply said, 'Hi, Honey. I've found us a nice self-contained B&B for the night in a village called Croft plus a place for dinner, the Horseshoe Inn. It is within easy walking distance of our lodgings. Doesn't that sound exciting?' Samantha held her phone so Molly could see where they were going.

'Yes, Mummy.'

The hairs on the back of Samantha's neck bristled as she sensed they were being watched. She bit down on her lip, trying to control the anxiety growing inside. Samantha coughed, then breathed in deeply.

It's nerves, Samantha, get a grip on yourself.

She took another deep breath, and her fear settled.

Okay, that's better.

Not wanting to raise suspicion, Samantha casually scanned the room.

'Are you alright, Mummy?'

'I swallowed the wrong way, that's all.'

'Who are you looking for?'

'No one, Molly, I'm just looking.'

'The man from the train?'

Samantha's heart raced. 'Have you seen him?'

'Nah.'

The food hall was full of people ordering from the many vendor windows, going about their business. Tables were occupied by families, couples, or individuals, some eating, drinking, reading, or chatting, while others talked on their phones or stared into the screen of a smart phone or laptop. An old man, wearing a beige flat cap and dressed in matching cashmere overcoat, slept, his head drooped and mouth hanging open. A fifty-year-old woman, her shoulder-length blonde hair resting on a white shirt, tied back with a yellow scrunchie decorated with brown dots, stared out of the window, lost in her thoughts. What Samantha would do if she spotted someone suspicious, she hadn't considered. Her eyes drifted around the room, lingering on one person, then another, seeking Chinese agents. Her gaze went unmet, and she noticed no Asians in the mix to cause her alarm. Samantha breathed out, unaware that she'd been holding her breath. Her fears put to rest, she said, her tone light, 'I'm hungry, aren't you?' Before Molly could respond, she added, 'Let's book into the B&B and then get some dinner. What's your fancy?'

'Um, nuggets and chips.'

Samantha scrunched up her face. 'Let's see, shall we?' Molly recognised her mother's subtle code. Molly, you can have anything you like, as long as it comes with either salad or vegetables.

Samantha stood and extending her hand towards Molly. 'Come on, let's be going.'

'I'm fourteen, Mum, we don't hold hands.'

Samantha opened her mouth, closing it again. There was no point in arguing.

Molly grinned, proffering her hand.

Ellen Goldsworthy, the woman that Samantha had spotted wearing a yellow scrunchie, studied Samantha and Molly from their reflection in a window. She saw Samantha take Molly's hand and walk from the food hall. To ensure her movements would go unnoticed, Ellen Goldsworthy waited ten seconds before following them outside, whilst leaving a discrete distance between them. She watched her targets enter their car before returning to hers. Although she didn't know where they were heading, she knew that there was no need to rush because the Chinese Security Service was electronically tracking the pair's movement.

Ellen Goldsworthy had been recruited as a teenager into the services of the Chinese secret service. She was born in Hong Kong to English parents when it was under British rule. Her father was a senior bank executive and her mother worked in HR. Like many wealthy foreigners living in Hong Kong, she'd had a privileged upbringing with staff undertaking everyday chores: a cleaner, cook, nanny and driver, plus she had attended an international school. Like many teenagers, she wanted to grow up quickly and strove to impress her friends. Adolescence was turbulent, and she argued constantly with her mother, Ellen, defying all household restrictions, wearing wild clothes, staying out late and sleeping until the afternoon. Her father, Peter, was more sympathetic, viewing their testing times as a rite of passage into adulthood. Despite rebelling, Ellen's academic grades held up and, were it not for her behaviour, she could have been a school captain. Her journey into the world of espionage started at sixteen while staying at her friend's Sue-Lin's house. Reflecting on her recruitment now, Ellen Goldsworthy couldn't recall how the elements came together, only that the Chinese exploited her vulnerabilities. It was October 1987, the time of the infamous Black Monday Stock Market Crash, which rocked the world, when the Hong Kong Market dropped nearly forty-six percent. The crucial banking sector went into a tailspin, pushing the financial system towards an imminent danger of collapse. Her father, as a senior banking executive, was under tremendous pressure and this played out at home. Breaking into her father's study and photographing his papers started as a dare, an outlet for her anger. In truth, she'd unwittingly committed espionage on behalf of the People's Republic of China. It was because of her love for her father that Ellen Goldsworthy continued her relationship with the Chinese, initially through a handler. She had been offered a choice; walk away and her father's career would be ruined, or become a well-paid agent in the world of espionage, and her father would be spared. Ellen had chosen the latter.

From inside her car, Ellen Goldsworthy watched Samantha and Molly drive from the Service Centre back onto the motorway and, maintaining her cover, waited a couple of minutes before following. She used the time to file a report by calling her office and speaking with Chen Li.

'They are on their own.'

'Are you sure they are receiving no support from British Intelligence?' Chen Li asked.

'Yes, Sir. Samantha Liew is like a cat on a hot tin roof, as they say in Britain, meaning she's jumpy and has the clumsy behaviour of someone operating out of their league. I'm in no doubt, Sir, that Samantha Liew is on her own and has no outside help.'

'Perhaps, Ms Goldsworthy, or it's an orchestrated show for our benefit. If Samantha Liew feared being followed, why does she carry her phone? Are you sure, Ms Goldsworthy, it is not we who are being watched?'

Though nobody could see her, Ellen Goldsworthy shook her head. 'Samantha Liew is an amateur. She's naïve, doesn't know that we are tracking her movements through her mobile. I've seen no one else and, Sir, she wouldn't voluntarily involve her daughter. Do you want me to pick them up?'

Chen Li had a niggling feeling of unease. His years of experience told him they weren't fully on top of the situation. He hesitated before answering, 'Not for the time being. I want you to rattle her cage, to force her hand, if she has one to be forced. We will watch and eavesdrop on her phone.'

'If you wish, Sir, I could pay a visit tonight while she's sleeping? That would unsettle her.'

'No, I'm thinking of something more dramatic. If she is a professional, I want to force her to act like one. I also want to know if someone else is lurking in the shadows.'

'Yes, Sir.'

Chen Li sensed his agent's hesitation. 'Is something bothering you?'

'I'm in no doubt that Samantha Liew is operating alone. If we delay bringing her in, Claudia may get wind of the pending rendition; it will be she who comes out of the shadows. That woman is a nasty piece of work and will operate outside of her government's guidelines. Were she to stick her nose into this matter, it would get messy.'

'You know Claudia well and you're right to be wary of her. I am reliably informed, however, that she's in Moscow and out of harm's way. I've instructed Michael Tan and Kang Long to drive up tonight and join you. Make your plans for tomorrow. In the meantime, keep a watchful eye on Samantha and Molly Liew.'

'And Snowflake, the cat?'

'I don't appreciate attempts at humour, Miss Goldsworthy.'

Chen Li ended the call.

***

Samantha awoke at seven thirty, feeling surprisingly relaxed. The phone call to Richard the night before had gone off without a hitch and from their conversation, she was confident he still believed the cover story that they were at school camp. The meal at the Horseshoe Inn had been fine and, best of all, she and Molly hadn't fought. On their return to their accommodation, with Molly tucked up in bed, Samantha planned the following day's journey. After breakfast, they would drive for an hour and ten minutes to the service centre near Lancaster. The stop was earlier than she wished but, as a precaution, Samantha wanted to keep the car's fuel tank above half full. At Knutsford, she'd forgotten to top up. From Lancaster, they would drive the two and a half hours to Hamilton on the outskirts of Glasgow. From there, either after an early lunch or late morning tea, depending on the time, Samantha would push on for the final one hundred and seventy miles, or two hundred seventy-three kilometres, to Inverness, their destination. Samantha's goal was to arrive around four o'clock in the afternoon.

Having showered and dressed, Samantha checked her watch and reckoned that it was time to wake Molly. In Molly's room, Samantha spotted Snowflake curled up on the end of her daughter's bed with Molly sleeping soundly, a scene of tranquillity in an unsettled time. She placed her hand on Molly's shoulder, ready to wake her up, but, upon sensing her daughter's rhythmic breathing through her fingers, changed her mind.

Let her sleep in until eight. We have plenty of time.

Snowflake opened one eye to glance at Samantha, then lazily closed it again, a confirmation that it was too early to move.

It was just shy of eight ten when Molly, in her red polka dot pyjamas, rubbing the sleep from her eyes, wandered into the kitchen. Snowflake following behind. Samantha had already poured the cereal left by the B&B host into a bowl and needed only to add the milk.

'Do you want to get dressed first?' Samantha asked, but Molly, still groggy from sleep, shook her head.

Free of London, the secrecy of yesterday lessened, and Samantha outlined the journey ahead to Molly, showing the route on her phone over breakfast. Molly studied the map, noticing how far Inverness was from London. She felt uneasy. How would Olivia find them? She needed to drop another stone with Inverness emblazoned on it, and soon, if Olivia was to arrive by the following day. Without finishing her cereal, Molly said, 'It's a long drive Mommy, we should get going.' She jumped up from the breakfast table.

'Where are you going, Molly?'

'To get dressed.' Molly's answer was partially true, but she also wanted to write INVERNESS on the back of a pussy cat playing card, ready to post when they stopped at Lancaster.

Samantha was delighted about not having to hound Molly to ready herself. 'It's a long day, Honey. Finish your breakfast first.'

Molly was about to complain, but thought better of it. She was a secret agent like Claudia and Olivia and grumbling could compromise her cover. She finished the bowl of cereal, then asked for a piece of toast. *That's what Claudia would do*, she thought.

It was nine forty-five, later than Samantha intended, when they loaded the last of their luggage into the boot. It was Molly who spotted the flat front passenger side tyre as she was about to jump into the car.

'Damn it!'

Samantha came around to inspect the wheel. She couldn't remember ever having a flat tyre before, but knew that they had roadside assistance for eventualities like this. But this was not their home car, it was a hire car. After rummaging through the glove compartment and inspecting the hire car policy, she was still unsure if it was part of the package.

'I'll have to ring them.'

Plonking herself in the passenger's seat, she stuffed the agreement documents back into the glove compartment, slamming it shut with a thud. Taking a deep breath before phoning the hire car company, Samantha pushed her head back into the headrest when she noticed, high on the windscreen on the far-left edge, a sticker– Roadside Assistance, with the prominent phone number.

The tyre change took ten minutes, but the wait for help took an hour. As she pulled away from the curb, Samantha glanced at the time on the car's infotainment system. Five minutes past eleven.

'Damn, Lancaster will be a lunch stop now.'

'Mummy, is damn a good or bad word?'

'Sorry, Honey.'

The drive to Lancaster was like the day before, mostly in silence with Samantha and Molly, unbeknown to each other, ruminating over their own issues. Not wanting to repeat the Knutsford mistake, Samantha headed straight for the petrol station as she entered the services. Molly waited for her mother to begin filling the car before seizing on the opportunity to drop the next stone. Grabbing her colouring book and pencils, Molly opened the car door and said, 'I'll meet you inside the service centre.'

Without catching her daughter's eye, Samantha responded, 'No!'

Molly snapped back, 'No is not an answer.'

Samantha, watching the gauges on the petrol pump tick over, her fingers clenched on the trigger, gave Molly a side glance. 'You haven't used that line since you were four or five.' The observation that Molly was acting like a child found its mark. Pouting, Molly returned to the car.

What would Claudia do?

With the fuel tank full and payment made, Samantha drove off, seeking a place to park. With no COVID restrictions in place, the service centre was hectic, with vehicles manoeuvring in and out, parked cheek to jowl. Wary of someone opening their door into the hire car, leaving a dint she would have to pay for, Samantha searched for a parking bay that would offer some protection. On her second lap, she noticed cars had overflowed into the heavy vehicle parking bays; even as a Londoner, Samantha knew truckies would frown on the practice.

Do I do another circuit or risk the wrath of a disgruntled driver?

She peered at her watch and sighed.

I haven't time for this mucking around. If someone complains, I'll have to flutter my eyelids.

She told Molly to leave the rear window slightly ajar to allow fresh air to enter for Snowflake and they headed to the Service Centre eateries, with Samantha striding out in front, calling back to Molly to keep up. Inside, Samantha scanned around for a table away from the hustle and bustle. Twelve-twenty-five was bang on lunch time and Samantha knew she would be forced to take whatever was free. After weaving around people for three minutes doing the circuit of the eatery, she spotted a table about to become vacant. Her find coincided with that of another couple who made the same observation. A race for possession ensued, the opponents having the advantage of being closer to the target.

Pointing, Samantha said, 'Quick, see that table, go grab it, Molly.'

Like a rabbit at the starting gate of a greyhound race, Molly dashed away, arriving moments before her competitors. Pretending not to see them, she plonked herself down in one of the seats, placing her colouring book and pencil case on her lap as she crossed her arms. The couple altered course, veering away to continue their search.

'Good girl,' Samantha said, as she arrived.

Inspecting the table, Samantha said, 'Oh, what a mess.' Gritting her teeth and speaking so that Molly couldn't hear, she muttered, 'Some people are such pigs!'

The previous occupants had departed without removing their rubbish, leaving behind three hamburger boxes, one with a quarter eaten burger still inside, four large hot chip cups–empty, four half used squeeze-on tomato sauce packs, two empty bottles of coke, and a half-drunk bottle of water. Samantha peered about, hoping to spot a person cleaning the tables, but no one was present. Fortunately, the diners had conveyed their mealtime cuisine to the table on two plastic trays. Samantha stacked the trays with the garbage before disposing of the rubbish in large bins that adorned the eating area.

'Yuck!'

Returning, Samantha, hiding her displeasure, smiled at Molly and said, 'That's better. Now you have room for your colouring book. Wait here while I get us something to eat.'

Molly opened her mouth, ready to utter, 'Don't I get to choose,' but snapped it closed again, realising that her mother's absence was the opportunity she'd been waiting for. As a super spy, she would slip away, post the card and be back before her absence was noticed. Samantha swivelled around and strolled towards the food stalls. Molly opened her colouring book, flipping through until she found a blank page at the very back. She glanced at her mother, making sure Samantha's back was facing her so that she wouldn't be seen. Conscious of not wishing to lose their hard-won table,

Molly took a black colouring pencil and wrote in large letters **RESERVED**, and positioned the handmade sign in the middle of the table.

That will have to do.

Ready to leave, Molly stood, but hesitated.

It's not enough, Molly. What else would a secret agent do? Oh, I know!

Molly took a red, blue, green, and yellow pencil from her pencil case, placing one in front of each of the four vacant chairs.

That's better.

From across the room, Ellen Goldsworthy watched Molly's actions with bemusement.

What on earth is the child up to? From the way she's acting, checking that Samantha isn't watching, her behaviour seems secretive. Now what? Molly, where are you going?

Ellen Goldsworthy glanced first to Samantha, then back at Molly, deciding whether she should follow the girl.

No, best stay on the mother. Whatever Molly is up to, it is only child's play.

Molly had spotted with her sharp eyes a post box when she'd accompanied her mother to pay for the petrol. To avoid being seen by Samantha standing in a queue, Molly took a longer route, exiting the building and sprinting around the outside, then back the way they had come. The journey took longer than Molly hoped and, as she re-entered the building, her mother was already heading towards their table. It would be a race to see who arrived first and Molly, fearing that she would be seen, frantically searched for an excuse, settling on a tried and tested one: She had had to visit the toilet.

Samantha, dining tray in hand, scanned the room on her return, focusing on the tables either side of theirs, looking for anything suspicious. Her eyes skimmed over their table, settling on the other side of the room. She was struck by a disconcerting feeling.

Our table is empty?

She glanced back and Molly was there. Shaking her head at her own silliness, she continued to the table.

'Here you are,' Samantha said, placing the food tray down.

Molly was still packing away the pencils, reaching across the table to pick up a red one which was in her mother's place.

'What are you doing?' Samantha asked.

'Just playing.'

These simple words uttered from the mouth of a child but lost in adolescence, were a universal "get out of gaol free card".

'Oh,' her mother said, curiosity satisfied. Placing Molly's lunch in front of her, she said, 'I bought you a salad and ham roll.'

Ordinarily, if accompanying her mother, although not her father, Molly would huff, then roll her eyes at having to eat salad. Not today; she was on a top-secret mission.

Samantha opened the plastic packaging and removed her chicken and salad sandwich, giving it the once over before taking a first bite. For a mass-produced object, it was surprisingly tasty. As they ate, Molly thought of Olivia, believing that she would be in Inverness by the following day and that everything would return to normal. Samantha contemplated the next part of their journey and was conscious of the need to keep moving. She stole a glance at her watch; it was approaching a quarter to one.

'We need to get going.'

Molly nodded.

Samantha took another bite from her sandwich when, like at the Knutsford Service Centre, the hairs on the back of her neck bristled. Again, she felt like they were being watched. Resting the half-eaten lunch on its plastic packaging, Samantha scanned the room on the lookout for anything suspicious, her trepidation rising. She let out a muffled squeal as her phone rang.

Molly looked at her mother. 'Mummy, what's wrong?'

Samantha wasn't aiming to ignore Molly, but her mind was elsewhere as she stared anxiously at the mobile phone screen, its caller ID reading, "Private Number." Believing they were being watched, Samantha feared the call originated from the Chinese State Security Service, even Chen Li, whom she'd met at the Shark Fin. Samantha's heart, already racing, increased its beat.

What should I do?

Disconnecting the call, Samantha scanned the room again in search of the caller. Her phone sounded, signalling an SMS had arrived. Fearing what the message might say, Samantha ignored it.

Molly watched her mother's reactions with increasing alarm.

'Mummy, you have to look at it. It may be from Oliv...' Molly stopped herself and backtracked. 'From someone important.'

In trepidation, Samantha lowered her eyes and read, "When Harry met Sally", a reference to a movie, the meaning only she and Olivia understood.

'Oh, my goodness, I've hung up on Olivia.'

Molly looked up and, with a voice brimming with excitement, exclaimed, 'Olivia!'

I knew you would come.

Samantha's heart leapt with joy and, with her eyes transfixed on the phone screen, thoughts of being watched were temporarily forgotten. Five seconds later, a chill engulfed her body when she realised she had seen *that* woman before. Without moving her head, Samantha cast her eyes to the side. The middle-aged, blond-haired woman was seated five tables away and, as Samantha examined her profile, she pondered.

Have I seen her before? Don't be silly.

Samantha's fingers tingled and her mouth went dry as the feeling of foreboding grew. With her mind elsewhere, Samantha was oblivious to her phone ringing.

Molly said, 'Mummy, answer the phone.'

Samantha knew it was Olivia on the phone, but her voice was still tentative when she said, 'Hello.'

Olivia breathed a sigh of relief. 'Dear me. Hello, Samantha.'

On hearing the familiar voice, tension drained from her body and a teardrop formed in the corner of her eye. 'Oh, my goodness, Olivia, I can't believe it's you.' As Samantha finished the sentence a realisation hit home. Letting out a gasp, Samantha said, 'The yellow scrunchie with the brown dots. Definitely, it's the same one as yesterday. We're being followed by a woman.'

Olivia gathered her thoughts. 'What woman, Samantha?'

Panic rising in her throat, Samantha repeated, 'We're being followed!'

Samantha gasped again, realising that Olivia was in Spain, not aware that she and Molly were on the run from the Chinese security services.

'Stay calm, Samantha. Can you see the person from where you are?'

Samantha glanced to where the woman was seated and, when their eyes met, Samantha said, 'Yes, and she's looking at me now.'

Olivia stroked her chin, thinking about what to say. Her voice reassuring, Olivia said, 'They are tracking your movements through your smart phone, which is how they know where you are. We must also assume they are eavesdropping on our conversation. Be careful what you say and I expect they will not allow us to talk for long.'

Samantha took a gulp of air.

Olivia, her voice steady, said, 'I want you to tell me where you are.'

The question caught Samantha by surprise because Olivia's manner implied that she could help. How could she when Olivia was in Spain? 'On the M6, at the Lancaster Service Centre. Where are you?'

'I'm on my way and not that far behind you.'

Samantha sobbed, 'How?'

At his London headquarters, Chen Li was listening to the conversation between Olivia and Samantha. Within seconds, with Olivia unaware of Samantha's whereabouts, he was satisfied that Samantha's disappearance wasn't part of an entrapment operation by MI6. If MI6 were now to be involved, it would be reactionary. He relayed his observation to Ellen Goldsworthy, the field agent at the scene.

'What do you want me to do?'

'Let's wait a moment longer, Ms Goldsworthy. We may learn more.'

Samantha sobbed, 'How?'

Olivia ignored the question and said, her tone authoritative, 'Samantha, you must leave. I'm going to give you my phone number. Do you have something to write it down?'

'Yes. Wait, give me a second.' Samantha motioned to Molly to pass her a pencil and the colouring book. 'Okay, I'm ready.'

'Good. Once you've written it down, you must destroy your phone, smash it if you have to. When you're safely away, buy a pre-paid phone and call me. I will then step you through setting up encrypted messaging. Are you ready?'

'One tick.' Samantha opened the colouring book from the back and placed it on the table in front of her.

Chen Li did not want to lose Samantha. Hearing Olivia's instructions, he gritted his teeth and, voice raised, commanded Ellen Goldsworthy, 'Stop Samantha Liew from obtaining Olivia's number. Do what you must, but stop her. Go now.'

Ellen Goldsworthy touched her pistol as she leapt to her feet. 'Good', she whispered.

Pencil in hand, Samantha was prepared to transcribe Olivia's number when her eyes were drawn to the word **RESERVED,** which was written in capital letters on the opposite page.

What on earth?

Samantha glanced at Molly for an explanation, but stopped as she spotted the woman with the yellow scrunchie jump to her feet.

Samantha dropped the pencil and reached across the table, taking Molly by the hand. 'Quick, we have to go.'

Molly grabbed her pencils as she was dragged from the food hall, banging into tables and chairs as they fled. In the car park, Samantha peered behind; scrunchie woman wasn't far behind. Panic-stricken, she yelled into her phone, 'Olivia, the woman is chasing us.'

Olivia had been apprehensive listening to the noises from the other end of the line. She breathed a sigh of relief, as she said, 'Thank goodness I thought I'd lost you. Are you ready for the number?'

'No Olivia, not yet. That woman is right behind us. We're running for the car.' Samantha swivelled to see if Scrunchie Woman was gaining ground and ran straight into a man coming in the other direction, the impact dislodging the phone from her grip, sending it spiralling into the air before crashing down onto the ground, shattering its screen.

The man, dressed in a tailored, vintage three-piece black pinstripe suit, recovered from the shock of the impact and said, 'Whoops-a-daisy. I am so sorry.'

As he was speaking, he noticed Samantha's broken phone lying on the ground and bent down to retrieve it.

CRUNCH.

With his fingers inches away, Samantha stomped on the phone's screen, grinding it into the ground. Confused by her actions, the man straightened, anticipating an explanation. Before he could say anything, Samantha grabbed Molly by the hand and hurried off. Motionless for a moment, he shook his head in disbelief as he watched the woman and child dash away. He turned and walked towards the food hall, inadvertently stepping in front of a middle-aged blond woman. They collided.

'Whoops-a-daisy,' he said for the second time in as many seconds.

Ellen Goldsworthy growled as she tried to push her way past. 'Get out of my way, you stupid man.'

She stepped to her right, and he moved left, each blocking the other's path. Angry, Ellen Goldsworthy placed her hands on the man's shoulders and twisted him out of the way. The delay gave Samantha and Molly a temporary lead.

Olivia, on the train to Manchester, was unaware of the events unfolding at Lancaster Service Centre and kept talking. 'I need you to stay calm. Can you do that for me?'

Olivia waited, but there was no reply. The phone line died.

'Oh no.'

***

Samantha let go of Molly's hand as they approached the car. She fumbled in her pocket for the key fob to unlock the doors.

'Hurry, quick, get in and put on your seat belt.'

Once inside, Samantha found the button to lock the doors, the *clunk* of its operation momentarily making her feel safe. She breathed a sigh of relief as she glanced in the mirrors, then out of the windows. Samantha scanned the vicinity for the scrunchie woman and, to her delight, she was nowhere to be seen.

'I think she's given up.'

Molly swivelled in her seat to check on Snowflake and released a high-pitched cry. Through the back window, she witnessed a lorry about to ram them. At the last second, the lorry peeled to the right, scraping along the driver's side of the car, stopping alongside, blocking Samantha's exit. Caught unaware, Samantha shrieked in fear as she reached for the engine start stop button to drive away. Before her finger could push the control, another lorry positioned itself close to the passenger's side. They were wedged in. Overcome with despair, Samantha bowed her head in defeat.

Molly, desperation etched in her voice, implored, 'Mummy, Mummy, push the windscreen out.' Samantha stared at her daughter and watched Molly, her back resting on the seat, legs on the dashboard and feet pressed against the windscreen, demonstrating what was needed. 'I don't have the strength Mummy.'

Samantha nodded and positioned herself, ready to copy Molly. Her feet in place, she pushed with all her might, but nothing happened. Samantha adjusted her stance for another attempt. With her back hard against the seat, feet firmly on the windscreen and groaning under the strain, she heaved.

POP.

The intact windscreen dislodged and fell onto the car bonnet.

I did it.

Straightening herself, Samantha commanded, 'Come on, Molly, we have to go.' She began crawling from the car. Molly started to follow then remembered that Snowflake wasn't with them. She turned to search in the back seat. Scared by the drama, Snowflake was perched on the rear parcel shelf out of Molly's reach, her lead dangling down.

Samantha shouted in frustration, 'Come on Molly, this is no time to muck around.'

With outstretched hand, Molly called to the cat, 'Snowflake, Snowflake, there's a good kitty. Come here.'

The cat stared back; its whiskers twitched. *This is not the treatment I expect.*

Molly pleaded, 'Please, Snowflake, you have to hurry.'

The cat jumped down and scooping her up, Molly tucked Snowflake under her arm and, for the second time, started crawling from the car. 'Oh no, I've forgotten the playing cards.'

Samantha stared in utter disbelief as Molly ducked back inside the car again, yelling,

'What are you doing? Come on!'

Molly reached inside, rummaged through her day pack and found the deck of cards. She stuffed them into her pocket before scrambling out of the car.

Driven by panic and with no escape plan, Samantha and Molly started running.

Before working for Maxfield Transport, Eric Rundell from Bingley in West Yorkshire, served in the British Army, Royal Logistic Corps, as a driver transporting supplies. He'd resigned after his second tour of Afghanistan to spend more time with his family. Today, he was transporting goods from Leeds to Preston and then onto Whitehaven, a port town near the English Lake District. He was parked up in the heavy vehicle zone of the Lancaster Service Centre, seated behind the steering wheel of his idling articulated lorry, eating his lunch, a curry pie to be washed down with a can of soft drink. Conscious of diabetes in his family— his father—ordinarily he took a homemade lunch with him and drank water. Once a fortnight, he allowed himself the delight of some junk food, although he often felt bloated afterwards, a price worth paying. As he savoured the rich, crunchy pastry of his pie, he was interrupted by the distinctive, crunching sound of metal on metal, as a truck began scraping along the side of Samantha's hire car.

Glancing in his mirror, he saw the lorry, saying aloud, 'What's going on?'

He was about to do a recce when, in his passenger side mirror, he watched another lorry drifting towards the car. Eric Rundell slid across the seat, opening the door for a better look. Absorbed, watching as the front windscreen was kicked out by a woman who then clambered on to the bonnet followed shortly by a young girl, he paid little attention when his half-eaten pie dislodged from his hand and fell to the ground. The woman and child started running in his direction.

What's in the kid's hand? Is that a cat? No way, it can't be.

His eyes were drawn back to the two lorries. From each, a well-dressed man in a business suit, looking nothing at all like lorry drivers, was climbing down from their rigs.

'This is not right,' Eric Rundell said to himself in his broad Geordie accent. 'Not right at all.'

Eric Rundell was born at the Royal Victoria Infirmary in Newcastle upon Tyne, living in Whitley Bay until his parents separated when he was twelve years old. He moved, with his fourteen-year-old sister, Kendra, and mother, to Abbeystead, a tiny village in the middle of nowhere, or so he thought at the time. Now, it's described as a "Picturesque village in the Forest of Bowland, an area of outstanding natural beauty, in Lancashire, England."

Despite the arguments at home before his parents split, Eric felt the loss of his father, though he failed to understand it at the time. With his move came a change of school; his grades suffered, as did his behaviour. Kendra, on the other hand, immersed herself in her studies, becoming dux and school captain. As brother and sister, they were total opposites, the yin and yang, although yin and yang are seen as complementary, a balance between two opposites. After the separation, Eric's mother struggled with her son's behaviour. That was until Eric dropped the F-bomb at school one too many times.

It was the day of Eric's sixteenth birthday and he was seated outside the school principal's office, already on his last and final warning. The latest incident meant that suspension was imminent. All of his tutors wanted Eric Rundell kicked out of school for good. Alex Branner, the Principal, had turned the school's performance around in the last three years. She stood for no nonsense and demanded that students and teachers alike followed the rules. Dress codes were strictly enforced, and non-compliance resulted in demerit points. Using profanities was forbidden, as were sexist language and taunts, with all transgressions viewed through the prism of the school's five values.

Community
Service
Excellence
Integrity and Respect
Learning for Life.

Teachers and students were expected to live the school values or find somewhere else more aligned to their outlook. Alex Branner was in her mid-forties, a slim, athletic looking woman, who dressed like the mythical school mistress of the nineteen sixties in a tweed suit, sporting tortoiseshell thick-rimmed glasses.

The door opened and Eric Rundell raised his head to see Alex Branner standing watching him. In her flat and measured tone, she said, 'Mr Rundell, come inside.'

Turning, she walked to her desk and, when Eric entered, she pointed to the vacant chair in front of her and told him to take a seat. She let the silence grow between them until, after thirty seconds, she began to speak.

'Mr Rundell, I won't insult your intelligence by asking you why you're here today. That report precedes you. If it has been your desire to leave the school, then you have succeeded.'

Eric knew he was on a final warning and the consequence of further wrongdoing had been made clear to him. The realisation that he was about to be expelled was still a shock. He felt a pit form in his stomach and he swallowed hard a couple of times.

Alex Branner looked at him sternly. 'What is it you hope to do?'

On the previous occasions that he had been before the principal, if he'd answered at all, it was with a shrug of his shoulders, but not this time.

'Join the army, Miss.'

Eric Rundell's engagement with her caught Alex Branner by surprise. Sensing hope, albeit remote, she hesitated before removing her glasses and placing them down on the table in front of her. 'The army, like your father?'

'No Miss, not like my father. He drank too much and didn't give a fu...whoops, sorry Miss. He didn't care about us and I'm going to be different.'

After years of working with children, Alex Branner could spot the difference between sincerity and a confidence trickster; she knew when she was being played and this was not one of those occasions. She sensed a glimmer of hope surfacing in a disengaged boy, struggling to become a man.

'I believe you will, Mr Rundell.'

Eric bit his lip, fighting to stop tears welling in his eyes.

Not wanting Eric to be embarrassed into shutting down the conversation, the Head fired off another question, 'What are the entry requirements to become a soldier?'

'I can join now at sixteen and there are no educational requirements. The recruitment officer told me that there's more chance of being accepted if I'm a little older.'

'Well, Mr Rundell, it seems you have a choice to make.'

'A choice, Miss?'

'Yes, Mr Rundell. You may finish your education with us or leave us now in the hope you will be accepted into the army. It's entirely up to you. If you choose to stay, it must be because you want to be here and be the best man you can become. And no more swearing at all.'

Alex Branner paused and donned her glasses again. 'Mr Rundell, I won't ask you for an answer now. I want you to go home and sleep on it. Look deep into your heart, Mr Rundell. Either way, come and see me at nine o'clock sharp tomorrow morning.'

To this day, Eric Rundell remembered the promise he had made to himself that night, to be a good person and loving father. The sight of the child, Molly, fleeing, fear etched across her innocent face, emboldened Eric Rundell. He watched as a blue SUV, driven by a blonde-haired woman, drew up alongside one of the men. He could see that they were working together, and it wasn't for anyone's benefit, but their own.

This looks like a scene straight out of a Mafia movie. Should I get involved?

He made his mind up. In her baseball hat and yellow sunglasses, Molly reminded him of his seven-year-old daughter, Natalie, and it triggered in Eric Rundell his protective instincts. Before he realised what he was doing, he called out to the woman running, obviously the child's mother, 'Hey, Lassie!'

Samantha heard a shout coming from somewhere in front of her, as she and Molly ran in fear. To her right, Samantha noticed the articulated lorry, and the driver was leaning from the passenger's side door.

He called out again, 'Hey, Lassie!'

Samantha, her mind racing, driven by adrenaline, tried to understand what was happening.

What should I do? He could be one of them?

She stole a glance over her shoulder and spotted the man who had followed them onto the train, talking with the scrunchie woman. In an instant, any doubts Samantha harboured about the woman being a Chinese agent vanished and, worse, the woman was Caucasian; the implications were obvious–anyone she met could work for the Ministry of State Security, not only those of Asian origin. The truck driver calling her. He could be on their pay; were they being herded into a trap?

'Hey Lassie, this way, quickly now.' He could see from the woman's expression that she was wary of him, and why wouldn't she be? 'You must trust me; they're coming after you.'

What choice do I have? Samantha thought.

Reaching for Molly's hand, she guided her towards the idling truck. 'We have to trust him.'

'I know, Mummy.'

Eric Rundell held out his hand for Molly to take and, without a moment's hesitation, Molly released her grip on Samantha and transferred it to Eric as he said, his eyes meeting Molly's, 'One, two, three, and up you come, Lassie.' Eric Rundell's strength lifted Molly clean off her feet.

'Ooooh,' Molly gasped, as she and Snowflake were safely deposited inside the truck cabin.

He called down to Samantha, 'Come on, Lassie, climb up here. Quickly now.' Eric slid across to the driver's seat and checked to see if Samantha was on board.

Samantha placed her left foot on the step of the truck and, taking hold of the grab rail, hauled herself up and, when she pulled the door closed behind her, the lorry was already moving.

Eric Rundell checked in his mirrors and watched a man, the one who'd been talking to the woman from the SUV, hurriedly climb into a truck driven by someone else. The lorry rolled forward and began to follow them. Speaking to himself, he said, 'I hope they are speed limited like I am or we'll be run off the motorway.' As he approached the Service Centre exit, Eric Rundell had to make a split-second decision, turn right for the M6, or left and Greaves Hill Lane which would take them into the countryside on narrow stone and hedge lined roads barely wide enough for a car, let alone a heavy articulated vehicle. He'd glimpsed the lorry driver trailing him through its windscreen and, like the man talking to the woman in the SUV, he wore a business suit. The driver didn't resemble a truckie, but he knew looks could be deceptive.

As a teenager, Eric Rundell had lived close to their current location, the village of Abbeystead. He knew the back roads well.

If I go left, they'll have difficulty passing me and I reckon I can outrun them.

Banking on his skills as a professional driver and his local knowledge, Eric turned left and accelerated away from the Service Centre, constantly checking his mirrors as he changed up through the gears.

'Now then, Lassie, what's going on?'

Samantha had not imagined a scenario such as this and pretended not to hear the question while she sought a palatable explanation. Telling this stranger that her husband was a spy wasn't an option. She realised that she'd have to say something or risk him stopping and handing them over to their pursuers.

Eric glanced at Samantha, indicating he was expecting a response, but it was Molly who spoke.

'My father is a spy, espionage, you know.'

Eric fought the urge to smile. 'Really? Are you spies as well and is this why you are being chased?' From the corner of his eye, Eric watched Molly's reaction. She scrunched up her face.

'Don't be silly, of course not. We didn't know that Daddy was one either, not until recently... when we were in Spain.'

'Molly!' Samantha interjected, her tone implying that she say no more.

Eric changed into another gear. *I could almost believe the child's story, or maybe they are practiced con artists. But that wouldn't account for why they were being chased... then again, it might.*

'Go on with the story... Oh, sorry, I don't know your names. I'm Eric, by the way.'

Molly blurted, 'I'm Molly, and this is Snowflake. Snowflake is my cat, and she helped save us in Spain.'

Samantha sighed and shook her head before saying, 'Hi, I'm Samantha.'

Eric nodded as he checked the mirrors, noticing those pursuing Samantha and Molly were close. 'Molly, tell me more of your spy story.'

Annoyed, believing Eric's tone suggested that she was telling a fairy tale, Molly mumbled under her breath, 'It's not a story.'

They were driving on a single lane road, barely wide enough for the lorry to fit. Visible through the front windscreen, an oncoming car suddenly appeared from around a corner. Samantha screamed.

Eric hit the brakes, and the nose of the truck dived as it slowed. Seconds before impact, the car swerved into a spot, an unofficial passing space that lined the roadway. Samantha expected the oncoming driver to toot his horn or wave a fist, but he held his silence. Sensing Samantha's puzzlement, Eric said, 'The locals are used to meeting buses and tractors on these roads. Most drivers will pull over when they see a vehicle approaching, or back up if that's not possible.' Eric changed gears. 'You were telling me, Molly, that you learned your father was a spy when you were in Spain?'

Molly looked first to her mother then at Eric, her demeanour showing she was going to reveal something secret. 'We learned my daddy *wasn't* a good spy.'

'Oh! I wasn't expecting that. And who's chasing you? The British or the....' He let the silence hang, inviting Molly or Samantha to fill the gap.'

Samantha sighed again. 'My husband works for the Chinese State Security Service and it is they who are chasing us.'

Eric glanced at Molly. From her hue, he'd guessed that she was of mixed race, Asian and European.

It could make sense. I'm inclined to believe Molly.

'What do the Chinese want with you?'

Samantha answered before Molly could respond. 'They want to take us to Beijing and we are afraid that if we go to China, we will never return. That's why we're on the run. From the Chinese and my husband.' Samantha folded her arms.

Eric had read in the newspapers of the Uyghur internment camps in China's Xinjian province in the far west of the country and of the souring relations between the United Kingdom and China. With the backdrop of Hong Kong and Huawei, he was inclined to believe the stories of Uyghur abuses, and feared that Samantha and Molly would be detained.

'What about the British security services, won't they help you?'

'My husband is a traitor.'

'Is anyone helping you?'

Molly held her tongue, though she wanted to tell Eric about Olivia.

Samantha shook her head. 'No, we are on our own.'

'Fair enough.' Eric checked in his mirrors; the lorry was directly behind them and, as they swung around a bend in the road, he glimpsed the following SUV. Slipping into a barely understandable Geordie accent, he said, 'Bugger this! We'll go down past old Henderson's place. There's a pothole on the corner that'll put you on your roof if you don't know it's coming! Best you hang on pets. I'll need to put some distance between them and us if this is to work.' He changed down gears to build up speed when an agricultural tractor, its driver unconcerned about other travellers, meandered out of a farm gate and turned in front of Eric, forcing him to brake heavily. Eric glanced at his speedometer; they were crawling along the road at fifteen miles an hour.

'Stupid bugger,' he cursed.

Honking the truck's horn, Eric yelled as the farmer ignored the commotion, 'Get out of the way!'

Kang Long, in hot pursuit of Samantha and Molly, narrowly avoided hitting Eric Rundell's lorry as it pulled up. His passenger, Michael Tan, saying, 'What's happening?'

'Beats me, can't see a thing.'

'Are they going slow on purpose?'

Kang Long shrugged his shoulders. 'Probably a slow-moving vehicle, tractor maybe, on this road.'

'You might be right.' His two-way radio crackled to life as Ellen Goldsworthy, travelling behind, demanded a situation report.

Michael Tan, his manner unhurried, shared Kang Long's observation, adding, 'They're not going anywhere.'

'What are you doing about it?'

Michael Tan peered at Kang Long, chuckled and said, 'She's getting her knickers in a real knot!' He pushed the talk button on the radio. 'We are monitoring the situation.'

I'll give you monitoring the situation.

Ellen Goldsworthy fired back her reply. 'Listen to me carefully, Mr Tan. I want you to climb from your truck on to the back of the one in front. Travel along the roof to the cabin and kill the driver while they are still travelling at a snail's pace. Do I make myself clear?'

Michael Tan looked at Kang Long. 'She's nuts.'

Kang Long nodded. 'She's also the boss and we all know what happens when you disobey: chop, chop. I'll nudge up as close as I can. You'll be able to jump off the bonnet and on to their truck.'

'That's easy for you to say.' Michael Tan took a deep breath. 'Okay, fine, just don't run me over if I fall.'

As Kang moved the lorry closer, Michael Tan opened the door and placed his feet on the railing. Manoeuvring along the step, he hauled himself onto the bonnet, and breathed out in relief.

We are going so slowly, it's easier than I thought.

Pushing himself upright, Michael Tan swayed until he found his balance, then walked to the front of the truck. The gap between the two vehicles was too wide for him to cross. He signalled for Kang to drive closer and, when they were all but touching, held up his hand for Kang Long to hold the position. Heart racing, Michael Tan stretched out his arms, ready to leap the gap.

It's now or never.

He launched himself into the air and landed, wrapping his fingers tightly around the door cam-bars that ran vertically up the trailer securing the doors. His weight supported by his arms; Michael Tan's feet hung in the air as he scrambled to secure a footing. He breathed out.

Got yeah!

Kang Long slowed his truck and drifted back ten yards in case his partner fell from the truck.

Using the bars like ropes, Michael Tan climbed. Reaching the top, he dragged himself onto the roof before crawling a couple of yards forward and standing. Their slow speed meant that the head wind was minimal, but the swaying and bumping of the truck as it drove down the uneven country lane made maintaining his balance difficult. Removing his pistol from its shoulder holster, ready for when he reached the target, he placed one step after the other and moved towards the cab.

Inside the driver's cab, Eric was unaware of the advance of Michael Tan as he tapped his fingers impatiently on the steering wheel.

Come on! He muttered inside his head, frustrated by their slow progress. With his local knowledge, Eric knew they were approaching the Chipping crossroad.

Turn off will you. Go left or right, I don't care.

The tractor travelled straight ahead.

Damn!

With Michael Tan on the roof of the lorry, Ellen Goldsworthy wanted to minimise the risk of escape, so she checked her GPS display, searching for a way around the vehicle transporting Molly and Samantha. The map showed that, if she turned left at Chipping Road and right onto Anyon Lane, she would cut them off at Dolphinholme. Once past Chipping Road, with no other turns from Greaves Hill Lane, Molly and Samantha had to come that way.

I've got you now.

Checking his side mirrors, Eric caught sight of the SUV as it raced off down Chipping Road.

'Darn!'

'What is it?' Samantha asked.

'The blonde lady in the SUV, the one following you, she's trying to cut us off.' He gritted his teeth in frustration. He knew the pothole wasn't far away but, if the tractor didn't move out of the way soon, it would all be over. 'I'll have to persuade the farmer to pull over and let us pass.'

Samantha said, 'What do you mean by persuade?'

'Best you both hang on because I'm going to give the tractor a gentle nudge from behind.' As Eric finished speaking, the tractor came to a standstill, causing Eric to brake heavily, the lorry rocking to a sudden halt.

'What the ...'

Before Eric could finish his utterance, the tractor turned right and drove into a farm gate, leaving the road ahead clear.

The sudden stop unbalanced Michael Tan and, losing his footing, he fell face first onto the roof of the trailer.

With the tractor gone, Eric put his foot on the accelerator. The lorry picked up speed, rocking left and right as it moved forward. The swaying motion caused Michael Tan to be tossed to the side and, before he could steady himself, he was thrown from the trailer, landing on a boggy grass verge running alongside of the lane. Winded, he was still for a moment, trying to gather his senses before sitting up, the soft ground having broken his fall. Kang Long watched his partner plunge and pulled up, expecting the worst. In disbelief, he saw his colleague as his head popped up from the grass.

Samantha asked, 'Are they still behind us?'

Eric changed up another gear as his lorry continued to build speed. He glanced in the mirrors. 'They seemed to have stopped.

No, hang on, they are moving again. We're not far from the Henderson's place. If we can build up a lead, enough so they don't see us brake, they may hit the hole and flip.'

The speed they were now travelling filled Samantha with fear and she reached for Molly's hand, but Molly didn't take it. In stunned silence, Samantha watched as they dashed along the narrow country lane, hedges racing by in a blur. She glanced at Molly, who was grinning as she calmly stroked Snowflake, barely able to contain her excitement. Noticing her mother, Molly said, 'I love this and so does Snowflake.'

'It's coming up soon,' Eric said, as he pumped the brakes, wiping off speed. A moment later, he accelerated again.

'Here we go, hang on tight.'

Eric fought for control as the front left wheel sank into the giant hole, lifting the right wheels clear off the ground. If he hadn't been gripping the steering wheel in anticipation, it would have been ripped free of his hands. Samantha gasped, her mouth hanging open as the trailer wheels smashed through the pothole. The lorry teetered on the brink of disaster as Eric battled for control.

'Come on old girl, back you come.'

The wheels on the right-hand side of the lorry crashed down onto the bitumen with a thud, sending the truck swaying right, then left. For a moment, Samantha thought that Eric had lost control.

Eric Rundell shot a glance at Molly and then Samantha as he said, his voice calm, a contrast to the way he was feeling, 'That wasn't too bad, was it?'

He eased on the brakes to slow the lorry while checking in the mirrors to see what was about to unfold behind them.

From the cabin of their lorry, Michael Tan glimpsed the truck across the fields. Pointing, he said to Kang Long, 'The boss won't be pleased if you let them get away. Step on it.'

Kang Long grinned. 'If I'd known you were such a backseat driver, I'd have left you in the ditch. In case you haven't noticed, I'm gaining on them and I'll have...'

BANG.

CRUNCH.

While speeding through a sweeping corner, the lorry's front wheel hit thin air as the road disappeared into a mammoth pothole, the sound of the impact echoing through the cabin. The steering wheel was ripped from Kang's hands and, before he could react, the lorry altered course, heading towards a field. Kang, regaining his grip, turned the wheel violently in the opposite direction while braking, a combination that unsettled the truck's balance.

It began to topple.

All Kang Long could do as they went over was to yell, 'Hang on!'

CRUNCH - SMASH - BANG

The lorry hit the ground on its side, slid along the road and came to a halt, its nose resting against a hedge.

Eric watched his pursuers come to grief and eased his lorry to a standstill. Turning to Samantha, he said. 'Lassie, that woman in the SUV is coming the other way. There is no way forward or back if we stay on this road.' He pointed out of the passenger side window. 'See those trees? If you follow them, you'll come out on Anyon Lane. On the other side of the road is a farmer who might help you. If you two want to get away, there's no time for discussion. You need to go, and now. I'll try to delay her for a bit.'

Samantha hesitated.

'Go!'

'Come on Mummy. Snowflake and I are ready and you must be too.'

'Good luck,' Eric Rundell called as Samantha and Molly climbed down from his lorry.

He waited for them to climb over the hedge and into the field before pulling away. The junction in Dolphinholme, where Anyon Lane and Greaves Hill Lane met, wasn't far up the road and, although he didn't expect to make it there before the SUV, he still hoped that he might. To his surprise, he arrived first and watched the SUV fast approaching on the left. Knowing that the woman would expect Samantha and Molly to be on board, he drove through the intersection to lead her on a merry chase and away from Molly and her mother.

Ellen Goldsworthy hit the steering wheel with her fist in frustration as she slowed, coming to a standstill, expecting the lorry driven by her associates to be in hot pursuit. As she waited and watched Eric Rundell drive off into the distance, she picked up the radio and snapped. 'Where are you?'

Michael Tan answered, 'We've come to grief.'

'Are you injured?'

'Nothing broken, only cuts and bruises, but the truck's a mess.'

Although tempted to continue on her own, Ellen Goldsworthy weighed up the situation and decided against it.

'Alright, I'll head for you.'

She wasn't concerned about the wellbeing of her associates, but she wanted to retrieve them before the police arrived. Were they to be taken into custody, the incident could turn messy and create an embarrassing diplomatic incident. As Ellen Goldsworthy turned down Greaves Hill Lane, she muttered to herself, 'Don't think you've outsmarted me, Samantha Liew. Nobody does that, especially some upstart, bloody amateur.'

Eric Rundell was surprised when the SUV didn't pursue him. He slowed the lorry in contemplation of going back for his passengers. *No, Eric, they are safer without you. Samantha, Molly, and Snowflake are on their own now.* He sped away; his mind filled with doubt.

CHAPTER 14
Troubled Mind

Olivia sat impatiently on the train to Manchester which, after the aborted conversation with Samantha, was taking an eternity. When she arrived, she needed to make her way to the Service Centre in Lancaster, their last known location, before she could start the search. She'd rung Claudia when Samantha's call ended abruptly and left her a cryptic message. Knowing that she was operating without help from MI6, though Stephen's recent intervention may have changed that, she ruminated for an hour before calling James. Olivia was not surprised when he told her that Samantha's phone was no longer transmitting, either turned off or broken. She took a deep breath and, with nothing to lose, asked whether MI6 was going to or had gathered intelligence from the Service Centre, which would be useful in tracking Samantha.

James said, 'We are looking into it, but it's still early days. I'm sorry, Olivia, but I can't share anything without Stephen's authorisation. Now that he knows of your involvement, I'm sure he'll want me to assist you. I will ask him, I promise.'

'As always, James, you've been most generous. If I may ask another question? I tried calling Claudia, but to no avail. Is this something to be concerned about?'

'No. As part of her current assignment, we expected this to happen. She's been out of reach for three days now and we are not concerned.'

Hanging up, Olivia closed her eyes, hoping that a nap would speed the journey. Restless sleep eluded her and the trip dragged on until the PA system gave the news Olivia wanted.

The next stop is Manchester; Manchester is the next stop.

Olivia exhaled in frustration.

Other than driving to Lancaster, what else can I do? This situation is hopeless. I'm hopeless.

Is this despair I hear, my love? See what happens when I'm not about? You catch Max disease.

If I may, kind Sir, please exchange your banter for a solution. Otherwise, would you kindly leave my head?

You, my love, require the assistance of the Agency. I suggest you try our friend Inspector Axel and ask him to apply some pressure.

Why didn't you suggest that earlier?

Olivia dialled the Inspector, and to her relief, he answered. 'Sorry, Inspector. It sounds as though I've woken you. It's Olivia.'

Inspector Axel looked at the clock on the bedside table. It was almost midnight. 'That's alright Olivia. I'm in Tokyo, so it's night here, but it's always a pleasure to talk with you.'

Olivia felt her heart sink. She'd known that Axel was overseas, but Tokyo was on the other side of the world, too far away to proffer help. 'Likewise. Japan, Inspector. That's a long way away.'

'Yes, and I'm flying to Istanbul in Turkey tomorrow morning. I've been tracking Linda Orr. She flew to Berlin, New Delhi and onto Japan, where I lost contact with her in Nagano City in the Chubu region. I've been here for three days. This evening, a report came in that she has taken a flight to Turkey, which is why I'm heading there next.'

Olivia felt compelled to issue a word of caution to her friend. 'I fear that Linda Orr is leading you to Sumela Monastery. It would be wiser to concentrate your efforts on where she went in Nagano City and why she was there.'

'That may be so, Olivia, but Stephen has directed me otherwise.'

'Sumela is possibly a trap. Be careful.'

'Yes, I will. Now Olivia, I doubt you've rung me for a social chat, though I would be pleased if you have.'

'I have a dilemma, Inspector. I've lost contact with Molly and Samantha, and Claudia isn't answering her phone.' Olivia sighed and then explained all that had transpired.

'Well, Olivia, you have had a busy day. I'll call James and persuade him to share what they know from the Lancaster Service Centre with you. That might give you a lead.' Inspector Axel paused. 'If Molly and Samantha are heading to Scotland, perhaps hoping to hide in a remote location, I know someone who can help: Detective Sally Mars from Stornoway, we worked together following the disappearance of Charles Scott who went missing from Barra Island in the Outer Hebrides and who was linked to the death of John Moss. I'll text you her number and call her for you. I will also leave a message for Claudia, which will give me a chance to tell her where Linda Orr is directing me. Sorry I can't be there with you, Olivia—I know I'm not much help from here.'

'You've been more than helpful, Inspector. Now, I think I'm keeping you awake, so I'll bid you a good night.'

'Before you go, Olivia, I hope you don't mind me asking but, how are you since the passing of Max?'

Olivia sighed. 'As well as can be expected. I appreciated your wishes of condolence, along with the many others.'

'When Claudia and I are back in the UK, we will get together and drink a toast to the wonderful man.'

Olivia felt a lump rise in her throat. 'I would like that very much, Inspector. Because of COVID, Max didn't have a proper sendoff.' Olivia swallowed, pushing down the emotion which threatened to break in her voice. She coughed. 'Excuse me, Inspector. I've organised for his ashes to be sent to the UK. He wished to be buried in the churchyard where we were married, with its sweeping views of the ocean. I would be honoured if you and Claudia would join me there.'

'It will be our pleasure.'

Manchester. Manchester, the train is stopping at Manchester station.

'I have to go. We've arrived. Good bye, Inspector.'

Putting her phone away, Olivia stood and looked around for her luggage.

Oh, that's right, I don't have any, not even my day pack with my smalls, I've left that somewhere. This is going to be another Operation Underpants with no clean undies!

The thought of it made Olivia shiver with her memories.

Stepping from the train and onto the platform, Olivia let the crowd thin before making her way out of the station. She paused in the middle of the footpath.

I've had all this way to decide my next course of action and I still don't know what to do.

I miss you, Max. What would you do?

That's obvious, Olivia, have a cup of tea.

'Yes, a cup of tea, Britain's answer to everything.' Olivia smiled. A cup of tea was always Max's solution.

That's my Olivia. There's no point driving to the Service Centre. With nothing else to do until Molly posts another card, find a hotel room for the night. A nice one, of course, suitable for Lady Olivia Suzanne Elizabeth Huggins.

I feel so helpless, Max. What happens if Molly doesn't post another card or worse, the Chinese have apprehended them?

Olivia felt a light touch on her arm. A woman, no more than twenty-two said, her voice kind, 'Can I help you? You seem lost.'

Olivia smiled. 'Was I talking to myself again?'

'Yes, I think you were.'

'This morning at the airport, a kind man asked if I was okay, and now you have done the same. My faith in humanity has been restored and I thank you for your concern. I recently lost my husband of over sixty years to COVID and I've taken to talking to him as if he is still here. I'm told it's quite normal.' Olivia raised both of her eyebrows and grinned. 'Thankfully, I haven't yet started answering myself back. I'm not from these parts. Is there an agreeable place where I can have a nice, hot cup of tea?'

'Yes, there's a quaint tea house that I think you will enjoy and it's close. If you like, I could walk with you, unless someone is meeting you.'

With the memories of the morning fresh, Olivia chuckled. 'I'm Olivia. What's your name, Love?'

'Eileen.'

'The man of this morning asked me the same thing, Eileen. I must look like a lost soul.' Olivia held her arm for Eileen to take. 'As my good friend Claudia would tell me if she were here, *Lead on Macduff.*'

Olivia and Eileen had been walking and chatting easily for ten minutes when Eileen pointed at a sign.

'Here it is, OHAYO TEA. My friends love this place. It has fruit teas and a wide selection of bubble teas, plus their signature Brown Sugar Tapioca Milk and original Milk Tea. We come here all the time and I know you are going to love it. Oh, you do like bubble tea, don't you?'

Ha ha, I'm so looking forward to this.

Olivia had never heard of bubble tea, let alone tasted it. Not wanting to appear ungrateful for Eileen's generosity, Olivia said. 'I discovered bubble tea a couple of years ago. My departed husband, Max, and I were late converts. What's your favourite, my dear?'

A late convert? I don't think so.

'Go away.'

Eileen looked at Olivia, disappointment written across her face.

Mortified, Olivia placed her hand on Eileen's arm. 'Not you, my dear.'

An insightful countenance replaced Eileen's disappointment as she said, 'Max, your late husband, you were speaking to him?'

Olivia nodded.

'Is he still annoying, even though he's...' Eileen put her hand over her mouth. 'Oh, that's insensitive of me. Sorry.'

Olivia laughed, 'No, no, you got it in one.'

I resemble that remark. That's a joke, Olivia.

Ignoring Max's voice, Olivia said. 'Now, my dear, you were telling me your favourite tea.'

Eileen grinned. 'Oh, it has to be Honeydew.'

'Honeydew! What a coincidence. That's exactly what I was going to order. How spooky is that?'

'That is freaky.'

Eileen walked Olivia to the door before bidding her farewell. Olivia stood for a moment and watched Eileen away into the distance before staring at the OHAYO TEA sign and stepping inside. *Max, bubble tea is not what we were expecting.*

I thought you were a late convert, Ha ha. Might I suggest you forgo the Honeydew and try a fruit tea instead. Best not ask for an English Breakfast or Earl Grey.

Olivia smiled.

Even though she'd been sitting for four and a half hours on the train after the walk from the station, Olivia was pleased to take the weight off her feet. With Honeydew tea in hand, Olivia watched the world go by outside the window, her mind churning her conundrum. 'What now, Max?' Olivia said aloud.

Patience, my Love.

Her phone sounded, making Olivia jump and causing her to spill her tea.

James MIT.

'Hello, James,' Olivia said excitedly, hoping Inspector Axel had been persuasive.

'Hi, Olivia. Where are you?'

'I'm at a teahouse in Manchester. And James, I never thought I would live to see this day, but it's a teahouse where you drink your tea through a straw and the tea has floating things in it.'

James laughed. 'Bubble tea, a trendy fad like those so-called gourmet speciality doughnuts which are ordinary doughnuts glazed and coated with toppings at three times the price. I only wish I'd come up with these ideas. Then I would be sailing a yacht to the south of France rather than sitting here at my desk.'

'Yes, James, but you wouldn't have the pleasure of talking to me.'

'That is so true, Olivia. Now, why I called. Ten minutes ago, the person emptying the post box at the Lancaster Service centre accidentally dropped the bag and a playing card with a cat motif fell to the ground. It had no postage stamp but was addressed to MI6, so the postie rang us to see if it was something important. Scrawled in large letters on the back was the word Inverness. Molly and Samantha are heading for Inverness, Scotland.'

Olivia breathed a sigh of relief, momentarily forgetting Molly and Samantha were being chased. 'Any news of them after Lancaster?'

'You know Inspector Axel rang me?'

'He told me he would.'

'He insisted we take care of you, as if we wouldn't, Olivia. Anyway, back to the reason I called. We have accessed security CCTV footage from the Lancaster Service Centre and it shows Samantha and Molly getting into a lorry. The lorry is owned by a company called Maxfield Transport and was being driven by an Eric Rundell. Samantha and Molly were being pursued by two known Chinese operatives, Michael Tan and Kang Long. Interestingly, they were operating with a woman who we don't know, although we are working on it. To cut a long story short, Olivia, we've spoken to Eric Rundell. Having evaded the pursuers, he dropped Molly and Samantha in farmland near Dolphinholme. We are making a working assumption that Samantha and Molly are free and are making their way to Inverness. By what means, we don't yet know.'

This was the news that Olivia had been waiting for, yet it set her mind racing and panic coursed through her veins.

Inverness, what do I do now?

Having not experienced anxiety before, Olivia struggled to understand her reactions and her feelings were not something she was willing to share with James. After all, she was the famed Olivia. Shaking her head from side to side, Olivia tried to clear the fog that was clouding her mind.

Pull yourself together, Olivia!

It's okay, my Love. We will do this together as we always have. Team Olivia and Max.

James, having finished speaking, waited for Olivia's response. He let the silence hang for ten seconds before asking, fearing that her mobile phone had lost its signal. 'Are you there, Olivia?'

Her voice strong and oozing with confidence, Olivia said, 'Sorry, James, my mind was elsewhere, deciding whether I should rent a car and drive to Inverness this evening.'

'Hire a car Olivia? Why would you want to do that? I have taken the liberty and booked you on a flight from Manchester to Inverness. It's just over an hour's journey.'

Olivia glanced at her watch. 'When?'

James detected a sense of unease in Olivia's voice, contrasting the confident persona she was trying to project. 'In the morning, Olivia. No point in rushing up there tonight and we don't believe that Samantha and Molly will arrive until tomorrow. You've had a long and harrowing day—an early flight from Spain, a kidnapping, a car crash, and now a journey to Manchester. You've accomplished more in a single day than most of us could in a lifetime. Tonight, you'll be staying at the Stock Exchange Hotel, in the luxurious Board Room Suite. I've reserved a table for you at seven in their renowned restaurant, The Bull and Bear. The flight in the morning is at nine thirty and a taxi will pick you up from the hotel at eight, the driver meeting you in the lobby. When you arrive at Inverness Airport, a hire car will be waiting there for you. The best I could do at short notice was a Kia Sportage. I understand they are quite good. If Claudia were here, she'd want some V8 Supercharged thing. How that woman will manage in the coming Electric Vehicle world, I have no idea. Also, Stephen has approved the monitoring of Samantha's bank accounts. If she makes any transactions, we'll inform you right away.

Olivia was overwhelmed with relief, and her fears dissipated. 'That sounds perfect, James. Thank you. I am slightly confused. Why the sudden change in heart? What's changed?'

'Yes, Olivia, you're right, something has altered. Stephen wants to speak to you; hold the line and I will transfer you.'

James has always been a good man.

Olivia took a sip of tea and nodded and said, 'Yes, he has.'

James scrunched up his face. 'Sorry, Olivia, I missed that. What was it you were saying?'

'Oh nothing, James. I was talking to the waiter. She asked me if I'd finished my tea, and I told her I had.'

'Okay, good luck, Olivia. I'm transferring you. Bye.'

There was silence before Stephen Walls said, 'Good afternoon, Olivia.'

'Hello, Stephen.'

'I hope you are recovering from this morning's ordeal and have had a relaxing train journey to Manchester.'

'Yes, thank you, Stephen. On both accounts.'

'Good. Well, Olivia, as is the way in the world of espionage, things have changed markedly. We operate in a dynamic environment, where getting an orderly picture is hard. When I dropped you at the station, we didn't appreciate that an unknown female Caucasian Chinese agent is operating on UK soil. The Foreign Secretary is concerned, especially at this time when we have heightened tension in the UK-Chinese relationship. As you will be aware, the friction between the United Kingdom and China has been growing in recent months over a series of issues, including the tech firm Huawei, the political future of Hong Kong and human rights in Xinjiang. In retaliation, China has increased its activities against Britain, in what our military planners call the *grey zone*. This refers to aggression somewhere between traditional concepts of war and peace, like cyber-attacks and disinformation campaigns. The HMS Queen Elizabeth aircraft carrier with 18 F-35B stealth fighters, is leading the largest contingent of warships since the Falklands War of 1982, through Asian waters on port visits to Japan and South Korea. This carrier strike group, known as CSG-21, includes two Type 45 destroyers, HMS Defender, and HMS Diamond; two Type 23 anti-submarine frigates, HMS Kent, and HMS Richmond; and the Royal Fleet Auxiliary's RFA Fort

Victoria and RFA Tidespring. Accompanying the strike group is a Royal Navy Astute-class submarine fitted with Tomahawk cruise missiles and American destroyer USS The Sullivans, outfitted with the Aegis missile-defence system and the Dutch frigate HNLMS Evertsen.'

'The recent security and foreign policy review, *Global Britain in a Competitive Age*, describes China as the biggest state-based threat to the UK's economic security. It also characterised China as an authoritarian state with a different value system that poses challenges to the UK and its allies. We will continue to work with China on some global issues, but we are increasing the protection of our critical national infrastructure, institutions and sensitive technology, and strengthening the resilience of our critical supply chains so that we can engage with confidence. We will not hesitate to stand up for our values and interests where they are threatened.'

'This maritime deployment is part of the UK's positioning in the Indo-Pacific and a response to the rising threat of China. The carrier strike group will conduct freedom of navigation operations in disputed areas of the South China Sea and take part in military exercises along with the U.S., France, Canada, Australia, and Japan. CSG-21 will arrive in these waters soon. The Chinese Government in response to what they see as Britain's provocative action, has been steadily ramping up its anti-UK rhetoric and its retaliatory threats. As the Australian Home Affairs secretary, Michael Pezzullo said, "The drums of war are beating". Scotland, HMNB Clyde is the home of all our submarines, while RAF Lossiemouth is our Quick Reaction Alert Station North and the home of three Typhoon squadrons.' Stephen paused...

'As part of a new historic Australia-UK-U.S. alliance, Britain and the United States are set to announce a nuclear submarine deal with Australia. Only a limited number of countries can run nuclear submarines, so Australia will join an exclusive club. This announcement will anger some of our allies, the French in particular. Needless to say, the Chinese will be furious and will slam the move. This is not the time to have Chinese agents wandering around in Scotland. So, track this woman down, find out who she is and, if she or any of her associates, Michael Tan and Kang Long, go near any of our military bases, you are authorised to take whatever action is necessary. This is now a matter of national security.'

As Olivia listened to Stephen, she felt that war talk about China was juvenile; if he'd told her this to instil a sense of urgency in her, the sentiment was wasted. When Stephen finished speaking, Olivia said, 'The Chinese will be in Scotland because of Samantha and Molly, not a carrier strike group sailing through the South China sea.'

'It's a risk we are not prepared to take. The order stands.'

'I understand, Stephen. From the Service Centre footage, do you have a picture of this woman?'

'It won't be of much help. It's very granular, not something we could use in making a match, but I'll have James send it, along with photos of the two men she's working with, which we have on file.'

Olivia felt her frustrations rising. 'What of Samantha and Molly? Did the Foreign Secretary agree to their protection?'

'She is still considering the request, Olivia. I believe it is looking promising.'

Olivia was from a generation that didn't argue with superiors but felt that Samantha and Molly had become pawns in a wider game. 'Are MI6 about to use Molly and Samantha as bait to lure this mysterious woman into the open? They are innocents; such a move would be reprehensible.'

Stephen was surprised by Olivia's observation. 'Bait, how so?'

'By delaying protection.'

'The granting of protection is a matter for the Secretary, Olivia. It takes time. It is not linked to this woman, but she is connected to Samantha and Molly, as are you. That's why the task is assigned to you as a British agent.'

Weasel words

'Max!'

Stephen waited for Olivia to continue but, from her tone, the word *Max* sounded like a statement rather than the beginning of a sentence. It made no sense.

After a momentary pause, Olivia said, 'Max, would agree with you, Stephen.'

'Indeed.'

'He would. Which reminds me. Stephen, I'm currently unarmed and without official identification.'

'I'm aware of that, Olivia, and have asked James to make the necessary arrangements. If there are no further questions, I wish you good luck and, as always, be careful.'

'Thank you, Stephen.'

Olivia placed her mobile phone on the bench in front of her and stared out of the window, taking in what Stephen had told her. She took a mouthful of tea. *Max, this bubble tea is like sipping sago through a straw.*

I won't say I told you so, however you did choose honeydew!

Yes, I liked the name.

I rest my case your worship.

CHAPTER 15
Land Rover

A Field Near Dolphinholme

Molly, with Snowflake trailing behind on a lead, looked over her shoulder and called, 'Come on, Mummy, keep up or the nasty people will see us. You, too, Snowflake.'

The cat raised its head, as if to say, *You could carry me.*

'Okay', Molly said, scooping the cat up in her arms.

Samantha let out a muffled cry, her foot finding another muddy puddle. Peering down at her sodden shoe, she didn't notice the fresh cow pat until she stepped in it. Samantha squealed, 'Yuk.'

Molly bit her lip to stop herself from laughing. 'Come on, Mummy.'

Samantha, now on firmer ground, stared at her daughter, imploring her to wait. One at a time, Samantha wiped her shoes clean using the long grass. As Eric Rundell had instructed, they followed the tree line until they reached the hedgerow and Anyon Lane. Across the road, two hundred yards to their left, they spotted the farm yard; three hundred yards to the right were the town limits of Dolphinholme.

Samantha, to herself said, 'Which way, left or right? There will be a bus stop in the village where we could catch a bus to a larger town, one with a railway station. We could then catch a train to a city or hire another car.'

Pleased with her reasoning, Samantha headed towards a wooden farm gate partially hidden by a hedge. She intended to walk along the road into Dolphinholme and had taken a few steps when she realised Molly wasn't following. Samantha turned and, copying her daughter, said in good humour, 'Come on, Molly, keep up.'

Molly's face was stern as she held Snowflake in one hand and planted the other on her hip. She shook her head in defiance and spat, 'No!'

'No?'

Molly pointed to the road. 'Look, Mummy, we can't wander along the road as if we don't have a care in the world. That nasty woman is driving around and waiting at a bus stop. If that's your plan, meandering around in a tiny village for who knows how long is asking for trouble. We are on the run, Mummy, not on a leisurely Sunday stroll in the park. We need stealth and cunning if we are to get away.'

Samantha copied her daughter, placing her hands on her hips. 'Do we now? And you have a better plan?'

'As it happens, I do. We need cover, so Mummy, we stay on this side of the hedge until we are opposite the farmhouse. When the road is clear, we cross over and knock on the farmhouse door, right? We tell them we have broken down and ask if they can call for a taxi. Look at us, mother, daughter and cat. We won't be viewed with suspicion. We might even be invited in for afternoon tea while we wait.' Molly smiled, 'There are some advantages of living in a sexist world; if you've got it, then flaunt it.' She fluttered her eyelids comically.

Samantha scrunched up her face but smiled. 'Sexist world, meandering along the road, stealth, cunning, where on earth has all of that come from?'

Molly opened her mouth to tell her mother that she reads a lot but Samantha continued, 'Anyway, your plan won't work. Where's our broken-down car?'

'Okay, my plan is not perfect. What would you say to the farmer?' Molly put Snowflake on the ground.

The question took Samantha by surprise. ''Well... that I had a fight with my husband and demanded that he stop and let us out, but accidentally left my phone in the car. I feel a little foolish now so would prefer to take a taxi home, rather than face humiliation by ringing him to come and pick us up.'

'Oh, Mummy, well done. That's an excellent story. I wish I'd thought of that. Let's do it.'

Before Samantha could respond, Molly walked along the hedge towards the farmyard. Rooted to the spot, she watched her daughter and shook her head in disbelief.

What just happened?

Shrugging her shoulders, Samantha said, 'Oh well, as Molly said, let's do it.'

She fell in behind her daughter and, when they reached a gateway in the hedge opposite the farm, stopped. Molly lifted Snowflake into her arms before scanning the road. When she was satisfied that the coast was clear, she said, her voice a whisper, 'Let's go, Mummy.'

The farm yard led to a traditional eighteenth century, double storey, brick-built detached farm house with adjoining barn and ancillary agricultural buildings nearby. They looked about and, seeing no one, Molly led Samantha to the white front door of the house, stepping back as she said, 'Okay, Mummy, you knock.'

Samantha raised her fist and, as she was about to knock on the door, Molly called, 'Wait a moment, Mummy!'

Molly passed Snowflake to her mother and removed her hat and sunglasses, placing them in her pocket. 'That's better, Mummy.

It's best if I look like a child, as young as possible.' She gave a childish grin and held out her hands for Snowflake as Samantha passed the cat to her daughter. 'Okay, Mummy, now you can knock.'

Tap, tap, tap.

Samantha tapped her knuckles against the door. When there was no response, she thumped harder. She took a step back and waited, but the house remained silent. 'Looks like no one is home.'

'They are probably in the farmyard, Mummy.'

'We can't go snooping around.'

Molly placed Snowflake on the ground, holding the lead with one hand and tugging at her mother with the other.

'Come on.'

'No.'

'Come on, Mummy.'

The farm yard was peppered with agricultural sheds, its surface wet and muddy. At the centre was an old green Land Rover, paint peeling from its bonnet. The driver's door was open, suggesting that someone was nearby. 'Go on, Mummy. Call out.'

'What?'

Molly shook her head in frustration, whispering while pretending to yell, 'Is anybody here?'

'HELLO!'

The appeal was met with silence, except for the sounds of birds tweeting and regular country noises.

'HELLO. IS THERE ANYBODY HERE!'

Still, there was nothing.

Molly led Snowflake to the Land Rover and poked her head inside. The keys were in the ignition. She beckoned for her mother to come over.

'Let's take it, Mummy.'

Samantha's jaw dropped open at her daughter's suggestion and she peered nervously about in case they were being watched or had been overheard.

'Steal it? Oh, I don't know, Honey. That is breaking the law and, besides, it's been a long time since I've driven a manual car.'

As Samantha spoke, Molly let go of Snowflake's lead. The cat jumped into the driver's seat of the Land Rover, while Molly strolled round to the passenger's side and climbed into the vehicle 'Are you driving, or is Snowflake?'

Samantha breathed out heavily. 'I suppose, in for a penny, in for a pound. Move over Snowflake.' The cat jumped onto Molly's lap then gazed back at Samantha, as if to say, *What are you waiting for?*

Samantha took a last look about the farmyard before sliding in and closing the door. Turning the key, she let out a yelp as the starter motor engaged the flywheel and, with the Land Rover in first gear, it jerked forward.

'Clutch, Samantha, put your foot on the clutch,' she said to herself.

When she turned the key again, the vehicle roared to life, its rusted muffler providing little silencing. Fearing being heard, Samantha lifted her foot off the clutch while applying the throttle, sending the Land Rover hopping forward in a series of leaps and bounds. Thumping her foot back on the clutch, the Land Rover rolled to a halt at the farm gate. Looking right then left, Samantha wondered to herself, *Which way?*

'Where are you going?' Molly asked, when Samantha turned left towards the village of Dolphinholme and not towards the motorway.

'They will expect us to head back towards the Service Centre. Instead, we'll go the other way.'

'Do you know where this road will take us?'

'No, but probably to a town where we can dump the Land Rover and catch a train.' Samantha glanced at her daughter. 'There's nowhere in the UK that's far from a train station.' Samantha's statement was accompanied by a grinding noise from the transmission as she tried to change up a gear but forgot to engage the clutch. 'Ouch!'

'Mummy, we don't have a map.'

'We'll use the GPS on my phone.'

'What phone, Mummy?'

The ancient Land Rover, with its worn tie rods and steering box, didn't track straight but wandered over the road, needing constant steering correction to stay on their side of the road. When Samantha spotted a vehicle approaching from the opposite direction, she tightened her grip on the steering wheel. As the SUV approached, Samantha tracked it with her eyes, her gaze locking with the other driver. Scrunchie Woman! A feeling of dread washed over Samantha as she held her breath and checked the mirrors.

Please, I hope she hasn't seen me!

Ellen Goldsworthy couldn't believe her luck as she braked. 'Well, well, well, gentleman, this is our lucky day. Did you see who just drove past going in the opposite direction?'

Michael Tan and Kang Long answered in unison. 'Yes.'

Her eyes darting left and right, Ellen Goldsworthy searched for a place to spin around. 'Samantha Liew is more resourceful than we gave her credit for.' She checked the rear mirror. The Land Rover was still in sight. 'Where's a gate when you want one? Ah, there you are.'

Having executed the turn, she was confident of catching the slower vehicle. Ellen Goldsworthy halted at the side of the road to plan her attack. She zoomed out on the map from the sat-nav. 'This is excellent, gentleman, just excellent. With a bit of a nudge and push, we can force Samantha to drive into the Forest of Bowland, an area of gritstone fells, deep valleys and peat moorland; quite desolate. When she's on one of its deserted tracks, we intercept, subdue, tie up and transport. The Bowland Fells are boggy and wet, the ideal location. So, gentleman, your incompetence has played to our advantage.'

Samantha saw the brake lights of the SUV illuminate. 'Shit!'

'Mummy, you can't say that word.'

'Never mind that. Did you see that car? It was Scrunchie Woman.'

'Scrunchie Woman?'

'You know who I mean, Molly. I will explain later, haven't time now. Damn, they are turning around. I'll have to try and outrun them. Shit!' As she pushed her foot hard down on the accelerator, the Land Rover gained speed only sluggishly. As it did, Samantha had to work hard to keep it travelling in a straight line.

In Dolphinholme, Samantha barely slowed as she veered left towards Abbey Stead Rd, sending the Land Rover onto the wrong side of the street, narrowly missing parked cars, as she negotiated the corner. Checking the mirror, Samantha watched the SUV speeding towards them. By the time they passed the Dolphinholme Methodist Church, it was right behind. Ahead were two roundabouts, one almost immediately after the other, the type painted on the roadway without a physical structure. The quickest way through was to go straight, straddling the circles painted on the bitumen. Samantha glanced in her rear-view mirror. The SUV had vanished, but she spotted it in her peripheral vision, lunging up on the inside.

'Shit!'

To avoid a collision, Samantha adjusted her line, veering down Abbey Stead Road, which ran off to the right.

Ellen Goldsworthy smiled as she watched the Land Rover veer to the right. 'Do you see that, gentlemen? That is how it's done, with gentle persuasion, and your foe does the rest for you. Now we ease back a little and let her run for a time. Mr Tan, from my examination of the map, there are two turnoffs to our left before we reach a T-junction where I want her to turn right. To encourage Samantha to head in the correct direction, I will drive up on her inside as we approach the intersections. I want you to forewarn me of their approach.'

Michael Tan adjusted the GPS map on the infotainment centre so that it provided a better overview. 'Okay, Boss. You will see some buildings coming up on your left. Yeah, there they are,' Michael Tan said, pointing out the windscreen. 'When they end, there's three hundred yards to the turnoff, Procter Moss Road. From the map, it's looks like a ninety-degree turn. Unless she slows, they have to keep going straight.'

Ellen Goldsworthy nodded. 'Okay, to keep her momentum going, I'll move up and apply some pressure.' Easing on the accelerator, the SUV closed in. When negotiating a corner, the Land Rover ran wide. Ellen Goldsworthy pulled up on the inside, forcing Samantha onto the wrong side of the road. Laughing, Ellen Goldsworthy accelerated, ready to pull alongside.

As the SUV and the Land Rover raced side by side, Michael Tan said, 'Boss, we've just passed Procter Moss Road.'

Molly, peering over a stone wall and around the corner in front, noticed an approaching vehicle. She screamed, 'Mummy, there's a car coming!'

Pinned on the wrong side of the road, Samantha glanced to her left. Scrunchie Woman stared back at her, grinning.

'Bitch!'

'Language, Mummy!'

'Hang on, Molly, I'm going to ram her.'

Molly's eyes opened wide in alarm as she cried out, 'Not with my side of the car, you're not!'

Focused on her adversary and not hearing Molly, Samantha turned towards the SUV.

'Take that, Bitch.'

Ellen Goldsworthy stomped on the brakes, the SUV nose-diving as it rapidly wiped off speed. In less than a second, the oncoming vehicle was gone, narrowly avoiding the Land Rover as it swerved across in front. Coming off the brakes and positioning herself behind the Land Rover, Ellen Goldsworthy laughed. 'She's got more spunk than I gave her credit for.'

Molly breathed a double sigh of relief; they hadn't hit the SUV, and they had also avoided a head on collision. 'Gee Mummy, that was close.' Looking at her hands, Molly realised she'd been squeezing Snowflake. Relaxing her grip, Snowflake flicked her tail in annoyance.

Samantha looked in the rear-view mirror and gritted her teeth.

'Gentlemen,' Ellen Goldsworthy said, 'Right about now, Samantha Liew will think that if she slams on the brakes, we will smash into the back of her. Now is the time to show that I won't tolerate such nonsense. On the next straight, I'll pull alongside the Land Rover and you will point your pistol at her, Mr Tan. I'll then give her a little kiss on the quarter panel, so keep your finger away from the trigger. We wouldn't want that gun of yours going off by accident, would we?'

The SUV roared into life and Ellen swerved to her right, sliding alongside the Land Rover. Molly let out a shriek.

'Mummy, the man's got a gun!'

Startled, Samantha glanced to her right but, before she could take evasive action, Ellen Goldsworthy wrenched her steering wheel to the left, smashing into the side of the Land Rover, sending it rocking from side to side.

Ellen Goldsworthy laughed as she eased back on the accelerator to pull in behind the Land Rover. Looking at Michael Tan, she snapped, 'How far to the next road?' He studied the map before saying, 'Ah, don't worry about it, Boss. Plantation Lane is on a corner. It's another ninety-degree turn. She won't go that way.'

Biting her tongue to control her anger, Ellen Goldsworthy snarled, 'Mr Tan, I am neither asking for nor seeking your opinion.'

'No, Boss.'

Her voice raised, Ellen Goldsworthy said, 'Well? When is it?'

'Do you see the farm on your left?'

'Yes.'

'After that, drive through a forested area, then it's one hundred and fifty yards on your left. The T intersection is a mile further on.'

'You are right, Mr Tan; she is travelling too fast to take Plantation Lane.'

Samantha looked in the rear-view mirror. 'They've dropped back a bit.'

Molly nodded. 'You know they are herding us?'

'Herding. What do you mean?'

'They are pushing us towards the heather moorland and bogs of the East side of Lancashire and North Yorkshire. We studied the Forest of Bowland last year at school and I remember reading that you can walk for miles without seeing a soul. So, it makes sense for them to push us that way. There will be no one to see what happens to us.'

Samantha bit her lip as she tried to think. They were fast approaching a T junction. It wasn't her intention to share her concerns, but she said aloud, 'Which way do I go?'

'Do what they want, Mummy. If the SUV comes up on your side, go left. If it's on my side, turn right.'

Samantha wanted to ask Molly why she thought that, but the intersection was fast approaching and her focus was on survival; there was no time to reason. Looking in the mirror, she saw the SUV nudging up on Molly's side of the car.

'They want us to go right.'

Gritting her teeth, Samantha changed down a gear making the engine roar. She yanked on the steering wheel, causing the Land Rover's tyres to squeal as they flew into the intersection on two wheels. Fighting to maintain control, the vehicle fishtailed down the road before finally straightening. Samantha breathed out in relief; her palms sweaty from the stress.

CRASH!

The SUV rammed them from behind, rocking Molly and Samantha forward in their seats.

'Now what?'

'Do what they want, Mummy.'

Samantha felt her anger rising. 'I don't understand Molly. What do you mean? It makes no sense to me.' She started to cry. 'None of this makes any sense.'

Furious at losing control, Samantha's thoughts raced.

Pull yourself together, woman. You're the adult here.

'Sorry Molly, what I meant to say w...'

BANG!

They were hit again. Taken by surprise, Samantha lost control of the Land Rover, causing it to shoot over to the right. Just as it was about to smash into the stone wall lining the road, Samantha wrestled it back, sending them hurtling towards the wall on the other side. Pulling on the steering wheel again, while flicking her foot off the accelerator, the old vehicle settled and raced down the road.

Molly, her voice steady despite the panic she felt, said while pointing out of the window, 'See the barren hills over there?'

'Yes.'

'Take any road that leads that way.'

'Why, Molly?'

'From the pictures the teacher showed us, there are rocky tracks that cross the blanket bog. If you can find one of those tracks, we will have the advantage. We are in a Land Rover and they have a city SUV.'

'You clever thing. I think that may just work.' Samantha smiled, but her relief evaporated when she realised they were already heading to where Scrunchie Woman wanted them. The road they were driving was deserted, with isolated moors on either side. With the Land Rover going as fast as it could, Samantha took her eyes off the road and glanced in the rear-view mirror.

Molly screamed.

A push bike rider was directly in front of them. With no time to break, Samantha swerved to the right. Simultaneously, having instructed Michael Tan to shoot out the Land Rover's rear tyre, Ellen Goldsworthy accelerated to pull alongside.

CRUNCH!

The sudden move of the Land Rover caught Ellen Goldsworthy off guard, the two vehicles colliding, smashing the left front fender of the SUV, knocking the guard onto its front tyre. Both vehicles narrowly missed the cyclist, the near miss sending them sliding across the asphalt while the women struggled to regain control. The road had narrowed to barely the width of a single car. With the front tire billowing smoke, Ellen Goldsworthy eased off the throttle, settling in behind the Land Rover. Fearing a puncture, and Samantha and Molly eluding capture, she ordered Michael Tan to shoot at the Land Rover wheels. He wound down the window, leaned out, and took aim.

With her foot to the floor urging the Land Rover to go faster, Samantha said, 'Come on.' She glanced in the mirror, spotting the hand gun pointing from the SUV. 'He's about to fire!'

'Swerve, Mummy, swerve! Hang on, Snowflake.'

The road was narrow, and Samantha risked running into a ditch, but there was no choice. She jerked the steering wheel right, then left and right again, setting in place a pendulum motion, causing the Land Rover to spin one-hundred and eighty degrees and face back the way it had come. The SUV raced past, miraculously, without colliding. Instinctively Samantha had put her foot on the clutch so, when the Land Rover came to a standstill, the engine was still running. Shocked, Samantha was dumbfounded.

'That was cool, Mummy. Go!'

'What?' Samantha looked at her hands, they were shaking.

'Go, Mummy, go!'

'Oh, okay.' Raising her clutch foot caused the Land Rover to almost stall, confusing Samantha until she realised the vehicle was in fourth gear. She fumbled with the gear stick, then after a couple of failed attempts, engaged first and began driving away. Glancing the mirror, she noticed the SUV was yet to turn around.

Ellen Goldsworthy lifted her hands from the steering wheel in frustration. 'How did she do that?' With the road too narrow for a three-point turn, Ellen knew she needed to find a gateway or track and turn around if she was to continue the pursuit. She edged slowly forward, seeking a suitable spot to turn the SUV around.

From the back seat, Kang Long said, 'You could try a handbrake turn.'

Her patience at its wits end and voice dripping venom, Ellen Goldsworthy said, 'Could I now? How would you suggest I do that when the car has an electric handbrake and its bloody electronics won't let it engage while we're moving?'

BEEP! BEEP! BEEP!

'What now!' Glancing at the SUV's instrument cluster, Ellen Goldsworthy noticed the tyre low-pressure warning light flashing. The left front had deflated.

Kang Long bit his lip to stop himself from chuckling.

CHAPTER 16
Carlton

'That was cool, Mummy, Go!'

'What?' Samantha looked at her hands, they were shaking.

'Go, Mummy, go!'

'Oh, okay.' Raising her clutch foot caused the Land Rover to almost stall, confusing Samantha until she realised the vehicle was still in fourth gear. She fumbled with the gear stick, then after a couple of failed attempts, engaged first and began driving away. Glancing in the mirror, she saw the SUV was yet to turn around. Spurred on by fear and with adrenaline pumping through her veins, Samantha muscled the old Land Rover at its maximum speed around the twisty narrow road. Blanket bogs gave way to a country lane bordered by stone walls, sheep grazing in the fields. Further on, a broken white line appeared in the middle of the road, separating two-way traffic from her. She checked in the mirror and released a sigh of relief as her heartbeat settled. Samantha eased back on the accelerator. Cresting a rise in the road, Molly and Samantha spotted dwellings in the distance, a jogger running towards them; all were signs they were about to re-enter civilization.

'What's the plan, Mummy?'

Samantha glanced at her watch, realising that they couldn't make it to Inverness that day. 'I'm not exactly sure, Honey. We must be close to Lancaster so we could dump the Land Rover, catch a train to Glasgow, stay the night and take a bus the rest of the way in the morning.'

Molly thought for a moment. 'If I were the bad people, I'd watch for us at the Lancaster Railway Station because it's not far from the Service Centre where they started following us. We should take a train from somewhere not as obvious.'

They were entering a small hamlet and Samantha spotted a street sign which pointed straight on for Lancaster, right to Carlton and left: Bay Horse.

'That showed some insight Molly and I agree, it's an excellent suggestion.' Samantha glanced at Molly and smiled. 'I'm beginning to think that you really are fourteen and not eight.' Easing back on the accelerator, Samantha indicated and then turned right. 'I'm not sure if Carlton will have a train station, but let's find out.'

'Mummy, do you think Carlton will have some shops?'

Samantha shrugged her shoulders. 'I don't know. Why, Honey?'

'Because, when we ran, we left all our stuff in the car.'

A look or horror spread across Samantha's face. Letting go of the steering wheel with her right hand, she patted her trouser pocket. Feeling her wallet, with its assortment of cards and cash inside, she sighed with relief.

CHAPTER 17
The Bus from Glasgow

Olivia awoke refreshed after a hearty evening meal and a good night's sleep. The night at the Stock Exchange Hotel was made even better when, after dinner, the night porter knocked on Olivia's door.

'Good evening, Madam. This has arrived by special courier, so I thought I would bring it up to you.'

He held up her day pack, and the porter was lost for words when Olivia responded, 'Ah, thank goodness. Manna from heaven, clean knickers.'

After breakfast, a taxi driver was waiting in the hotel foyer to take Olivia to the airport. When he opened the back door for her to enter, the attempted kidnapping of the previous day played in her mind, and Olivia hesitated.

What choice do I have? One way or another, I must get to the airport.

She sighed.

Somehow, things were easier when there were two of us.

'Madam, is there a problem?' the driver asked.

Olivia uttered the first words that popped into her mind, and they were poignant, being both true and untrue. 'No umbrella.'

The driver gave Olivia a double take. 'No umbrella, Madam?'

'In case it rains.' She climbed into the back of the taxi.

Her apprehension faded as they left the hotel and, by the time she arrived at Manchester Airport, was forgotten. Except for activating the security metal detectors twice, for no apparent reason, and with only carry-on luggage, the check-in procedure was a cinch. Olivia scanned the busy departure lounge to find a quiet seat away from the others, where she could wait alone for the flight to be called. No sooner was she seated than her phone buzzed, alerting her to a text message.

Call James.

Confident that she wouldn't be overheard, the conversation muffled by the constant hustle and bustle of the noisy airport, Olivia pressed the *return call* icon.

'Good morning, James.'

'Olivia. I trust you slept well.'

'Even better after your late-night gift arrived.'

'We aim to please. Now Olivia, if I may, let's get down to business. Samantha used her credit card this morning, purchasing two bus tickets from Glasgow to Inverness. It departs soon, ten past nine from the Buchanan Bus Station, and arrives at twelve forty-five this afternoon at the Inverness Bus Terminal. The timing is perfect, as you will be in Inverness before them.'

Olivia was curious how Samantha and Molly had travelled from Dolphinholme to Glasgow but held her tongue, a conversation for a later time. Besides, James may not know the answer. In the background, she heard her flight being called.

Passengers on flight LM 592 travelling to Inverness. Your plane is now boarding.

'James, they are calling my flight so I don't have long. Stephen told me you were organising some items for me when I arrive in Inverness.'

'Absolutely, Olivia. James, the quartermaster at your service. In the glove compartment of your hire car, you will find a weapon and ID. Card. On the back seat, a laptop and MI6 surveillance kit– powerful camera, listening and GPS tracking devices. When I hang up, I'll send you the app to install on your phone.'

'Perfect as always, James. One last thing if I may? Is there any news on the Chinese agents?'

Not much Olivia. The SUV that the blonde woman was driving was found dumped and burnt out near the village of Quernmore, three miles east of Lancaster. Two vehicles were reported stolen from Lancaster last night, neither recovered. Our operating assumption is that they took one of them, but it's unlikely they're still using it. Samantha and Molly may be in the other, but that is irrelevant now. We must assume, if we know Samantha and Molly are making for Inverness, the Chinese Security Service do as well. You will need to be on your guard, Olivia.'

'I can assure you of that, James. Goodbye.'

This is the final call for passengers on flight LM 592 travelling to Inverness. Your plane is ready to leave.

Olivia stood and made her way towards the departure gate.

'Excuse me, Madam!' A woman's voice called. 'Excuse me!'

Olivia turned.

A cleaner, judging by her clothes, was pointing at a day pack next to where Olivia had been sitting. 'Is this yours?'

Olivia looked at the woman meekly. 'Oh, my goodness, I would forget my head if it wasn't screwed on. Thank you. Really, thank you. Olivia knew that protocol dictated that the cleaner, on seeing an abandoned bag, should have called security. The airport would have been shut down and her flight missed. She had almost screwed up in a big way.'

Ha, Ha, Ha. Almost left your knickers behind. Again!

Max, stop it. This is no laughing matter. I'm losing my marbles.

Loneliness increases the risk of dementia by forty percent.

Even from the grave, you're a curmudgeon. Olivia sighed, which sounded more like a moan. *I am lonely and I miss you, my love.*

A man in a uniform, possibly a flight attendant, approached. 'Are you Olivia?'

'Yes.'

He breathed out with a sigh of relief. 'That is wonderful. May I see your boarding pass?' Olivia held it for him to see. 'They are holding the plane for you, Madam. This way, please.'

***

Inverness Scotland

After landing at Inverness Airport, Olivia picked up the hire car and drove the seven and half miles to the bus station positioned in Farraline Park, near the city centre, an area that could be accessed from either Margaret Street or Stothers Lane. Because Olivia was driving, and with Farraline Park designed for one-way traffic, she came in off Stothers Lane, stopping at the first of the parallel parking spots in front of the public library, a building of Greek Revival architecture with a wide central pedimented portico and Doric columns in Moray sandstone, the best classic structure in Inverness. Her position provided an uninterrupted view of the bus station with its four terminal bays. Olivia scanned the area; hers was the only vehicle. Of the five people she could see, none looked suspicious: a woman with a pram, two elderly gentlemen and two teenagers. She checked her watch. The bus was due in fifteen minutes.

Where are you, my espionage lovelies?

Movement in the mirror caught Olivia's attention. A dark blue transit van was entering off Stothers Lane driven by a man of Asian appearance, a middle-aged woman in the passenger's seat. Olivia surmised that a third man was in the back.

'Here we go. I have company,' Olivia said aloud.

The van drove past Olivia and parked in front of her, a vacant space between them. Staring at the back of the van, Olivia was uneasy, knowing that they would attempt a snatch and grab, either at the bus station or when Samantha and Molly were walking along the street. Her feeling of trepidation grew.

There are three of them and only one of me. How on earth do I stop them?

Olivia rubbed her chin and sighed.

Why am I lost for ideas?

Olivia checked her watch again; ten minutes to go.

I can't ring James or Stephen because, as Max would say, that wouldn't be cricket. Claudia, it has to be Claudia.

Olivia dialled, but like the time before, the call went to voice mail.

Her voice firm and confident, Olivia said, 'Hi Claudia, it's Olivia. I'm at the central bus station in Inverness, Scotland, hoping to intercept Molly and Samantha. An abduction team has been sent by the Chinese Ministry of State Security, so we are in a race to see who gets to them first. Call me if you can, otherwise, I'll keep you posted.'

Olivia, your mission is to identify and track the female agent and not allow yourself to be distracted. If you focus on that, the rest will naturally follow.

Max. I'm not using Molly and Samantha as bait.

How else will you draw the woman out into the open?

What are you suggesting?

Move your cute little bottom out of that seat and attach a tracking device to the transit van. Then sit back and watch. If the woman gets out, take some happy snaps, otherwise do what surveillance is famous for, watch and wait. When Samantha and Molly arrive, the agents will follow them in the van before grabbing them off the street. From there on, it's simple. Ring the police and report the kidnap attempt while following the vehicle. If, at worst, you lose them, the tracking device won't.

When the police intercept the van, show them your MI6 identification and take Samantha and Molly into your protection. They stay with you at Claudia's apartment until granted protection. When arrested, the cover of the female Chinese spy will be broken and all three of your mission parameters will have been successfully completed. Once more, the nation will owe you a debt of gratitude.

Three? Olivia asked.

Yes, my Love. Protect Molly, identify the female agent and safeguard UK assets. Now then, Lady Olivia Suzanne Elizabeth Huggins, shake those tail feathers and get that tracking device attached to the van before the bus arrives.

You make it sound easy.

As you have always done, my Love. Now it's time to go to work.

Olivia removed the magnetic GPS tracker from the case of goodies provided by James. Gadget in hand, she left her vehicle and approached the transit van directly from behind, keeping herself hidden from its mirrors. Bending, she slipped the device under the bumper bar. Letting go, she watched in dismay as it fell to the ground. Olivia shook her head.

Bloody modern vehicles. They are all plastic, nothing for it to grip.

Carefully lowering herself, Olivia kneeled on the ground, and stretched her arm under the van, fumbling about, trying to feel the tracking device with her fingers. Gripping it firmly, she held it against the underside of the vehicle until she felt a strong magnet bite. Using the back of the van for support, Olivia slowly rose and, after wiping the dust from her knees, strolled back to her car. Satisfied that her exploits had gone unnoticed, Olivia opened her phone and checked that the GPS device was transmitting a signal. The current location was displayed on the screen map.

'Excellent.'

The passenger door of the van opening caught Olivia's attention, and she spotted the female spy alight. Expecting the agent to check her surroundings, Olivia dropped her head forward and opened her mouth, mimicking an old woman dozing in the front seat while watching through half-closed eyes. She surmised that the Chinese agent was positioning herself to follow Samantha and Molly to coordinate the snatch and grab from the ground.

Ellen Goldsworthy scanned the bus stop for risks before checking her lapel microphone. 'Testing, one, two, three.'

'Okay, got you, Boss,' Michael Tan said.

Ellen Goldsworthy adjusted her earpiece.

Watching, Olivia waited for the woman's eyes to move off her car before reaching across to the passenger seat and taking hold of the camera. As the woman moved off, she pointed its auto focus lens at her target, held her finger on the shutter button and fired off ten shots in rapid succession.

Thank you. Now turn the other way dear, so that momma can get a nice profile shot. Oh, there's a good girl.

Olivia squeezed the shutter button again and then zoomed in, taking ten more photographs.

Wary of being recognised by Samantha and Molly; Ellen Goldsworthy wrapped a brown scarf around her neck and pulled a black velvet bucket hat from her pocket. She added it to the mix before moving closer to the parking bays.

Olivia, satisfied with her photography, secured the camera back into its equipment case and placed it on the floor in the back seat next to the laptop, out of harm's way. She checked her pistol.

'I'm ready.'

The bus from Glasgow turned from Stothers Lane into Farraline Park, stopping in parking bay number two. Olivia watched as the bus door swung open and passengers began disembarking.

Condensation streamed from the exhaust of the transit van, telling Olivia that the engine had started. She watched as the female agent moved into her final observational position. The Chinese Ministry of State Security abduction team was poised to strike.

CHAPTER 18
Taipan

Monya Molilevick's Mansion in Moscow, Russia

Claudia was on her sixth lap of the twenty she'd been running twice a day since arriving at Monya's compound, when Fabian, Monya's private secretary, waved at her to stop.

'Good afternoon, Claudia. The meeting of the Brotherhood has concluded and Monya would like to see you. He's waiting in the Zmei Cave.'

Slightly out of breath, Claudia replied, 'Thank you, Fabian. I would like to freshen up first if I may.'

'Monya will see you *now,* so that isn't necessary.'

***

Monya stood when Claudia exited the lift and he beckoned for her to join him at the Chesterfields, gesturing for her to be seated. Making herself comfortable, Claudia glanced about the underground hideaway.

'The dragon's lair. There's something about this place that I like.'

Monya laughed. 'So, you've used your time with us to study Russian mythology, have you? Alexandria believes that *Zmei Cave* means *My Cave*, which isn't such an outrageous proposition.'

Claudia grinned. 'Zmei was a benevolent dragon. I thought that perhaps Azhdaya would be more apt.'

Monya chuckled. 'The demonic version of a Zmei dragon that spits fire and devours humans and cattle?' He tilted his head to one side. 'In Russian folklore, the evil dragons are female, as I'm sure you're aware, Claudia. Azhdaya is a name that would suit yourself, though rumour has it you're becoming more benevolent with age.'

'I do so love fairy tales.'

'Many of our beloved fairy tales have their roots in people and places–real people, I mean.' Monya paused. 'But enough of this idle chatter. The Brotherhood has noticed a shift in the structure and organisation of our competitors in the underworld, and there are rumours of consolidation between otherwise rival groups. Triads are transnational, prominent in China, Taiwan, Hong Kong, Singapore, but have presence in most countries of the world. Triad structure is loose, unlike the pyramidal hierarchy of the Mafia or Yakuza. Although there is a hierarchy to Triad Leadership, rarely are the activities of smaller Triad gangs directed by the heads of a larger Triad. This has allowed local gangs to partner with non-Triad members. Unlike us, the profit benefits individual gangs and not the organisation as a whole. There's lots of money floating around, but it's spread thinly across many gangs. Triads are your traditional gangsters: cruel, uneducated–the low life, if you like. In Hong Kong alone, there are fifty Triad gangs with a membership of eight thousand. Triad groups like the Wo Group have multiple subgroups, each specialising in different types of activities. There is a Triad hierarchy, but until recently, it was difficult to say how it was used. Neither the Triads nor Yakuza are at their peak of influence, so the Brotherhood has considered them benign when it came to our global activities. That is changing because of the rise of a person called Taipan. Taipan is bringing these formerly loosely associated Triad gangs together to increase the scope of their illegal activities and broaden its transnational character.'

Claudia nodded.

'The Yakuza, unlike the Triads, operate almost exclusively in Japan and, unlike the Triads, are professional and highly organised with centralised syndicates. Just as I pulled the various Mafia families together to form the Brotherhood, Tomoe is uniting the Yakuza, as Taipan is the Triads. Individually, Taipan and Tomoe pose a threat to my dominance, even ignoring integration with The Firm. The Brotherhood is being awoken by this new threat. With what I've learnt, the Principal at its head, The Firm structure, looks something like this.' Monya rotated a sheet of paper to face Claudia. It read:

Jasper–the banker

Cosy Bear–cyber warfare/ransomware

Sun-Tzu–military

Davros–information technology

Tomoe–Yakuza

Taipan–Triads

'Each member brings a particular asset to The Firm.' Monya paused. 'Claudia, do you see what's missing?'

'Ah, this is where I hope the missing Avatar isn't a dragon.'

'Precisely. It may well be a dragon, perhaps Azhdaya, but it's not Zmei. Before your arrival, the Brotherhood had discussed the emergence of a shadowy figure called the Principal, and we knew already of Taipan and Tomoe. It was your conversation with me that started joining the dots. I saw how these names fitted together and it wasn't until I was discussing Cosy Bear with my colleagues that I realised we had a missing Avatar.'

'The Mafia.'

'Until your visit, I hadn't realised that the Firm posed a direct threat to me as head of the Brotherhood. If the Principal's tentacles reach inside the FSB to Cozy Bear, then they will touch the Brotherhood, possibly even MI6. They are everywhere. If there's not already a Mafia Avatar, it's only a matter of time before one is in place. At today's meeting of the Brotherhood, I quickly dismissed your Cosy Bear proposal, Claudia, and moved to the next item of business.'

'You fear a coup?'

'If someone sees the opportunity, undoubtedly they will seize it. A move under the auspices of The Firm would provide the resources needed to execute a takeover–of me and of the others.'

Claudia nodded her agreement. 'It's unlikely to be bloodless. Have you considered whether the missing avatar could be genetics or a biological weapon and not the Mafia, after all?'

'That may be so but, for the moment, I will stick with my instincts. They've always served me well. Genetic engineering and biological weapons are undoubtedly part of the mix of The Firm, as are robotics and artificial intelligence. They may exist in its structure now or they are still to arrive. I sense that The Firm's universe is in its formation stage. Still in its infancy.'

Claudia crossed her legs and leaned back into her seat, the words of Andrei Gorbachev resonating in her mind, sending a shiver down her spine.

Amassing economic, technological, political and military capacity, capable of threatening nations.

'If the Brotherhood has discussed Taipan and Tomoe, do you know where to find them, Monya?'

'I haven't searched with the vigour that is now warranted. Nonetheless, I did put the feelers out. However, with this new insight, it would be wise to question the reliability of that intelligence. That aside, Taipan is rumoured to be in the Dângrêk Mountains of Cambodia at a place called Preah Vihear Temple. Have you heard of it?'

Claudia shook her head.

'I'm not surprised, neither had I. This is what I found on the internet:'

> 'Preah Vihear Temple is an ancient Hindu temple built during the period of the Khmer Empire, situated atop of 525-metre (1,722 ft) cliff in the Dângrêk Mountains in the Preah Vihear Province, Cambodia. The temple sprawls along a clifftop near the Thai border with breathtaking views of lowland Cambodia below. The temple is laid out along a north-south processional axis with five cruciform gopura, decorated with exquisite carvings, separated by esplanades up to 275 metres long. In the early 1980s it was the site of an atrocity when thousands of repatriated Cambodian refugees who had fled the Khmer Rouge were killed or maimed in the minefields around Preah Vihear.'

'I think you will agree Claudia, it is the perfect place for a hideout and it is where you will begin your search for Taipan.'

Claudia raised an eyebrow. 'I take it you will be reciprocating?'

'My benevolence is driven by self-interest and self-interest alone, and it's an inconvenient truth that the ally I can trust is also my enemy. Using your analogy from the other day, The Firm must be dismantled, one most wanted card at a time. If you go to the

Dângrêk Mountains in search of Taipan, I will, in return, seek the identity of Cosy Bear. I expect to be kept informed of your progress.'

Claudia nodded. 'I'm confident Stephen will agree to that.' She put her hand on her chin. 'When you had the feelers out, did Turkey, or more precisely the city of Trabzon or Sumela Monastery, surface?'

'No. Why do you ask?'

'It turned up several times recently. Tomoe, or someone purporting to be Tomoe, left the words Altindere Vadisi on a card for me. Altindere Vadisi is a national park and Sumela Monastery within is of note. Trabzon, a city near the Sumela Monastery, came up with my chat with the head of the Russian Federal Security Service, Andrei Gorbachev. They were looking into Sun-Tzu and, of the FSB agents sent to Turkey, none have returned.'

Monya pursed his lips and breathed out heavily, giving Claudia a wry smile. 'We operate in a world of deception; seldom are things as they seem. If all trails lead to Turkey, Sumela Monastery may be a well-lit beacon. Like moth to a flame, they are drawn to bright lights and, no matter how many perish, they keep coming. Sumela Monastery is a place to stay well clear of, but I doubt that MI6 or the FSB can resist its fatal attraction.'

Monya took Claudia's mobile phone from his pocket and tossed it to her. 'Now, if you will excuse me, there are other matters that require my attention. You are welcome to use my study and Fabian will assist with your travel arrangements.'

***

Claudia made herself comfortable in Monya's high-backed dark grey Italian leather chair, placing her phone, which had been idle for the duration of her stay, on the glass topped executive desk.

Fabian had been waiting for her when she ascended from the Zmei Cave and offered to bring a beverage while she made her calls. A hot cup of tea delivered, she waited for Fabian to leave before switching on the phone. It beeped several times, alerting her to missed calls and messages. There were four missed calls with voice mail; two from Olivia, one each from Inspector Axel and Stephen Walls. Stephen's the most recent. Claudia thought she would start with Olivia's voice mails played in time order.

> *Hi Claudia, it's Olivia, with a quick update. I arrived in the UK this morning to the news Molly had posted a card. I talked to Samantha briefly on the phone before communications were lost. She was at the Lancaster Service Centre on the M6 and reported being followed. I'm en route.*

Claudia took a sip of tea and reflected on what she'd heard. There was something in Olivia's tone that worried her and she sensed a feeling of unease, as if Olivia was uncertain.

I'm sorry Olivia, I didn't envision Molly needing you so soon.

She checked the next message, received that morning.

> *'Hi Claudia, it's Olivia. I'm at the central bus station in Inverness, Scotland, hoping to intercept Molly and Samantha. An abduction team has been sent by the Chinese Ministry of State Security, so we are in a race to see who gets to them first. Call me if you can, otherwise, I'll keep you posted.'*

Claudia breathed a sigh of relief; Olivia sounded more like her old self—a woman back on top of her game. However, the news of a developing abduction team weighed heavily on her mind. She hoped MI6 was providing Olivia with the support she needed and resolved to discuss the matter with Stephen, and forcefully, if necessary. Contemplating a trip to Scotland, she took another sip of her tea while deciding whom to call next: Inspector Axel or Stephen. Ultimately, she chose to contact Inspector Axel first, hoping to gain a complete understanding of the situation before speaking with Stephen.

> *Claudia. Hi, it's me, Axel. Two things. First, I assume you know Molly has activated her call for help and Olivia is trying to find her and Samantha before the Chinese do. I've spoken with Olivia and felt she was experiencing some difficulties, which I put down to her loss of Max and to Stephen Walls being less than forthcoming with support. I'm about to ring MI6 and give them a piece of my mind. Second, I'm in Japan but on an early morning flight to Turkey. I'm still following Linda Orr and my guess; she will lead me to Altindere National Park and Sumela Monastery. Take care. Bye for now.*

Claudia shook her head. 'A moth to a flame, Inspector. You must not go to Sumela Monastery.' Claudia took a sip of tea. 'Olivia, I'm also worried for you, Molly and Samantha. I fear my friends, each in different parts of the world, are in grave danger. How can so much happen in a short time and what can I do? Before you make a decision girly, best to find out what Stephen wanted, then I'll start calling them back.'

> *Claudia. It's Stephen. Call me ASAP.*

'Well, that was short and to the point, for which Stephen, you go to the end of the queue. Inspector, you are first.'

Claudia keyed in Inspector Axel's number, the call diverting to voice mail.

'Inspector, it's Claudia. Call me back as soon as you can. Oh, and Inspector, beware of Sumela. I fear Linda is leading you into a trap.'

Next, Claudia tried Olivia, which also went to voice mail. She left no message. It was Stephen's turn. The phone rang twice before Stephen answered.

'Ah, Claudia. You're back in the world of the living.'

Humour, Stephen, how unlike you.

'Stephen, it's good to talk to you, too.'

'Indeed. Has your visit been fruitful?'

Direct and to the point. Much more like Stephen.

Calling on her skills as a spy, Claudia reported succinctly but accurately, first on the Sun-Tzu discussions with Andrei Gorbachev, then Monya's bargain that she hunts down Taipan for discovering the identity of Cosy Bear. Claudia told Stephen of the likelihood that Sumela Monastery was being used by The Firm to lure those poking around into a trap and alerted him to Inspector Axel's impending danger. She held her tongue about Olivia, intending to raise the subject towards the end of their conversation, where it couldn't be lost in the exchange. Stephen listened to her account without interrupting.

'Claudia, I'm not sure if you're aware but there has been another major ransomware attack in the U.S. Fuel pipeline operator Colonial Pipeline has been forced to shut its entire network, an 8,900-kilometre pipeline, the source of nearly half of the U.S. east coast's fuel supply. We've already seen a price spike, panic buying, and supplies are running low. The White House is saying that this is as close as anyone can get to the jugular of infrastructure in the United States. Petrol stations from Florida to Virginia are running dry. North Carolina has declared a state of emergency and other states are considering doing the same. The U.S. President said that a Russian-based group was behind the ransomware attack and the FBI has identified DarkSide, a shadowy operation originating out of Russia, as being responsible.'

'DarkSide, Stephen. Not the work of Cosy Bear and The Firm?'

'We believe this criminal gang is affiliated with The Firm. Critical infrastructure is becoming increasingly appealing to ransomware operators and attacks are growing more sophisticated, frequent, and aggressive. Our incremental improvements in cyber security are inadequate. More than ever, we need to strike back Claudia. National Cyber Force (NCF), the joint initiative between the Ministry of Defence and British intelligence, part of our new offensive capacity, will take down computer servers of DarkSide tomorrow, restoring oil supplies.'

'Excellent Stephen. It seems everything is under control.'

'This latest cyber-attack has sharpened the focus of our U.S. ally. They want Cozy Bear shut down. We need Monya's cooperation, so I want you on the first flight to Cambodia. Find and eliminate Taipan.'

'I appreciate the urgency, Stephen, but I am concerned about Olivia. Protecting Molly seems to have become more arduous and dangerous than I envisaged.'

Stephen's voice was firm as he said, 'The situation on the home front is fluid and changing rapidly. Time doesn't permit detail; however, Olivia is now operating with the full authority and resources of the agency.' He softened his tone. 'I have every confidence in Olivia and she has been doing this kind of work since before you were a twinkle in your parents' eyes.'

Claudia's inquisitive and mistrustful nature needed to understand the change in circumstances that made protecting Molly and Samantha of interest to MI6, but she resisted the urge to ask. 'Ordinarily Stephen, I would agree. Olivia is an exceptional agent. In the aftermath of Max's death, it may be prudent to offer Olivia assistance. She is, after all, used to operating with a partner.'

'Indeed. Your guidance is noted.'

The change in Stephen's tone told Claudia that the subject was closed. 'Speak to James about the intelligence and resources you will need in Cambodia and call me when you touch down. Have a safe flight and good luck.'

Stephen ended the call.

Claudia slipped the phone into her pocket and began walking a lap of Monya's study, her mind awash with conflicting thoughts, unsure of the right decision.

Do I go to Cambodia and Preah Vihear Temple in search of Taipan or, with Inspector Axel's life in danger, Turkey and Sumela Monastery? Do I honour my promise to Molly and help Olivia in Inverness, Scotland? I can do only one.

CHAPTER 19
Scotland The Brave

The bus from Glasgow turned from Stothers Lane into Farraline Park, stopping in parking bay number two. Olivia watched as the bus door swung open and passengers began disembarking. Condensation streamed from the exhaust of the transit van, telling Olivia that the engine had started. She watched as the female agent moved into her final observational position. The Chinese Ministry of State Security abduction team was poised to strike.

Ellen Goldsworthy saw the last of the passengers step down from the bus, and, having seen neither Samantha nor Molly, whispered into her radio, 'I'm going to take a closer look.' Met by friends, family, or making their own way, travellers began dispersing as Ellen Goldsworthy broke cover and mingled, searching in case Molly and Samantha were hidden from her sight. Scanning the area, she said into the lapel mike, 'I still see nothing, so will speak to the driver.'

'Okay, boss,' Michael Tan replied.

Olivia made the same assessment as the Chinese. Molly and Samantha were not on the bus. She observed as the female spy approached the driver who had been unloading luggage from the bus. After a brief conversation, the woman returned to the transit van, which drove slowly away. Olivia faced a split-second decision: follow or talk to the driver.

Olivia, my love, follow and you do so blindly. Intelligence is king, or queen, if you prefer. Besides, with the tracking device, you will know where to find them.

Max, you're right. Leaving her vehicle, Olivia strolled towards the driver while checking that the transit van was being monitored by her phone's GPS tracking app. A teenager on his new motorised electric skateboard didn't spot Olivia, who was hidden by the front of her car until she stepped out in front of him. The youth swerved to his left, attempting to avoid the collision as Olivia stopped abruptly and threw her hands out in front of her to steady herself. She tried to take a step backwards, but the change of direction unsettled her balance. The skateboard rider collided with the hand holding the mobile phone, ripping it from Olivia's grip. With the phone wedged against his chest, the skateboard rider zoomed past, transporting it with him, the phone falling to the ground and smashing to pieces as he came to a halt. The boy shook his head, angry at the silly old lady, the annoyance quickly replaced by concern. After checking his victim was unharmed, he gathered up the broken pieces of the phone, picked up his board and walked towards Olivia.

Her heart racing, Olivia's feet were welded to the ground by the shock of the near miss.

This is nothing. Shake that tail feather, my Love, or the bus driver will be gone before you can speak with him.

Holding the broken phone towards Olivia, the teenager said, his voice quivering, 'I'm so sorry lady. I didn't see you. You came from nowhere.'

Olivia took the phone and, smiling, said, 'It's a lucky thing that you're a switched on, alert and nice young man, otherwise things may have turned out much worse than a broken phone.' She looked at the electric skateboard tucked under his arm. 'I wish we had those when I was your age. They look like tremendous fun. If you will excuse me, young man, unless you want to dink me home on the back of your board, I have a bus to catch.'

Olivia checked that there were no other vehicles coming and crossed the road, arriving at the bus parking bay as the driver, having closed the luggage storage compartment under the bus, was climbing back on board. The skate board rider watched Olivia leave. He shrugged his shoulders and, placing the board on the ground, accelerated away, the incident forgotten as quickly as it had happened.

Poking her head through the bus door, Olivia said. 'Excuse me, I'm looking for a woman and child, Samantha and Molly, who caught the bus in Glasgow. The child is Anglo-Asian in appearance and had a cat with her.'

The driver was startled, a confused look appearing on his face. 'A police woman just asked me the same thing. Who are you?'

'My name is Olivia. I'm with the British Secret Service and that woman wasn't with the police. What did you tell her?'

The bus driver looked Olivia up and down.

No way is this old bird with the British Secret Service. I don't know what her game is, but this black duck is keeping his mouth shut.

'Madam, without the consent of the passenger, I'm not permitted to provide any details.'

Removing her identity card and holding it in front of her, Olivia climbed up the steps and onto the bus. 'Did you ask to see the woman's warrant card?'

The bus driver studied the licence sized card Olivia was holding. Next to the Royal Coat of Arms of Great Britain, in capitals, one word under the other, was embossed SECRET INTELLIGENCE SERVICE and, next to the word Service, was MI6. He studied the photograph and then the name: Olivia Bishop.

Olivia repeated her question. 'Did you ask to see the woman's warrant card?'

Sheepishly, he shook his head.

'I ask you again, what did you tell her?'

'That they got off at Aviemore. At the railway station.'

'Go on,' Olivia said, her voice firm.

'She asked about the trains between Aviemore and Inverness and I told her they run every hour and forty minutes and do the journey in thirty-seven minutes. We take forty-five minutes, so it is possible that they are already here, or will arrive sometime this afternoon. That's if they are coming to Inverness.'

Olivia nodded before saying, 'What's your name?'

'William Pace.'

'Well, Mr William Pace, you know better than to speak of this conversation? With anyone.'

'Yes.'

'Good. Then we understand each other.'

Olivia turned, and holding the handrail, descended the steps onto the pavement. As she was about to leave, William Pace called after her, 'The lady pretending to be a policewoman. Who was she?'

Olivia paused and raised a finger, which she wiggled from side to side in front of him. The message was clear: *that question is not to be asked.*

The public car park that serviced Inverness Railway Station was virtually opposite, although she had to drive around the block to reach it. Leaving Farraline Park in search of the blue transit van, Olivia turned left on Academy Street, then left into Strothers Lane but, instead of turning left again and into the bus station, she drove straight on to the railway station car park.

It started raining. Olivia switched on the windscreen wipers, saying as she began circumnavigating the car park, 'Where are you, my murky friends?'

A blue vehicle on her right caught Olivia's attention, and she swivelled her head to stare at it through the side window.

BEEP! BEEP! BEEP!

With her foot still resting on the accelerator, the vehicle's autonomous emergency braking system activated, bringing the SUV to an abrupt standstill. Out of the windscreen, Olivia spotted a middle age man standing directly in front of her.

He mouthed, 'Sorry,' and kept walking, oblivious that it was the car's driver assist system that saved his life, not Olivia's reactions.

Pay attention, Olivia.

She moved off again and paused at a gate displaying a sign that read *Inverness Station Car Park (For Rail users only)*. Driving in, Olivia cruised to the other end before turning round and driving out again. 'Damn, they're not here. Now what?'

Use your ingenuity and resourcefulness, my love

Yeah right. Like what?

You could start with the laptop.

Olivia groaned, and said aloud, 'Of course, the laptop. I can track them on that and ask James, via the MI6 chat room, to find out if a woman and child took a taxi from Aviemore to Inverness.'

And that, my Love, may give you an address. At this rate, you will be a detective like Inspector Axel.

I'm finding you equally annoying in the afterlife as I did in person.

You miss me.

Yes, I do. Enough of being sentimental. As the old adage goes, Max, it's time for less pace and more haste. I need a place with easy parking and not in the centre of town to stay, to regroup my thoughts and prepare for an offensive.

That's my girl. Do you remember, we once lodged at a nice place on the other side of the river? It's close, just off Ness Walk. It has a nice little restaurant, and at your age, you must keep your strength up.

I need to keep my strength up! That's a bit rich coming from a dead person.

Oh, I forgot, you don't believe in an afterlife, so it's best we lock you up now, a crazy woman talking to her deceased husband.

Secretly.

Not always.

Leaving the car park and joining Railway Terrace, Olivia turned left onto Longman Road, using Friar's bridge to cross Ness River. She followed the A82 for a while before taking a left at Bishops Road, which led to Ness Walk. Olivia knew there was a quicker way to the hotel but didn't want to find herself lost, so took the route she remembered. Max's cover as a spy had been as a doddering old vicar, which was why Bishops Road stuck in her memory. And it was her name.

Checked in and inside her hotel room, Olivia freshened up before getting down to business. Opening the laptop, she logged into MI6 and downloaded the photographs she'd taken of the mysterious woman into the system. Moments later, the facial recognition software found a match on the Driver and Vehicle Licensing Agency data base. The woman was Ellen Goldsworthy.

'Bingo,' Olivia said, knowing that, armed with a name and photo, the security analysts at MI5 and MI6 would soon know all about Ellen Goldsworthy.

Next Olivia placed a video call to James and, when he didn't respond, she posted a message.

> *James. Urgent. I need to know (ASAP) if Samantha and Molly caught a taxi or similar from Aviemore, Scotland today and where they were dropped. The Chinese female Caucasian agent is Ellen Goldsworthy. I've uploaded her details. I have attached a tracking device to her blue transit van. PS My phone is broken.*

Olivia finished typing and waited, but not for long.

BING! James replied.

> *Well done, Olivia. I'll make the necessary enquiries. Give me thirty minutes.*

Olivia smiled to herself.

That's the old Olivia.

Next, she opened the map on the laptop for the GPS tracking device, wanting to see where her adversaries were located. They were at the Eastgate shopping centre car park, near the railway station.

'

'They know no more than I do,' she whispered, concluding that they were likely enjoying a late lunch to give the Chinese Security Service time to conduct the same inquiries as MI6.

Picking up the laptop to take it with her to the restaurant, Olivia muttered, 'This is going to come down to a race, so perhaps I'll skip the glass of wine with lunch.'

Ha ha, the way you drive, a glass of wine or two may help. Make it a bottle.

Shut up Max.

***

Olivia was enjoying cucumber and cream cheese sandwiches while watching the map on the laptop for signs of movement from her adversaries. She'd told the waiter, 'The bread needs to be soft but not soggy, cucumber sliced thinly without its skin and just a little salt and pepper, not overpowering plus a little dill. Dill is your friend. Leave the crust on as it helps my hair curl.'

After Olivia's precise instructions, her attempt at humour about the crusts on the sandwich fell flat, the waiter ignoring her comment. Inwardly Olivia chuckled, enjoying the game as once she and Max had, although she was often embarrassed by his antics. As the waiter turned to leave, Olivia added, 'I expect my sandwiches to be served on the best china and, if you have a silver platter, that will do perfectly.'

BING!

A message from Stephen Walls. 'The boss,' Olivia said, 'this must be serious.'

She minimised the tracking map and clicked the icon for the encrypted messenger service.

The woman you identified as Ellen Goldsworthy is an ex-Special Branch and has been involved in counterespionage. She resigned six months ago after a long and distinguished career and is booked on a flight leaving the UK in two days' time. This is a major security breach for the UK and it's imperative that Ellen Goldsworthy is arrested and that we speak with her.

Scotland, as with every other Police Force in the United Kingdom, has a Special Branch, although this is not the terminology they use. As you know, the Special Branch has a primary role to gather intelligence, work with and pass information on to the Secret Intelligence Service (MI6) and the Security Service (MI5). Ellen Goldsworthy's history in policing means it's imperative that Special Branch and MI5 are kept in the dark until we know who we can trust. They cannot know or be part of the pending operation. Our footprint within the Scottish Police force must be kept to a minimum.

I've had discussions with the Chief Constable. The plan is to use the Specialist Firearms unit to make the arrest. Detective Sally Mars, who has worked with MI6 before, is being flown by army helicopter from the Isle of Lewis to Fort George and will head up the police side of the operation. The command centre is being established at the military base of Fort George; meantime, we have activated our command centre here. Sally Mars reports to you.

Samantha and Molly Liew were dropped by taxi half an hour ago at 63 Torness Road, Inverness. We are monitoring the tracking beacon you placed on the transit van, and it seems the Chinese don't yet know Samantha and Molly's whereabouts.

I want Samantha and Molly removed from the equation. You are to pick them up and transport them to Fort George. They have been granted protection.

Your termination authorisation is rescinded and the new directive is to capture and hold. We want Ellen Goldsworthy alive.

Be careful Olivia, Ellen Goldsworthy is extremely dangerous.

Stephen Walls.

PS, James wants me to add, there is a new phone waiting for you at Fort George.

Olivia maximised the map on her computer. The GPS tracker still had Ellen Goldsworthy at the Eastgate shopping centre. She minimised it again before typing a quick reply.

Message understood. Olivia.

Olivia understood Stephen's reasoning. The Intelligence Services had failed to uncover a traitor in their midst, one with access to counter espionage material. It was a major security breach and an embarrassment for the British Government. They desperately needed to know the secrets she had revealed. Capturing her would also help limit the Intelligence Services' reputation damage with its Five Eye security partners.

Jotting down the address on the back of a napkin, sixty-three Torness Road, Olivia closed the lid to her laptop. Grabbing hold of the computer and the last uneaten sandwich, she returned to her room.

'Well, that was a quick stay,' she said to herself, while packing her vehicle with her limited belongings.

Entering the address into the Kia's GPS, Olivia smiled. Torness Road was close, two miles away on the opposite side of the river. As she rolled out of the hotel driveway, Olivia glanced at her watch. If everything went according to plan, she would be at Fort George within the hour. Back on the A82, Olivia turned left at the roundabout towards Raigmore Hospital, then left again on the A8082 towards Culduthel, using Holm Mills Bridge to cross River Ness and drive into Holm Mills. She turned left at Dores Road before making the last right turn onto Torness Road. To read the house numbers, Olivia slowed to a crawl, stopping in front of number sixty-one from where she had a clear view of sixty-three. The target house had a broken-down picket fence, grass was unmown and a derelict 1960 Triumph Herald was abandoned on its lawn.

Olivia muttered to herself as she got out of the Kia. 'This doesn't look right.'

After knocking on the front door, it opened to reveal a pot-bellied man in his late forties supporting three-day beard growth and wearing a stained white singlet, grey chest hairs oozing from the top. He stared at Olivia but said nothing.

'Good afternoon. My name is Olivia and I'm looking for Samantha, Molly and Snowflake.'

The man scratched his head. 'Never heard of them,' he said, a missing front tooth evident as he spoke.

Olivia hesitated, wondering whether he was covering for them, or Samantha had given the taxi driver a false address? She contemplated showing her MI6 identity card and asking to look around, but thought better of it.

'It seems, Sir, I have the wrong address. If they do drop by, please tell them that Olivia is looking for them.'

She turned and made her way slowly back to the SUV, hoping that if Molly and Samantha were hiding inside, when the man said Olivia, they would come out. At her vehicle, she edged forward and stopped in front of number sixty-three, where she paused for three minutes. When no one came, she concluded Samantha had been clever and given a false address. She moved off, knowing that Samantha, Molly, and Snowflake were close by, probably within walking distance. However, without a surveillance team, only luck would discover them.

Olivia pulled over to think.

Okay, this new development calls for a change of plan. Eliminate the threat to Molly and Samantha by picking up Ellen Goldsworthy and her cronies. Then you can concentrate on finding the Liew's.

Checking the GPS map, Olivia saw she was on the right side of the river for Fort George and could follow the A8082 to the A9 and then take the A96 for the drive out to the Fort. She decided that being unfamiliar with the area and with its distance; the drive was too long to be assigned to memory and that the destination should be programmed into the GPS, a task that proved more complicated than imagined. With what should have been a two-minute task taking five, she set off. Approaching the Inshes Roundabout with its twelve entries and exits, the Carlton Bingo building on her right and Police HQ on her left, she slowed to give way to traffic. As she was entering, Olivia saw a blue transit van exiting, travelling in the direction she had just come.

'Gees, that's them,' Olivia said aloud.

There was nothing Olivia could do but complete the circle on the roundabout and, by the time she was facing back the way she'd travelled, the van was nowhere to be seen.

Put your foot down, my Love, or you will lose them.

Be quiet Max, I don't have the time for you. Olivia pulled onto the footpath and parked, putting her hazard lights on as if she had broken down. Taking the laptop from its bag, she set it on the passenger's seat and switched it on.

'Come on,' she grumbled impatiently as the system slowly came to life. If they went to Torness Road, she would continue her journey to Fort George. Any other address and she would be there within minutes.

CHAPTER 20
Molly

Aviemore Railway Station

'Wake up, Molly.'

Molly yawned and stretched her arms. 'Are we there yet, Mummy?'

'No, we are getting off the bus here in Aviemore, to take a taxi the rest of the way to Inverness. It's my plan to foil those following us.'

Molly stroked the cat and said, 'That's clever, Mummy, isn't it Snowflake?' Snowflake nuzzled Molly's hand.

The bus stop was to the north and on the opposite side of the road to the railway station. Samantha and Molly disembarked, waiting for the bus to depart before checking their surrounds. On the left, Samantha spotted some small shops with a larger Tesco's supermarket a little further along the road. Behind her, back towards the railway station, she saw a taxi waiting in a bay behind a blue *Do-not-Enter* sign.

Her voice ringing with confidence, Samantha said, 'Molly, this is going to be easier than I thought. How about we get a drink and a snack to stop the worms biting before continuing our journey?'

'Yeah!'

Refreshed after a meal and toilet break, which included Snowflake, Samantha, with Molly all ears listening for the address to write on the next playing card, negotiated a cash price for the thirty-mile journey to Inverness. As they entered the taxi, Molly whispered, with an edge of urgency in her voice, 'Mummy, you told the taxi man where we are staying. What if the bad people find him?'

Samantha beamed and whispered back. 'I'm not as silly as you think. The address I gave him is near to where we are staying, but it's not correct. I had a false address in case we needed it, and we did. Come on.'

I still don't know the address.

Molly released an audible sigh, which she quickly changed into a yawn so as not to arouse her mother's suspicions.

You are a super spy, Molly. As we get close, keep a watchful eye out for a post office so you know where to find one.

Like on the bus, the hum of the road and motion of the vehicle made Molly drowsy. She fought the urge to close her eyes, but in the end couldn't resist and fell asleep.

Samantha rocked Molly gently, whispering, 'We are almost there. It's time to wake up, Sleepy Head.'

Realising that she'd fallen asleep, Molly panicked and sat bolt upright, swinging her gaze to look outside just as they were passing a corner building with a sign that read *Drumblair Post Office, General Store*. Next to a phone booth was a red post box. One street later, they turned onto Torness Road and Molly breathed a sigh of relief.

Fantastic, a post box this close to where we are staying. Even if I have to climb out the bedroom window, if I can get a message off tonight, Olivia will be here in the morning. Sneaking out is what Claudia would do, so I can too.

Dropped at number sixty-three, Samantha waited for the taxi to leave before guiding Molly, Snowflake following behind on the lead, two blocks further. She stopped on the footpath and pointed towards a front door.

'Ta-da, this is ours.'

Molly made a mental note of the street number. Next to the front door was a push button combination key lock box into which Samantha entered the code *2222* and then removed the house key. Inside was a nicely furnished, modest, three-bedroom home with a separate kitchen and lounge. It was as comfortable as it had appeared in the pictures from the internet. For the first time since leaving London, Samantha felt safe and did a pirouette as she said,

'Your home is your castle, even if it's a holiday rental.'

Molly laughed at her mother's antics. 'I like it Mummy and so does Snowflake.' Snowflake head-butted Molly's leg in agreement.

'Good, I'm pleased. The lady I hired it from did some shopping for us and we even have cat food for Snowflake. If you want to go and play for a while, I'll make us some lunch. Oh, and the lady told me that in the lounge room there is a cabinet containing games, pencils, colouring books, all the things you like.'

'Okay, Mummy. Come on Snowflake, let's explore.'

Samantha checked the kitchen pantry and fridge before creating a healthy lunch of grilled salmon wraps with lettuce, tomatoes, onion, dill, mayonnaise, and grated cheese. Folding the ingredients into warmed tortillas, she placed the finished product onto plates before putting them on the table. She smiled, satisfied with her work.

'Molly's favourite. Oh, I forgot the drinks.'

From the fridge she took a bottle of sparkling water, placing it on the table along with two glasses. 'Molly! Molly! Lunch is ready.'

There was no reply.

Samantha drifted into the lounge, calling as she went, but still no reply. Fearing the silence, her pulse raced, panic seeping into her body as she opened the back door and glanced into the garden. She couldn't see anyone, but called out anyway.

'Molly!'

Dread building inside, Samantha looked out the lounge windows to check the front garden. She screamed out in alarm,

'NO.'

Richard Liew was walking through the gate.

He's taken Molly.

Samantha knew Richard had her precious Molly and was coming for her. She couldn't help herself. Driven by rage and the protective instincts of a mother, Samantha flung open the front door and raced towards him, fists at the ready.

'Where is she?'

Richard Liew was struck twice on the chest before he gripped Samantha's hands, stopping her blows, trying to understand what she was yelling amongst the tears. The sound of a van door opening caught his attention, and he turned his head. Michael Tan was standing alongside a woman that he didn't recognise.

She was holding a pistol.

'Quick,' Richard Liew said to his wife, 'Inside the house.'

He dragged Samantha towards the front door.

The moment the transit van drove past Torness Road, Olivia jumped on the accelerator, bouncing her SUV off the footpath, causing an approaching car to brake heavily to avoid it running into her as she cut out in front. Two minutes and twenty seconds later, having broken most of the traffic laws, eyes darting from the laptop to the road, she rounded the corner to where the transit van was sending its tracking signal. Easing up, Olivia spotted first the blue van, then Samantha Liew's back as she vanished inside the house, and finally Ellen Goldsworthy with Michael Tan at her side. They were advancing towards the front door. Swerving in front of the transit van, she shoved the Kia into reverse and floored the accelerator. With wheels spinning, the reverse collision alarm activated.

BEEP BEEP BEEP.

Red lights flashed on the dash.

'Don't you dare auto-brake on me.'

Even though her foot was already to the floor, she increased her pressure on the accelerator.

SMASH!

The impact of the collision shoved the transit van backwards, its headlights shattering, the tow bar from the Kia rupturing its radiator, sending water cascading to the ground. Olivia's SUV halted; its tail embedded into the front of the transit van. She calmly pushed the electronic park button for the automatic transmission, unbuckled her seat belt, and opened the driver's door, removing her pistol from its holster as she alighted. Gun held out in front, Olivia rounded the SUV and took aim at Ellen Goldsworthy while moving towards her. Ellen Goldsworthy countered by levelling her pistol at Olivia.

'Hello, Sweetie,' Olivia said, using Claudia's tag line.

Ellen Goldsworthy knew Olivia wasn't the ruthless assassin Claudia, but the utterance of the name *Sweetie* sent shivers up her spine.

Recovering her poise and, with all the nastiness she could muster, said, 'Why, if it's not the old broiler, Olivia. I thought I recognised you at the bus station but dismissed it, thinking that you were still in Spain. Forgive me, Olivia, but I find all dribbling geriatrics look the same. Speaking of which, how is Max? Oh, that's right, he's dead. How insensitive of me.'

Without moving her eyes or gun from Ellen Goldsworthy, Olivia smiled and, demonstrating that she also knew who she was dealing with, said, 'Ellen, my dear, have you bothered to look in the mirror recently? Probably not, but you're no spring chicken yourself... At my age, I shouldn't be allowed a licence. I'm afraid my interesting parking technique will have alerted the neighbours and the police will arrive soon. It's time to put your weapon down and surrender. I'm sure the Chinese Government won't want a scene.'

'You're quite the eternal optimist for someone at your stage of life. I offer a simple trade. The child Molly, in exchange for Richard Liew.'

Olivia did her best to conceal the confusion in her face, reconciling Molly as a captive and Richard Liew being nearby. She was about to ask for proof when, as if reading her mind, Ellen Goldsworthy held a playing card with a cat's motif on it for her to see.

'Please, take it.'

Olivia edged forward, taking the card while maintaining her aim. Turning it over in her hand, she saw that *TO MI6* was written in red pencil and underneath was the current address.

Laughing, Ellen Goldsworthy said, 'I know what you're thinking, Olivia. How is it we have Molly? Is that right? We stumbled upon her and that stupid cat of hers at the post box preparing to post the card to you, I presume. She's in the back of the van, unharmed after your little escapade, I hope. Now be a good girl and give me your car keys, as mine seems to be in a state of disrepair. Then I'll take my leave while you think about my proposition.' Ellen Goldsworthy smirked. 'Be under no illusion, Olivia. If you try to stop me, Kang Long will have no hesitation in killing her.'

Olivia lowered her weapon and removed the key fob from her pocket.

'Mr Tan, if you will take the fob from her. Excellent.'

A grin spreading over her face, Ellen Goldsworthy waved her pistol towards the transit van, an invitation for Olivia to look. Kang Long, pistol drawn, bundled Molly out of the back, Olivia could see that Molly was scared, too frightened even to raise her head. The sight of the distressed child tore at Olivia's heart strings.

Kang Long said, his tone menacing, 'Move it, kid.'

He pushed Molly in the back; the force causing her to stumble. As she tried to regain her balance, Molly's head turned slightly sideways, her eyes meeting Olivia's. Instantly, the fear etched across Molly's face vanished. She raised herself to her full height and, her voice assured, said, 'Olivia is here. Now you're in for it.'

Kang laughed, 'You're dreaming, kid.'

He opened the rear passenger door of Olivia's SUV, forcing Molly inside, before climbing in himself. Ellen Goldsworthy holstered her weapon, calling as she walked towards the SUV, 'A trade, Olivia. Richard Liew for the kid.'

'Where?'

'I'll call you.'

Unseen by Ellen Goldsworthy, Olivia scrunched up her face.

I don't have a phone.

'I will call on Richard's phone as I hear that you have butter fingers.' As Ellen Goldsworthy reached the SUV, she turned and said, her voice dripping with irony, 'Bye Sweetie.'

Olivia judged that there was little she could do without endangering Molly, so remained rooted to the spot, watching helplessly as Ellen Goldsworthy drove away.

I'm coming for you Molly, that's a promise.

We're coming for you Molly, that's our promise.

Movement caught Olivia's eyes as Snowflake, lead attached, jumped from the back of the transit van onto the pavement. Patting her leg, Olivia called, 'Snowflake, Snowflake, come here, there's a good kitty.' Cat hair pointing straight up, taking on a spiked appearance, a sign of anger, Snowflake sprinted to Olivia's side, the message unmistakable. *They've taken my Molly!*

Olivia bent down and picked up the cat. 'Don't worry, we will get her back.'

Inside the house, Samantha broke free of Richard's grip and rushed outside before he could prevent her, stopping dumbfounded when she witnessed Olivia holding and stroking Molly's cat. Richard followed his wife, but stopped when Samantha, standing halfway between Olivia and Richard, started firing off a series of disjointed questions. 'What's going on? Where's Molly? Olivia, what are you doing here? How did you find us?'

She turned to face Richard. 'And you, how did you find us? Who are those people? Are they with you? Oh, Molly, where's Molly?'

With Samantha's emotions overflowing, Olivia walked towards her, then, as she had done in Spain, placed a calming hand on her arm. 'Samantha, with all the ruckus, someone will have called the police. For Molly's sake, it's vital that we leave immediately. You must trust me. Richard, where's your car?'

'It's parked around the corner.'

Olivia, her voice strong and confident, a woman in control of the situation, said, 'That's perfect, Richard. We have no time to lose. Lead us through the house, out of the back door and to your car. We need to plan how to rescue Molly. Samantha, take Snowflake from me, and I promise to answer your questions once we are away from here. We have work to do, so let's go.'

Samantha sobbed. 'What about Molly?'

Olivia gripped Samantha's hand and, in a reassuring voice, said, 'We are going to get her.'

That's my girl.

***

Like he had done in Spain, as if leading a military patrol, Richard Liew raised his hand, signalling to Olivia and Samantha to stop. Nearing an intersection, he spotted a police car, its lights flashing but no siren, fast approaching. When it had passed, he said, 'Okay, keep moving. My car is just around the corner.' Samantha followed in silence, stewing over her barrage of questions that had gone unanswered. At the car, as Olivia climbed into the back seat, she joined her, leaving Richard in the front on his own.

Starting the motor, Richard glanced at Olivia in the mirror. 'What now?'

'Your appearance, Richard, has altered the equation, something I need time to digest. Move away from here and find a safe place to stop while I consider our next move.'

Richard nodded, and they moved off.

Listening to the matter-of-fact exchange between her husband and Olivia, Samantha could hold her tongue no longer.

'Altered the equation!!! that sounds like something that woman Claudia might say. I don't mean to be rude, but what about Molly? And Richard, why are you here?' Before Olivia could reply, Samantha added, her tone settling, 'Oh, Olivia, forgive me for comparing you to Claudia. I apologise as I am so glad that you're here, truly I am. How did you find us?'

Olivia saw Richard glance at her in the mirror as he raised an eyebrow; he too wondered how she'd found Samantha. 'Now isn't the time to answer your questions in any detail. There will be time enough for that when Molly is safe. I will tell you what I can. I'm here because Molly summoned me. She understood that were on the run from the Chinese government and needed help.' Olivia saw Samantha open her mouth, ready to ask the obvious questions. Not wanting to mention Claudia, Olivia held up her hand 'The arrangements between Molly and I are for later as we have more pressing matters at hand. Samantha, you must forgive my words as they may sound calculating, not reflective of my heart, the love I feel for you and Molly.' Olivia took a deep breath. 'It's been my experience that, in situations like these, as counterintuitive as it sounds, we need to consider the Chinese Security Service' concerns, fears and objectives. We need to look at the world through their eyes. Until recently, they viewed Richard as a loyal servant. After the events of Spain, he was no longer an effective agent in Britain. His knowledge of their activities in the UK meant they had to send him home–to what fate, we can't know. You and Molly were a loose end to be tied. It is possible that they believed you were an MI5 spy, Samantha. It doesn't matter whether you are or are not. The best way for the Chinese State Security to control the risk you posed was for you to accompany Richard to China. When you and Molly fled, an operation was launched for your capture, a clean-up exercise. Sometime between you leaving and now, their faith in Richard's loyalties to the Communist Party has collapsed and they now fear that he will reveal secrets to the UK intelligence agencies. Other than bargaining chips, you and Molly are no longer important to them. They want Richard at all costs, hence the offer of the exchange: Molly for your husband.

Samantha nodded solemnly. 'When we do the exchange, will they kill him?'

Richard glanced at Olivia in the mirror, keen to hear her answer.

'No, not at the exchange site, at least. Ellen Goldsworthy, that's the woman who has followed you, knows MI6 is hot on her trail, especially now she's seen me. She is also aware, if Richard turns, he is a high value asset for British intelligence. They will keep him alive in case she needs a bargaining chip herself. Somewhere in Scotland and close to here, the Chinese State Security Service is putting together a hurried extraction point for her and the team. Ellen Goldsworthy will keep Richard alive until she's safe herself.'

'Will I get Molly back?' Samantha asked.

Richard piped in from the front seat. 'Samantha, I agree with everything that Olivia has told you. When we do the exchange, Molly will be released and you will be free. What I don't understand is how they knew I was here? I took precautions. A new phone, picked up the hire car last night and haven't used my credit card since leaving London.'

Olivia shrugged her shoulders. 'All I know is that Ellen Goldsworthy knows your new mobile number and will call us with the handover location. Somewhere on you or the car or through the phone, we are being tracked. And we can turn that to our advantage.'

Richard Liew glanced at Olivia in the mirror. 'This looks like a suitable spot coming up. Do you want me to pull over there?'

'Yes, that will do nicely. I will need to use your phone.'

Richard indicated to the left, preparing to stop as Samantha asked him, 'How did you find me?'

'In your side drawer next to our bed was a pad indented from your writing on the page you ripped out, where you had scrawled the Inverness address. When you moved the pen over the page, it went through to the second page. Like in the movies, I examined it to expose the writing underneath, not by rubbing a pencil over the page, because that may have damaged the indentation. I angled it to the light and copied it down.' As he finished speaking, Richard pulled into a car park and switched off the engine. 'We wait now, I suppose?'

With things changing so rapidly, Samantha was swamped by contradicting emotions. She wanted Molly, but did she also want Richard? 'Olivia, I need to speak with you alone.'

'Of course. Let's stretch our legs. Now, what is it dear?'

'I feel like a silly schoolgirl. With Molly's life at stake, I have to decide if I want to stay with Richard. Worse, a part of me hopes he loses his life during the exchange so that I don't have to make a tough decision. That's awful, I know.'

Olivia looked at Samantha with sympathetic eyes. 'What is it you wish me to say, my dear?'

Samantha shrugged her shoulders, 'I don't really know...' She sighed... 'I would appreciate your opinion.'

'When we marry, and Max and I were the same, we want a fairy tale *happy ever after* ending. On the days after the wedding vows, we are shrouded in a Hollywood or Jane Austen feeling of love. It doesn't take long for the truth to set in; relationships are hard work and exist in a mundane world of daily grind. The spark fades because the marriage was built on an illusion of idealism. He's my soul mate, he will change, I will never stop loving him, for better or for worse, our marriage will be different. The list is endless. Laziness or quirky behaviours that were once tolerable become beacons of annoyance. For some, the husband has an affair, or work is the mistress. For you, Richard had a secret life as a foreign spy. Regardless, there is a third *person* in the marriage. We may follow different routes but, at some point, on the journey we arrive at the same place.'

'Do we stay or go?'

'Despite this, marriage is still popular. People looked rosy eyed at Queen Elizabeth and Prince Philip, who met in 1934 and married on November 20, 1947. They were married for seventy-three years, had four children, countless grandchildren and great-grandchildren. He walked in the footsteps of his Queen, always three steps behind and, when he passed away aged ninety-nine, it was the end of a modern-day love story that lasted seventy-three years. It is no surprise that the divorce announcement from Bill and

Melinda Gates, after twenty-seven years and three children, fascinated us. Melinda Gates wrote, "he's had to learn how to be an equal and I've had to learn how to step up and be an equal," and that they could no longer grow together. My take on life, Samantha, is nothing in life is fair or equal and that it's a fool's paradise to think otherwise, plus a road to certain unhappiness. After all, Prince Philip walked three steps behind his Queen, equitable but not equal. Literature leads us to believe that marriage is one of the most beautiful and precious of human institutions, perhaps that's why unhappy people stay together for reasons they rarely understand themselves: for the kids, financial stability, security over independence, to protect their sunk resources, only leaving if it is worth it. Infidelity, or other serious problems like yours, are a powerful motivator. You are not the first woman to think of leaving your husband, and certainly not the last. It is not my place to give advice, though that's what you are seeking. However, today I will. To leave a marriage is a decision equal to the one taken when you marry. In your circumstances, where Richard's behaviour has put you in danger, but he himself is not a danger to you or Molly, it's a choice to be made at a different time, when you are *all* safe.'

Samantha, in her heart of hearts, knew that this wasn't the time for a decision, and hearing Olivia say so brought comfort to her otherwise troubled thoughts. 'Thank you, Olivia. How do these exchanges take place?'

Olivia touched Samantha gently on the arm. 'Well done. Ask me again when we are in the car.'

Richard's heart ached as he watched Samantha through the windscreen speaking to Olivia. After Spain, there were so many words he should have whispered into his beloved's ear. I love you; I need you; I want you; I'm sorry for all that has befallen you and Molly. He'd remained mute, as he must now.

Returning to the car, Samantha asked, 'How do these exchanges take place?'

Olivia rubbed her chin. 'Typically, trades involve both parties looking at each other across a vacant space, a bridge is often best, then the people to be swapped walk towards each other and pass in the centre. Often, one side or both will plant armed personnel to ensure that the exchange goes smoothly and sometimes to enact a double cross.' Olivia looked at Samantha,

'Our chess game is playing out live, with both sides adapting and responding to a rapidly changing situation. It would be a challenge for either of us to plan a double cross but, if we are to secure both Molly and Richard, we must.' Olivia turned her gaze to Richard, who was watching at her in the mirror.

'This is a hard question for you and my help will not be conditional upon the answer. However, MI6 will ask me, so I must ask you too: will you cooperate with the British security services?'

Richard Liew didn't hesitate in his answer. 'If you secure Molly's release and I live, I'm yours.'

Olivia nodded. With resolve ringing in her voice, said, 'Okay, I've never lost a person on my watch before and I'm not starting today. We have work to do. Richard, pass me your phone.' This time Olivia's memory didn't fail her, and she punched the number for MI6 and James into the phone. He answered after two rings.

'James, this is Olivia with a priority one call. Patch me through to the command centre.' The phone was silent for three seconds until Stephen Walls spoke. 'Go ahead, Olivia.'

'Stephen, you are on speaker phone. The situation on the ground has changed markedly. I have in my company Richard Liew and Samantha. Ellen Goldsworthy has taken Molly hostage and wants an exchange for Richard. We are waiting for the details of how that will work. Is Fort George operational?'

'Indeed Olivia, things have altered dramatically.' He paused ... 'Fort George will be another thirty to sixty minutes before it's ready, even slightly longer, as Detective Wells is yet to touchdown.' Stephen hesitated... knowing all those present could hear him. 'This is an unexpected turn of events. Do we know Richard Liew's intention?' Olivia started to respond when Richard spoke over the top of her.

'Sir, if you save Molly and keep my family safe, by which I mean protection, I will tell you more than you can ever imagine.'

With no time to prepare and limited resources—if any—at Olivia's disposal, Stephen was under no illusions about the enormity of the task ahead: securing Molly and Richard safely. Of all the agents he had, if anyone could pull off the seemingly impossible, it was Olivia. 'What's your plan, Olivia?'

'Firstly Stephen, locate my SUV which Ellen Goldsworthy has taken. The hire company told me that the car came with a *find my car* function and to activate it, I needed to log into the portal with a password and then enter the registration number. The password is the rental contract reference number, which James will have.'

'Right, Olivia. James has joined us in the control room and is working on it now.'

'Thank you, Stephen. I'm operating under the assumption that the Chinese agents have a nearby safe house where Ellen Goldsworthy is planning the exchange and extraction of her team from the UK. I doubt we have long before they make a move, so we can't wait for Inspector Wells and her team. My plan is to go to the safe house and secure Molly while Richard and Samantha follow

Ellen Goldsworthy's instructions for the exchange until I tell them otherwise. The Chinese are tracking Richard and believe I'm with him, I will have the element of surprise. This is Richard's phone and will remain with him and Samantha. Track it. I will acquire another so you can monitor me.'

Ordinarily Stephen wouldn't approve such an audacious plan. The SAS would be sent in to free Molly, not a sole agent in her late eighties. However, these were not ordinary times or circumstances. 'Alright, Olivia. James is texting the address of your SUV now. You only have a narrow window, so it's best you make haste. Ask Mr Liew to share the exchange point as soon as he is aware of it. Good luck everyone.'

Olivia instructed Richard to drive slowly around the nearby back streets, asking him to stop when she saw a young man in his twenties, wearing a Glasgow Rangers football jumper, washing his Ford Focus in the driveway.

'He will do nicely,' Olivia said, then telling Richard and Samantha to leave her, not wanting them to be identified as working in collusion. As Richard was about to drive away, Snowflake leapt from the car. 'Sorry Snowflake,' Olivia said. 'I have to do this on my own.' She lifted the cat back into the car.

Olivia walked into the driveway holding her MI6 Identification.

'Excuse me, Sir. I'm with the Secret Intelligence Service and I need your vehicle.'

The man looked her up and down and if his obscene language decorating every second word was filtered out, he said, 'I don't fucken think so, Lady.'

Olivia withdrew her pistol. 'Oh, I do think so, son.'

He shook his head in resolute indifference. 'You will have to shoot me first.'

This is going well, Olivia.

Not now Max.

I suggest, my dear, a change of tack. Appeal to his obvious... adventurous spirit.

Olivia, her voice resolute, said. 'Son, I need to rescue an eight-year-old girl being held hostage by Chinese agents, then protect her father who has vital information about foreign operatives' espionage activities here in Britain. This is a matter of national security and you can either drive me or I will shoot you. The choice is yours. Oh, and I also want your phone. I will count to three.'

The man's indifference vanished, his face turning a whiter shade of pale as he stammered, 'Why didn't you say so? Best get in. I'm fucken Thomas by the way.'

'Olivia.'

***

The Chinese Ministry of State Security safe house was in Milton of Leys, a residential settlement three miles southeast of the Inverness city centre, a location with easy access to the A9 and other routes of escape. Olivia contacted the MI6 control room whilst Thomas drove and confirmed that her targets were still present. She also learned the location of the exchange point, a single-lane bridge over the River Spey, half a mile from Avie. This meant that Molly would be on the move soon. As they pulled into the street, Olivia spotted the battered SUV and instructed Thomas to drive past and stop four houses further along. She sighed unconsciously and whispered, 'Max, how am I going to do this without putting Molly at risk? There is no time for disguise and my age makes stealth near on impossible.'

Thomas, assuming that Olivia was talking to him, having heard one side of Olivia's conversation with MI6, wiped his nose on his sleeve and said in his broad Glaswegian accent, 'I'll stop them leaving for you while you go in and get the kid.'

Surprised by the remark, Olivia glanced at Thomas. He smiled while plucking from his pocket a folding blade knife. 'I'll slash their bloody tyres.'

'Are you sure?' Olivia asked, concerned about the young man's safety.

Thomas laughed, 'Look Lady, I grew up in Glasgow, once dubbed the murder capital of Europe. These people are fucken nothing. While they are swapping the tyre, you go inside and get the kid. I'll drive round the back and meet you.'

As Thomas opened the door to exit, Olivia called after him, 'Slash the back right?'

'Yeah, the one away from the curb.'

That's what I was going to do, Thomas muttered to himself.

Olivia adjusted the car's rear-view mirror so that she could watch his progress. With no hesitation, Thomas strolled past the SUV and, in a quick flowing motion, bent down, punctured the tyre and kept on walking. Even if someone was watching, such was his speed and agility, that it would have been easy to miss what happened.

He's done that before.

After crossing the road, Thomas returned to the car. 'All right Lady, you're up.'

Olivia looked at him questioningly.

'Shit lady. Fucken stash yourself in the driveway next door and wait for them to come out. Haven't you done a burg before?'

You picked yourself a burglar. How fitting.

'I have an eye for talent, Max.'

'What did you say, lady?'

'I said that I have an eye for talent and it's *My Lady* or *Olivia* if you don't mind. I'll meet you round the back.' Olivia opened the car door and pulled herself out, accompanied by a groan from old age, a twinge in her back.

Was that a bit of arthritis, dear?

A little pain is better than being dead.

Oh, that was harsh!

From her vantage point, hiding in the garden next door, Olivia had a view of the SUV and watched as the front door of the safe house opened. Moments later, Ellen Goldsworthy emerged, holding Molly by the hand, leading her to the vehicle. Ellen Goldsworthy opened the passenger side rear door of the SUV and shoved Molly inside before climbing in next to her. Kang Long jumped into the driver's seat with Michael Tan seated alongside.

Kang Long pushed the start button.

BEEP! BEEP! BEEP!

The sound of a low tyre pressure warning sounded, accompanied by a picture of the right rear on the display. He opened the door and hung his head out. 'Damn, we've a flat. Must have been when the old bag used the car as a battering ram.'

Ellen Goldsworthy spoke through gritted teeth. 'Not again. That Olivia is proving to be a real pain in the arse. I'll take Molly back inside while you two change it and be quick about it. We don't have long.' Softening her tone, and taking Molly by the hand, she said, 'Come on.'

'You're hurting me.'

Ellen Goldsworthy loosened her grip. 'I'm sorry, Molly. I don't mean to hurt you. Is that better?'

'Yes.'

'Good.'

Olivia watched as Molly and Ellen Goldsworthy headed inside.

Ellen Goldsworthy accompanied Molly to the bedroom where they had been holding her, shutting and locking the door. From the kitchen, she called Chen Li, head of the Chinese Ministry of State Security operations in the UK, to update him.

Pistol drawn from her hiding place next door, Olivia waited for Michael Tan and Kang Long to disappear behind the SUV, one loosening the wheel nuts while the other placed the jack under the car. Slipping from the cover, Olivia crossed into the front yard of the safe house and followed the fence line until she was standing beside the building, where she moved along its edge, peering in the windows, holding her breath, hoping not to be seen. At the third window, Olivia popped her head round the corner and gasped when her gaze met the eyes of someone peering out. A second later she realised it was Molly. A grin of relief decorated her face. Molly smiled back at her, silently mouthing that she believed Olivia would rescue her. Olivia understood she had mere seconds to extract Molly before they risked being caught. Gripping her pistol by the barrel, she prepared to smash the glass.

Olivia, no Stop! The sound of breaking glass will wake the dead.

You're right, Max.

Holding the pistol by the butt, she pointed its barrel at the window latch and mouthed to Molly to fetch a chair and open it. Holstering the gun, Olivia helped Molly slide up the window while trying to open it quickly without making a sound. Molly threaded herself through the gap, throwing her arms round and hugging Olivia the moment her feet touched the ground. Olivia met the embrace, then held her finger to her lips, requesting that Molly keep quiet. Whispering, she said, 'Follow me.'

Olivia began leading Molly into the rear of the garden, heading for the back fence.

'Where's Max?' Molly whispered.

Olivia stopped at the paling fence and scanned left and right for a gate, but there wasn't one. 'Max got sick and passed away.'

Molly put her hand to her mouth and said, 'Oh! I'm so sorry.'

'You weren't to know, Molly.'

'Will you take me to his grave so I can say goodbye?'

'There is a special place in Cornwall with a view over the ocean where he wanted to be laid to rest. When this is over, we will go there together. Now, my young super spy, this fence is too high for an old chook like me to climb. Like you did in the tunnels in Spain, I need you to be brave and you must do it alone. Climb over and you will see a red Ford Focus parked on the side of the road. The driver is Thomas, wearing a football jumper. His language is a little colourful, but he's a good man and will take you to safety.'

Molly scrunched up her face, her eyes wide open. 'No! I won't leave you.'

In a firm but tender voice, Olivia said, 'We don't have time for an argument, Molly. If you want to protect your family, you must go and now.'

A teardrop formed in the corner of Molly's eye and ran down the side of her face as she nodded.

Olivia smiled. 'I'm an old hand at this Molly and will be fine. So, my young super spy, off you go.'

Olivia waited as she watched Molly scamper over the fence before retracing her steps. Hidden by the side of the house, she paused as Michael Tan walked up the path. She heard him open the front door and call out, 'It's done, Boss. Kang is tightening the nuts, then we can go.'

Ellen Goldsworthy was still speaking to Chen Li when she heard Michael Tan. Finishing the call, she made her way to the bedroom to fetch Molly. Unlocking the door, she let out an audible groan in despair. Molly was gone, and the window was open. Ellen Goldsworthy checked the back garden before spotting the back of Olivia vanishing around the corner onto the footpath.

'Doesn't that geriatric ever give up? I'm going to kill her, I am, I'm going to kill her!' Pulling her head back inside the house, she yelled to Michael Tan, 'She has Molly, stop her!'

'Who?' came Michael Tan's confused reply.

Goldsworthy rolled her eyes. 'Santa Claus! Who do you bloody think? Olivia.'

Molly Liew, spotting the Ford Focus where Olivia had told her it would be, approached and peered inside, tapping cautiously on the side window to attract the attention of a man wearing a football jersey. The man beckoned towards her and Molly opened the door, saying.

'What's your name?'

'F**...' he stopped himself from swearing. 'Um, my name is Thomas and you must be Molly.'

Molly nodded.

'Best get in then.' When Molly was in the car, Thomas asked, 'Where's the old woman?'

When Molly explained what Olivia had told her, Thomas put the car in first gear and began moving off as he said, 'Are you up for fucken fight Molly?'

'Absolutely.'

'Buckle up then and let's go and get her!'

Molly clicked her seat belt into place and the front wheels of the Focus squealed as Thomas slammed his foot to the floor. At the end of the street, he swung left, the speed of the car causing it to under-steer onto the wrong side of the road as he changed up a gear and raced towards the street where the safe house was located.

Approaching the intersection, vroom, Thomas double de-clutched, blipping the throttle as he changed down gears, throwing the Focus sidewards into the next street and straightening as he saw the SUV. On the footpath, just in front of the vehicle, he spotted Olivia hurrying away.

'There she is,' Molly yelled.

As the Ford Focus raced past the safe house, Thomas caught sight of a woman flanked by a man dashing down the garden path, obviously in pursuit of Olivia. Hitting the brakes while honking the horn, Thomas skidded the Focus to a stop alongside Olivia, who barely had enough time to pull herself into the back seat before the car was moving again.

Breathless, after her quick sprint, Olivia said, 'Thank you.'

Thomas nodded, 'Fasten your seat belt, they're after us.'

A burglar and a racing driver... No, a car thief more likely. You choose well.

He reminds me of you.

Ha ha. He's not that cute.

Olivia turned and glanced out of the back window. Ellen Goldsworthy was stepping into the SUV.

Kang Long had the motor of the SUV idling when his boss and Michael Tan leapt in.

'What are you waiting for? We need that girl.'

The engine of the Ford Escort screamed as Thomas swerved around a slow car, changing down a gear and turned right. Molly was surprised by the lack of urgency in Olivia's voice as she said, her tone jovial, 'Thomas, I take it you are a car thief and a burglar?'

'I know these fucken back streets and should be able to give them the slip.'

'Language Thomas, please. Molly and I are pleased that you are such an accomplished driver and that you know your way about but would prefer if you didn't kill us. Isn't that right, Molly?'

Molly hesitated, torn between being frightened out of her skin and having the most fun she could ever remember. She settled on a simple, 'Yes.'

Thomas laughed, 'I like you, Lady.'

Olivia grinned even though Thomas couldn't see her, her tone conveying the humour, 'It's My Lady, Thomas.'

'Yes, My Lady.'

After a quick glance in the mirror, Thomas turned south on the B862, which ran along the east side of Loch Dochfour. Thomas saw the SUV was still with them despite him swerving between slow vehicles and making sudden direction changes on the back streets.

Olivia asked Molly to pass Thomas's mobile phone, which was where she left it, in the centre console. She called the control room at MI6 and spoke to Stephen Walls, who told them they were only minutes away from tracking them on a live satellite feed. Meanwhile, they were following events via Thomas's phone and the *Find my car* app of the Kia SUV until the satellite came into position.

At Molly's request, Olivia asked about her mother and father, Olivia relaying that Detective Sally Mars had landed at Fort George and that an armed response team had been sent to the River Spey bridge. Her parents would soon be secured. The helicopter was being refuelled and Detective Mars, with a second armed response unit, was being sent to their aid.

'In the meantime,' Stephen Walls said, 'keep heading south and, whatever you do, Olivia, stay away from Ellen Goldsworthy until help arrives.'

'That is our intention, Stephen.'

Approaching the hamlet of Dores at speed, a town he knew well, Thomas overtook a motorbike while ignoring the thirty miles an hour sign, planning to veer left at the approaching junction, staying on the B862 to Fort Augustus. He let fly a barrage of profanities when he caught a truck just before the intersection. Not wanting to lose his slender lead over the SUV, he altered course, going straight ahead on the B852 to follow the banks of Loch Ness to Foyers. The road to Fort Augustus would have been a speedier route and easier to elude their pursuers. No sooner had they left the town limits of Dores than the road narrowed to a country lane where they risked being slowed by oncoming vehicles, and overtaking, if they caught someone, was a near impossibility, except at one of the passing bays.

In hot pursuit, egged on by Ellen Goldsworthy, Kang Long approached the B862 and B852 junction. Not slowing, he shot across the road, causing an oncoming vehicle to swerve as he cut across in front of it.

'At last,' Ellen Goldsworthy said, 'they've made a mistake. Close up and push them off the road.'

Up ahead, Kang Long saw that recent rain had left a large puddle with mud washed across the road. Sensing an opportunity to make the Focus spin on the slippery surface, he squeezed on the throttle. The gap between the vehicles closed effortlessly, and the SUV rammed into the back of the Ford.

'Take that,' Kang Long said while grinning.

A flurry of profanities accompanied Thomas's steering wheel corrections as the car slid to the side, fishtailing before straightening again. Rounding a sweeping bend, Thomas was greeted by the back of a slow-moving car, sightseers enjoying the views of Loch Ness. If he braked, the SUV would hit them again. A yellow sign flashed into his peripheral vision: *Passing Place.*

Holding his breath, Thomas gambled on the tourist not noticing him and veered left into the pullover space, not more than a couple of car lengths long. He overtook the vehicle on its inside before swerving in front of it. Checking the mirror, Thomas could see that the SUV was held up, and he breathed out heavily. A light flashing on the instrument panel caught his attention; the low fuel warning light.

As they drove, Olivia communicated their predicament to Stephen. Low and flying north up Loch Ness, two Tornado jet fighters, roared into view.

Olivia's heart leapt at the magnificent sight, and Molly pointed. 'Stephen, have you sent the RAF?'

'No, Olivia. It must be a training flight.'

Olivia's spirits momentarily sank, but Thomas refocussed her attention.

'We are running on fucken fumes. If help doesn't come soon, we're ...'

Olivia interjected, 'Language, Thomas.'

Stephen, listening from the MI6 control room, glanced at the map. 'Olivia, Detective Mars and the armed response team are flying over Loch Dochfour. They are only minutes away. You must hold on. In fifty yards, on your left, is a dirt track. Take it. It will lead you past a property and then into a clearing. It's a dead end but, with luck, you will have lost them and the clearing is somewhere we can land a helicopter.' Olivia shared the instructions with Thomas.

Not wanting to leave a dust trail behind, Thomas slowed, turning off onto a dirt track that was surrounded by trees. He crawled past a dwelling before coming to the large clearing where he drove until the road ran out. He executed a U-turn and parked up to wait for the helicopter. They'd stopped for only fifty seconds when Olivia's battered SUV came into view and crawled towards them. The ground on either side of the road they'd drove in on was unstable and the track only wide enough for one car.

They were trapped.

'Everybody out,' Olivia commanded, and when Thomas and Molly hesitated, she snapped, 'Now!'

Olivia walked to the driver's side of the Focus and got in. 'I need to buy you both a little time. The cavalry will be here soon so head towards the trees and hide until the help arrives.'

Molly guessed that Olivia's plan was to ram the SUV head on and she shook her head in disbelief. 'What are you going to do, smash into them?'

'It's okay, Molly. Thomas will look after you until the helicopter comes.'

'No, you mustn't.'

'Remember Molly what I said about Cornwall, the place with a view over the sea?'

Tears flowed down Molly's cheek. 'No, you mustn't do it.'

'There's no time for an argument Molly.' Olivia revved the engine.

Molly placed her hand on Olivia's shoulder, kissing her tenderly on the cheek.

Olivia smiled and looked at Thomas. 'Mind your P's and Q's and look after this girl.'

She pulled the door closed and hit the accelerator.

Ellen Goldsworthy watched as Olivia drove towards them. 'What is that geriatric thinking? Ram her off the road. Let's grab the kid and get the hell out of here.'

Kang Long grinned, driving head on at speed towards Olivia in a game of chicken, confident that she would yield first because he was braver. As they approached each other, he squeezed on the throttle to increase his speed.

Max, I must stop them... Dead.

I know, my Love.

Kang Long felt a bead of sweat drip down the side of his face as the two vehicles raced towards one another. They were so close that he could see Olivia through the windscreen and watch as she took her hands from the wheel and closed her eyes.

Olivia would not yield.

At the last second, he stomped on the brakes and threw the steering wheel to the right. The SUV left the track and bounced to a stop at the side of the road, its bumper bar coming to rest, touching a large rock. He breathed a sigh of relief before wiping his sweat ridden hands dry on his trousers.

Olivia peeked through a half-open eye, not sure if the cars had missed each other or whether she was dead. In front the road was empty but, before she could place her hands back on the wheel, her car left the dirt track, launching itself into the air, smashing down on the uneven surface. The airbags activated, hitting her in the face and side as the car rolled, flipping upside down before coming to a stop.

Thwap-thwap-thwap-thwap

The blades of a military helicopter cut through the air as it swung inland, having followed the shoreline of Loch Ness to circle over the clearing. Detective Mars spotted the SUV of Ellen Goldsworthy reversing from the shrubbery and back onto the dirt track. A hundred feet from the SUV was a young girl, Molly, she assumed, and a young man, both waving up at them. A hundred and thirty feet the other way was a car on its roof.

'What are your instructions?' the pilot asked through the intercom.

'Put us down between the girl and the SUV.'

'Roger.'

Ellen Goldsworthy knew better than to send a volley of shots up at the helicopter; the armed response unit would counter the return fire, resulting in their deaths.

'Drive,' she commanded Kang Long.

As the helicopter touched down, the armed police, followed by Detective Sally Mars, disembarked. Molly ran to Sergeant Williams, the first person she saw, crying out, 'Olivia, Olivia, she's in the car.'

His voice reassuring, Sergent Williams said, 'Okay, young lady, come with me.' He led Molly to Detective Wells.

Detective Wells crouched down, trying to hear what Molly was saying over the noise of the rotors. She acknowledged Molly with a nod. 'Sergeant, you with me. Tell your men to protect, Molly.'

Molly shook her head. 'I'm coming with you.'

Detective Mars dropped to one knee. 'I know you want to help Molly, but you must let me do my job, which is to get Olivia out of there.'

Sergeant Williams asked Detective Sally Mars, as they hurried towards the upturned car, whether the helicopter should be sent to follow the Chinese agents.

'Not until we know how Olivia is.'

Leaving the track, Detective Mars feared for the worst. Every panel on the Focus was damaged and its rear wheels were still spinning in the air. She stood back to let Sergeant William's force open the driver's door. Olivia was strapped upside down in the driver's seat, her eyes open.

'Can you hear me, Olivia?' Sergeant Williams said.

Olivia nodded and, with adrenaline contributing to the discourse, said, 'This is most undignified; my knickers are wrapped around my teeth. If you would kindly lower me down, I would find it most appealing.'

Olivia's manner caused Sergeant Williams to smile, but he hesitated, conscious of the potential for a back injury. The smell of leaking petrol made him change his mind. He summonsed Detective Mars with a wave of his hand.

Sergeant Williams placed his arms under Olivia's shoulders, asking Detective Mars to unclip the seat belt on the count of three. Supported by his powerful arms, he guided Olivia from the car. As he lowered her feet to the ground, Olivia let out a cry of anguish, her ankle broken.

Sergeant Williams said, 'Olivia, we must move away from here in case the car explodes. It seems your ankle is injured. I'll have to carry you. Is that okay?'

Olivia didn't respond. Detective Mars thought she appeared dazed and feared that she would pass into unconsciousness.

Sergeant Williams said, 'Olivia, I'm going to pick you up.'

As he lifted Olivia from the ground, Detective Mars whispered, 'Sergeant, if you can manage it, carry her to the helicopter. We need to get her to a hospital.'

'Should we wait for an Air Ambulance?'

Detective Mars shook her head. 'There isn't time.'

Molly burst into tears as Olivia was lifted on board the aircraft. She threw her arms around Olivia, who was still in Sergeant Williams's arms.

'Careful there, Lassie. We don't want to hurt her.'

***

The battered SUV stopped at the bitumen, steam hissing from its damaged radiator, sustained while dodging Olivia. It turned left onto the B852. Two miles up the road, the SUV spluttered and slowed. Kang Long looked at the dashboard, which was lit up like a Christmas tree, warning lights flashing everywhere. 'We're in limp home mode.'

Ellen Goldsworthy wound down the window to listen for the helicopter and, satisfied that the sky was silent, said, 'Stop the car in the middle of the road and pop the bonnet.' Sticking her pistol into the top of her pants, hiding it with her jacket, she exited the vehicle, opened the bonnet, and peered at the steaming engine.

Tina Little was driving her brand-new car, a present from her parents at her twenty-first birthday party the night before. In front and blocking the road was a middle-aged blond woman, the bonnet of her car in the air, steam snaking from it. Tina slowed, bringing her new car to a standstill. Through the windscreen, she saw the distressed woman mouth *sorry* and indicated with her fingers *do you have a phone*.

Tina nodded and wound down her window as the woman walked up alongside. 'Hi Love, Silly me, left my phone at the hotel. Would you mind calling the RAC?'

'Sure,' Tina said.

372

As Tina reached into her purse for the phone, Ellen Goldsworthy ripped the pistol from her pants and rested its cold barrel against Tina's temple.

'Nice car.'

***

Thwap-thwap-thwap-thwap.

The rotor blades built up speed as the helicopter prepared for take-off. Speaking through his intercom, the pilot asked, 'Where to?'

Without a moment's hesitation, Detective Mars said, 'The Aberdeen Royal Infirmary, the major trauma hospital and radio ahead, to let them know we are coming.'

The sound of the blades cutting through the air resonated inside the cabin and there was a judder as the helicopter lifted from the ground.

Olivia felt unwell and groggy, shock setting in; she had an overwhelming desire to close her eyes and sleep. Fighting the urge, Olivia bit down hard on her lip. Molly, distress etched across her face, watched Olivia, her heart aching. When their eyes met, Olivia found the strength to smile and beckoned with her fingers for Molly to come to her.

Molly sat beside Olivia, resting her head on the old lady's bony shoulder.

A creeping cold began to envelop Olivia, causing her to shiver. Ignoring the discomfort, she summoned warmth into her voice, though it came out weak. 'Do you know what, Molly?'

Olivia felt Molly shake her head, moving it from side to side as it rested on her.

'This is the second time in as many days that I've ended up in the hospital. I'm starting to worry they might think I enjoy the place.' The effort of speaking took Olivia's breath away, and her eyelids grew heavy, pulling her toward the irresistible allure of slumber. 'Molly, the old Olivia needs a little rest.'

Molly smiled, a teardrop forming and rolling down her cheek. She whispered, 'It will be alright Olivia. Max is here.'

Olivia shivered.

I'm cold Max.

It's okay, my Love, I'm here with you.

I wanted to say goodbye to Claudia. I thought she would be here.

We've had our time, my Love and what an adventure it has been. Inspector Axel needed her more.

***

CHAPTER 21
The Promise

Two Years Later

Unlike the previous year's anniversary, where the sky and sea merged on the horizon in a brilliant mix of blues, giving the illusion of no beginning or end, today the savagery and wonder of nature was on full display. Poseidon, in homage to the brave people who called the sea home, whipped the ocean into a frenzy, sending white horses crashing into the shore with the sound of a thousand hooves thundering on the ground.

Molly, Snowflake tucked under one arm, a bunch of flowers in the other, stood in front of the grave and breathed in the salt air and remembered her promise. Placing Snowflake on the ground, she kneeled and positioned the flowers next to the headstone.

'Thank you.'

Molly had kissed Olivia goodbye on the cheek and vowed that every year she would visit the place where you could see the ocean from the churchyard. The remains of Olivia and Max had been buried together in their special spot where many, many, many years prior, they had been joined as one.

'Till Death Us Do Part.'

THE END

LOVE LETTER FROM DRESDEN

MARK A. BIGGS

Modern day fairy tale.

A love story unearthed from a shoe box leads a daughter on a journey for the truth. Set between WW2 and modern day and told through the eyes of several characters, Love Letters from Dresden is a beautiful tale of friendship, survival and love.

"With the winds of time, love letters drift from our lives, taking their secrets with them."

OPERATION UNDERPANTS

Book #1 Max & Olivia Series

MARK A. BIGGS

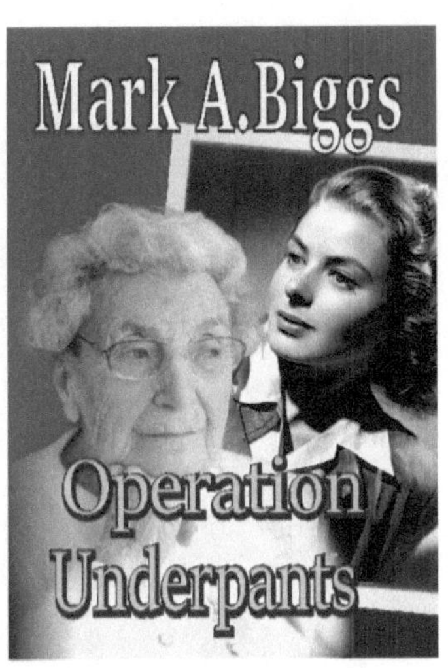

Growing old is peculiar to the individual

Unceremoniously dumped in a retirement home by their children, international spies Max and Olivia languish forgotten and waiting to die. After finding a secret message in the newspaper they must escape and travel to the UK with the fate of London and much of the world hanging in the balance.

CLAUDIA

Book #2 Max & Olivia Series

MARK A. BIGGS

The adventures of our eccentric old spies, Max and Olivia continue in the exciting sequel to Operation Underpants. *Claudia* is an uplifting story full of danger, fear, good vs evil, never being too old, never giving up hope, and having ultimate faith in others.

Feared assassin Claudia doesn't kill Max but takes him with her - putting her at war with herself and a past she hoped to forget. Meanwhile, Olivia must escape the watchful eye of MI6 to track her beloved husband Max across Europe, leaving in her wake a delicious trail of chaos.

OPERATION OBE

Book #3 Max & Olivia Series

MARK A. BIGGS

Novichok Nerve Agent, Gutenberg Bible, Russian Oligarch

Max and Olivia face their greatest challenge

Living their remaining days onboard the Queen Mary 2, Max and Olivia are suddenly dragged back into the world of international espionage and an undeclared war with Russia.

A story of adventure, humour and love set against the happenings of the world today.

St Mary's Dating Agency

Book #4 Max & Olivia Series

MARK A. BIGGS

Espionage and foreign interference are insidious

St Mary's Pi-Ski, with its ageing and declining congregation, enters the game of online romance to save the church. John Moss, photographing himself in exotic locations for his romance profile, collides with Lucy, aka Claudia, a beautiful spy in possession of an item sought by ruthless Chinese agents. John becomes an unwitting mule, drawn into a dangerous game of espionage masquerading as love.

OPERATION ORIGAMI
The Ire of Claudia

Book #5 Max & Olivia Series

MARK A. BIGGS

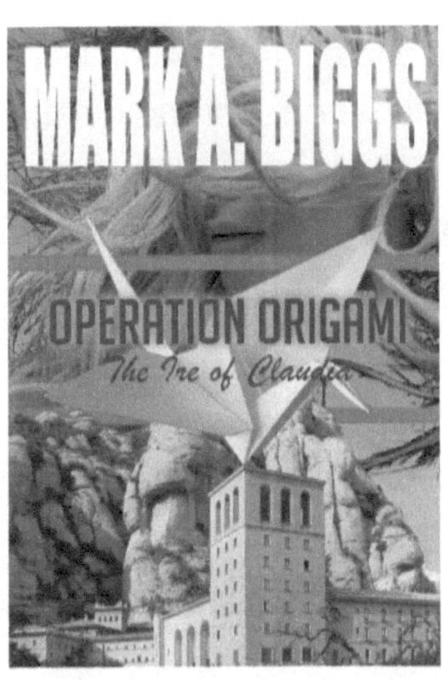

A riveting fast-paced story

John Moss was the victim of the charms of Claudia, a British Secret Service Agent. His mission? To carry a national secret stolen from the Chinese government into the United Kingdom. Claudia planned to leave him high and dry once she retrieved the Quantum Cube. Falling in love was never part of her plan. The explosion in which he died wasn't part of her plan, either.

Concern is growing that Claudia's desire for personal vengeance will ignite a war between both the Chinese and the British intelligence sectors. What her superiors can't see is that the two intelligence agencies are already at war. Killing John was only adding fuel to a steadily growing fire.

Now Claudia is on a hunt for the Crane – the assassin that killed John and has avoided identification for years.

With her superiors breathing down her back and tracking her every move, Claudia must be discreet in her mission. She must use what contacts she has, all while watching her back. At a moment's notice, it could all be over for the spy.

Claudia isn't the only one being hunted. Two older spies are being tracked by Davros, who works for The Firm, a new organisation to the espionage game. Danger lurks around every corner for both the young and the old, each embarking on a mission that could end with casualties on both sides.

When Claudia is captured in Spain and held captive in the dungeons deep below Montserrat Abbey, two old friends must rescue her. Coming out of retirement in the midst of a pandemic wasn't the thrill octogenarians Max and Olivia were looking for.

And then, of course, there's Molly and Snowflake the cat.

In the world of espionage, assassins, and national secrets, nothing is as it seems.

www.ingramcontent.com/pod-product-compliance
Lightning Source LLC
Chambersburg PA
CBHW021954130726
47903CB00014B/1356